Also by Barbara Hambly

A Free Man of Color

Fever Season

Graveyard Dust

Sold Down the River

And coming soon in hardcover:

Wet Grave

GRAVEYARD DUST

"Seductive . . . Sweeps from lavish balls on elegant river plantations to voodoo rites in Congo Square and savage brawls in mean waterfront dives. . . . January proves the ideal guide through these treacherous social strata."
—*The New York Times Book Review*

"A richly detailed murder mystery with a little bit of voodoo mixed in for flavor. Don't miss this powerful series." —*Mystery Lovers Bookshop News*

FEVER SEASON

A *New York Times* Notable Book of the Year

"A notable writer of mystery fiction . . . This one grips the reader from start to finish." —*The Washington Times*

"From the highborn Creoles in their river mansions to the uncivilized Americans brawling on the levee, Hambly speaks all their languages, knows all their secrets, and brings them all to life." —*The New York Times Book Review*

A FREE MAN OF COLOR

"Magically rich and poignant . . . In scene after scene researched in impressive depth and presented in the cool, clear colors of photography, Hambly creates an exotic but recognizable environment for January's search for justice." —*Chicago Tribune*

"A darned good murder mystery."
—*USA Today*

Die Upon a Kiss

Barbara Hambly

BANTAM BOOKS
New York Toronto London
Sydney Auckland

This edition contains the complete text
of the original hardcover edition.
NOT ONE WORD HAS BEEN OMITTED.

DIE UPON A KISS

A Bantam Book

PUBLISHING HISTORY

Bantam hardcover edition / June 2001
Bantam mass market edition / May 2002

ISBN 0-553-58165-1

Published simultaneously in the United States and Canada

Bantam Books are published by Bantam Books, a division of Random
House, Inc. Its trademark, consisting of the words "Bantam Books"
and the portrayal of a rooster, is Registered in U.S. Patent and
Trademark Office and in other countries. Marca Registrada. Bantam
Books, 1540 Broadway, New York, New York 10036.

PRINTED IN THE UNITED STATES OF AMERICA

OPM   10 9 8 7 6 5 4 3 2 1

For Adrian

Special thanks, as always, are due
to Pamela Arceneaux and the staff
of the Historic New Orleans Collection;
to Paul, Bill, Sand, and Norman
at Le Monde Creole; to Emily Clark;
to Rebecca Witjas; to Kate Miciak;
to Laurie Perry; to Stephanie Hall;
to Bob Moraski for all his time and knowledge;
to Jill and Charles for helping me through
much awfulness; and to George.

James Caldwell's American Theater

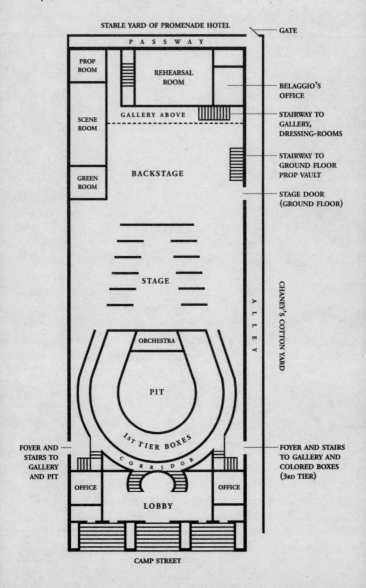

Die Upon
a Kiss

ONE

—∞∞∞—

". . . nigger," muttered a man's voice, hoarse in the dark of the alley but very clear.

Benjamin January froze in his tracks. Would this, he wondered, be the occasion on which he'd be hauled into court and hanged—or, more informally, beaten to death on the public street—for the crime of defending himself against a white man's assault?

The gas-jet above the American Theater's stage door was out. A misty glimmer beyond the alley's narrow mouth showed him that the gambling-parlor at the City Hotel on the other side of Camp Street was still in operation, and above the wet plop of hooves, the creak of harness, a man's voice sang jerkily in English about Ireland's em'rald hills. It was past three and bitterly cold. Even in Carnival season, New Orleans had to sleep sometime.

January considered turning immediately back to the stage door and retreating through the theater and out to the street by one of the side-doors that admitted patrons to its galleries or pit. He was a big man—six feet three—and built on what the slave-dealers at the baracoons along Baronne Street liked to call "Herculean" lines; he could have taken most assailants without trouble. But he was also forty-two years old and had learned not to take on *anybody* in a pitch-dark alley less than five feet wide, especially when he didn't know if they were a) armed b) white or c) alone. Words had been uttered: that implied one auditor at least.

But Marguerite Scie, ballet mistress of the Theater's new Opera company, had locked the alley door behind him. By this time, she'd have ascended from the prop-room on the ground floor to the backstage regions immediately above. She and January had been catching up on seven years' worth of old times since rehearsal had ended at eleven, and January wasn't sure there was anyone else in the building to hear him pound the door and shout.

And he'd learned that when white men got drunk enough to go around looking for black ones to beat up, flight was effective only if you were damn sure you'd get away. It was like escaping from a pack of wild dogs. If you acted like prey, you'd become it.

For a time he stood listening in the darkness.

Anger smoldered in him that he'd even contemplate flight. In Paris, where he'd lived for sixteen years, he'd been assaulted once or twice, coming home late from night surgery at the Hôtel Dieu. Later, after his marriage, he'd played piano until the small hours at society balls, at the Opera or the ballet—jobs that paid more than a junior surgeon ever earned—and had walked through darker streets than this. But even in the Halles district, or the St. Antoine, few of the local *orgues* were dim-witted enough to take on someone who bore that close a resemblance to an oak tree.

In New Orleans a white man would do it—and expect to get away with it—if his victim was black.

Music gusted over the alley's rear gate. That led to the stable yard of the Promenade Hotel, and would be locked, too, at this hour, though the gaming-rooms were still running full-cock. Even in the slack days of summer, when yellow fever stalked the town's fetid streets, the gambling-rooms were open, and it was Carnival season now—January couldn't imagine what it would take to close them down.

Another carriage rattled by up Camp Street, its occupants blowing horns and banging tin pans. *The hell with this.* January pulled off his gloves, shifted his music-satchel to his left hand, and balled his right into a fist the size of a cannonball. *I can always tell the judge I couldn't tell if they were white or black, in the dark.* He took off his hat, and that annoyed him, too: if it came to fighting, he'd probably lose it, and it was new. The old one had been demolished by a gang of drunk upriver Kentucky ruffians who'd cornered him one night last October on his way back from playing at a ball. Hat and satchel in his left hand, right hand freed and ready, heart hammering in his breast, January put his right shoulder to the theater wall and moved forward again.

He'd seen no forms silhouetted against the street's dim glow. Only one niche broke the hundred feet of brick theater wall between him and the alley mouth—the door from which stairs ascended to the slaves' section of the gallery, and the half-tier of boxes reserved for the free colored. He cursed himself: Why couldn't he remember if there were two or three doorways in the wall of Chaney's cotton yard on the other side, or where they were, after all the times he'd been up and down this alley?

Cursed himself, too, for coming back to New Orleans at all—to a town where he could be beaten up by white men with impunity.

Wondered, for the thousandth time since coming back thirty months ago, why he hadn't stayed in Paris. Going insane from grief couldn't be that unpleasant, could it?

The creak of boot-leather, in touching-distance of his own long arm. Stale sweat, stale liquor, dribbled tobacco-spit, and long-abiding dirt . . .

Beside him in the dark.

Behind him in the dark.

Nothing.

To turn and look, much less to break into a run, would invite attack. His breath sounded like a bellows in his own ears and his heart like a bamboula drum.

Nothing.

The dim radiance from the street strengthened before him. Still no squish of striding boots in the horse-shit-smelling black stillness at his back. Not even a spit-warm wad of tobacco juice on the back of his neck. He slid out into the flame-dotted murk of Camp Street and turned immediately right, taking shelter behind one of the marble piers that flanked the American Theater's front stairs.

At that point, he reflected later, he should simply have crossed the street and made his way back to his lodgings in the old French town on the other side of Canal Street like a good, uninquiring nigger should. Then he would have been able to say, with perfect truth, *I know nothing of murder, I know nothing of blood, I know nothing of why anyone would crush skulls or burn buildings or try to kill me and my friends in the dark. . . .*

But the circumstance of not being attacked—not even spit on—by at least two drunk river-rats at three in the morning in a back alley was so unusual that January set his hat and music-satchel safely out of the way on the marble steps, settled himself farther back into the pier's inky shadow, and waited to see who they *were* after.

And in doing so, almost certainly saved Lorenzo Belaggio's life.

The eight gas-lamps that so brilliantly illuminated

the theater's facade earlier in the night—its owner, James Caldwell, was also part owner of the new municipal gasworks—were quenched. Now and then a carriage rattled by, driven full-speed by improbably costumed Mohicans or Musketeers on their way to one last drink, one last round of faro or vingt-et-un after whatever party or ball had occupied their evening, but no one gave him a glance. A blue-uniformed representative of the City Guards, January supposed, would be along shortly to demand an account of his business so long after curfew and a look at the papers that proved him a free man.

But before that could happen, he heard a man shout *"Dio mio!"* and then, *"Merdones! Assassini!"* and recognized the Milanese voice of the impresario who'd spent the evening taking orchestra and company through the first rehearsal of his new opera, *Othello.* January lunged to his feet, down the alley, hearing rather than seeing the flopping, wrenching suggestion of struggle, the thud of bodies on the brick walls, and the grunt of impact.

Then he smelled blood.

He grabbed the nearest form—coarse wool and greasy hair slithered under his fingers—heaved the man off his feet, and flung him toward Camp Street. Indistinct forms writhed in the murk; a man shrieked in pain. He grabbed again, slipped in the muck of horse-shit and rainwater. Edged metal bit his arm. He seized the attacker's hand and twisted it; a moment later, arms hooked around his body from behind.

He dropped his weight, turned, grabbed the front of a rough shirt, hauled his assailant into a punch like the driving-rod of a steamboat's engine. More blood-smell and the crash of a body against the wall. Someone opened the gate at the end of the alley, said, "Holy Jesus!" and slammed it again, and voices hollered confusedly on the other side of the wall. The same instant light speared from the stage door and Madame Scie called, "Who's there?" Almost under January's feet, Lorenzo Belaggio screamed, "Murder!" again.

Someone blundered into January, throwing him against the wall. Footsteps pounded and he saw two forms—he thought there were two—stagger against the smudgy glow of the street. A startled horse whinnied; a man cursed in English, cracked a whip.

"I'm killed!" howled Belaggio. *"Dio mio,* I am dying!"

January knelt in the filth at his side.

"Hideputa!" In the jerking flare of two whale-oil lamps the darkest-voiced of the Opera company's three sopranos, Consuela Montero, strode up the alley a step behind Madame Scie, velvet skirts hitched high above plump knees.

"Is he all right?"

"Oh, I am dying!"

"Scarf," said January tersely. "Ruffle, kerchief, anything you've got."

Madame Scie thrust the lamp at her companion, flipped up her schoolgirlish gauze dancer's skirt to get at a petticoat-ruffle. Yellow light glistened on blood. Most of it seemed, in fact, to be coming from Belaggio's left arm rather than his torso, but January jerked the black long-tailed coat back from the impresario's bulky shoulders, searching for telltale spreading red on the white of his shirt, the azure-stitched gold of his waistcoat. Before the ballet mistress could rip free her ruffle, a male voice said, "Here," and a mauve silk handkerchief was passed down over January's shoulder by a man's hand in a mauve kid-skin glove: "Did you see who did it?"

January glanced around and dimly recognized one of the gentlemen who'd come to watch the rehearsal. Handsome as Apollo, French Creole by his speech, wealthy by the cut of the mauve velvet coat. Even the buttons on its sleeve, and on the glove, were amethyst, flashing in the lantern-light as he stretched a hand down to Belaggio. "Are you well, Monsieur?"

"Lorenzo!" shrieked Drusilla d'Isola, the prima donna, and fainted in the Creole gentleman's arms.

"Get him inside." January's own arm ached damnably from the knife-slash he'd taken and he still couldn't find any wound on Belaggio other than the cut on his arm, which he bound up with petticoat-ruffle and purple silk. He got a glimpse of a bloody skinning-knife lying in the mud, but lost sight of it as Madame Scie stepped back to make way for first violinist Hannibal Sefton—hired, like January, for the Italian opera's first season at the American Theater—and Silvio Cavallo, tenor.

The sight of young Cavallo seemed to miraculously revive the swooning impresario. "Assassin!" Belaggio cried, jabbing his forefinger at the tenor, then sagging dramatically back against January's injured arm like a dying steer. "Murderer! Conspirator! *Carbonaro!*"

Cavallo, who'd stepped forward to help support him—Belaggio was nearly January's height and anything but slender—fell back, dark eyes flashing, and Hannibal said reasonably, "Not conspirator, surely? Conspire with whom?"

As if to answer the question, Cavallo's friend from the chorus, a dark, squat Hercules named Bruno Ponte, appeared panting from the darkness.

"They have conspired to murder me . . . !"

Belaggio was definitely not wounded anywhere but in the arm. "Begging your pardon, Signor," January pointed out as they lugged the impresario in through the stage door to the vault where the props were kept, "Signor Cavallo's clothing is unmuddied. I believe that you knocked down one of your attackers in the fray." With a Creole gentleman present—tenderly depositing the unconscious d'Isola on a Roman dining-couch while young Ponte and Hannibal dragged a gilded daybed out of the jumble of flats, carts, lampstands, chairs, statues of Aphrodite, and stuffed or carven livestock that crammed this low brick vault beneath the theater itself—he wasn't about to admit to having laid a finger on white men.

"Argue it later," commanded Madame Scie. "We need more light."

"Go upstairs and get candles," ordered Cavallo, giving Ponte a shove toward the stairs. "Get bandages, too, and brandy from the wardrobe room. I'll fetch the City Guards."

"If you can find any sober at this hour," Madame Scie retorted as the tenor bolted through the outer door. Madame Montero located a box of fat yellow candles among the props for the castle hall scene in the upcoming *La Muette de Portici*. "Good. Thank you." The Creole gentleman still sat on the edge of the banqueting-couch, gently chafing d'Isola's fragile hand. "Are you hurt, Benjamin?" Madame was the only one, apparently, who had noticed.

"Just a scratch."

"Dear Virgin Mary, help me!" Belaggio sagged back onto the striped cushions, clutching his arm again. "Brandy!"

The Creole gentleman withdrew a flask from his pocket—mauve Morocco leather with an amethyst on its silver cap—and held it out. Hannibal took a hearty swig before passing it on to January, who put it to Belaggio's lips.

"Lorenzo, Lorenzo!" Drusilla d'Isola sat up and pressed

lace-mitted hands to her bosom. "Ah, God, they have killed him! Without him I shall die!" And fainted again. Gracefully, wrist to brow, into the mauve Creole's powerful arms.

"Hannibal, fetch cloaks from the wardrobe." Marguerite Scie was fifty-seven years old and had seen, from a garret window, her father and two of her brothers go to the guillotine. Histrionics did not impress her. "You, Benjamin, sit down and get your coat off. M'sieu Marsan—" This to the Creole gentleman bent tenderly over La d'Isola, the lamplight new-minted gold on his shining curls. "Where might we find M'sieu Caldwell at this hour?" In any city but New Orleans, at any time but Carnival, the answer to such a question at this hour would be, self-evidently, *Home in bed.* But there was no telling. Considering Caldwell's former profession as an actor, and his current involvement in a dozen other money-making schemes in the American community of New Orleans, the theater owner could be anywhere.

"Check the Fatted Calf Tavern," advised M'sieu Marsan, raising his head. The Creole's voice was both light and melodious, with the soft slur to his speech. His eyelashes were dark, making his sky-blue eyes all the brighter. "I believe he was going there with M'sieu Trulove to confer about the Opera Society, but they may have gone on."

As he eased Belaggio out of his coat and waistcoats— the impresario affected the dandyish habit of wearing two—and made another futile search for anything else resembling a wound, January wondered what any of these people, let alone all of them, were doing in and around the American Theater at twenty minutes after three in the morning.

Himself, and Marguerite Scie, he understood. While

a twenty-four-year-old student of surgery in Paris, he had made ends meet by playing piano for the ballet school at the Théâtre de l'Odéon. Though close to forty then, Madame had still been dancing, precise and perfect as Damascus steel. They had been lovers, the first white woman he had had. When, much later, he had met and sought to marry the woman he loved, it was Madame who had gotten him a job playing harpsicord for the Comédie Française—the job that had let him and Ayasha wed. Madame had, over the next few years, sent piano pupils his way, and had recommended Ayasha's skills as a dressmaker to both the Comédie's costume shop and to the actresses of the company: even in the heartland of Liberté, Egalité, and Fraternité, there were few who would choose a surgeon of nearly-pure African descent over white Frenchmen.

When January had entered the American Theater yesterday to meet the opera company Mr. Caldwell had brought to New Orleans from Havana, Marguerite Scie's first words to him had been *I grieved to hear of your wife's death.*

They had had much to talk about.

The others . . .

January wrapped Belaggio's shuddering bulk in a kingly cloak of beggar's velvet and dyed rabbit-fur someone handed him, and tallied the faces in the candle-light.

Hannibal Sefton's presence, if unexplained, at least wasn't sinister. January had known the fiddler for two and a half years now and knew the man didn't have a violent bone in his opium-laced body. Through the evening's rehearsal, as he'd sat at the piano, January had heard Hannibal's stifled coughing behind him, and whenever he turned, it had been to see his friend's thin face white and set with pain. As usual when his consumption bore hard on him, Hannibal had taken refuge in laudanum to get him through rehearsal, and January guessed, by the creases in his rusty black coat and the way his graying hair straggled loose over his back from its old-fashioned queue, that he'd simply fallen asleep afterward in a corner of the green room. How he managed to play as beautifully as he did under the circumstances was something January had yet to figure out, but that was the only mystery about Hannibal.

The presence of the others was less easily accounted for.

Drusilla d'Isola, girlishly slim and frail-looking, he knew to be Belaggio's mistress, and it didn't take much guessing to place her there. Her dressing-room was on the second floor above the rehearsal-room and offices. According to company gossip, it included a daybed among its lavish amenities, as well as gas lighting—the only dressing-room so supplied—a gilt-footed bath-tub, a coffee-urn, a French armoire painted with cupids, and even a small dining table. Her hair, the color of refined molasses, was no longer in the elaborately upswept Psyche knot in which it had been dressed at rehearsal, and January could tell by the fit of her plum-colored moiré dress that it had been laced hastily—probably by herself—and that she wore neither corset nor petticoats beneath.

Consuela Montero's raven hair *was* dressed, shining with an unbroken pomaded luster in its fantasia of loops, tulle bows, and blood-red ostrich-tips, and the crimson gown that made her creamy skin glow almost golden was laced and trussed as only a maidservant's attentions could make it. The soprano had protuberant brown eyes that reminded January of a wild horse ready to kick or bite or bolt. At the moment she was regarding La d'Isola with undisguised contempt as the prima donna emerged with fluttering eyelids from her swoon.

"Are you all right?" Monsieur Marsan tenderly stroked d'Isola's wrists. Even his stickpin matched, an amethyst like a pale iris's heart set in a twilight-hued cravat. "M'sieu, the brandy, if you would . . ."

January passed the brandy back to Hannibal, who took another gulp before returning it to Marsan. *"It is not so deep as a well, nor so wide as a church door,"* observed the fiddler, leaning over January's shoulder as January checked Belaggio's hammering pulse. Fortunately he spoke English, since the wound so described in *Romeo and Juliet* had proved fatal and Belaggio was making a sufficiently Senecan tragedy of his injury as it was. "Shall I get more blankets, or shall we move him—them"—he glanced back at La d'Isola, whom Monsieur Marsan had wrapped in his coat—"upstairs, where it's warmer?"

"By all means." Marsan lifted the prima soprano as if she were a doll; La d'Isola sagged gracefully back so that her head hung over his elbow, her hair a rippling curtain halfway to the floor. January had seen her take the identical pose earlier that evening in the first rehearsal of *Othello,* when Staranzano the baritone bore her to the bed.

Marsan's dandyish ensemble had caught January's eye at rehearsal, added to the fact that he'd sat apart from the other members of the newly-founded St. Mary Opera Society. That separation, at least, was now made clear— January wondered how it came about that a Creole Frenchman was a member of the Society at all. As a rule, the French Creoles who owned most of the plantations and who still controlled the money and power in the city avoided the newly-come, newly-wealthy Americans, treating even the representatives of the best families of New

York, Virginia, Philadelphia, and Boston as if they were tobacco-spitting filibusters straight off the keelboats.

This antipathy was in fact the genesis of the St. Mary Opera Society. The money contributed by the wealthy inhabitants of that new upriver American suburb was what enabled James Caldwell to go to Havana and enlist Belaggio, to bring to New Orleans a company which sang in the sweetly musical Italian style—pointedly different, Caldwell and Belaggio both assured their patrons, from the more lavish, but more harshly sung, French-style opera presented by the French Creole John Davis at his theater on the Rue d'Orleans.

Curious, thought January, that a Creole like Marsan would be part of the St. Mary Society. . . .

"Is Mademoiselle better?" Marsan's boyishly handsome face creased with concern as he touched La d'Isola's hair in the candlelight. "Come, we will take you somewhere warm and comfortable. . . ."

Well, perhaps not so curious at that.

"I faint!" croaked Signor Belaggio when January tried to get him to his feet. "I die!"

January had the distinct impression that the impresario was angling to be borne upstairs like a slaughtered hero. January could have done it—he'd lugged and manhandled bigger men in his years as a surgeon—but his slashed arm smarted and he was beginning to feel lightheaded himself. "Signor Ponte," he called out as the chorus-boy darted down the stairs with voluble excuses about not having been able to find bandages or brandy or anything else where they should have been. "Help me, if you would be so kind."

"Keep him from me!" Belaggio directed a withering glare at Bruno Ponte. "It was he, he and his keeper, who attempted to assassinate me! You think he would not take the moment of holding me up to slip a little dagger between my ribs?"

Ponte's cupid-bow lips pulled back in rage. *"Pisciasotto!"*

"Recchione!"

"Fregatura!"

"Gentlemen!" Hannibal shoved two candles into Ponte's hands and went to help January himself. "There are ladies present." And it was a good bet, thought January, that though La d'Isola was unconscious, both Madame Scie and Madame Montero knew enough Italian—even the highly dialectical Sicilian and Milanese—to understand what was being said.

Between them they got Belaggio up the wide stairs that ascended from the brick-pillared gloom of the propvault to the backstage. This cavernous space was already a jumble of wings and flats, cupid-bedecked gilt furniture from next Tuesday's presentation of *Le Nozze di Figaro* mixed with blue and green glass lamp filters and a nearly full-sized gondola from the melodrama *The Venetian's Revenge,* which had been staged that evening for an audience that consisted largely of Kentucky backwoodsmen, filibusters, gun-runners, and riverfront rowdies. In the background loomed the half-finished plaster sections of what would hopefully become Mount Vesuvius in time for next Friday's performance of *La Muette de Portici,* though at the moment the ramshackle collection of lathe, canvas, and sheets of red and orange silk bore little resemblance to the fire-spewing colossus that dominated the posters pasted to every wall in town.

"Would someone stir up the fire in Signor Belaggio's office? Madame . . ." Hannibal suggested as Belaggio jerked the key back from Ponte's extended hand.

With a sigh, Madame Montero took the key and

went to open the office, the ballet mistress following with still more candles. Since these were tallow work-candles from the chorus-men's dressing-room, the office quickly filled with their faint, sheep-like odor. January and Hannibal deposited Belaggio in the massive armchair beside the desk, then withdrew to the backstage again.

"I've taken the liberty of carrying Mademoiselle d'Isola to her dressing-room." The planter Marsan descended the stairs from the gallery off which the principals had their dressing-rooms, resplendent in waistcoat, shirtsleeves, and a pale-purple glitter of amethyst and silk. "Perhaps if you would be so good as to see to her, Madame . . ." Marsan divided his glance equally between Mesdames Scie and Montero; Hannibal bowed tactfully to Marguerite and said, "Might I escort you up, Madame? The stairs are very dark." He took a candle and guided her out; the Mexican soprano's scarlet-painted lips twisted with scorn and January reflected that it was just as well Montero wasn't going to be left alone in a room with the unconscious prima donna—not that he supposed for a moment Drusilla d'Isola's swoon to be real.

"Five cents says La d'Isola's back inside ten minutes." Hannibal clattered down the steps again and led January to the carved and gilded throne of the Doge of Venice. "Seven, that she faints again the minute she's got an audience. I nicked Belaggio's brandy from his desk." By the light of his single taper he eased January out of the rough jacket he'd put on for the walk home, and picked the slashed and sodden shirtsleeve away from the cut. *"What bloody man is this?"* he added, dropping from French to Shakespearean English, something Hannibal did with even greater facility than January, who was himself long used to switching from French to Spanish to English and back.

"It looks worse than it is."

"It better, or we'll be calling in the undertakers." He doused January's handkerchief in the brandy, took a gulp from the bottle, and daubed the wound. January flinched at the sting of it. Behind them in the office, Belaggio's groans, gasps, and accusations continued for the benefit of Madame Montero and M'sieu Marsan. "Did you notice young Ponte changed his coat?"

"Are you sure?"

"Fairly." Hannibal tried to open the folding pen-knife he'd taken from his pocket, but his skeletal fingers were unsteady; January took the knife from him, opened it, and handed it back to cut away the sleeve of his shirt. "He and Cavallo both were wearing long-tailed coats at rehearsal, and I think they were in the same outfits when I first saw them in the alley. Cavallo was, I know—a blue cutaway with a velvet collar." He nodded toward Ponte, emerging from the office to hurry up the stairs. The chorus-boy's boots were mud-splashed, January noticed, but the dove-colored trousers above them spotlessly clean. Even Hannibal, who'd come out of the theater only in the battle's aftermath, had fresh spatters of mud on his calves.

Working carefully, and turning aside now and then to cough, the fiddler sliced the clean lower portion of the linen sleeve from the bloodied, and used it to form a bandage. His breath labored in the silence, but he seemed better than he had earlier in the evening.

"You, boy." Marsan's tall form blotted out the light of the office doorway. "We need water in here to make coffee."

Sixteen years ago, before he'd gone to Paris, it hadn't bothered January to be addressed by strangers by the informal *tu*. That was just something that white men did when addressing slaves—though sixteen years ago most

French Creoles were fairly careful to use the polite *vous* in speaking to men they knew were free colored, albeit they occasionally forgot and called black freedmen *tu*, as they would slaves, horses, children, or dogs. In Paris, everyone had spoken to him in the polite form—*vous*. He'd felt a kind of elation in it, as if it were a mark of an adulthood impossible in New Orleans. It surprised him sometimes, after two and a half years, how much he still minded.

Sometimes it surprised and shamed him that he didn't mind more.

"M'sieu Janvier was hurt saving Signor Belaggio's life," said Hannibal, and he stood up, his hand unobtrusively on the back of the throne for support. "I'll get the water." He picked up the single candle and turned away toward the stairway down to the vault, where the big clay jars of drinking water stood. He hadn't reached the stair, however, when the outer doors banged below, and lantern-light jostled over the brick of the walls.

". . . borne them upstairs," Cavallo's voice said in his lilting English, and boots clattered, first on the soft brick, then hollow on the wooden steps.

"Them?" The light, scratchy tone of Abishag Shaw, Lieutenant of the New Orleans City Guards, veered skittishly between the Milanese's faulty pronunciation of a French plural subjunctive and his own idiosyncratic comprehension of the language.

As two blue-uniformed Guards, Shaw in his stained and sorry green coat, and Cavallo came into view, Hannibal explained. "Signorina d'Isola was overcome by the sight of the blood—" He switched from French to the Spanish that he was fairly certain only January would understand, and added, "—and I daresay by the spectacle of someone other than herself holding center stage." He dropped back into French again to include the handsome young tenor and the guards. "M'sieu Janvier was injured, too, but not badly. Coffee for everyone?"

He rattled down the steps to fetch the water, coat-skirts billowing around him, like an underfed and slightly pixilated grasshopper. January carefully kept himself from smiling at the expression of alarm that flashed across Marsan's face at the prospect of sharing refreshment with one who was—by his slouched hat and straggling hair, his drawling river-rat English and the tobacco he spit casually on the floor—the brother-in-arms of every Kaintuck, keelboatman, filibuster, and Yahoo that had drifted down-river to invade what had been for so many years the haven of French civilization in the New World.

If there were a form of address less respectful than *tu*, January reflected, leaning back in the deceptive gold-crusted cushions of the throne and closing his eyes, Marsan would use it to Shaw. He wondered how soon it would occur to the French Creoles to write to the Académie Française and ask that one be invented.

Closing his eyes was like letting go of a rope and dropping into warm water fathoms deep. *Full fathom five thy father lies . . .*

His arm throbbed, and reaction to the fray tugged him down.

Coffee, he thought. There was an urn and spirit-kettle in the green room. Probably Italian-style, strong and bitter, but still nothing to the Algerian black mire Ayasha had made.

His beautiful Ayasha. His wicked-eyed desert *afreet* whose death in the cholera had sent him, in grief too great to bear alone, from Paris back to New Orleans. Back to the only home he knew.

Two years and six months. The fifteenth of August

1832. He recalled it to the day, and each day without her since, not yet quite a thousand of them. Beads of blood-stained jet on a string that might extend another thirty years before he reached his allotted threescore and ten.

There had been a time when he'd wondered how to endure a single one of them.

He had endured, of course. One did. He had learned to breathe again, and learned to laugh. Even to love—though the love he bore for the dear friend of his heart now was as different from Ayasha's as a poppy in sunlight differs from the heavy beat of the summer ocean. But it was like learning to walk on wooden legs after a crippling injury. He couldn't imagine ever not knowing exactly how many days had passed.

"Let's get you home." He smelled coffee, and Hannibal's voice broke into the stillness of his thought. The fiddler set the cup on the floor beside the throne. "You look all in."

"I'll stay."

"Shaw knows where to find you."

Behind them in the office Marsan was saying, ". . . some business with Monsieur Belaggio. I remained for a time after rehearsal. . . ."

For three and a half hours? What business couldn't wait for day?

"I think I need to speak with him tonight."

". . . shall manage somehow to be here in the morning. Never would I oblige Signor Caldwell to one day of worry, one hour, over the obligations which we have to his opera season here in New Orleans. *È vero,* I can conduct rehearsal from a chair, if I can but be borne in from my carriage. . . ." Belaggio's voice faltered artfully, like a tenor dying at the end of Act Three.

"They're going to try again, you know."

"What?" Hannibal paused in the act of collecting his long hair back into its straying pigtail.

"To kill him." January opened his eyes. "Have you read the libretto of the opera we rehearsed tonight?"

"*Othello?*" He thought about it, and something changed in the coffee-dark eyes. "Ah." He coughed. "Yes."

"It's probably the most beautiful setting I've ever encountered for that play," said January quietly. "The version Belaggio has written makes Rossini's look like a second-rate *commèdia* at a fair. Everything Shakespeare said, or implied, about jealousy, about passion, about the meanness of heart that cannot abide the sight of good . . ."

"And all the audience will see," finished Hannibal, "is a black man kissing a white woman." He coughed again, and dragged up a gilt-tasseled footstool with a kind of swift, unobtrusive urgency.

"Kissing her." January glanced back through the lighted doorway of the office, where Belaggio, forgetful of the fatal gravity of his wound, was on his feet, declaiming the details of the fray to Shaw. "And then murdering her out of a love too great for his heart to endure."

"Hmmm." Hannibal chewed for a time the corner of his graying mustache. Though the fiddler never spoke of his family or home, January guessed from things he had said—from the lilt of his speech—that Hannibal came of the Anglo gentry that had lands in the Irish countryside and a town house in London, the gentry that sent their sons to Oxford to become good Englishmen on money abstracted from a peasantry that eked out a starving living on potatoes and barely understood a hundred words that were not in Gaelic. Raised on Shakespeare and on the classics of Rome and Greece, it was almost beyond the fiddler's comprehension that one man would feel revulsion for another of equal merit for no other reason than the color of his skin.

"And you think someone told him not to put on that particular opera?"

"You think someone didn't?"

Hannibal picked up the coffee-cup again, offered it to January, then, when it was refused, sipped it himself. "And he doesn't understand."

"Could you have written a piece that perfect," asked January softly, "and not want to put it on? Not *have* to put it on?" His eyes turned toward the black door of the rehearsal-room next to the offices of Belaggio and Caldwell. There the company had spent most of the evening familiarizing themselves with the libretto of the new piece that would be the center of Caldwell's Italian season. The other six operas—not all of them Italian, but sung in the melodic Italian style—were in repertory, having been performed at one time or another, somewhere, by everyone in the company. Even small towns in Italy had their opera houses, and for every production at La Scala or La Fenice, there were hundreds of minor *Figaros* and *Freìschützes* and *Barbers of Seville*, done two or three a week.

But every season had its new opera, its premiere. The one no one in town had yet seen. John Davis, at the French Opera, had invested a great deal of money and time in arranging to premiere *La Muette de Portici*— which Belaggio, out of sheer effrontery, had selected to present as the second opera of his own season, on the night before Davis's scheduled production.

Othello, Belaggio's own work, was thunder no man could steal.

". . . seizing the man, I hurled him from me," Belaggio boomed, swept away in the torrent of his own *récitatif.*

"But he rose out of the darkness and fell upon me like a tiger with his knife. . . ."

What, think you I'd make jealousy my life?
And chase the moon's dark changes with my heart. . . .

The doomed Moor's heart-shaking aria sounded again in January's mind, the soar and dip of the music that pre-saged Othello's plunge into the very madness he scorned. The building tension that made the listener want to leap up on the stage and shout *No, don't heed him . . . !* Knowing inevitably, tragically, that Othello would. Othello understood passion and war, but he did not understand the pettiness of soul that was his undoing.

Blood, Iago, blood!

. . . *nigger,* the men in the alley had said, and let him pass.

Had they meant, *That's a nigger, we're waiting for a white man?*

Or had Othello been the nigger of whom they spoke?

"Don't die on us now, Maestro."

January opened his eyes with a jolt. Lieutenant Shaw stood before him, the coarse, narrow planes of his face illuminated now only by the lantern in Hannibal's hand. "We'll need a ox-team to haul you home." The lamp in Belaggio's office had been quenched. The backstage was dark, and cold.

"Belaggio . . . ?"

"Gone back to the City Hotel with a couple Guards to make sure he gets there all in one piece. The ladies, too, all of 'em." Shaw slouched his hands in his pockets, spit toward the sandbox in the corner, and missed it by a yard—a tall, stringy, shaggy-haired bumpkin who looked like he should have been harvesting pumpkins somewhere in Illinois, until you saw his eyes. "You want me to help you all the way back to your rooms, or are you satisfied Mr. Cavallo here won't try to assassinate you on the way just to keep you quiet?"

Cavallo looked genuinely alarmed at this jest, as well he might—in Milan under the rule of the Austrians it was no joking matter. January said quickly, "Of course not. That's absurd. The men who attacked Belaggio were Americans, I'll swear to it."

"You seen 'em? Heard their voices?"

January hesitated. "I heard one of them whisper 'nigger,'" he said at last. "And I smelled them. Smelled their clothes."

Shaw nodded, noting this piece of evidence behind those gray, lashless eyes that, for all their seeming mildness, were cold as glass.

"They dropped a skinning-knife in the alley." January staggered a little getting to his feet, and his arm ached hideously under Hannibal's makeshift bandage. Someone had fetched his music-satchel and hat from the front of the theater. With another wary glance at Shaw, Cavallo put an arm under January's good shoulder: the young man was almost as tall as he, clear-browed and hawk-featured, and wearing, as Hannibal had pointed out, a short tweed roundabout instead of the nip-waisted blue cutaway he'd had on when first January saw him in the alley.

"Did they, now?" Shaw wriggled a candle free of the mess of wax on the table around it, picked away a straggle of charred wick, and lit it from the lantern, to precede them down the stairs. Ponte came around to January's other side and carefully supported him without touching his injured arm. He, too, watched Shaw, not with Silvio

Cavallo's ingrained wariness, but with deeper and more virulent hate. In any of the many dialects of the Italian peninsula, *sbirro*—policeman—was the foulest of insults, and with good reason. Hannibal followed, holding the lantern high.

Very softly, as they descended the plank steps to the prop-vault, January heard Ponte whisper a question in Sicilian—". . . guesses," January made out the word.

Cavallo answered immediately *"Silencio,"* and nodded back at Hannibal. And to January, in the standard Italian in which the various Neapolitans, Milanese, and Lombards communicated with one another and outsiders, "Where is it that the Signor lives?"

"Rue des Ursulines," replied January. "At the back of the French town. Hannibal can guide you. It's about a mile. I'm sorry we can't take a cab, but for men of my race in this city, it is forbidden by law." His knees felt weak, and by the time they reached the end of the alley he was glad of the support.

At this hour of the morning even the final revelers of Carnival had at last gone home to bed. The brass band that had been playing in the Promenade Hotel behind the theater had fallen silent. Even in the Fatted Calf Tavern, just up the street, the lights were out, and in the gambling rooms of the City Hotel. The distant clamor of the levee, audible from the street before the theater at most hours, was stilled, although in less than an hour the markets would begin to stir. The thick air smelled of the river, of mist and the livestock markets close by at the foot of Lafayette Street.

The city slept.

Gorged and drunk and sated. Dreaming its dreams of wealth and fever, sugar and cotton and slaves, beside the slow, thick river. Slaves and French and Americans and the free colored *sang mêlés* united for a few hours in their human need for rest.

Glancing behind him, January saw Lieutenant Shaw still pacing back and forth in the wet murk, ill-burning candle in hand. He'd stoop now and again to study something in the indescribable muck of churned-up mud, old straw, and trampled horse-droppings. By the lopsided glow January could see the dark niche of doorway where the two assassins had concealed themselves.

But there was no sign anywhere of a knife.

TWO

＊

As a slave-child on a plantation called Bellefleur, Benjamin January had lived in music as naturally as a fish lives in water. His earliest memories were of his father whistling in the freezing dark as he washed in the trough behind the cabin that two families shared: every morning a different tune. Some were those African tunes men sang in the fields, songs whose meaning had been lost over the years but whose haunting melodies still moved the heart and the bones. Some were the bird-bright cotillions heard once or twice, when the Master had company at the big house and folks would loiter in the yard to listen to the fiddle played within. January's father could whistle a tune back after hearing it once. When January grew older— freed by his mother's new master and given proper piano lessons in the light-handed Austrian mode from an émigré—he was astonished at how many of those tunes he instantly recognized.

What would Antonio Vivaldi have thought had he known that his "Storm at Sea" concerto would be whistled by a tall black man with tribal scars on his face, walking out to the sugar-harvest with his cane-knife in his hand?

Why this should return to January's mind as he entered the New Exchange Coffee House on Rue Chartres slightly before noon the following day he wasn't sure. Perhaps because he'd learned to look at music as a sort of armature, a core or frame of reference around which other perceptions of the world were built. Perhaps because he knew, after playing the piano for a thousand dances and ten thousand lessons, how music can slip past the guards that the mind puts on itself, how it can alter the shape of thought before the thinker is aware of the change.

Else why the anger over Beethoven's symphonies? Why the riots over *Fidelio,* whose young lovers weren't intriguers tricking an old husband or doting father, but patriots standing forth against tyranny? Why in Milan and Parma and Venice could one be arrested for whistling the barcarole from *La Muette de Portici: My friends, the dawn is fair . . . ?*

It was only a tale of events centuries old, after all.

Words were dangerous enough. In most of the United States it was now forbidden to teach slaves to read since the big slave revolts of 1828 and 1831. But music gave words power. Music made them memorable. Burned them like the R brand for *Runaway,* into the flesh of the heart.

Thus it was that though January woke with his cut arm hurting so badly that he had to tie it into a makeshift sling in order to walk, he dressed and made his way to the headquarters of the City Guard in the Cabildo, in quest of Abishag Shaw.

And the men at the Cabildo directed him here.

January hated the New Exchange.

As the brightly painted sign above its doors proclaimed, the front room was a coffee-house. The velvet aroma of the beans as they were roasted competed pleasantly in the dim spaces of vaulted plaster with the stinks of hair pomade, sweaty wool, cigar smoke, and the

comprehensively uncleaned gutters of the Rue Chartres.
January stepped through the tall French doors that lined
two walls and searched for sight of Shaw among the men
clustered on the backless benches, the rush-bottomed
chairs around trestle tables. Well-dressed men for the
most part, muttering in low voices and scratching figures
in memorandum-books. Sober coats of brown or blue—
Carnival did not penetrate to the New Exchange. Over in
the corner a flash of delicate sky-blue announced Vincent
Marsan's exquisite presence. High-crowned hats of beaver
or beaverette or of the more modern silk. Chiefly white
men, though January recognized Artemus Tourneval, a
well-off free contractor of color, and noted another im-
maculate gentleman picking his way among the tables
who, though nearly as light as some of the Neapolitans
and Sicilians in the opera chorus, definitely had African
ancestors as well as white.

Neither Tourneval nor this other man—probably a
planter come to town from the Cane River country—
made any move to sit down. Nor would they have been
served if they had, even if only with each other. When
they spoke to the white men—as they did, dickering and
figuring and speculating about interest and credit—both
remained on their feet, while the white men sat, and neither looked the white men in the eye.

January wondered dourly if they were addressed as
vous or *tu*.

The only other men in the room of African descent
were the waiters, and an occasional porter from the yard
beyond. Neither Tourneval nor the colored planter gave
them a glance.

When one aspires to mastery, one does not acknowledge cousinship with slaves.

Tu, thought January. *Beyond a doubt.*

In the big back room the auction hadn't yet begun. Kegs, bales, boxes, were stacked around the whitewashed plaster walls, and on out into the sunlit yard. Nails, tools, seed, foreclosed from failed businesses. Small boxes on the long sawbuck tables contained the deeds to city lots, houses, shares in cotton-presses or sugar-mills or boats. In the yard, mules and horses, ranging from sleek bloodstock to spent ewe-necked nags—foreclosures, probates, the breakdowns of men who'd miscalculated their incomes or debts.

Slaves.

"Open your mouth, Deacon, let him see your teeth." Jed Burton—January recognized him as one of the St. Mary Opera Society—waved his merchandise forward. A man in cheap homespun turned the slave in question half-around, to get better light in his mouth while he peered and thrust his fingers inside.

Dressed up in their best, the men in jackets of blue corduroy or wool, even those who were obviously field-hands. The women wore dresses of bright cotton calico, chintz, or sometimes even silk, their hair wrapped in the colorful tignons that the law required all women of color to wear. All smiling, cheerful-looking. Nobody wants a sullen slave, and a "likely" attitude might be the difference between working as a yardman in the city and being sent upriver to cut cane. In a corner a man with leg-shackles on his feet and an "R" burned into his cheek clasped a woman's hands. Small children clung to their mothers. Older children—ten and up—looked like they wished they could. But they hovered close, and gazed up at the white men with a look in their eyes no child should even know exists. January knew exactly the dread they felt, the dread of that first night in a strange house with no one they knew around.

Just because the law said *Ten years old* didn't mean

that private sales weren't worked all the time for children of six and seven and eight. Besides, the law also said *Where possible.*

He looked around again for Shaw. This time saw him: the Kentuckian was within a thumb's-breadth of January's formidable height and they were generally the two tallest men in any gathering. Hands in pockets, his battered orphan of a hat shoved onto the back of his head, Shaw looked like any small-time teamster or cracker farmer out after a bargain. The yard was full of such, prying open the mouths of mules or field-hands, peeking into casks of tar or nails, testing an ax-head or saw-blade from job-lots with the edges of horny thumbs. A yard to January's left a man said, "Shuck down, honey" in drawling flatboat English to a stout young female slave; she unbuttoned her blue-flowered frock and let it drop around her feet, so that the man could knead her belly and pinch her breasts. Her children looked on.

"Maestro." Shaw slouched up to January and spit under the hooves of a mule held by a coffee-house servant. "I was just fixin' to call. You all right?"

January glanced over at the buyer and the woman who had been wearing the blue-flowered dress. "A little sick to my stomach." He reminded himself that to go over and strike the man—or even tell him to behave like a gentleman—would be pointless. The next buyer would do precisely the same. "They told me I'd find you here."

"For all the good it's like to do." Shaw led the way across the yard to the gate onto Rue St. Louis. "As if anybody smugglin' in Africans behind the law's back would sell 'em in a public exchange." He jerked his thumb toward the seller of the woman in blue, haggling now with the cracker in curious archaic French: a little dark, thin-featured man with the bump of an old break in his nose, a knife scar on his cheek, and mustachios down past his chin. He wore a home-made shirt of the blue-and-pink weave typical of the Acadians of the southwest parishes, his long black hair bound back like Hannibal's in a queue. "One day I might just ask you to help me on this as well, if'n you got the stomach. I speak French right enough but it all sounds pretty much the same to me whether a man's speakin' it like a Frenchman or like a Spaniard."

"That's where they're smuggling them in from?" January watched the dark-mustached Acadian, the pot-bellied cracker shaking his head. "Cuba?"

"Cuba, Puerto Rico. Sometimes they lands 'em at Veracruz or Matamoros an' changes the bills of ladin'. It's all very well to outlaw importin' slaves, but as long as sellin' 'em on the open market's no crime, all you do is drive the price up." Shaw's drawling voice was soft, but January could see the hard lines of distaste in the corners of the man's unshaven lips. "And of course, when ol' Captain Chamoflet there brings in slaves to sell, they's always Creole, born an' bred here—an' if he didn't pay their owners for 'em, they're too scared to say."

A few streets away in the Place d'Armes the Cathedral clock began to strike. From the brick vaults of the Exchange's back room a man's voice called out: "Lot Number One for the day, Court of Probate auction of the possessions of the late Anne-Marie Prudhomme." Another voice repeated the words in English, and a general stir passed through the coffee-room, men rising, readjusting galluses or hats. Moving through to the back.

"A woman named Lacey, aged twenty-three, trained in cooking, laundry, ironing, and embroidery—let your dress slip, girl, show 'em what you got—warranted of sober and modest disposition and in good health. What am I bid here?"

"Three hundred," called out a voice that January recognized as Vincent Marsan's.

Anger swam in January's head and he put out a hand to the rough plaster of the wall. His arm throbbed again and he felt breathless and giddy. "Yes," he said. "When you need help against smugglers, count on me." He took a deep breath. The grayness retreated from his vision. "Is Belaggio all right?"

"Fair to middlin'." Shaw's eyes narrowed. "Leastwise he ain't claimin' them two songbirds tried to peck him to death in the alley no more." He held out a copy of the *Louisiana Gazette* to January, a paper much favored in the American community. "You sure what you seen an' heard, Maestro? I was in that alley soon as it got light an' I went through the mud there with a seine, an' didn't find no knife nor nuthin'."

Guesses, the chorus-boy Ponte had whispered, and Cavallo had replied, *Silencio.*

Who guesses?

Guesses what?

"I think so," said January. "I heard only one word, *nigger,* and that in a whisper. But I'd swear in court to the smell. Not," he added with bitterness in his voice, "that my testimony would be admitted against white men."

"Now, Maestro," chided Shaw in his mild voice, "you know it ain't come to that. You's a free man. It's only slaves they don't let to testify."

"And what white juryman," asked January, "would vote against a white plaintiff on the word of a man of color?"

"Not knowin' personally which particular juryman

you're speakin' of," said Shaw, and he spit in the direction of the gutter, "naturally I couldn't say. And like as not any lawyer'd point out a man can wear a dirty coat to do dirty work. An' *nigger* is damn close to *nero*—comes from the same word, in fact." He folded his arms, chewing ruminatively, like one of those scrawny, deadly Mexican steers that will gore a man on horns eight feet tip to tip. A carriage clattered past, the coachman maneuvering between a mule-dray loaded with chairs and a cart trying to make the corner into the New Exchange yard: January glimpsed the occupants, faces vaguely familiar from the French Creole balls and parties he played at. A well-off planter family, the Master springing lightly down to go into the Exchange. The mistress—stout from too much good food and the bearing of too many children—called out reminders about when to meet for supper. A daughter and a son-in-law and grandchildren, all of whom probably lived beneath the same roof both on the plantation and here in town during Carnival: close-knit, inextricably part of one another's lives, for better or for worse.

January's mother, that avid student of town gossip, could have told him the names of the free colored mistresses of both father and son-in-law, and what the men had paid for their contracts of placement—*plaçage*—and probably what the mother and daughter had had to say on the subject, if anything. In the doorway of the Exchange the planter paused to greet Fitzhugh Trulove, linchpin of the St. Mary Opera Society, a big, fresh-faced Englishman with beautiful silvery hair and a decided partiality for the loveliest and least competent member of Madame Scie's corps de ballet.

At length Shaw said, "You speak Italian, don't you, Maestro?"

"I do," said January. "Not as well as Hannibal—you can't shut him up in any language. I couldn't write poetry in it."

"I surely wouldn't ask you to," replied Shaw gravely. "Only enough to sort of ooze around backstage and listen for who in that company might have wanted to hire a couple of Salt River roarers to ventilate their boss's gizzard for him." From behind the unwashed strings of his dust-colored hair, Shaw's gaze changed a little at the way January stiffened. "You don't think so?"

"I don't think it was anyone in the company," said January, and he told Shaw what he had told Hannibal the previous night: about the grandeur of Belaggio's version of *Othello*, and the soaring beauty that would render it a target for hate. He spoke hesitantly—it was the first time he had talked to Shaw about music and he wasn't entirely sure he would be understood. In fact, he realized that he was taking much for granted in supposing the Kentuckian's acquaintance with music extended beyond "Turkey in the Straw." "Have you asked him whether anyone warned him not to put *Othello* on?"

"Didn't even know about it." Shaw eased his verminous hat back a little and leaned one bony shoulder against the wall. "If'n anybody did, Belaggio didn't think fit to mention the matter."

"He wouldn't," said January. "He's a Milanese. He doesn't understand the custom of the country." His voice twisted a little over the phrase and he glanced through the Exchange doors, where the auctioneer was crying the virtues of four pure-bred mules, a wagon, and Negro driver. . . .

"He's only been in this country for what? Three days?" Shaw tilted his head a little to one side. "Who-all would know what operas he planned to do? Caldwell?"

"Caldwell and the members of the St. Mary Opera Society," said January. "That's Fitzhugh Trulove, Jed Burton . . ." He nodded at the coarse-faced little man visible in the yard, "—the Widow Redfern, Dr. Ker from Charity Hospital, Harry Fry, who just bought the steamboats *Alameda* and *Oceana*. Vincent Marsan, Hubert Granville from the Bank of Louisiana . . . maybe two or three others. And their wives," he added, aware of who was the real power in any cultural society in the American quarter. "Caldwell himself. His theater managers, Russell and Rowe. And whoever else they might have mentioned the matter to. Caldwell's been talking for years about challenging John Davis's French Opera by bringing opera to the American Theater. Marsan was the one who heard Belaggio was putting on a season in Havana, I think, but it was Trulove who put up most of the money for Caldwell to bring them here lock, stock, and barrel for Carnival."

"An' you think if any of 'em—Granville or Trulove or the Widow Redfern—was to take offense at this *Othello* thing, an' say *Why don't you just pick somethin' else? . . .* Belaggio wouldn't?"

January was silent, turning over in his hands the folded copy of the *Gazette*. Remembering the music he'd heard for the first time yesterday, the music that had turned his heart inside-out. Remembering what he had seen of Lorenzo Belaggio in the three days since the man had arrived in New Orleans. The man whose life he had last night saved.

"I don't like Lorenzo Belaggio," he said at last. "Maybe I'm just fastidious." His mouth turned down as an image came to his mind, brief and sharp as a miniature on ivory. He'd come suddenly up the narrow steps to the principals' dressing-rooms on an errand, and found Belaggio pinning Nina, the slave-woman who looked after the company's wardrobe, against the wall. One of the impresario's beefy hands was pressed over the struggling woman's mouth while the other groped down the front of her blouse.

January shook his head, trying to force aside both the memory and his disgust. "Then I read the libretto for *Othello*, and played through the score. And I didn't know what to think." His words slowed, almost stammering as he tried to fit what he felt into what he knew. "This isn't just a story being told. You don't write music like that just to fill seats, or show off your soprano's cadenzas. Not this kind of music. You write it because it's inside you, and it will kill you if you don't bring it out."

He glanced aside as he said the words, annoyed at himself for speaking his heart. Belaggio had scowled petulantly as he let the slave-woman loose, then shrugged with a grin of complicity. *We're both men, eh?* And against that, like the surging through-line under Baroque counterpoint, the terrible, terrifying duet of Othello and Iago. *Farewell the tranquil mind, farewell content. . . .*

"Well, Maestro." Shaw scratched with absent-minded thoroughness under his right arm. "I'll take your word for it. You're a musician, an' it'd be as silly for me to say you don't know what you're talkin' about as it'd be for me if I said so to some doctor who pointed out the difference between the cholera an' food-poisonin', which look pretty much alike to most people. But all the same, I surely would like to know if some of the members of that company got their own reasons for wantin' the man put to bed with a shovel. Somebody had to know he was gonna be comin' up that alley, long about that hour of the night."

Clouds were moving in overhead, fantastic floating mountains, like fleeces in a stream, such as January had seen nowhere on earth but in this land of his birth. Chill flowed before them, and the scent of rain. Men emerged from the Exchange, Marsan saying over his shoulder, "Have it delivered to my plantation. Roseaux, across the river on Bayou des Familles. I'll have my factor draw a draft. . . ." The cracker who'd bargained with Chamoflet checked his stride, came over to Shaw.

" 'Scuse me introducing myself, friend, but the name's Jared Tucker, I'm a dealer. I's wonderin' if you'd brought your boy here to the Exchange for purposes of sale?" He indicated January with a gesture of his cigar.

"Mr. Tucker." With a little wave of apology, Fitzhugh Trulove broke from his companions and interposed his soft, pear-shaped bulk between the slave-seller and January before January or Shaw could utter a word. "Please allow me to introduce Mr. January, one of the free musicians who plays for the Opera. Mr. Tucker."

"Pleased," lied January in English through lips that felt like wood.

Jared Tucker inclined his head, not in the least embarrassed. "My 'pologies," he said, an upriver nasal twang. "No offense meant."

"None taken." January averted his eyes from the dealer's, proper for a black man, but not before he caught the glint in them of annoyed regret. *Eleven hundred, maybe eleven-fifty, gone to sheer waste.* January could almost hear the thoughts spoken, as he'd heard them spoken, not once but many times, in the corners of crowded ballrooms where he and the other musicians played for white men's parties. Not even anger there. Only the expression of one who sees an acquaintance buying a bishopped horse or squandering an inheritance. *Damn shame. . . .*

January set his teeth hard as Tucker and Trulove strolled back to Marsan and the others: ". . . draw a draft on the Louisiana Bank for the balance in three months," January heard Marsan say, resuming the conversation exactly where it had left off. The slave-dealer nodded as if nothing out of the ordinary had taken place. "Or I'll have Mr. Knight get in touch with you. . . ."

Shaw spit, wordlessly eloquent. After a little silence he said, "Be too much to ask for you to get me a copy of this liber-etto you talk about—I guess that means the words they's singin'?"

"It won't do you much good." January became aware his hands were balled into fists in his jacket pockets. He made them relax, fingers seeking the rosary of blue glass beads that never left him. Passing along—or trying to pass—to God an anger that he understood would eat his soul if he let it.

With a sigh, he shook his head. "For one thing, it's in Italian," he went on. "For another, words are the least of an opera. They have to ride the music: it's the music that tells the story. Come to Madame Bontemps's house— Bontemps is my landlady. She lets me hold my piano classes in her parlor. Come Sunday afternoon, after dinner, and I'll take you through some of the libretto with the music, and try to show you what I mean."

"Obliged." Shaw ruminated a moment more, while the auctioneer inside rattled off the dimensions, location, and terms of sale for six plots of land along what would be a new railway route from the river to the lake, if the city ever decided which contractor was going to build it. January guessed that the property, developed from one of the nearer plantations, was under a foot and more of water at the moment.

"I'll surely ask Belaggio if'n anybody's spoke to him on the subject of changin' the repertoire. In the meantime . . ." Shaw extended a forefinger like a knotted cane-stalk to tap the grimed and smeary newspaper that he'd handed January. "You might want to have a squint at that."

A FEARFUL ESCAPE FROM DEATH

The bloodstained histories of Macbeth, and the fearsome rivalries of the Borgias, pale in comparison to the dreadful enmities and dark deeds perpetrated in this very city. Signor Lorenzo Belaggio, newly arrived in New Orleans to bring to it a spectacle of opera never seen here before, was assaulted last night as he emerged from James Caldwell's American Theater, by villains hired by a rival to work his ruin.

Belaggio, who though badly wounded in the affray bravely fought off four assailants, will present under Mr. Caldwell's auspices a season of seven operas at Caldwell's unsurpassed American Theater. "It is the first time that Italian Opera shall be seen in this city as it was meant to be seen," Belaggio declared.

And indeed, the American Theater, larger and more handsomely appointed than its rival, Mr. Davis's Théâtre d'Orleans, bids fair to eclipse Mr. Davis's customary offering as the sun eclipses the pallid stars. Though Davis was heard by many to utter murderous threats against the courageous Italian, the City Guards have dismissed as absurd the possibility that rivalry—nay, defeat in the lists of art—played some part in the hiring of bravos to incapacitate the key figure in the upcoming spectacles. Still . . .

·   ·   ·

Perplexed and faintly nauseated, January set the paper on the edge of his piano, gazed through the spotless white-curtained parlor windows at the Rue des Ursulines, milky silver now under the shadow of approaching rain. Two of the street's namesake nuns hurried along the banquette, the rising wind snapping at their magpie habits; a woman selling asparagus from a wicker tray dropped them a curtsy and a smile.

The article went on—January had already read it twice, once on a bench in the Place d'Armes, where he'd stopped to rest after parting from Shaw, and once after he'd returned to Madame Bontemps's—to insinuate that, in fact, John Davis—Parisian-born and French to his fingers' ends—had done precisely what "the City Guards have dismissed as absurd": hired men to injure— *"though surely even a beaten rival would not have the calculated malice to utterly make away with"*—Lorenzo Belaggio.

January had worked for James Caldwell often enough to know the flamboyant former actor wouldn't stoop to this. To stealing, or helping Belaggio steal, his rival's thunder by putting on the same opera, yes, of course. To buying up all the red silk and flame-colored glass in town, so necessary for the fire-effects of the volcano, certainly. But this—accompanied as it was by harrowing accounts of the Roncevaux in the alley—had to have come from Belaggio himself.

January turned to the keyboard, and shaped the ghostly echoes of that final, heart-shattering duet. *Kill me tomorrow, but let me live tonight.* . . .

And yes, he told himself, *Beethoven was a horrid-tempered domestic tyrant and yes, Rossini is a sharp and money-clever entrepreneur and Balzac doesn't bathe and sleeps with every woman he meets, but still* . . .

But still . . .

Why persist in the childish belief that beautiful art must come from a beautiful soul?

What was there in this music that shouted to him, *I understand what it is like to be outcast. What it is like to be so damaged in my heart that I cannot believe in even the beloved's profession of love.*

How could Belaggio understand that, and yet be behind the mean-minded insinuations that peppered the article in the *Gazette*?

Or was he himself, thought January wryly, guilty of the Venetian Moor's own brand of disillusionment, that cannot bear to see the beloved as less than perfect? *This woman's love stirs my heart, therefore she must be without flaw; this music shakes my soul, therefore the man who wrote it must be good. . . .*

"Benjamin?"

The deep, pleasant voice was accompanied by a light rap on the French door's small panes. As January rose from his piano-stool and opened to the short, stocky gentleman who stood on the high brick step, he flung up his hands in mock terror and gasped, *"Dio me salve! Assassino!"*

And John Davis rapped him sharply on the elbow with another folded copy of the *Gazette* and burst out laughing.

January stepped aside to let the theater owner in. In doing so, he nearly collided with his landlady, who had emerged from her bedroom in her usual silence and fastened both men with a stare of unwinking disapproval. "People aren't supposed to come into the parlor now," Madame Bontemps announced in her odd, flat voice. The round brown eyes rested on Davis. "M'sieu Janvier should have told me you were coming. I want to know when someone is going to come into the parlor." She was a

small woman with an indefinable suggestion of crooked-
ness to her narrow shoulders, clothed as usual in a dress
cut after the fashions of her girlhood triumphs at the
quadroon balls. This was a style toward which January ordinarily felt a wistful nostalgia—he'd grown up looking at
women clothed in high-waisted, narrow-cut gowns of
clinging gauze and thought women nowadays dressed like
idiots—but on Madame Bontemps's stocky little frame
the costume, executed in brilliant green chintz, was impossibly grotesque.

Nothing daunted, Davis bowed, removed his rain-
flecked beaver, and kissed her gloved hand. "My dear
Madame, I apologize most abjectly for not writing ahead
to inform M'sieu Janvier of my coming. . . ."

"M'sieu Bontemps wants to know who will be coming into his parlor," she proclaimed, M'sieu Bontemps being the protector who, fifteen years ago, had put her aside
on the occasion of his marriage. In spite of the dismissal
she had kept his name, as many plaçées did. There were
times when January wondered if his landlady remembered she *had* been turned away. "I'll have to write him
about your coming in. I write him every Sunday." M'sieu
Bontemps had died three years ago in the cholera. January
knew his landlady still *did* write her former protector,
whose parting stipend to her had shrunk almost to nothing, courtesy of the white man's widow. It was this latter
circumstance that had forced her to take in boarders, including himself.

"And very wise of you, Madame," Davis agreed
gravely. "M'sieu Bontemps is a great friend of mine, you
know."

"I know." She peered up at him from beneath the immense red-and-yellow mushroom of her bizarrely-fash-
ioned tignon. "But I have to write him nevertheless. Until

he writes me back, M'sieu Janvier, you have to speak to M'sieu Davis down at his office."

"Of all the ridiculous things." Knowing, evidently, that argument was pointless, Davis stepped amiably back down to the brick banquette, and gestured with the *Gazette* as January took an umbrella from beside the door. They made their way toward the corner through the lightly pattering rain, Madame Bontemps watching them from the step. By the way she'd kept her distance from Davis, January wondered whether she'd read the article also and seriously suspected his friend of hiring bravos to murder Belaggio after all. Except, of course, that her suspicions could as easily have stemmed from the color of Davis's waistcoat—"You can't trust a man who wears too much green," she'd informed January darkly that very morning—or an objection to the hearts-spades-diamonds fobs that decorated his golden watch-chain.

"Lieutenant Shaw tells me you were responsible for saving Belaggio's life last night," Davis went on, hopping the brimming gutter of Rue Bourbon. "He says you may have seen the men—"

"I didn't," interrupted January. "Only heard one of them whisper. Have you been in that alley next to the American Theater? It's like being locked in an ammunition box."

"I've been there." Davis paused when they reached the far side of the street, rested his hand on the iron support of a gallery.

It seemed to January—and he'd known John Davis since the first year he'd played piano professionally, at the age of sixteen, in the old United States Hotel that the man had owned down near the Navy yard—that since the death of his wife, Davis had aged. And he did not look well. The once-ruddy face was blotchy, and showed the marks of strain. Not surprising, January thought, considering the seven or eight lifetimes the little entrepreneur had packed into his sixty-two years of gambling, importing, dodging rebel slaves in Saint-Domingue and Cuba, and running two theaters, three gaming establishments, and several ballrooms in New Orleans. Ordinarily Davis was one of the liveliest men he knew, seeming to bustle even in repose. For the first time, January thought: *He's tired.*

And then, seeing the grayish tinge of the round, heavy cheeks, the sweat that filmed so suddenly along the shoreline of that crisp gray hair: *He's ill.*

"Are you all right, sir?"

Davis looked up at him, like one caught in a lie. He gestured with the *Gazette* again—the rain had run the print—and made a business of unsnagging the fobs that depended from one of his watch-chains from the second, foppishly redundant chain that looped below. "No, no, I'm well. I'm fine. It's just this . . . this farrago of lies . . ."

"You don't think anyone's actually going to believe it? Anyone who knows you . . ."

"I'd like to credit my friends with more brains than that, yes." Davis sighed. "But the town isn't what it was, Ben. You know that. I used to know everyone in this town. They'd come to the opera, or to the subscription balls. I'd see them at the Blue Ribbon Balls with their plaçées. . . ." He dug in his coat-pocket for a handkerchief of spotless linen, took off his hat to pass the cloth over his sunken face. Rain pattered in the gutter, stirring up the stench of garbage; a small brown frog hopped out and sat on the banquette, staring up at the men with black bright-sequin eyes.

"I know it's every Creole's lament that the Americans

are at the bottom of his woes," said Davis. "But they out-number us a dozen to one these days. Most of them have come to town in the past five years. All they know about me is what they read in rags like this."

"Even so," said January, troubled more now by the older man's weariness, by the slump of his shoulders and the sweat that beaded his face despite the chill, than by his words. Davis was one of his oldest friends in the town. The first man to hire him, he remembered, to play as a musician. When January had left for France, Davis had come down to the wharf—the only white man there save for St.-Denis Janvier himself and one of few people to come at all—and gave him thirty Spanish dollars: *You use this to go to the opera when you get to Paris,* he'd said. *Man doth not live by bread alone.*

He was the only one who'd understood that.

"You have friends. . . ."

"And I have enemies." The little man straightened his shoulders with an effort, and put his handkerchief away. "And more than that, I have debts. I took an opera com-pany to New York last season and didn't make a dollar—I owe this city over a hundred thousand dollars, in credit and loans, and Caldwell's beating the pants off me at the American Theater. *And* hiring away my best musicians." He cocked a playfully accusing eye up at January.

"Oh, I understand why you're playing for his produc-tions—including that damned *Muette* next week, damn him!—and not mine this season. He's paying twice what I can. He's got the American audiences. . . ."

"Vaudeville and melodrama." January's voice tingled with contempt.

Davis leaned close, and with a conjurer's flourish pretended to pluck a Mexican silver dollar from behind

January's left ear. "You know who had this dollar before I did?" he asked.

January shook his head.

Davis twirled it in his fingers, tucked it into his waistcoat pocket. "Neither do I, my boy," he said wisely. "Neither do I." He sighed, and with the fading of his bright, quizzical look, his face grew old and sad.

"I can't afford this, Ben. I'm trying to recoup where I can—my construction company has a bid in on that new steam railway-line out to the lake—but the Americans on the City Council are trying to force me out. This isn't going to help. Mind you," he added with a grin, "I probably shouldn't have said *I'll cut his heart out in a church* when I heard about his *Muette*. . . . They probably didn't even recognize the quote."

"Can you move your performance up?" Garish bills advertising Belaggio's production of the Auber opera adorned the wall behind them: Vesuvius belching flame and the eponymous Mute Girl hurling herself into its crater. In fact, Belaggio's first performance would be *Le Nozze di Figaro,* but January couldn't imagine what playbill would draw Americans into the theater to see that. Cherubino flinging himself three or four stories from the Almaviva balcony into a particularly savage rosebush?

Davis shook his head. "My tenor and my soprano don't arrive until the twenty-ninth. And Caldwell's bought up every firework and flare and bolt of red silk in town, damn him. So when Mount Vesuvius erupts, I'm going to have to ask the audience to use their imaginations—not that the Creoles have them. . . ."

"Oh, give me a muse of fire!"

Davis laughed, a bright, infectious sound in the quiet street. "Or at least tell me where to hire one for the night," he said. "And you know, I suspect three-quarters of the Americans in this town actually believe that's a perfectly reasonable excuse to kill another man? Idiots, all of 'em."

"What do you want me to do?" asked January, and Davis clasped his hand gratefully. "Shaw's already hinted he'd be glad if I kept my ears open. . . ."

"Oh, nothing more than that," said Davis. "I'm certainly not requiring death-defying leaps or hand-to-hand encounters with tigers. And I daresay it'll all blow over, as King Louis said to Marie Antoinette. But I'd feel better knowing you were keeping an eye on things."

"That I'll do, and gladly." January folded up the umbrella as the rain softened and eased. On the other side of the street, two children clothed as prince and princess in anticipation of some Carnival festivity peeked from a carriageway between two shopfronts, and squealed as the last raindrops plinked into their small, extended hands. "I still can't imagine anyone taking these accusations seriously."

"Neither can I," said Davis. "Unless these assassins— whoever hired them—succeed next time."

THREE

⸺∽⸻

"Who would murder Belaggio?" Madame Marguerite Scie rose from her plié and stood by the rehearsal-room barre with her thin arms folded, such morning sunlight as managed to trickle between the back of the theater and the wall of the Promenade Hotel's stable yard picking out streaks of silver in her tightly-bound fair hair. "Anyone in the company, I should imagine, with the possible exception of the little d'Isola chit. He isn't well liked."

She flicked her long legs into fifth position, demipliéd twice, and sank, flat-backed and upright, into a deep grande, her long fingers barely touching the support. She'd been eleven years old, and a pupil of the best dancing-masters in Paris in preparation for her eventual Court presentation, when the Bastille had been stormed in 1789. She still moved like a girl.

January rested his chin on his folded arms on the back of the chair he straddled before the piano. "You behold me agog, Madame."

She smiled sidelong, like an amused snake. "It's no accident he was putting on a Christmas opera season in Havana, of all places." The inflection of her deep, velvety voice made the Spanish colonial capital sound like a muddy hamlet on the Mississippi. "I think the only reason he's still able to do seasons in Milan is because his brother is a Commissioner of Police there, and can get the Austrians to make trouble for his rivals. Look where he works."

She sank, and rose, in a graceful port-de-corps, the muscles of her back like a fencer's above the short-sleeved camisole, the abbreviated corset, and schoolgirl skirts. "Milan, Florence, the Veneto . . . and America, where people haven't heard of him. Lorenzo has a reputation for not having his books balance. If the Carbonari ever do manage to run the Austrians out of the peninsula, he'll be behind a barrow in a market-place the following morning, urging housewives to buy tomatoes."

Before his encounter with the assassins in the alleyway, January had intended to dine Friday night with his dear friend Rose Vitrac, a young, former schoolmistress at the moment earning her living by correcting Greek, Latin, and science papers for several of the young gentlemen's academies in town. By the time he'd returned from his talk with Davis, however, and had taught his day's piano lessons, January's injured arm ached as if hacked with a sword and he'd felt feverish and weak. "I'm ashamed of you, Benjamin," Rose had said, peering at him severely through the thick lenses of her spectacles. "A mere cut on the arm sends you to ground? A brief pummeling by villains drives you to seek your bed? I'll have you know that young Mr. Saltearth, the friend of the hero in *All for Glory, or, A Patriot's Triumph,* currently being presented at the American Theater, managed to drag himself fifty miles through the snow in the dead of winter despite being shot through both lungs by Tories, in order to warn General Washington of a prospective attack on Valley Forge."

"You know a lot about it"—January shaded his eyes

to squint up at her from the chair where he'd been resting on the gallery outside his tiny room—"for someone who considers even Dumas's plays too silly to watch." The patchy clouds had broken by then, sweeping the low pastel houses of this part of the French town with pale sheets of light, and Rose, perched on the gallery rail, had looked more than ever like a very young wading-bird, gawky-graceful and ready to fly away.

"I was given a complete account of this—er—epic by Marie-Philomène, who has the room next to mine behind Vroche's Grocery," she had retorted. In the end they'd compromised by going downstairs to Madame Bontemps's kitchen and making sausage and rice under the landlady's silently disapproving eye. Upon leaving, Rose had promised to make inquiries at the Fatted Calf and various other cafés in the vicinity of the American Theater about whether two young men answering the descriptions of Signori Cavallo and Ponte had been seen.

It was, January had reasoned, a starting-point. "They can't have spent the entire time from the end of rehearsal at—what was it, eleven? eleven-thirty?—until past three cramped in that doorway," Rose had said. "I can do a very passable imitation of a lady's maid, searching for information on where Young Michie might have been at that hour and who he might have been with. It isn't," she'd added with grim wisdom, "like the waiters at the cafés have not heard such inquiries before."

"I can't see errors in bookkeeping being grounds for murder," January said now, mentally comparing Rose's slim, scholarly awkwardness with Marguerite Scie's knife-blade poise. He had told the older woman of his love for Rose, and his hopes that she would one day marry him: one day when he made enough money to live somewhere other than in a rented room in Marie-Claire Bontemps's garçonnière. One day when past wounds in Rose's soul had sufficiently healed.

"It depends upon the size of the error," returned the ballet mistress. "And the circumstances of the murder." She pointed her toes in a couple of swift tendus, bowed forward again, arm precisely curved. "Paying bravos to slaughter a man in an alley, no. For one thing, I should imagine bravos come rather expensive, even in New Orleans."

Past the rehearsal-room door, footfalls creaked the floor of the backstage—the scrape of something heavy being moved, the squeak of a pulley, suddenly brightening light, and a stink of burning gas. Caldwell's American Theater was the largest in the city, and if rude by European standards was far more modern than the rival Théâtre d'Orleans. "A few days before everyone took ship from Havana, Signor Belaggio surprised Cavallo searching his office, and accused him of trying to rob the cashbox. Cavallo in turn accused Belaggio of keeping duplicate books. High words were exchanged."

"It's still a long way from high words," countered January, "to a dagger in an alley in the night."

The corps de ballet was coming in, in twos and threes, arms around one another's waists or glancing daggers at rivals. Gossamer skirts, tight-brushed hair. *Did you see him looking at you from the wings, chérie? I could see the love in his eyes. . . .*

"Little rats," they were called in Paris. Some of the Sicilian girls were as dark as Rose was, the Milanese nearly as fair as Madame Scie. Many had been hired in Havana, and having failed to find wealthy protectors in Cuba had come to try their luck in New Orleans—Spanish girls, or octoroons fair enough to claim Spanish, with names like Columbina or Ignacita or Natividad. There were one or two French girls, and French Creole girls hired locally, and they looked at the Habañeros and said things like "chaca" and "catchoupine." *I hate to be the one to tell you, sweetest, but I'm your friend and someone has to. . . .*

Among them, like a splendid flamingo among doves, moved the gorgeous flame-haired, long-limbed Oona Flaherty, whose admission to the corps had been the price James Caldwell was willing to pay to have Fitzhugh Trulove in the St. Mary Opera Society.

Darling, he treats me just like I was a princess! We had ices at the Café Venise, and rode in his carriage along the levee. Afterward . . .

January wasn't sure, but he suspected that the choice of *La Muette de Portici* had had as much to do with Trulove's passion for Oona as with Belaggio's desire to steal a march on John Davis. In that passionate tale of Spanish domination, Neapolitan revolt, seduction, romance, and volcanic eruption, La Flaherty was dancing the part of the Mute Girl, a prospect to make anyone shudder.

"Were it not for the dagger you saw," remarked Madame Scie, counting off the girls with a chill gray eye, "I would wonder if perhaps the intention was mayhem rather than murder. It is, in fact, common enough in the South"—she meant south of Rome—"for a nobleman, if annoyed by a plebeian, to have his lackeys chastise the offender for his presumption. It was done in France as well, of course, in my father's time. But I agree," she added, glancing at the bandaged lump under January's left sleeve with the condescension of eleven generations of marquises de Vermandois, "that the knife came into use quickly."

"Has that ever happened to Belaggio?" January turned

around in the rush-bottomed chair and commenced warming up his hands with the simplified version of the "Rondo à la Turque" that he used for his students. In keeping with everything else in the American Theater, the piano was the best to be had, a massive iron-framed Babcock grand with the heavy action typical of English instruments.

Madame Scie shook her head. "For the simple reason that he worked with Incantobelli. His partner, you understand." She walked to the barre again, and taking second position, sketched a couple of demi-pliés, which the more perceptive of the girls watched and imitated at once.

"A man not only talented, but brilliant. And charming—he had the dukes and princes of Naples, the senators of Venice, quarreling like schoolgirls over who would sit next to him at receptions. When I worked with the two of them at the San Carlos in Milan in 'twenty-seven, it was obvious Belaggio could barely endure it. He was never one to be outshone. Perhaps it was only that which finally caused the break between them. I don't know. Girls!" She clapped her hands sharply. "Two demis and a grande, port-de-corps— So. First, second, fourth, fifth. Sixty-four bars, if you would, M'sieu Janvier."

January played snippets of polonaises, *valses brilliantes,* and simplified rondos for the dancers to warm up, during which time he was conscious of a constant coming and going around the rehearsal-room door. Lions gazing at gazelles, it was called in Paris. Fitzhugh Trulove quite frankly brought in one of the chairs from the orchestra to watch his red-haired inamorata, hands clasped before his pink-flowered waistcoat and a smile of fatuous content on his round pink face. Jed Burton appeared shortly thereafter—January wondered what both of those planters had told their wives about where they were going this morning—and, a little while later, young Harry Fry, the steamboat owner, looking as always as if his collar were buttoned too tightly. It amused January to note how the girls took greater care in the pointing of their pink silk toes, with the men standing in the doorway watching, and how preoccupied they became with perfecting the curves of their arms. Once he caught Marguerite's sardonic eye and almost laughed.

Did the girls know, he wondered, that these gentlemen who took them for ices and for rides along the river road, who watched from the wings "with love in their eyes," all had plaçées? Free women of color for whom they had bought houses along Rue des Ramparts and Rue Burgundy, whom they had established as second wives?

Would it make a difference if they knew?

The St. Mary Opera Society, he thought, and his eyes returned to the little group again as Marguerite explained a complicated ronde-de-jambe. The first ones to know that Belaggio intended to put on an opera of *Othello.* At least a few of them had been at Thursday night's rehearsal, and had read the libretto. Who felt, or guessed, the power of the music. Which one, he wondered, might have taken it upon himself to "chastise" the Italian "for his presumption"?

Trulove? The man was reputed to be brainless, and in two and a half years of playing at the parties of the wealthy, January had not seen the smallest evidence to the contrary. But his wife was a cold, clever woman, ruthless and strong. And in any case, it didn't take brains to desire or plan such a crime. Only hate.

Was there hate concealed behind Trulove's bland pink countenance?

Stubby and brick-faced beside Trulove's tall, silver-haired amiability, Jed Burton spit into the sandbox just

outside the door and leaned down to whisper something
to the Englishman, nodding as he did so toward the girls
at the barre. Trulove flung back his head with a smile. January tried to remember what his mother, that fount of
all gossip and scandal—French or American or free
colored—had to say about Jed Burton, and could recall
only that the man was a contractor, involved in a lawsuit
of some kind about a plantation his first wife had inher-
ited on Bayou des Familles. Burton had been a planter
himself, and hadn't made a go of it—January was well
aware that men like Trulove, ostensibly so wealthy, lived
in debt from year to year, borrowing money from their
factors against crops only barely in the ground, dependent
on the frost and the harvest and the resistance of their
slaves to disease.

Burton had a wife now, named Ludmilla—his
second—whose father was of the Virginia planter aristoc-
racy, and it was undoubtedly she who actually wanted the
box for the opera season. January had the impression Burton himself didn't know Othello from Punchinello and
didn't care.

But Americans were full of surprises. He'd learned
that much from Shaw.

Young Harry Fry was quite frankly gazing at a sweet-
faced Cuban girl named Felina with his heart in his eyes.
January recalled hearing someone—his mother? Uncle
Bichet?—mention the young man's interests in brokering
sugar and cotton crops as well as transporting them; in
buying furs from the trappers in the mountains of Mexican territory. Anything to turn a dollar. Son of a Boston
banker, Fry had been sent here to claim a share of the
enormous revenues pouring into the city. With the
breakup of the old Spanish Empire, money and precious
metals that had previously gone straight to Spain were up

for grabs. Legally or illegally, they were coming through
New Orleans from Mexico, from Cuba, from the new nations of New Grenada, and it was through New Orleans
that guns and supplies had gone to Bolívar, Guerrero,
Iturbide. January had seen young Fry at a dozen American parties and as many or more of the Blue Ribbon
Balls—the quadroon balls—at the Salle d'Orleans, alter-
nating his polite dancing or wholehearted pursuit of the
free colored demimonde with serious-faced conversation
among the businessmen of the town.

A young man eager to advance, thought January. At
any cost, perhaps. He was negotiating with several friends
of January's mother for their daughters' contracts of
plaçage, but as far as January had heard hadn't settled on a
mistress yet.

At the conclusion of the ballet rehearsal, January
emerged from the rehearsal-room to find Hannibal Sefton
perched halfway up the Count Almaviva's pink marble
garden steps, playing a wistful West Irish planxty on his
violin. The music floated gently above the babble of
voices, like sun-spangles on water: five different varieties
of Italian; slurry, lilting Viennese German; the sloppy
Creole Spanish of Havana; and several sorts of French.
The green room, dark as a cave and barely twelve feet
square, was good only for making coffee in—besides being tacitly off-limits to the little rats and most of the musicians.

"I hear we're going to need to count the money twice
after every performance," January remarked just loudly
enough that Silvio Cavallo, sitting a little lower down the
steps with a couple of other Lombard members of the
company, turned his head.

Hannibal sighed, and said, "That'll teach you to ask
before you rescue anyone." In the flickery glow of the

gasoliers, he looked a little better than he had Thursday night, but dangerously thin: shabby in his skirted coat and long hair, like something that had wandered out of an old portrait.

"You think that Austrian's whore hasn't learned to keep double books?" Cavallo rose, and moved close to speak without being overheard. He'd been speaking Milanese with his compatriots, but switched to the Italian that January knew better. "Look them over if you will, Signor. He's learned enough from that brother of his, that Viennese *sbirro*, that his books will smell of lilies, like the Book of Judgment in Paradise." He cast a glare across the dusty brown dimness of backstage at Belaggio, ascending the steps from the prop-vault. A black silk sling supported the impresario's arm, though January's wound had improved sufficiently in thirty-six hours that he'd been able to dispense with his. La d'Isola tripped lightly at Belaggio's side, exquisite in a flutter of black-ribboned white organdy. She tugged the stage-hand Pedro away from bringing up flats to fetch Belaggio a chair, and made Nina abandon her adjustment of Madame Montero's costume to find a cushion for his arm, and in general fussed as if the impresario had just struggled up from his deathbed.

If young M'sieu Saltearth in All for Glory *can manage to drag himself into action,* thought January, *surely Lorenzo Belaggio can do no less.*

"But if you believe I would conceal myself in an alley with a knife because of it . . ."

"I don't," January told Cavallo, mildly and not entirely truthfully. "I was just curious as to why Belaggio thought you might have. And who you think would. Did you know Bellaggio's partner Incantobelli?"

"I thought it is this Señor Davis, this owner of the French Opera, who is supposed to have done this thing."

Consuela Montero flounced furiously over to them, the old antidote Marcellina's fussy pink gown and enormous panniers fitted awkwardly over her black satin petticoat. "As for Incantobelli, there is a man who truly understands the opera. He would not have put *that*"—her lace-gloved hand flicked scornfully in the direction of d'Isola—"anywhere but in the chorus. And as for that carrot-haired Hibernian slut . . . *Madre de dios!*"

At that moment Vincent Marsan came up from below, bending his golden head in conversation with the Widow Redfern, and a third member of the Opera Society, a thin little flaxen gentleman whom Hannibal later identified as Marsan's factor and business agent, Erasmus Knight. La d'Isola straightened up from adjusting the cushion under Belaggio's arm—January saw her eyes seek Marsan's.

As the planter's back was to him, January didn't see what was in his face. But he saw him pause, and tilt his head a little, at the long-lashed, dark passion in her gaze.

"Do you know why Belaggio and Incantobelli parted?"

Montero shrugged. "He left the year before last, at Christmas. I was doing a season at La Fenice, singing Fiordiligi and Leonore—decent roles, leading roles, not this collection of waiting-women and old maids that lying Milano traitor has . . ."

"We were speaking of Incantobelli?" suggested Hannibal, taking Montero's hand. And when she glared at him in haughty dudgeon, he added in Spanish, "If I hear more of his iniquities toward you, *guisante mia,* I shall have to call him out, and then what would the company do for a first violin?"

She rapped his knuckles with her spangled fan. *"Es ver-*

dad. In any event, Incantobelli was the first singer with whom I appeared upon a stage. It was at La Pergola in Florence, in ... well, I forget the year." She waved airily. "I was one of Cleopatra's waiting-women to his *Guilio Cesare.*"

Which explained, thought January in a flash of enlightenment, why Incantobelli wouldn't have been as receptive as Belaggio was to Drusilla d'Isola's wide-eyed charms.

"Don't listen to Madame Montero when she speaks ill of Drusilla—of Mademoiselle d'Isola," said Cavallo as the Mexican soprano rustled away to seize back Nina's services during her rival's moment of distraction. "She's no Malibran, but she has very fine feeling, a very spritely manner on-stage, that makes up for it." He watched the young soprano with brotherly tenderness as she hovered at Belaggio's side, her gaze flickering to Marsan, shy as a child's. Belaggio was recounting his battle in the alley to Claud Cepovan, the Austrian bass; Marsan made his way across the backstage, stood looking down at d'Isola, lips curving gently beneath the close-clipped golden mustache.

"Concha Montero was Belaggio's mistress before he met La d'Isola. I imagine that's what she was doing at the theater so late on Thursday night."

"Spying on Belaggio?"

"Spying on La d'Isola, more like." Hannibal coughed, and dug in his music-satchel for the inevitable bottle of opium-laced brandy. *"Those pretty wrongs that liberty commits / When I am sometime absent from thy heart ...* I mean, the lovely Montero *knows* what Belaggio's up to."

Belaggio struggled gallantly to his feet to take the Widow Redfern's hands. She was forty-two, built like a treestump, and wearing approximately five hundred dollars' worth of pearls on one wrist alone. Madame Montero stepped up to his other side, elbowing the still-enraptured d'Isola out of her way.

"Not being blind," Hannibal went on, "I'm sure Consuela's noticed the direction of La d'Isola's eye when M'sieu Marsan's in the room."

After one final smile at Marsan, Drusilla turned back and grimly slipped around Montero, with a solicitous adjustment to Belaggio's sling.

"Marsan was supposed to meet Belaggio Thursday night, but at what time? If Montero could prove he'd come early or late to rendezvous with La d'Isola . . ."

"As a favor to me," said Cavallo, laying a hand on Hannibal's bony shoulder, "would you limit the number of people before whom you air that particular theory, Signor Sefton? And as a favor to yourself," he added, his grip tightening. "If you think Belaggio would have the slightest compunction about dismissing her—a girl of twenty-two, with neither friends nor family, in a country where she does not speak the language—I can only assure you that you are wrong."

He moved away to join his young friend Ponte, who was passing around a bottle of red wine with a half-dozen of the other Neapolitans of the chorus on the slopes of Vesuvius. They had presumably selected the dismantled volcano not so much from homesickness as because the properties manager, a hard-faced little gnome named Tiberio, hailed from Salerno. While he fussed with his pots of sulfur, charcoal, and nitrate of strontia, Tiberio shouted instructions to Pedro, one of the two stage-hands Belaggio had brought with the company from Havana: instructions and curses, since Pedro spoke only Spanish and couldn't have understood the wizened Sicilian's thick Arabic-flavored dialect even if he *had* known Italian.

In fact, as he leaned on the *faux marbre* balustrade and observed the backstage at large, January was reminded strongly of some of Rose's chemical demonstrations: elements separating out, Lombards chattering in the brisk tongue of Milan, Florentines ignoring them and conversing in Tuscan pure as Carrara marble, Romans looking down their aquiline noses at the Neapolitans and Sicilians, and everybody cutting the Austrians. He'd seen the same phenomenon at balls given by French Creole planters: Orleanistes wouldn't speak to Legitimistes except to occasionally join in slanging Bonapartistes. . . . And none would speak to the Americans—except Vincent Marsan, for purposes of business—while the *gens du couleur libre* like his mother wouldn't exchange a word with first-generation freedmen, let alone slaves. . . .

Then he recalled his own prejudice against Shaw, and grinned at his pose of philosophical judgment.

"If La d'Isola goes on like that," remarked Hannibal, following the prima with his eyes as she gazed after the retreating Marsan, "it's going to come to being left here, whether I mention the matter to anyone or not. I notice she's already figured out the quickest way to Marsan's heart—that outfit she's wearing couldn't possibly clash with any ensemble he might care to sport."

January looked again, and almost laughed, because it was true: the girl's stylish white and black blended beautifully with the symphony of silvers and grays the dandy had chosen that afternoon. Marsan should have looked ridiculous, but he didn't: broad-shouldered, beautiful, graceful, and tall, he looked literally like a prince of moonlight, a knight sheathed in silver.

No wonder d'Isola was smitten.

"Molte bene!" Belaggio flung up his hands in delight as the company's soubrette—the dainty and silvery-voiced

little Madame Elisabetta Chiavari—made her appearance
on the arm of her husband, a baritone named Trevi who
bore a striking resemblance to an amiable toad. "Now, I
trust we all know our way around *Le Nozze di Figaro* for
Tuesday night. . . ."

He herded everyone into the rehearsal-room again.
January and the other musicians carried in the straight-
backed orchestra chairs for themselves, and traded gossip and chat: who was playing the ball at the Hermanns'
that night, who'd go on from rehearsal to the reception
Fitzhugh Trulove was giving for the Opera Society at his
great handsome house on the Bayou Road. "You coming
to my place after that, Ben?" asked Jacques Bichet in an
undervoice, unwrapping his flute from its box, and January nodded. It would make a late night—the Trulove
party probably wouldn't end till past two—and the gathering at Jacques's would, like any after-curfew gathering of
the free colored, the *libres,* be completely illegal. . . .

But what else was Carnival for?

As old Uncle Bichet liked to say—tuning up his cello
with its sweet conversational voice—You can sleep during
Lent.

"It's wonderful to see everyone here looking so well!"
James Caldwell paused in the rehearsal-room door to
make an entrance, a tall man, handsome and energetic,
his flowing brown hair and carefully-groomed sidewhiskers a souvenir of his own days on the stage. All his
gestures seemed rehearsed. "I'm sure we're all prepared to
make this opera season, the first Italian Opera in this city,
a special and spectacular event."

Several members of the Opera Society applauded,
mostly because Caldwell seemed to expect it. Marsan
leaned down to exchange words with Mr. Knight—whom
January recognized vaguely from his days in Paris, though

his name hadn't been Knight at the time—and was nearly pushed out of the doorway by Madame Rossi, the costume mistress, her arms full of satin and false hair. She was trailed by her assistant, Julie, with Nina, the slave-girl, bringing up the rear.

"And where he got the money to purchase that girl," muttered Montero, clothed once more in prune-colored velvet and emeralds, "I should like to have made clear. A slave-girl, solely to look after that *lagarta*'s wigs and gowns and make-up, while all the rest of us must make do with Julie . . . !"

"Slaves are cheap in Havana," January pointed out. "A girl you'd pay nine hundred dollars for here can be bought for one or two hundred. He probably spent more on the dress La d'Isola's wearing."

"And where did he get the money for that, eh?"

"Same place he got the money for your bracelets?" suggested Hannibal, and the dark Aztec eyes flashed in an unwilling grin.

After years of working around the chronic shortage of musicians in New Orleans—of doubled-up violin parts, rewritten horns, and covering deficient woodwind sections with piano—it was good to hear Mozart's score more or less as written for once. Caldwell hadn't stinted on his orchestra, as January knew Davis was obliged to do. Most of the musicians were free men of color, trained, like January, at the expense of white fathers—or in January's case, his mother's white protector—and able to make a fair living playing cotillions, schottisches, and Chopin waltzes at the parties of the rich. What they played for themselves—or for organizations like the Faubourg Tremé Free Colored Militia and Burial Society—was another matter. The two young Bratizant brothers, Creole French seeking the experience of playing for the opera, and the

Bavarian Herr Pleck on his bass fiddle, were perfectly acceptable additions, and, of course, Hannibal could play anything. But January privately reflected that there were things about music that white people simply didn't understand.

Early in the rehearsal it became obvious to January that the aspersions cast by Madame Montero on Mademoiselle d'Isola's singing had not been gratuitous. She was, as Cavallo had so kindly put it, no Maria Malibran.

"A little more simply, Elisabetta my dear," urged Bellagio, during Susanna's Act Two duets with the Countess. "Susanna is a simple girl, she must sing simply. . . ."

"She must sing simply so that witless hussy's so-called ornamentations won't be shown up as the nursery-rhymes they are," muttered Montero savagely, standing, arms folded, beside January's piano. "Yet when Elisabetta Chiavari and I sing together, it is 'Let me hear you both soar.' Countess, huh! That Neapolitan bitch d'Isola has no business in such roles. I sang the Countess last year for Belaggio in Turin, and there was none of this, 'Sing more simply.' " While everyone else scrabbled around in their music, looking for the beginning of the ballet, she studied January speculatively, then lowered her voice.

"Señor," she went on in a different tone, "I understand that you give lessons as well as play for the opera? In other words, that you have your own piano, and a place to teach?"

"I do."

Montero glanced around to make sure she was unobserved, then set a gold half-eagle on the top of the piano with a rich clink.

"Might you be free for—oh—three hours tomorrow morning? Before rehearsal here?"

January's first thought—*If that five dollars is for an*

amorous interlude, you're certainly flattering me, Madame—glanced aside at the veiled calculation behind those long lashes. Even cutting short his time at Bichet's, it would mean he'd have almost no sleep. But he'd never forgive himself—certainly neither Rose nor Hannibal would forgive him—if he didn't find out what was going on.

"Ten?" he said, and the red-lipped smile broadened. "Ten it is."

FOUR

———◈◈◈———

"Othello?" Lorenzo Belaggio's heavy brows scrunched and his jaw thrust forward. "Why speak to me of *Othello?*" Rehearsal was over, not more than an hour behind schedule. All around them, the musicians were packing up their satchels, gathering their instruments for a quick dinner at jambalaya stands in the market, at the cafés that catered to the free colored, or the less formal groceries that sold bowls of dirty rice out the back doors, before the evening's engagements.

Flashes of half-heard merriment. Snatches of conversation.

"Gonna be at Jacques's tonight?"

"Cynthie said she'd bring along her pound-cake. . . ."

". . . fixed ol' John up with that sister of hers . . ."

"That sister? The one with all the shoes?"

Tiberio could be heard cursing the hosepipes that would run from the proscenium gas-jets into Mount Vesuvius's hollow bowels—at least January thought that's what he was cursing—and from the prop-vault below, a rich Gaelic voice grated, "Greedy god-damned Italians thievin' all the red silk—now I'm askin' what are we to do for Act Three tonight?" Posters all over town advertised the presentation of *A Maid of Old Scotland, or, A Prince's Escape* at eight. Presumably someone's castle was scheduled for fiery destruction.

"Did someone warn you not to put it on?" asked January quietly. "Or ask you not to put it on?"

Belaggio, who had begun to breathe noisily at the first mention of his opera, drew himself to his six-foot-plus burly height. "Who would dare speak so to me? Who would dare say to me—to *me*, Lorenzo Belaggio—what I should and should not have my people perform? My *Othello* is a great opera, truly great. Do you deny it?" He glared at January as if at an accuser. "Do you?"

"No," said January. "Not at all . . ."

"In Naples they wept, yes, they wept in the very streets when Desdemona died." His voice rose to a shout, causing Mr. Caldwell to turn from the door, where he was bidding Mrs. Redfern an obsequious farewell. "When the great Moor gathered her into his arms for one final kiss, to die upon that kiss . . . Who has dared to imply that it should not be sung? That there is any reason why it should not be given?"

Dark eyes blazing, the impresario caught January by the arm, dragged him past the startled theater owner, past Redfern and Knight and Redfern's vulpine business manager, Mr. Fraikes, and into the small office next to the rehearsal-room that Caldwell had given to him. "Who has spoken of this to you?" He kicked the door shut behind him. "What have you heard?"

"Nothing," said January, a little startled by this excessive reaction. "No one has spoken."

"Then why do you speak?"

"*Idiotes,*" raged Tiberio's voice. "Do you not understand plain Spanish? That Habañero *cornutu* warranted you understood Spanish and you have no more Spanish than my grandmother's seven-toed black cat, who is also a blockhead . . . !"

"Please forgive me, sir, for mentioning the matter," January stammered. "I fear someone may have asked you not to have *Othello* performed because Othello is a Moor—and because he is great. Because the play treats of the love of a white woman for a black man . . ."

"Boh!" The Milanese drew back, with a dismissive swipe of his hand. "Ridiculous! Every one of those men in the Opera Society has a Negress for a mistress! Even that scoundrel Marsan, who—"

"That is not the same thing, sir."

"And not the same thing as yourself and Madame Scie, eh?" Belaggio winked, and dug him familiarly with his elbow in the ribs. His breath was a swamp of rotten teeth and violet pastilles. "All those years ago, eh? And still she pines for you."

January blinked, trying to imagine Marguerite pining for *any* member of her regiment of discarded lovers. Did Belaggio assume La d'Isola would remember his name a week after their parting? "Signor," he said patiently, "I fear that it was because of *Othello*—because of what it portrays—that you were attacked in the alley. Because someone might have told you—"

"I know well enough who it was who attacked me." Belaggio glared around him, as if he could see through the little office's walls. With the door closed, the room was at once chill and stuffy, the yellow gleam of a single gas-jet showing up untidy piles of libretti and ledgers, novels and correspondence, and playbills reeking of ink. "You do not understand, my friend," he assured January. "You do not understand the madmen one finds in the peninsula these days. So-called intellectuals, students who deceive themselves and others with their rhetoric." He brought his kid-gloved finger up to tap the side of his own bulbous nose. "Carbonari—bah! 'Young Italy' they call themselves. Bandits, revolutionaries, ne'er-do-wells! They opened the gates of our cities to the Buonaparte and would open them again to worse! Disciples of anarchy and terror. All this I have seen before."

"Signor . . ."

"No more." Belaggio clapped January jovially on his wounded arm. "My good honest fellow, forget your fears. A dozen of the men of the Opera Society have received copies of my *Othello.*" He gestured to the heap of slender green-bound volumes on the desk. "Beautiful, eh? I had them printed specially." He picked one up. "I have had no complaints, either on account of the book or on account of the score. Who could complain? It will be a great success in spite of those hotheads, those Carbonari madmen. . . ." He pushed open the door and threw a venomous glare at Cavallo, who stood by the green-room door in Don Basilio's out-at-elbows lavender coat while Ponte adjusted his absurdly curled wig. "And that scoundrel Davis, who would see the whole of my opera season destroyed." He threw wide his arms—evidently forgetting his black silk sling and just as clearly in no discomfort—and expanded his great chest. "Fear not! Lorenzo Belaggio is more than capable of dealing with the likes of such as they! *Bellissima!*" La d'Isola—who'd been surreptitiously checking the angle of her stylish "Gothic" hat in one of Tiberio's reflectors—spun, with an expression of heart-melting joy. "You were magical this afternoon—perfect! If you sang so at La Scala . . ."

"If she sang so at La Scala," remarked Hannibal, slipping around the doorframe and watching the impresario plant half a dozen wet salutes on his protégée's face and throat, "she'd be rinsing egg out of her hair for a week. Not that it'll matter much Tuesday night. It's hard for one person to really botch up Mozart."

"How much attention were you paying to the Letter Duet?"

"Argutos inter strepere anser olores, as Virgil once put it. . . . Unfortunately I think Signor Belaggio actually believes that because the girl's pretty and will sleep with him that she can, in fact, sing. Not a good failing in an impresario."

"Not an uncommon one, though." January found his music-satchel where he'd left it, on the Contessa Almaviva's white-and-gilt writing-desk, extracted from it the shabby jacket of brown corduroy he'd bought while a medical student in Paris, and pressed in its place the black tailcoat he'd wear again later, at Trulove's. "Would you care to take supper with me at my mother's?" he asked Hannibal as they descended through the gloomy cavern of the prop-room, and so into the alley, where a couple of carters were trying to maneuver a wagonload of hay through the Hotel Promenade's stable-yard gate. "She was asking after you the last time I encountered her in the market."

January's mother was Livia Levesque, a slim woman still beautiful in her late fifties, whose pink stucco house on the Rue Burgundy had been given her by that same wealthy sugar-broker who had purchased and freed her—and made her his mistress—when January was eight. Upon January's return from Paris she'd charged him five Spanish dollars a month to sleep in the room he'd had as a child: when, in the wake of one too many acts of emotional blackmail, he'd informed her he was moving out—"To board with Marie-Claire Bontemps of all people!"—she'd threatened to distrain his piano on the grounds that it had been given him by St.-Denis Janvier when he, January, was a minor.

January had assumed, when he'd had a lawyer send her a letter demanding the instrument, that it was the last he'd ever hear of her except through the gossip of his younger sister, Dominique.

He had underestimated his parent. The morning after New Year's he had encountered her in the market, where she'd greeted him with polite effusiveness, as if he'd been away on a short journey but was now back in town: *How is your health, did you settle in satisfactorily in your new rooms, isn't Marie-Claire Bontemps the craziest old coot imaginable, and does she still converse with the candlesticks?*

Lawyer? January had wondered at the time. *Piano? Was that all a dream?*

But he'd answered her goodwill in kind. She'd invited him to Twelfth Night dinner, a welcome treat, since Madame Bontemps did not include board with the rental of his room and moreover had the disconcerting habit of coming across the yard to the kitchen and watching, soundless as a turtle, while he cooked anything. After that he'd been invited to dine at his mother's house on the average of once a week, frequently with Rose or Hannibal— January had yet to meet a woman who was proof against Hannibal's courtly and vulnerable charm. He was astonished at what good company his mother could be once he was no longer obliged to live under her roof.

". . . used to catch moths in wineglasses," Livia said as her servant, Bella, brought in the savory étouffé for January, Hannibal, and Dominique. The last golden daylight still lingered in the Rue Burgundy, but candles had been lighted on the table and in the lustres around the wall. He and Hannibal, January guessed, would be in good time to reach Trulove's, and with luck Rose would find him at Jacques Bichet's, with information about whether or not those "hotheads and madmen," Cavallo and Ponte, had in fact spent the later part of Thursday evening loitering in the Fatted Calf. "Does she still collect moths and talk to them?"

"Mother!" laughed Dominique. "You're making that up!" Twenty-two years old and beautiful as a bronze-gold lily, the daughter of St.-Denis Janvier was herself the placée of a stout, bespectacled young planter named Henri Viellard. Her cottage lay only a hundred feet down from that of her mother; the petunia-colored silk of her dress and the pink-gold luminosity of the pearls around her throat attested to the care Viellard took of her. "P'tit, that isn't so, is it?"

"I don't know." January spread his hands. "She does wander around at all hours of the night without a candle, like a sleepwalker. . . ."

"As if I'd invent such a tale, Minou!" Livia tapped her daughter's immense "imbecile" sleeve with her fan. Past the archway into the front parlor, the tall French doors stood open onto the Rue Burgundy, where the last of the day's traffic mingled with the first of the night's: hogsheads of sugar and cotton being hauled from canal to levee jostled axles with the landaulets of well-dressed women, or phaetons full of lively young gentlemen got up as Renaissance lords or Knights of the Round Table, singing or blowing handfuls of flour in one another's faces. The red-gold scent of gingerbread baking some-where near-by vied with the choke of steamboat soot in the air, and the smell of brick wet from the light rain that had fallen while January was in rehearsal. More rain threatened, high-piled mountains of cloud sweeping in fast from the Gulf.

"You'd see her at the quadroon balls, with half a dozen young white gentlemen crowding around her," Livia went on, "—though I never thought her above average for looks myself, and that mother of hers was enough to scare anyone off—chatting and talking—this was when the balls were held over on Royal Street, before M'sieu Davis built the Salle d'Orleans. . . . And all of a sudden her eyes would wander off, and be following a moth around the lights of the chandelier, and you'd see her looking around for a wineglass, not remembering who she was talking to. One night a big one landed on the arm of Joffrey Duquille as he was asking her to dance and trying to learn if she was interested in something more with him besides—*Joffrey Duquille,* mind you, one of the richest planters on the river. . . . And all Marie-Claire could do was stare and stare at this big gray moth, walking up his coatsleeve. Finally she blurted out, *Pray, may I have your wineglass, sir. . . .*"

"I believe it," grinned January. His mother managed to capture his landlady's precise facial expression, the hypnotized bulge of her eyes, the hunch of her shoulders and the curious tone of her voice, at once flat and urgent.

"So she tosses down the champagne"—Livia Levesque gleefully mimicked her old rival's flicking gulp—"and slaps the glass over the moth on Duquille's sleeve, *whap!* Like that. Then whisks the glass and the moth over her palm and goes scampering out of the room. Her mother had been working for weeks to maneuver Duquille to the point of offering to be Marie-Claire's protector, and was fit to kill her. . . . I've heard Duquille's niece is going to marry your Henri, Minou."

Dominique dropped her fork with a clatter on the green-and-pink French china, fumbled to catch it, dropped it again. Her mother watched sidelong, eyes bright with veiled malice.

"Is that true?"

Dominique swallowed hard, breathed once, twice, her face averted. Then she turned back to her mother with a light, sweet, careless smile. "No, I hadn't heard that. Henri hasn't returned to town yet. They had a large crop at Viellard this year, and the boiling and packing has taken longer than they'd thought."

"I saw him and that mother of his today in the Rue Chartres." Livia Levesque harried a fragment of lamb judiciously around her plate before deciding it was a prey unworthy of her notice. "With all those sisters in tow, like a flock of sheep out hunting for a shepherd. Didn't you know? I half expected you'd send your regrets for this evening."

Dominique closed her eyes for a moment, her face seeming suddenly old in the warm amber of the candlelight. January remembered her telling him once that Henri would always come to see her—even for a short while, even if it was late—on the first night of his return from whichever of the family plantations he was obliged to visit, and wished it were possible to strangle their mother.

"It's a good match," his mother went on. No doubt, January reflected, she'd negotiated Dominique's contract of plaçage to Henri with that same cool, hard blitheness: a house worth so much, and so much maintenance money per month. As every woman of the free colored demi-monde negotiated their quasi-legal contracts with the white men who would be their daughters' protectors, lovers, the fathers of their children. No young man wants to bicker over money with the damsel he means to take to bed; it takes a woman who has passed down that road to know what provisions her child will need on the journey.

"Duquille's son never wed, you know, and both daughters died of consumption, in 'eighteen and 'twenty-one." Livia Levesque sipped her wine and made a face, though it was French and of good quality; her eyes never left Dominique. "Poor breeding, I call it. He should never have married a Blancheville. The whole family's weak and Julietta Blancheville—Duquille's cousin—looks like a rabbit. The St. Chinian girl's likely to inherit everything from that side of the family, as well as half-interest in the St. Chinian cotton press and a dowry that's certain to top a hundred thousand dollars."

She clapped her hands impatiently for Bella to bring the cheese, the port wine, and nuts. "So if your Henri puts you aside, make him pay."

"She didn't have to break it to you like that." January came quietly over to his sister when, a half-hour later, the meal was concluded and the party foregathered in the parlor for coffee. The early winter twilight had fallen—music sounded from one of the big town houses around the corner, a lively Chopin galop. The red glare of flambeaux in the Rue Burgundy made a shadowed pattern of curtain-lace flowers flit across his mother's face.

". . . Italians." Livia dismissed the peninsula with a wave. "Always killing one another over something—no wonder they think poor M'sieu Davis hired ruffians! As if the man doesn't have better things to do with his money, besides having plenty of friends who'd do it for free if he asked them. And well he should, the amount I hear he's in debt these days. What the Americans would want an opera for anyway, I can't imagine. . . ."

The little square box-clock of gilt and cobalt on the

mantelpiece chimed six-thirty. It would soon be time for January and Hannibal to go.

"Don't be silly, p'tit." Dominique reached up to touch January's cheek. "It took me by surprise, that's all. You know how Mother is."

". . . Aunt Semiramis had an Italian cook who was the toast of Dublin," Hannibal was saying. "She used to get three proposals a week, plus offers from my aunt's friends, smuggled in by every post, of better pay. . . ."

"And of course I've always known Henri was going to marry someone." Dominique decanted the coffee from the bright-hued pot into cups, and arranged, with unconscious artistry, Bella's beignets and jelly-cakes on the smaller plates to carry them to the others. Les Mesdames—Livia's two chubby yellow cats—rose from dozing by the hearth and padded, with artless artistry, to the sideboard, pretending they were simply taking a walk because they found the fire uncongenially warm and not because anyone was about to leave the cream-pitcher unguarded. "I'm just glad for his sake she—this girl—is disgustingly rich. I mean, yes, Henri is very wealthy himself." She handed January the tray, and intercepted the cats, tucking one under each arm. "But think how much he'll have to pay anyone to marry those sisters of his."

And she made herself twinkle, fragile glass pretending to be adamant.

At Fitzhugh Trulove's ball later that evening, January had ample opportunity to observe Henri Viellard from behind the trellis of ivy and silk roses that half concealed the musicians' dais.

He'd seen the obese, fair-haired, myopic young planter at any number of receptions and balls over the past two years, though his only direct dealings with him had been in connection with the birth of Dominique's child the summer before last. Henri, whose family's chief plantation lay just across the lake, had been at one of his mother's social engagements when Dominique gave birth. He had come when he could, and had held the infant in his arms before it died. This was more than numerous white men did for their plaçées, but January knew that his sister had spent many uncomforted nights in the wake of little Charles-Henri's death.

This was a choice a girl of color made, he understood, when first she dressed in her finest and went—almost invariably with her mother—to the Blue Ribbon Balls.

January's friends in the Paris demimonde—the courtesans whose lovers paid for flats for them in the fashionable St. Honoré district, not the streetcorner whores or the little grisettes who labored by day making hats—had asked him about the Blue Ribbon Balls, half expecting him to say that the women who attended them were slaves. January had disabused them of this notion—like most of the Parisian *demi-castors,* the majority of the plaçées had been raised by plaçée mothers with the hope and intention of entering a permanent relationship with a wealthy gentleman. Of "finding a place," or "being placed." The only difference lay in the fact that the plaçées, though free, were all women of color.

The ladies of the Rue des Ramparts implicitly understood the price they would have to pay.

To have a wealthy lover, but not a husband.

To love, maybe, and have love, but never to be secure in that love.

To bequeath to her children the property and education that they might not otherwise have. And with that property and education, to bequeath the fairer skin that altered the way people looked at you, white and black and colored alike.

Henri Viellard had done well by his sister, January knew. And yes, of course Minou had always known that one day the man she loved would take a wife, and do his duty to the family property, the family name.

Viellard was there with his mother, a massive woman nearly as tall as her six-foot son and swathed in a terrifying confection of eggplant-hued velvet. "There's never any keeping up with them!" Madame Viellard cried, surveying her audience, the French Creole portion of the company in the pillared ballroom, which had fractured along its usual lines. That the Creole French attended at all was a tribute to Fitzhugh Trulove's long residence in the town, dating back to the days of Spanish governorship. His position as a bridge between the two societies, as much as his wealth, was the reason the canny Caldwell had sought him for the Opera Society. "What should war in Spain have to do with the price of sugar, I ask you? What are they fighting about anyway? Or these ridiculous countries popping up in South America, always changing their names and fighting each other and making everything awkward for everyone? One simply cannot keep track of them."

The galaxy of candles—in mirrored sconces on the walls, on the double line of painted columns, in the four chandeliers, on girandoles like a forest of silver trees rising among the heaped platters of the buffet—picked a second galaxy of brightness in the diamonds on Madame Viellard's massive bosom as she turned. "They should make up their minds once and for all what sugar is to sell for and then hold to it! One simply cannot get business done any other way!"

"But one never knows," demurred Mr. Knight, folding small, neat hands gloved in dandyish lavender kid, "what the markets in Europe will demand in any given year."

On their side of the ballroom—the side that encompassed the buffet—the Americans present muttered in English of slave prices and the profits to be made from cotton in the newer states and territories of the north and west, of tight money and buying stock on credit, as if Europe didn't exist. The little stack of *Othello* libretti sat untouched on a marquetry side-table.

And perhaps for them, reflected January, between the light, flowing minuet from *Don Giovanni* and a sentimental rendering of a Beethoven nocturne, Europe *didn't* exist. Six weeks' steady vomiting in a cramped cabin if you went by steam packet, with high seas and bad food and the possibility of the boiler blowing up as lagniappe. Three weeks if you wanted to pay clipper prices. And to most Americans it was only stories: castles and churches and crowded streets, and we have all that and more and better in America, don't we? And for a quarter the price!

Descriptive words meant little. You *didn't* understand, unless and until you'd actually walked through the green magic of the Versailles gardens in morning fog, or come out from between those crowding soot-stained buildings to see Notre Dame's square towers soaring up and up above you for that first time. Until you'd heard real opera sung by professionals in a good hall with a full orchestra, or rambled from bookshop to bookshop to bookshop along a cobbled street delirious with the knowledge that you could find anything you wanted— *anything*—somewhere along the way.

"One *should* know, Mr. Knight," declared Madame Viellard. "That is precisely my point." One side of the huge double parlor faced out onto a formal garden, and with the heat of the hundreds of candles—Trulove would never subject his guests to the smuts and stink of gas— long windows had been opened, admitting the green scent of wet foliage and the occasional rattle-winged pal- metto-bug. The matron glared at her son as if demanding support, but Henri, consuming pâté in wretched silence, would not meet her eye.

"It's a dreadfully ill-regulated place anyway, Europe," laughed Trulove, and he cast a fond glance toward Oona Flaherty, done up in lilac tulle and an astonishing three- lobed topknot bedecked with artificial grapes, clinging dutifully to the arm of one of Mr. Knight's clerks. January smiled at the burly young man's expression of grim con- centration: it was one of the duties of a planter's business agent to purchase and send upriver whatever the family might require in the way of tools or supplies: chinaware, spices, salt, coffee, or wine. Presumably a screen for an employer's *amours*—Knight also handled the Truloves' business—came under the same heading.

"Nonsense," retorted Mr. Knight. "You have been away from it for too long, sir. Since the Congress, Europe has been one of the most peaceful and best-ruled places on earth."

"If one equates good rule with oppression," returned another voice, and January, eliding smoothly from schot- tische to waltz, broke off for a moment, turning his head, seeking the owner of the voice—

Knowing absolutely that it had to be Belaggio's for- mer partner, Incantobelli.

He could think of no other reason for a castrato—as the lead in *Giulio Cesare* had to be—to be in New Orleans.

"True enough, one does not see the blood of kings

washed down the gutters much anymore, nor hear the tocsins ringing through the night," that soft, sweet alto continued. All January could glimpse was a flash of white hair, something he'd already deduced the man must have: even during the early days of his stay in Paris the fashion for those heartstopping, magical voices had been a thing of the past. For Incantobelli to have had enough of a career to make him an impresario now, he would have to be sixty at least.

"Yet as the price for that peace was to hand the states of Italy and Germany around to the victors like petits-fours, to rule and tax as they choose and to infest with their secret police, one cannot but reflect that there must have been some middle ground."

A frilled ruffle of violin music at his back reminded January what he was there for: Hannibal covering up for the fact that the piano had fallen out of the waltz in mid-bar. He fumbled, pulling his mind back to the piece, annoyed and embarrassed, and when next he tried to listen for that curious combination of child's voice and man's, all he could hear was Jed Burton complaining to the banker Hubert Granville about a horse someone had tried to sell him.

"What happened?" asked Hannibal quietly when the waltz curtsied to its end. "I thought your piano had broken a string."

January shook his head. "Incantobelli's here."

"Half a reale says Belaggio calls him out," replied Hannibal with barely a pause for breath.

"Who's Incantobelli?" demanded Jacques Bichet, shaking the spit out of his flute. "I have five cents on Davis. . . ."

"Oh, I'm still covering Davis," said the fiddler. "I've

got my money down for ten-thirty, five minutes either way. Incantobelli's Belaggio's former partner."

"Two cents on nine-thirty," chipped in Cochon Gardinier, an enormously fat man who was probably the best fiddler, after Hannibal, in New Orleans.

"It's nearly quarter-past now." Hannibal glanced at the intensely ormolued case-clock that dominated the far end of the parlor. "And Belaggio hasn't even arrived yet. Incantobelli will have to be standing on the front porch for a challenge at nine-thirty. . . ."

"Considering Incantobelli wasn't invited," said January grimly, "that's probably exactly where he'll be." Not far from the leafy screen that half hid these negotiations from their employer, John Davis was gesticulating angrily and saying something to Vincent Marsan. Marsan, resplendent in pale jade-green down to his gloves and the emeralds in his breast-pins, nodded sympathetically and stroked his golden mustache. But the sky-blue eyes never left the doorway to the hall. January heard *"La Muette de Portici"* and "—accuses me of hiring men . . ."

"On the other hand," he said, and brought out the music to the first quadrille of the evening, "I'll lay you that Davis gets in with a challenge first."

"Never!" Cochon whipped a Mexican reale from his pocket and slapped it down on the corner of the piano. "I'm for this Italian."

"For shame, sir!" Hannibal drew himself up like a demented Irish elf. "A fip on Davis before him."

"Done, sir!"

"And I," added Bichet.

"Covered." January counted out eighteen pennies from his pocket, the rough equivalent in the various currencies available in New Orleans to cover the various bets.

"Gentlemen!" Uncle Bichet finished touching up the tuning-keys of his cello and regarded the other members of the little orchestra with a stern eye. "Didn't your mamas raise you right? It ain't polite to lay wagers on white men at their own parties." He spoke the gombo French, the "mo kiri mo vini" French of the cane-brakes and the slave-quarters—which most of the musicians would have sworn, in white company, that they didn't rightly understand. Behind his spectacles the old man's eyes sparkled, disconcerting amid a graceful criss-cross of tribal scars. " 'Sides, you all ought to know better than to bet on anythin' a *blankitte*'s gonna do. Now, let's shake these folks up a little. Ben . . ."

January grinned, and danced his fingers over the first bars of "La Bonne Amazone." As if by magic the crowd that jammed the room shifted, transforming from a wall of backs into an open aisle of non-dancers crowding aside between the pillars and around the buffet, and dancers forming up three sets—

—as cleanly divided along French and American lines as if on a battlefield. Anne Trulove, a biscuit-blonde in rigidly tasteful gray, took her husband by the arm and firmly steered him into the American set farthest from the one graced by Oona Flaherty and her lumbering cicisbeo. Henri Viellard, after an unsuccessful attempt at concealment behind one of the buffet table's silver epergnes, gracelessly led his middlemost sister into the French set. Vincent Marsan's wife, a colorless woman with the face of one who has neither laughed nor wept in years, made a move toward the French set, then flushed as her husband did not respond, and retreated hastily to the wall again.

Nowhere did January see anyone who might have been Incantobelli.

"At least we should have a lively evening," remarked Hannibal, and the orchestra whirled into the music like a thousand colored ribbons released at once into the wind.

Later that evening, crouched in the darkness with the stink of blood filling his nostrils, January remembered Hannibal's remark with rage, and bitterness, and despair.

FIVE

⎯⎯⟡⎯⎯

Lorenzo Belaggio made his appearance at ten, Mademoiselle d'Isola radiant on his arm.

"Guess Incantobelli didn't meet him on the gallery," taunted January as the impresario thrust aside the tawny velvet curtain that swagged the vestibule doors, held it back with a dramatic gesture that halted the dancers mid-pirouette, and drew all eyes to the dazzling figure framed there in her gown of white and emerald. One felt she waited for applause.

"The night's young." Hannibal rounded off the truncated waltz with a little flourish of notes, like a satin bow.

"I hope that six cents wasn't your rent."

Caldwell and Trulove made haste to bow to the young soprano, Marsan to kiss her hand. La d'Isola preened happily and uncomprehendingly at the compliments that rained about her in English, nodded earnestly to the French ones, and said, in her soft, sweet voice with its Neapolitan lilt, *"Merci . . . merci, Mi-sciou,"* like a child pronouncing her lessons. "Please. You are so kind." Though she had the air of one who certainly accepted the praise as deserved, she also thanked the giver of each compliment with a sparkling, genuine smile. She seemed more relaxed than she had at the theater—maybe because Consuela Montero wasn't present.

Few of the singers were. Madame Chiavari had come early with her husband, and had departed early; some of the ladies were distantly polite, but enough of a stigma still clung to a woman of the stage that even the Creole ladies weren't sure if they should be seen in conversation with her or not. The men, of course, had no interest in a woman so respectably wed. Other than Oona Flaherty, still on the arm of Mr. Knight's trussed-looking clerk, the only person January had glimpsed so far from the theater was Madame Scie, clothed in a rather old-fashioned gown of apricot gauze and listening politely to young Harry Fry expostulate at the far end of the refreshment table.

"What do the midwives do in this country?" she demanded a few minutes later, coming around the corner of the leafy musicians' screen. "Crush the bump that governs interest in anything they cannot eat, invest in, or take with them to bed?" She tapped the back of her head as if participating in a demonstration of phrenology.

"He seems to have heard of Napoleon, for which I suppose he is due some credit, but all else is either I have got such-and-such a bargain dealing for cotton, or How much is proper to spend on a gift for the Señorita Felina? What sort of jewels would best advance my suit? Mr. Fry knows, he tells me, where to procure them cheap. Would I take a message to her? Not that the girl can read, even should I permit myself to be used as a letter-box—or a bawd." Her thin wrist flicked in a gesture eloquent of exasperation and self-mockery. "I wept for your exile before, *mon vieux,* but I see now my tears were ignorant, falling far short of the truth."

"*The words of Mercury are harsh after the songs of Apollo,*" agreed Hannibal gravely. He and the ballet mistress had taken to each other at sight. "It's a malady akin to the cholera, I believe, borne upon the insalubrious air.

A man can be a very paragon of political theory while he lives in Paris, but within six months of stepping from the gangplank, he hasn't an idea in his head but what percentage of his next cotton crop can be invested in slaves."

January leaned an elbow on the edge of Trulove's grand piano. "White people in this town just don't have any idea how to have a good time. Especially during Carnival. That's the one bad thing about being good in this town: the whites pay you more, but if the pay were equal, I'd sooner play for the free colored militia and burial societies. Better food, better talk, better dancing, funnier jokes, and far, far, far better music."

"Would you care to accompany us to Jacques Bichet's party after everyone here goes home?" inquired Hannibal, who was by this stage of the evening weaving slightly with exhaustion and brandy. He picked from the dancer's hair a spray of the fragile straw-flowers that were its only ornament, and tucked them into his buttonhole like a skeletal wisp of smoke. "He did say we should bring whomever we liked," he added, seeing January's expression of shock that he should even make such a suggestion to a white woman, and the daughter of a beheaded French marquis at that. "Jacques, your good wife wouldn't have any objection to Madame Scie coming along to your place afterward and hearing real music, would she?"

The flautist's eyes widened. Like January, he was far more disconcerted at the average white lady's reaction to such a suggestion than at any danger that might attach. But Marguerite Scie was not the average white lady. She'd trodden the opera stage for too long to concern herself with scandal, and had long since, January knew, abandoned the convention of seeking a respectable protector who might be shocked at her behavior. The crowfoot lines around her gray eyes deepened with amusement and delight, and old Uncle Bichet, seeing this, leaned around his cello and answered for his flabbergasted nephew, "I think my nephew's wife would be pleased and honored, if this meets with your approval, Madame."

"Indeed it does." The ballet mistress inclined her head, first to the old man, then to Jacques, then Hannibal. "And considering the number of people here who have injured themselves in their haste to speak to a mere dance mistress, and an elderly one at that," she added dryly, "I shall count the minutes."

And as James Caldwell and Lorenzo Belaggio between them led La d'Isola toward the musicians, she strolled away, erect and solitary, to the pillar where she had stood before.

"Gentlemen," said Caldwell, "perhaps you'd be good enough to play for our beautiful nightingale to give our company here a taste of what's in store at the American Theater this season?"

Drusilla looked around her, startled, and tried to draw back, but Belaggio put a firm hand on the small of her back.

"That pretty song the Countess sings in Act Three of *Marriage,* perhaps?" suggested Trulove, coming up from the other side. His wife was beside him, her cool blue glance touching the soprano—and the way Belaggio held her—with impersonal contempt, flavored by the malice of a woman whose husband has been insulting her for weeks with an Irish opera-dancer.

Blushing, Drusilla shook her head in a nodding forest of green-and-white ostrich-tips. "Oh, no, you must sing, my dear," purred Mrs. Trulove. "What about that lovely aria in Mr. Bellini's *Norma*?" And she hummed the first few bars of "Casta diva," arguably one of the most difficult pieces ever written for a soprano.

"Do not be so modest, *cara mia!*" boomed Belaggio, tightening his grip as the girl showed signs of trying to slip away. "You must show these people what a spectacle awaits them in our opera season! I insist. Gentlemen, you have the music. . . ."

Pale under her rice-powder and rouge, La d'Isola looked around at the faces of the men, and of the women closing in, smiling with curiosity at this woman of whom they'd heard. And January, looking at the girl's eyes, realized, *She knows.*

She knows she's fit only for chorus work.

Separated from an audience by the footlights, masked in paint and surrounded by other singers, enmeshed in a spectacle of action and beauty, a mediocre singer can get by. Cognoscenti might compare her coloratura to others they'd heard, but in the main, the weak or dull thread is safe in the brilliant tapestry's web.

A vain woman wouldn't have noticed her own flaws, or feared exposure as no more than the impresario's mistress, the woman foisted on the company and the audience.

Tears filled d'Isola's dark eyes, but she took a deep breath, ready to go down trying.

January was never sure afterward why he reacted as he did. Asked beforehand what a girl deserved who had used her body to edge her way ahead of better singers, he would unhesitatingly have said, *Let her stand up and try to sing without anything to distract her audience. Let her try to sing in a small room, in an intimate setting, face-to-face. That should teach her.*

Maybe it was because only a few hours earlier he'd seen the pain in Dominique's eyes, and how she'd held up her head and smiled.

Maybe because of the woman in the blue dress, at the

New Exchange, and the way Belaggio had held on to Drusilla's arm and said, *I insist.*

Maybe it was just that she was young.

He said in Italian, "Perhaps the Signorina would care to sing 'Si profondo mi amore' from your own *Othello,* Signor?" And he named Desdemona's sad little canzone from Act Four, heart-tugging in itself, tragic in its sweet simplicity before Othello's terrifying entrance . . .

. . . and, he knew, just within the girl's range and capabilities.

For one instant her eyes met his, filled with gratitude and almost unbelieving relief that she would be spared. She swallowed hard, drew another breath, steadying herself. "Yes," she said, "yes, thank you, that is . . . that would be perfect."

"*Othello* is a new opera, Signor," added January encouragingly to Belaggio, who showed signs of holding out for "Casta diva." "And truly, the finest that I have heard."

"Well, well . . ." Belaggio puffed up like a mating pigeon. "It *is* a fine piece, is it not? One of my best. What about it, *Popola?*" He brought d'Isola's hand to his lips. January saw that her fingers were trembling.

Somewhere in the candle-lit golden shadows, a shrill Irish voice demanded, "If she's going to sing, why can't I dance?"

And silence fell on the room as La d'Isola took her place before the bower, silence seduced, a moment later, by the sweet, languid whisper of Hannibal's fiddle.

It is the music that makes up the feeling, January had said to Shaw. *The words themselves are nothing.* Indeed, he doubted whether five people in the great soft-glowing cavern of the ballroom even knew Italian. But the gentle wistfulness of the air spoke, the slow-building pulse of intensity and sadness; that terrible alternation of yearning and despair that a woman knows, who both loves and fears her man.

> *So deep my love, that even in his anger*
> *My heart leaps out; his stubbornness and frowns,*
> *These I embrace, the day and night together . . .*

When Cavallo spoke of her depth of feeling, of her ability to deliver, not a perfect song, but an emotional performance, January had been tempted to attribute the praise to the friendship between the two. Now he saw that the tenor had spoken the truth.

La d'Isola, though her training had clearly been adequate, might not have been more than a mediocre singer, but as an actress she was unsurpassed.

Or else, thought January—and he glanced sidelong at her lover's florid countenance, the pride-filled, possessive dark eyes—she sang from her heart.

> *My mother had a maid called Barbara.*
> *She loved a man, and him she loved was mad;*
> *And he forsook her, leaving her to sing*
> *This song of Willow; singing it she died. . . .*

Hannibal's violin feathered gently in as the girl's voice soared into a cadenza, freed for the moment of words at all, singing only feeling, like a dove flying into storm. Love that accepts the rage of the beloved as just; the heart too tender to defend itself or the life of its owner. Anne Trulove, who did understand—who like Hannibal had been raised on Shakespeare—glanced aside and down, acknowledging her malice defeated and chastised. Major plunged into minor like the night that stalks in the wings of a hurricane, notes unfurling like luminous pennons against a lowering sky.

    Sing willow, willow, sing willow,
    Sing willow, willow, sing for me. . . .

During this scene, the libretto instructed, Othello would be visible on the gallery, just outside Desdemona's door. Weeping as he listened, and turning away, repentant of his jealousy. And at that moment, around the flowering vine of the willow song, would twine Iago's theme, as Cochon and Uncle threaded it in now, vivid as blood dripped on bridal-silk, as the echo of a cry uttered hundreds of years ago.

    Lie with her, on her, what you will. . . . Hot as monkeys, salt as wolves in pride. . . . And like night returning, Othello would turn back to that lighted room. To vengeance, and his own doom.

    Now, now, very now, January's mind whispered the words of the first act, which Belaggio had taken intact into Iago's opening aria. *That old black ram is tupping your white ewe.*

    He had heard and read endless speculation on Iago's motive in bringing about his commander's downfall: rage at being passed over to make room for the place-serving Cassio; envy of the greater man's abilities. The mention in passing that "he hath sometime between my sheets performed my office" was clearly a throwaway, an excuse, brought up only once at the end almost as an afterthought—certainly Iago's wife, Emilia, never gave the slightest indication of interest in Othello throughout the play. And to January, the motive was clear, starting in that first scene.

Iago could not endure it, that the Moor dared love a white-skinned woman, and was loved by her in return.

And it mattered to him not a whit that it was a woman in whom Iago had no interest himself.

Sing willow, willow, sing willow,
Sing willow, willow, sing for me.

Which of those men, wondered January as the final grace-notes of d'Isola's simple fioritura climbed into the silence, agreed with Iago? It was all very well for them to have mistresses of color—as Henri Viellard, mammoth and solemn in his gray coat and flowered waistcoat, had Dominique—girls whom they would bull for years without ever considering them good enough to marry.

But a black man bedding a white woman? Marrying her? Loving her so desperately that the thought of her betrayal drove him literally mad?

Unthinkable.

And criminal enough, in the mind of at least one man almost certainly in the room, to justify a little lesson in the alley beside the theater.

Anne Trulove was the first to applaud, the first to step forward and take La d'Isola's hands. John Davis was immediately behind, his face filled with admiration and, as he turned to Belaggio, with unwilling envy. A lover of opera, Davis recognized greatness, even in a man he disliked—January saw him hold out his hand, saw his lips move in words.

Belaggio drew haughtily back, eyelids drooping, and said something that made Davis drop his hand. Then the crowd intervened, and Anne Trulove caught January's eye, and gave a commanding nod.

Obedient, he riffled the introduction to "L'Alexandrine" on the piano's keys. Fiddles and cello, flute and clarionette bounded after him like fauns. Men and women paired again—French with French, American with American, like some absurdly politicized Noah's Ark. Jeté and emboitté, glissade and pas-de-basque. The froufrou of taffeta silk and the amber slither of candlelight—kid-gloved fingers to kid-gloved palms. The rhythmed creak of slippers on beeswaxed oak. Belaggio was still handing out copies of his libretto to potential subscribers and didn't even notice as La d'Isola slipped, trembling, away to the curtained alcove of a window, gathering around her shoulders her white-and-gold lace shawl, as if suddenly exhausted and cold.

And no wonder, thought January.

Perhaps she had learned a lesson, after all.

Despite what he'd said to Marguerite about the music at the free colored balls being better, January thoroughly enjoyed playing wherever he was hired to play. Music was his fortress, the shining world to which he'd retreated during a painful childhood; the brilliant spine around which he'd rebuilt his life during the dark months after Ayasha's death. Listening and playing—especially a grand piano like Trulove's—was the greatest joy he could ask for. Watching, too. A hundred minor dramas skirmished along the fringe of the dance, like a dance in itself, or an interlocking set of dances.

Trulove, Anne Trulove, and Oona Flaherty formed a minor cotillion as the planter attempted to cross the crowded ballroom to the Irish girl's side, and his wife intercepted him with spun-steel graciousness, a sort of verso Odyssey in miniature. Pale little Mr. Knight performed a one-man *haie* as he encountered and spoke with every planter in the room who owned forty arpents or more—he evidently had scant use for lesser fry. A sort of ring dance developed around the Widow Redfern, bachelors of every age paying court to her available affluence, and like the illustration of a tract, Marguerite Scie stood alone. She wasn't young, and she wasn't marriageable, and unlike La d'Isola and Oona Flaherty, she had come without the patronage of a man. Only John Davis paused to chat with the ballet mistress in the midst of his own grand-right-and-left with the influential Creoles of the City Council. January saw her draw herself up in a burlesque of Belaggio's snub; he saw Davis laugh.

"Vincent Marsan tells me you have a couple niggers to sell?"

The soft-muttered words lifted the hair on January's nape, though he'd heard them in one form or another at every ball and entertainment given by white men that he'd ever played. As Shaw had complained yesterday, half the slaves sold in New Orleans never got near such public venues as the New Exchange.

"Ah, that I do, Signor Burton." That was the voice that made January turn his head. Made his stomach curl sourly, and the music clink harsh in his ears. "That indeed I do."

Punch-cup in hand, Jed Burton looked up into the face of Lorenzo Belaggio.

"Prime hands?"

The impresario kissed his fingertips, smiling proudly about the men he was selling as if he hadn't written a song about loving that minutes ago had opened January's heart like a scalpel. "They have cut the sugar-cane in Cuba, they have worked in stables, they are young, they are healthy—"

"How young?" Burton spit tobacco into the brass can discreetly tucked behind a potted fern. "And how healthy? Creole niggers?"

"Of a certainty," agreed Belaggio, though January had seen the tribal scars—country marks, they were called—on the faces of both the stage-hands the impresario had brought from Cuba. "Louis is perhaps nineteen, and Pedro, twenty-two. Both were born in Cuba, and are acclimated against the diseases of this hemisphere. They speak English. . . ."

Another lie. But January guessed, with even a hundred-dollar knock-off in the average price of a cane-hand, that Burton wouldn't care.

He turned his face away, as if the notes before him were a map that would lead him on to a better world.

At the age of ten he'd beaten up three of the quadroon boys from the St. Louis Academy for Young Gentlemen of Color, classmates he'd surprised in the act of drowning a puppy in the gutter. As the darkest boy in the school, January had little patience with those boys anyway—the ones who'd call him *bozal* and *country* and *cane-patch*—and he'd taken a split lip and a swollen eye in defense of the poor little cur, who had promptly slashed his wrist nearly to the bone and run away while its erstwhile tormentors howled with laughter at January's pain and chagrin. His mother had whipped him, too, for getting his clothes torn.

The dog had been run over in the street by a carriage the following day.

As he'd said to Shaw, he understood that the makers of sublime art were not necessarily sublime themselves. And it was not necessary that they be, he told himself. Only that the art—the passion and the glory of Othello's unwise love—be permitted to reach out to those whose loves were routinely denigrated, whose passions daily mocked.

Nevertheless he tasted bile in his mouth as his fingers skipped through the Pantalon.

"If only the man wasn't such a damn huckster, he'd be easier to take," sighed Davis, coming to the musicians' bower between dances a few minutes later, to sneak Hannibal some brandy. "You wouldn't have a friend or two in the Swamp, would you, who'd know where I could lay hands on fireworks?"

"I don't know about ready-made fireworks," said January, overhearing. "But if you can procure gunpowder and chemicals, Mademoiselle Vitrac—you remember Mademoiselle Vitrac, M'sieu. . . ."

"The teacher, yes." Davis nodded. "And a chemist, too, if I remember rightly. Where could I send her a note, to ask . . . ?"

"Puta!" Belaggio's bellow of rage cut across the music's opening bars. *"Puttana! Cattiva fica!"*

"Consarn, as the Americans say." Hannibal untucked his violin from beneath his chin. "Backed the wrong horse."

Across the room, Belaggio ripped aside the curtain that half concealed the window embrasure, thrust apart Vincent Marsan and Drusilla d'Isola with such violence that the girl smote the wall. The water-ice she'd been holding spun from her hand, glass splintering. Marsan lunged forward, beautiful face transformed by a snarl of demonic rage—the men nearest him leapt to seize his arms. He twisted free of them with a movement more animal than human, stood facing the Italian, the two huge men towering over the girl like maddened bulls. For a moment there was deadly silence; then Belaggio struck Marsan across the face.

"Keep your filthy hands from that woman, you bastard *stronzolo!*"

Marsan's colorless wife stepped a pace toward them, but fell back at the sight of her husband's face.

"Stay with your Negress concubines, for I do not take such an insult from any man!" Seizing d'Isola's arm, Belaggio shook her until her head lolled on her creamy bare shoulders, her face ashen with shock.

"Devil's whore! You will not dishonor me. . . ."

"You dishonor yourself, sir!" The Widow Redfern strode from her ring of suitors in a jangle of diamonds and crêpe. The men—who had applauded so wildly when the girl sang of how a true woman trustingly accepts abuse from her man—muttered and shifted and avoided each other's eyes. January had seen the same uneasiness, less outrage than a disapproval of the inappropriateness of it all, when a white man punished a slave in the presence of other whites.

Mr. Knight, who was one of those who'd held back Marsan's first killing rush, added in Italian, "Signor, we cannot have you speaking to a lady thus. . . ."

"Lady?" Belaggio let out a crack of laughter. "This lightskirt, with her wicked eyes?" He shoved d'Isola before him through the French door onto the broad terrace. Framed by the flambeaux on the balustrade, the girl seemed to hover for a moment like Eurydice on the threshold of Hell.

"Honestly!" Galvanized by visions of a season-wrecking scandal, James Caldwell moved to thrust himself between Belaggio and the infuriated Marsan, and Davis interposed his body in the embrasure of the window itself.

"Mademoiselle d'Isola surely never—"

"Keep back from me!" Belaggio retreated a pace from Davis and lifted his hand in a gesture hugely reminiscent of an overweight Don Giovanni confronted with the stone commander in his parlor doorway. "Assassin! I told you before this evening I have nothing to say to your blandishments. Will you call your hired bravos from the darkness now?"

Davis was so shocked, he stepped aside, open-mouthed, and Belaggio shoved past him and out into the pagan torch-glare of the terrace. "Bitch!" the impresario cried. *"Puta!* I'll teach you to flee from me . . . !"

In point of fact, d'Isola had lingered for perhaps two minutes on the terrace before she fled, clutching her shawl distractedly about her, like Desdemona, awaiting her lover's pleasure. As the tallest man in the room, January had watched her during Marsan's altercation with Belaggio. Even when she'd finally descended into the dark protection of the garden's hedge-maze she had paused, a glimmering white form in the blackness, turning back to watch . . .

. . . or to give Belaggio a chance to overtake her for a lovers' quarrel and reconciliation among the ornamental hedges of orange and box.

"Where are you, faithless hussy? Do not flee from me, for I shall find you . . . !"

Of that, January had not the smallest doubt.

Then two things happened at once. At the same moment that he felt a tug at his coat—Uncle Bichet nodding toward Anne Trulove's tight-lipped gesture to resume the music—January saw a lithe figure glide through one of the other French windows onto the terrace, a silver-haired man with the odd, almost boneless stature that characterized a eunuch.

Incantobelli. January dropped back onto the piano-bench, swung into the Lancers. . . .

And, as he struck up the first gay chord, saw John

Davis, after a moment's hesitation, disappear after Belaggio into the dark.

If it hadn't been for Mrs. Trulove stationing herself where she could keep an eye on both the orchestra and her husband, January might have tried to slip away after his friend and warn him not to put himself out of sight of witnesses, at least until the potentially murderous Incantobelli had been accounted for. But whatever might be going on in the garden, he had been hired to do a job, and would not be thanked for straying from that task.

Thus he had only a general idea of the subsequent chain of events in the room around him: couples trying to find their partners, their sets, their dance-cards, and their left feet; Vincent Marsan striding toward the French doors and being stopped by his factor, a spectacle rather like that of an Italian greyhound trying to down a charging stag. Marsan's wife joined her voice to little Mr. Knight's, and the planter lashed at her with words that sent her in white-faced silence back to the wall, where she'd stood for most of the evening, as alone as Marguerite. "I'd better go after them," boomed Trulove as if the thought had only just occurred to him, and strode, not into the garden, but through the big double doors that led into the rest of the house. "Oh, faith!" cried Miss Flaherty, seconds later, to no one in particular. "I seem to have left me fan in the lobby. . . ."

"Signore, I beg you reconsider." Caldwell joined Knight in his efforts to stay Marsan, but January could have told him he was wasting his time. He couldn't imagine a white Creole who'd forgive being struck in the face.

"Incantobelli's out there," whispered January to Hannibal, glancing around for Madame Scie, who was, of course, nowhere to be found. "Somebody needs to get Davis back in here. . . . M'sieu Chevalier—Mr. Knight," he corrected himself, switching back over to English. "Mr. Knight, there's a man who's gone into the garden after Signor Belaggio, a man named Incantobelli. . . ."

"Incantobelli?" Knight paused in mid-stride. "What's . . . who is that?"

"Signor Belaggio's former partner, sir." January faked along as well as he could with the other musicians in time. "I know it's none of my affair, sir, but I think someone ought to find Signor Belaggio, and warn him, before the situation grows worse."

"That I shall do." Eyes blue as pale china flicked toward the terrace doors, exasperated—as well they should be. The elegant jade-green figure of Vincent Marsan was nowhere in the room either now. Probably out in quest of seconds. If Belaggio were later found dead, and Marsan—or Davis—was without an account of himself . . .

January could see the swift calculation in Knight's colorless eyes.

"Thank you. And your name is . . . ?"

"January, sir. Benjamin January."

And that, reflected January wearily as the factor disappeared—like everyone else—through the French doors to the terrace and the leafy labyrinth beyond, was the most he could do. He looked around for Mrs. Trulove, but she, too, had vanished. *That's all we need,* he thought as the players whirled gaily into the *grande chaine. Incantobelli murders Belaggio in the garden* AND *Mrs. Trulove slaughters her husband and the première danseuse of Friday's performance. . . .*

Two dances later—a mazurka and the Basket Quadrille—Knight returned through the garden door with the air of a man who has supped on lemons. "Did you find him?" inquired Trulove, who had himself only just re-entered the ballroom, smoothing his silvery hair.

"I've been searching all through the house." He pretended not to see Oona Flaherty slip through the rearmost of the ballroom's doors and pause by one of the room's long mirrors to make sure the bows of her bodice were straight. They weren't.

"I convinced Signor Belaggio to return to his hotel," replied Knight. His colorless tongue peeped out as if he were readjusting the set of his disapproval. "I have just now seen him away in a hack." He went to the table by the corner of the musicians' dais and collected the three or four remaining copies of the green-bound libretto.

"And Miss d'Isola?"

"Was with him."

"Did all—er—seem well?" James Caldwell tried to look as if he were more concerned with La d'Isola's happiness than the possibility of his impresario either firing his soprano or being shot by a member of the Opera Society three days before the season opened.

"If," said Knight, his already long face further lengthening, "you can term my instructions to speak to Mr. Marsan's seconds 'well,' yes. Though I must say . . ."

"Mr. Trulove." Anne Trulove appeared at her husband's side, gloved hands demurely folded and murder glinting in her eye. "Our guests are departing."

And not a moment too soon, thought January. Belaggio would be lucky—Davis would be lucky—if the impresario lived to get out of New Orleans. "With luck Marsan will shoot him in front of witnesses," January muttered as the musicians filed through the discreet demi-porte to the butler's pantry. Richard, Trulove's major-domo, was counting out silver Mexican dollars while Cochon, Jacques, and the others furtively cadged leftover pastries and ham from the heaped trays that servants were already bringing in for cleanup. "Assassin indeed."

"*Rightly to be great is not to stir without great argument,*" said Hannibal gravely, licking sugar from his thin fingers, "*but greatly to find quarrel in a straw / when honor's at the stake.* Marguerite said she'd await us in the oaks at the end of the drive. Evidently no one offered to see her to the hotel."

Miss it? Marguerite had said to January once, many years ago, when they'd walked out to St. Cloud for a Sunday afternoon of riding the carousel and drinking water-lily tea. She'd pointed to the ruin of a beautiful gate-house on the way, and mentioned in passing that it, and the now-demolished *hôtel particulier* it had served, had belonged to her family. *Miss that constant enslavement to petty gossip, the unending conflict with social rivals—Who can steal a dressmaker from whom, how dare the coiffeur visit that bitch de Rochouarte four hours later than me on the day of Her Majesty's reception? Pfui!* She'd flung up her hand in disgust. *I saw the kind of women it made of my mother, and my sister: women who'd sleep with a man only because he was invited to the Queen's parties, or because some rival loved him that week. I saw the kind of woman it would make of me.* Bien sûr, she'd added with a cynical shrug, *one must pay for one's freedom. . . .*

And this, reflected January, thinking of that straight pale-gold figure standing alone in the corner of Trulove's ballroom—this was part of the price she paid.

Gusts of chatter, laughter, and the creak of carriage-wheels floated on the damp night air from the front of the house. A little rain had fallen during the early part of the evening, enough to sparkle on the brick of the yard, where the kitchen's lamplight strewed it. All the world smelled of greenness and damp clay. Steam, too:

servants crossed back and forth past January, their arms full of napkins, tablecloths, pale-blue Wedgwood dishes, hundreds of them; hollow-ware like fragile mountains of diamonds, all to be washed tonight. He took a candle from the sideboard in the pantry and walked around to the terrace.

Like everything else in that graceful old house on the Bayou Road, the garden was immaculately trimmed and tended. The paths were clay, here and there mixed with the broken shells that were dredged by the ton from the lake. January paused under the bare trellis of the arch that led into the velvet gloom of Anne Trulove's labyrinth, and crouched to see d'Isola's light track in the damp clay of the verge, and over it the heavy striding smear of Belaggio's wide pumps.

Davis's tracks were interposed on them, the shorter stride clearly showing that the square-toed pumps were his. Therefore, guessed January—straining his eyes in the flickering glow of a single unsheltered candle—the longer tracks, the narrower feet that followed would have to be Incantobelli's. Narrower than Davis's or Belaggio's— narrow enough for him to recognize again if he had to. For good measure he pulled his notebook from his pocket, and used two torn pages to mark the length and breadth of the foot, in case he'd need to prove at some place and time that Incantobelli had been in a certain lo-cale, and John Davis had not.

As Shaw had said, a free man of color could still tes-tify in the Courts of the State of Louisiana. If it was un-likely that a white jury would convict a white culprit on a *sang mêlé*'s testimony, there was still the probability they'd acquit on it.

He passed on into the maze. Its leafy walls were nine

feet tall, smooth-trimmed as if planed. It reminded January
of the cane-fields, where the hot, close-crowding plants cut
out all visibility, all sound, all air. The night seemed suddenly very silent.

Close by him, he heard the crunch of a footstep.
"Who's there?" he called. He raised his candle, and the
coarse pelt of the hedges seemed to drink its light. "Who
is it?"

No one replied.

January moved forward a few steps, toward what
seemed to be a gap in the hedge. Instead of a way through
to the next passageway, however, he found a sort of niche,
like a little bower, containing a marble bench, over which
lay a woman's white-and-gold lace shawl.

She'd waited here. Seated on this bench—he saw the
marks of her heels in the wet moss, where she'd scraped
them back and forth—then the clear print where she'd
sprung to her feet when Belaggio's huge dark form
emerged around the corner of the hedge.

She could easily have fled farther, thought January,
standing up again. Could have ducked into a less conspic-
uous turning, and waited for Belaggio to pass. Could even
have slipped back to the house. Emily Redfern or any of a
dozen gentlemen could have been appealed to for the loan
of a carriage.

Instead, she'd waited. Waited for her lover to come
storming around the turn of the hedge, as his tracks
showed clearly he'd done. Waited for the obligatory tears,
explanations, vows that would culminate in the inevitable
caress. *Chastise Aphrodite,* says Helen to Menelaus when
they meet in the sacked ruin of Troy and she gazes at him
with melting eyes through the tousled curtain of her hair.
I deserve to be excused in this.

And like Menelaus—to judge by the green-and-white ostrich-tips scattered around one end of the bench with its smirking cupids, the rucked moss where heels had dug for purchase—Belaggio had fallen on her like a dog on a bone.

January walked back to the house.

S I X

❦

"Concha Montero will tear her hair out," remarked Hannibal. "A few token strands of it anyway. If she'd been here tonight she'd never have let him go out looking for d'Isola after the quarrel."

"Does she care so much for him?" January reflected upon the Mexicana's remarks about Milanese pigs.

"She cares about not being relegated to roles beneath her talents," said the fiddler, hopping a little unsteadily over a puddle in the road and holding out a hand to steady Marguerite—who in spite of the tall iron pattens she wore over her shoes needed no more help walking than she needed help breathing. "Even in the wilds of Louisiana, she cares about who sees her sing Marcellina instead of the Countess."

The light of January's lantern glinted sharply on the water in the weed-thick ditches; the crushed clamshells of the Bayou Road crunched harshly underfoot. Sometimes a carriage, coming back in toward town from one of the other wealthy houses farther out toward the lake, would pass them, the jolting light of its lamps serving only to mark the vehicle rather than to illuminate anything in the velvet darkness: Marguerite looked after these without expression and January wondered again whether she missed the life of a woman of good family, a woman who could ride home from parties rather than walk.

A woman whom gentlemen—and ladies—would speak to at parties, rather than politely ignore.

"I think what rankles," Hannibal went on, "is that La d'Isola is really so bad. She carried tonight by sheer pathos, you know. She didn't have to fill a theater—only a ballroom. The galleries at Covent Garden would never have heard her."

"That would be no loss," returned Marguerite acerbically, and the two of them traded irreverent observations about the relative acoustics of La Scala, La Fenice, and the American Theater on Camp Street while January scanned the towering, inky wall of cypresses to their right, searching for the red gleam of light that would tell him they were coming to the outer fringes of the Faubourg Tremé.

"You do understand," he said to Marguerite, when at last he saw the first firefly glints of lamplight far off through the trees, "that the gathering we're going to now is completely illegal. Carnival or no Carnival, free or un-free, the whites—" he used the disrespectful patois term *blankittes*, "—have forbidden assemblies of people of color except when specifically licensed by the city."

"Tcha!" exclaimed the ballet mistress, disgusted. "So much for the truths that Messires Jefferson and Franklin held to be self-evident."

January, who had grown up hearing about the self-evident truths of the Declaration of Independence and being called *tu* by strangers, only shook his head. It was part and parcel of that web of unspoken assumptions about men of color, the assumptions that caused not only white men in New Orleans, but in Paris as well, to seek out white rather than colored surgeons. The assumptions that unconsciously turned even the free colored of New Orleans, such as his mother, to physicians of less wholeheartedly African hue than he.

And Rose, he thought, faced those same assumptions each time she sought employment teaching the chemistry, optics, and natural sciences that were her lifelong study. Without thinking much about it, the owners of schools would hire a man, mostly because it was a man who had taught them.

"We just ignorant folk here at the back of town," he said, in exaggerated gombo French. "The truths that are self-evident here are that the City Guards may show up, and if they do, put out whatever light you can reach, get back into the trees and keep out of sight until they're gone. Anybody there will help you."

"And you still ask me," grinned Marguerite, "why I would rather hear good music and funny jokes at parties that are not respectable, than talk of servants and dresses and the price of slaves, at parties that are?"

Returning from the garden maze, January had found the other musicians gone. Only Hannibal had waited for him, sitting with Marguerite on the back gallery step, drinking coffee and comparing notes about Mr. Trulove's quest for his red-haired Dulcinea.

"We won't stay long in any case. I must admit I'm consumed with curiosity about what Madame Montero actually wants with me."

"It will be the worse for La d'Isola, whatever it is." The ballet mistress didn't sound particularly concerned. In her heart, January knew, whatever she liked to say, Marguerite was still the unassailable daughter of the Marquis de Vermandois.

"O formosa puella, nimium ne crede colori." Hannibal stopped to cough; in the silence that followed, January heard the scrape and rustle of something moving among the cypress and palmetto near the road.

"Are you . . . ?" began Marguerite, and January held up his hand.

"Get to the center of the road," he said softly after a long moment's listening in which he heard nothing. "And let's keep quiet for a little." He listened again as they walked on, straining his ears for further sound.

Maybe only a fox, he thought. Or a slave, making his or her stealthy way to meet friend or lover in the swamp.

Or someone or something else that had nothing to do with the stealthy crunch of gravel among tall hedges in blackness.

But he felt better when through the inky night he descried again the golden needle of lamplight behind shuttered windows, and heard the muffled swoop and whirl of music. Instinct and familiarity rather than any visual clue led him across the Bayou Road to the entrance of Claiborne Street, a muddy and rutted track between rough board houses and long stretches of native cypress, swamp holly, creepers, and oak. He kept a hand firmly under Marguerite's elbow as he walked, and stopped now and then to let Hannibal catch his breath. Out here at the back of the Faubourg Tremé, the City Guards seldom patrolled, especially during Carnival. What few neighbors Jacques Bichet had were all *libres* as well, and all invited to his parties: nobody thought of making it their business to complain. The damp darkness, and the faint vanilla scent of Marguerite's perfume, brought back to January those expeditions to Monceaux or Mont Parnasse on the outskirts of Paris, to hear a fiddler or a singer said to be extraordinary, or to some cabaret in the St. Antoine district, where they'd sit talking half the night.

I'd always wonder how they lived, Marguerite had told him once in a wine-shop in Vincennes, sharing a bread-and-cheese dinner under a courtyard vine. *When I was a child, I'd look out the windows of the carriage and I'd wonder: what do they do when they go home at night? What songs do they sing? When we were at Vermandois—the château, you understand—and there'd be a wedding in the village, I'd watch the torches and the dancers from the window. Or I'd climb down the ivy of the wall. My mother beat me when they caught me. She said, You will never learn proper manners if all you see is paysan oafs.*

January had mimed a great start of astonishment and said, eyes round with feigned amazement, "My God, Marguerite, your mother . . . my mother . . . They must be sisters!"

"You are my long-lost cousin!" she had cried, and they'd spent the rest of the afternoon inventing a family history that included African royalty and the haughty de Vermandois.

"Well, here's our man at last!" called out old Mohammed LePas from the darkness as the three friends picked their way through the primordial waste-ground of palmetto and hackberry toward the neat four-room cottage set among the cypresses. January smelled chicken-runs and pigs, the ubiquitous stink of outhouses and the sudden lorelei caress of cooking gumbo; heard music like a color or a scent in the air, a cotillion re-cut to African rhythm like a servant's hand-me-down dress.

"Thought you'd gone home to bed, Ben." Dark forms barely visible in the leaked jackstraw light from shutters. A smell of sugar and rum.

"Yeah, he's givin' a opera lesson in the mornin'."
Ramesses Ramilles's light voice spun comic lasciviousness
into the words.

"I'll give you a opera lesson." January led the way
around to the back of the house, where hearth-heat rolled
forth like a summer blessing from the candle-lit kitchen.
Jacques's sister Penelope, resplendent in the remains of a
masquerade fairy gown from some earlier portion of the
evening, stirred something in a cauldron at the fire. Tres-
tles and planks lined the back wall of the Bichet cottage,
laden with bread-puddings and gumbos, fried oysters and
pralines white and brown, a scattering of burned-down
tallow candles and a thousand varieties of dirty rice.
Mixed in among everybody's home specialties were whatever those who worked at the Verandah Hotel or the Café
des Exiles had brought away from the kitchens at closing
time. Across the yard, red curtains muffled the cottage's
doors, but someone had tied them in knots to keep them
out of the way. Music rolled out the way heat did from
the kitchen, filling the candle-starred black gulf of the
yard, rich as tapestry and gold.

There were few candles in the yard, fewer still inside.
Dark forms swayed and whirled. Feet slapped creaking
floorboards. Loose happy voices: "Get them knees up,
Philo!" "Whoa, look at her!" "Get after her, Isaak, you
gonna take that from her?"

"This's Madame Scie, my friend from Paris," January
introduced Marguerite to those gathered around the
kitchen door. Hands extended, welcoming. "Is Mademoiselle Vitrac hereabouts?"

"Well, ain't *that* just like a man?" sniffed Cora
Chouteau, Rose's best friend, looking like a half-grown
skinny kitten. "Brings one lady and starts lookin' around

for another before his shadow even catches up with him on the ground."

"I'd get rid of that one, honey, if I was you."

"One accustoms oneself," sighed Marguerite in her grandest de Vermandois accents, and flipped open her fan.

" 'Scuse me, I think I hear trumpets blowing a retreat," murmured January, and he crossed toward the house, whither Hannibal had already gone to join Cochon and old Uncle Bichet in playing for the dancers inside.

Musicians and cab-drivers at this hour, mostly, after the white folks had danced themselves exhausted and gone home to bed. The party would have started out larger, all the carpenters and milliners and furniture-makers of color, the *libre* craftsmen and artists, the workers in iron and marble and silk who made up this neighborhood at the back of the French town. Men and women whose work transfigured this low pastel city and embellished the lives of the rich. There would have been children earlier, too, racing around underfoot, sticky-handed with candy and shrieking with laughter, dancing dances of their own invention, now long carried home and put to bed. Old M'am Bichet's bed would have been heaped with babies. It was the die-hards who were left, the ones who loved to dance more than they loved food or sleep.

From the doorway January tried to pick out Rose from the press of people inside. He saw his full sister, Olympe, two years his junior, face sheened with sweat—the little room was like an oven—and all her cool iron toughness dissolved, dancing the *pilé chactas* with her husband, a grin on her face like Judgment Morning. Though Paul Corbier had to wake early to get to his work, January knew he'd dance the world's end to a standstill if he could do so with Olympe. Other friends were there, too, Isaak Jumon, the marble-carver, and little Vachel Corcet, the attorney, and Crowdie Passebon, who sold perfumes, dancing with the beautiful Mamzelle Marie, queen of the voodoos, her tignon off and her astonishing hair loosened down over her shoulders and her wise, wicked eyes bright. Paul and Olympe had been masking—half the people in the small double parlor had—and still wore bits of costumes. Olympe had gold-striped veils wound around her crimson dress and Paul wore old-fashioned doublet and hose.

In the corner near the street door Cochon Gardinier and Hannibal leaned back-to-back against each other, knees bent, eyes half shut, fiddle-bows flying so that the music spiraled and soared like mating dragons—Jacques and Uncle and every other musician from a dozen balls and parties had assembled here and whirled along behind them, the glory of the music fast and heartstopping and wild. January shut his eyes and let the sound fill him, and for a time he understood again why after Ayasha's death—when the whole world stood open to his empty heart—the only place he could come to was here.

Music. The flesh that robed his soul's chilled bones.

Family. Helaine Passebon's dirty rice on a couple of sheets of newspaper and the sound of laughter in the shadows.

New Orleans on a Carnival night, at the back of town.

"Get on over here, Ben!" called Uncle Bichet, and everyone waved. Someone held up a guitar. January shook his head, got booed and shoved, sighed resignedly, and edged through the press along the walls. He put his foot on a chair and swung into the *chactas* mid-bar, fingers leaping and fretting and hammering at the strings, chasing the fiddles, dancing rings around the tune. Cochon winked one twinkling piggy eye at him and Hannibal grinned like a sweat-drenched Celtic elf, and everyone swooped into one more crazy chorus before the dance crashed to a conclusion amid laughter and panting and gourd cups of tafia punch.

"And what's this I hear about you coming here with another woman?" Rose appeared at his side in a himation of bedsheets and a cardboard spear and Gorgon-decorated shield. Her nut-brown hair was plaited in those dozen soft little braids that adorned the maiden statues of ancient Greece.

January rolled his eyes. "Seems like people in this town mind everybody's business but their own." His face ran with sweat in the hot dark and he handed off the guitar to Jacques.

"You should thank the stars they do." Rose retreated with him to one of the front parlor's darker corners as the music struck up again. "The woman who works in the kitchen of the Fatted Calf remembers Silvio Cavallo and Bruno Ponte very well. They were in and out, she says, all the evening, in turns—first one sitting quietly and drinking coffee, then the other. She was most affected by the story of my putative mistress's distress. *Would that it were another woman,* she said. Another woman, you just go get some steel dust and honey from the juju doctor and that's that—something *I'll* evidently have to try. . . ."

"Madame Scie has no more interest in me these days than she has in Belaggio."

"So *you* say." Rose regarded him severely over the tops of her spectacles, which far from detracting from her personation of Owl-Eyed Athène in fact in a curious fashion increased it. "In any case, just before three, Ponte—whose turn it was evidently to keep watch—appeared in the doorway, gestured peremptorily to Cavallo, at which Cavallo rose and hastened from the room."

"This woman didn't happen to note what they were wearing, did she?"

"Cavallo wore the blue long-tailed coat that you described him wearing at rehearsal, with the velvet collar. I asked about it when I described him."

"In other words," said January, "he changed it at the theater, when he saw everyone there."

"If he and Ponte were watching the place, waiting for everyone to leave so they could search Belaggio's office," said Rose reasonably, "he'd have wanted to rid himself of anything that shouted 'I've been here since the end of rehearsal.' "

"Maybe," agreed January. "But equally, Cavallo could have been—"

From outside the shutters, a voice called, "The Guards!"

The music stopped with a jerk and a squeal. A dozen dancers seized the nearest candles and snuffed them to oblivion, quite clearly forgetting that they needed at least some light to beat a retreat out the back; January cursed, and grabbed Rose by the hand. Bodies blundered in the dark. He heard Olympe call "Out! This way. Give me your hand . . ." and someone squeaked and laughed.

One hand on Rose's wrist and the other against the wall, he groped through the darkness. The dimmest possible glow marked the rear door behind a heaving wall of shoulders. Astonishingly, the exodus was made in close to complete silence—curious, thought January, considering how few of the revelers had actually ever themselves been slaves.

They've only been treated like them, he thought as he

and Rose swiftly crossed the darkness of the yard and ducked into the deeper night beneath the trees beyond. You didn't have to belong to someone if you more or less belonged to everyone; if everyone together had a reason to keep you down. People like Rose, and Crowdie Passebon, and Cochon Gardinier, second- and sometimes third-generation *libres,* still had the slaves' instinct for swift, stealthy retreat. Their self-preserving watchfulness had been ingrained from a lifetime of working around the restrictions of the whites: you can't smoke cigars in public (the yard and house had reeked with them); you have to cover your head. Don't be uppity. Never look a white man in the eye.

Whatever you do, *whatever* you do, don't fall foul of a white man at law. Because you will not, you cannot, win.

Silence fell on the yard. Those among the pitch-black shadows under the trees watched and listened, attention strained toward the yard. From here in the fleeting starlight, it looked like even the trestle tables and the food were gone—*Somebody had presence of mind.* A dry rustle of palmettos off to his right; a twig cracked underfoot to his left; a woman giggled. The other women in the kitchen must have hustled Marguerite into the woods with them: *That sound you hear,* he could almost hear her saying, *is Grandmère de Vermandois rolling over in her grave. . . .*

After fifteen minutes or so, when no torches came into sight around the corner of the house, January saw a dark figure—probably Jacques's mother—leave the shelter of the woods and cross back to the kitchen. A light went up there—somebody must have simply clamped the fire-bell over the blaze on the hearth at the first alarm—and a moment later Old M'am Bichet emerged with a candle in her hand and went around to the front of the house.

"If this was one of your nephew's practical jokes," breathed Rose, "I hope his mother makes a gris-gris that turns him into a toad." January tried to recall whether it had been a man's voice that had given the alarm, or a boy's, and couldn't. It was the sort of thing his nephew Gabriel—or a half-dozen of the boy's cronies—would have considered hilarious, now that he thought of it.

Or himself, he thought, at the age of twelve.

A minute later their hostess came back around the corner of the house, shielding the candle in fingers edged in pink light. Uncle Bichet and Jacques and Jacques's wife, Jane, left the black wall of the swamp at three separate points and converged on her. Jacques lifted one arm, signaling all was clear. "I'm going to wear those boys out," promised January grimly. It was probably past four, and if he was going to give "a opera lesson" of unspecified duration to Madame Montero, and play at a Blue Ribbon Ball for Davis at the Salle d'Orleans tomorrow night, he'd have to attend early Mass—a thought that made him groan inwardly.

Why couldn't he be a heathen like Hannibal, and laugh God to scorn?

Others, it appeared, were also mindful of the nearness of dawn. As January and Rose returned to the yard, parties formed up for the walk home, Olympe already regarding her eldest son with deep suspicion. Penelope and Jane wrapped up dishes of food in sheets of clean newspaper for those to take home who would. "You take some dirty rice, Ben?" inquired Alys Roque, one of Olympe's friends. "I hear M'am Bontemps don't board."

"Would you *really* want to eat anything she'd cooked?" retorted Cora Chouteau, and got a general laugh.

"Hannibal, where'd you go?—Take some of this, please. I swear I could put you in a candle-mold and have room for the wick. . . ."

"I didn't yell 'Guards,' " protested Gabriel's voice over the general hushed babble of departure. "I swear I didn't. . . ."

"Marguerite?" January scanned the faces limned by the threads of candle-light, but saw no twist of graying blond hair starred with flowers. "Have you seen my friend Madame Scie?"

"I was talking with her." Mohammed LePas frowned. "Then some idiot whose name I won't mention knocked over the candle in the kitchen. . . ."

"I told you it was an accident," retorted Philippe duCoudreau. "You try movin' around in there with ten other people and somebody yells *the Guards is comin'* . . ."

"I thought you came in and grabbed her, Ben," said Cora.

"He did," confirmed duCoudreau, nodding. "I saw him."

January shook his head. "I was inside with Rose."

Silence. And those looks that go back and forth between people, when nobody wants to be the first to say *Uh-oh* . . .

They found every candle still long enough to sustain flame and spread out in the swamp. At this time of year, January found himself thinking, it was too cold for alligators—too dry for them to come up this far from the nearest water, which was Bayou Gentilly. . . . Besides, if someone were seized by a 'gator, he couldn't imagine it would have been silent.

Someone. As he edged through the harsh three-foot shields of the palmetto, the twining tangles of hackberry between the cypresses, January reflected uncomfortably on the way his mind phrased that thought.

Not *Marguerite* . . .

Just *someone.* Spindly light glimmered greenish

through dagger-shaped leaves, edged creepers snaking around the oak-trunks and the pointed goblin heads of the cypress-knees thrusting through last year's dead leaves. Bobbing glints in the darkness, like unseasonable fireflies, and an occasional hushed voice: "M'am Scie . . . m'am, can you hear . . . ?"

Gabriel's voice. "Here she is."

Damn it, thought January, hearing in his nephew's tone what the boy had found. *Damn it, no . . .*

She lay at the foot of an oak-tree. A little blood smudged a low-bending bough where her head had struck. But the wound was on the back of her skull, and the shoulder of her golden dress was torn. There was no possible way she could have simply run on the limb in the dark. The white flowers, fallen from her hair, strewed the dead leaves around her head. When January and the others bent over her and held the candles close, they could see the darkening bruises on her throat.

Huge hands. January had never met another man who had hands like that.

He didn't need to turn his head to see people look at one another. Didn't need to hear their silence. It was as if he felt the draw of everyone's breath.

Gently he felt her wrist. There was no pulse under the thin white skin, but he thought he detected a fragile beat in the vein of her neck. When he plucked the skeletal nosegay from Hannibal's buttonhole and held it before her lips, he saw the paper-fine petals stir. "Somebody, get a plank." He wondered why there was no expression in his voice. "An old door, or a tabletop. Anything to lay her out straight to carry her back to the house."

"Her neck broke?" Olympe knelt at his side, shrugged off her shawl. Hannibal brought up Marguerite's gray cloak, all snagged with dead leaves and twigs, found among the oak's twisted roots.

I should be feeling something, January told himself, not remembering how many nights had passed between Ayasha's death and the first onslaught of that hammering pain. "I don't know. She has a concussion, how bad I don't know." He saw Philippe duCoudreau, and one or two others, draw back a little when he turned, and said again, "I was with Rose."

"He was," agreed Rose, and duCoudreau nodded, with eyes that said, *And you're the woman who hopes to wed him.*

Isaak Jumon and Crowdie Passebon came back then from the house with one of the planks from the buffet. Holding Marguerite's head steady, January and Mamzelle Marie eased the ballet mistress onto the makeshift litter, covered her with cloaks and shawls.

"What do we say about this?" asked Mohammed. People looked at each other again, then at Jacques and his family.

Whatever you say, thought January, *it sure as hell can't be the truth.*

No one spoke for a time, as the implications of January's former relations with Madame Scie—known to a number of the other opera musicians present and almost certainly common knowledge by now among everyone at the party—and his present relations with Rose, sank into everyone's consciousness.

"We say a carriage struck her," said Mamzelle Marie at last. The voodooienne knelt on the other side of Madame Scie, listened to her chest, and gently touched her face and throat. "You know how crazy people drive, late, along the Bayou Road. You and Hannibal were walking her home,

Ben, and a carriage struck her, going fast without lights. You carried her here." She straightened up to her knees, regarded the fiddler with those dark, wise serpent eyes. "That sit with you, Hannibal?"

January felt Philippe duCoudreau looking at him, heard the silence louder than a thousand whispers.

The voodoo queen's gaze passed from face to face of those standing in the raw dark of the swamp. "That sit with all here," she asked, "until we can find the real truth?"

Uncle Bichet cleared his throat. Like everyone else there, the old man feared and respected Marie Laveau, but he had been, once, a prince of his tribe. He had been raised to love justice. "And what happens," he asked, "when we find that truth?"

"Depends," replied the voodooienne, "on what it is."

With Jumon and Mohammed and half a dozen others keeping watch all around for the City Guards, they carried Marguerite through the streets of the old French town to Olympe's house on Rue Douane. There they put her to bed in the rear bedroom, white and still as a corpse.

When January finally slept, much later in the day, he dreamed that he stood on a worn marble terrace in Cyprus, and through archways curtained in gauze heard Marguerite sing *Willow, willow, sing willow for me* in Drusilla d'Isola's sweet, despairing voice.

SEVEN

—◦◦◦—

By the time January left Olympe's house, after ascertaining that Marguerite's neck was not broken, the dense, misty blackness of the night had begun to thin to gray. In kitchens and slave-quarters all over town, men and women crept shivering from straw-tick pallets in unlighted rooms to kindle up the fires they'd prepared last night. To heat water so that Masters—or husbands— could wash their faces, or oil to fry rice, flour, and egg for *callas*. Along the levees, at the foot of Market Street, and St. Joseph, and Madison and St. Philippe, pirogues and canoes and fishing-boats put in, unloading aubergines and apples by the yellow cresset-glare, beans and winter lettuces and crates and barrels of black oysters and silvery pungent fish. A glory of baking bread and coffee blessed the air.

Crossing through the pre-dawn bustle of the Place d'Armes, casting despairingly this way and that in his mind for something else he might do, some other treatment he might add to those futile efforts already made, January felt again the iron cold of other dawns, the damp, mossy stink of the morning streets of Paris. Marguerite beside him, sinews and heart loosened with the sleepy content that the young feel when they've made music three-quarters of the night and love for the rest of it, in quest of coffee among the grimed echoing torchlit stone vaults of Les Halles.

Don't let her die. Virgin Mother of God, don't let her die.

There's not much you can do about a deep concussion, Dr. LeBel had told him—the head surgeon at the Hôtel Dieu in Paris. *Just nurse them, and get them to drink if you can once the danger of vomiting's past.* He'd lifted back the eyelids of the man he and January were examining then, a laborer whose thin breath reeked of decayed teeth and cheap wine, to show the mismatched dilation of the pupils, their fixed, unseeing gaze. *It's surprising how long they'll last, unconscious, if they can be made to sup a little gruel or water.*

One priest—probably Father Eugenius, January guessed—was already hearing confessions at the Cathedral of St. Louis. Three or four women in the gaudy, faded calicoes of the market waited on the benches near the wooden cubicle, hands folded in prayer. Only a few candles burned in all that shadowy space—at the far front of the church, votive lights before the Virgin's altar picked out the beauty of a curved eyebrow, the intricate life-maps of wrinkled and arthritic hands. Where was that quiet beauty, January wondered, in music? Why did opera celebrate only the loves of the young and noisy?

He confessed himself, and sat on the benches at the rear of the church that were reserved for people of color, until a sleepy altarboy came out and touched flame to the candles at the high altar, and Father Eugenius emerged in a robe of white and gold to say Mass. Only a handful of market-women were present, and a dozen slaves at the rear of the gloomy side aisles. The places of the whites in the center aisle were empty.

A veiled and fashionably-dressed woman knelt near

him, her elaborately-wrapped silk tignon proclaiming her
in all probability a plaçée. She did not take Communion,
but when January rose to leave, comforted as always by
the words of the blessings and the prayers, she remained,
rosary glinting faintly in her gloved hands.

Praying for expiation, he wondered, of a sin that the
white man's law would not permit her to rectify? Pleading
for the well-being of others in her family, who might rely
on her protector's largesse to give them a security they
might not otherwise have? Most of the plaçées, if they attended Mass at all, came to the eleven o'clock Mass—the
fashion-show, it was called. A parade of silk frocks and
new bonnets for the whites, of jewelry and stylish varia-
tions in color and wrap and feathers for the tignons of the
free colored women.

Not that many came. Mostly the ladies of the Rue des
Ramparts would exhibit their finery at the Salle d'Orleans
tonight.

The image of that penitent, whoever she was, stayed
in January's mind as he crossed the Place d'Armes, like the
air of a song that repeats over and over. He bought a bowl
of jambalaya and a cup of coffee in the market, and sat
watching the sea-gulls quarrel over shrimp dropped from
the baskets on the levee, trying to wake up.

In the blue gloom of the market hall the last torches
were extinguished. Light smote the waters of the river and
tipped the leafless branches of the sycamores around the
square with gold. Protestants and Americans said in
hushed, disapproving tones that the population of New
Orleans kept the Sabbath the way Bostonians kept the
Fourth of July, and as if to prove this, slaves stopped to
laugh and chat on their way to the market for their Masters, fishermen and stevedores sang in the morning chill as
they worked, their breath puffing white. A melismatic

holler was passed from crew to crew along the ranks of the steamboats unloading at the wharves, the words lost in the rise and fall of the voices: "Wayaaaaay, yooooo. . . ." January could follow the sound down the levee like the cloud-shadows that ran over the dark seas of standing cane.

At ten o'clock Consuela Montero would present herself for her session, and January knew from experience that it was easier and less exhausting to stay up than to get up. He could sleep in the afternoon—before or after returning to Olympe's house to check on Marguerite—so as to be clear-headed for that night's quadroon ball.

You can sleep during Lent. Last winter, having gotten on the wrong side of a powerful Creole matron, January had lost nearly all his students and had been hired to play very few balls; Mardi Gras was the harvest of his year, far less grueling than the sugar-grinding seasons of his childhood. You didn't sleep in either case, but at least at Mardi Gras you went to interesting parties.

You got her, Philippe duCoudreau had said in the lightless confusion of the Bichet kitchen last night. The candles had been out, the fire covered—jostling shoulders, crowding heads, features obscured in shadow. January passed his hand across his unshaven face, wondering how duCoudreau had been so sure. There was only one person at the party last night anywhere near January's size, and that was his brother-in-law, Paul Corbier, who would scoop up the gross brown four-inch palmetto-bugs on a piece of newspaper and pitch them gently outside rather than crushing them like every other person in town did.

Why would Philippe have accused him? The worst January knew of the man was that duCoudreau was the most hapless musician in New Orleans, and relations had never been anything but cordial between them. January felt a deep uneasiness, and anger at that uneasiness: anger that he would have to so deeply fear the possibility of any-one mentioning the truth to the police.

Struck by a carriage? He grimaced at the childishness of the lie. And what would the police say if they happened to see the huge bruises around Marguerite's throat?

You were her lover, you who love another now. Why would a white woman have gone with you to Bichet's except to demand something of you?

Of course your friends will all lie for you.

The people at the back of the Faubourg Tremé weren't so very different from the Milanese and the Sicilians who said *sbirri* with that look in their eyes. It does something to you, to know in your bones that justice is something other people get.

Someone had tried to strangle her. Someone had seized her by the shoulder and slammed her against the low-hanging tree-limb when she fought free.

What would Philippe say if someone started asking questions of those who'd seen Madame Scie leave Trulove's ball with himself and Hannibal last night?

Consuela Montero appeared on Madame Bontemps's doorstep on the stroke of the hour, a copy of the score to *Le Nozze di Figaro* in hand. *"Mil reniegos* that I declined to go to the house of Señor Trulove last night!"

News, reflected January, *travels fast.*

She folded back the mantilla that sheltered her round, determined face from the winter sun and inciden-tally from the chance notice of passers-by. "Not that there were not some in the Opera Society who begged me to meet them there, but to go listen to *Americanos* tell one another about cotton and slaves, *qué fastidio!* How would I know the girl would be so stupid as to displease her patron so in public?" She opened her little purse of gold mesh and laid a stack of five Mexican silver dollars on the corner of January's square six-octave piano. "Just so! One can only hope that foolish as d'Isola is, she will contrive to bring him to his senses herself."

Briskly, she set the score on the music-rack, and removed her black-and-gold velvet pelerine. "It is as well to be ready if she does. *Buen' dias,* Señora." She nodded and offered two lace-mitted fingers to Madame Bontemps, apparently not in the least discomposed by that woman's silent appearance at her elbow.

"Madame." January selected one of the silver dollars and pressed it into his landlady's palm. "This is Madame Montero, who is paying me for a private singing lesson this morning. You remember I sent you a note of this, yesterday afternoon?"

"I don't forget things." Madame Bontemps continued to hold Madame Montero's extended fingers in her damp grip. "Even seeing the Devil last night doesn't make me forget. I saw the Devil last night," she added, released her hold, and settled herself into one of the nearly threadbare—but spotlessly neat—green grosgrain chairs that decorated the front parlor. "It's ten o'clock." She folded her hands in her lap. "At ten o'clock I sit in the parlor."

January glanced at the soprano, who was studying herself in the pier glass between the windows and making sure that the lacquered curls on her forehead remained perfectly symmetrical. If Montero heard the landlady's intention, it didn't bother her. And there would be odder distractions than that, he reflected, at the theater Tuesday night.

To do her justice, Consuela Montero was a far better Countess than La d'Isola. She had, as she'd said, sung the role only the previous year, and needed only to be taken through it. January, who had a very passable baritone, sang the parts of both Figaro and the Count for her, accompanied occasionally by his landlady, who had a habit of chiming in with fragments of "Fleuve du Tage" and "Les bluets sont bleus." "You are good," Montero told January after their Act Four garden duet. "Better than Señor Staranzano, who just stands there, waiting for the world to swoon at his feet. You would make a good Almaviva—always supposing Almaviva was a Moor. It is you they should put in *Othello,* and not that Austrian buffoon in black paint."

That really WOULD *have them burning down the theater,* thought January, too amused at the notion of the reaction to such casting to feel much anger at the fact that in America it simply could not be. Probably not in Paris either, he thought, and be damned to your Liberté, Fraternité, and Égalité. "Maybe you could tell me," he said, shuffling through the score to locate the point at which the Countess reveals her true identity to her baffled husband. "Was there someone in the Opera Society who tried to get Belaggio to change *Othello* for some other opera? Tried to get him not to put it on?"

The elegantly-plucked black brows pinched. "Not put it on?" Montero's voice had the note of a queen who has been informed that her carriage isn't ready due to the drunkenness of the grooms. "*De qué,* not put it on? It is a very good opera. Beautiful. And we have no other premiere, unless you will have *La Muette* as such. But *La Muette* is years old, and is everywhere done. One must have the premiere."

"There are those in this city," said January, "who would not thank a man to put on-stage the love of a black man for a white woman. You do not know how it is here," he added, seeing in her face the same incredulity he had seen yesterday in Belaggio's. "I assure you, there are men who would do what they could to prevent it, as being 'indecent.' And I know Signor Belaggio is proud of it, as well he should be. But the pride could put him in danger."

Montero's red lips curled. "If what you say is true, Señor, I think you'll find that Señor Belaggio is the last man who would place his life before his pride. And *á la verdad*, I don't know what cause he has to be proud. It isn't as if he wrote *Othello.*"

"*What?*" Even as the word came out of his mouth, January knew she spoke the truth. A man doesn't have to be good to write great music. But there must be something about him that is great.

And that, he understood, was what bothered him about Belaggio.

He was petty. A petty man can write excellent music, he knew. But not the aria La d'Isola had sung last night.

"*De verdad.*" The soprano shrugged her fleshy shoulders. "Did you not know? Incantobelli wrote it. Why else do you think he made the threats he did, of murder and ruin? Why do you think Belaggio had that brother of his denounce Incantobelli to the Austrians so that he can never return to Milan? And even so," she added, settling the finale score before January on the piano-rack, "Belaggio still dared not remain in Europe, knowing Incantobelli could be as close to him as Naples or Rome. No, he must come to Havana."

Her onyx eyes flashed with a sudden ugly glint. "And like a fool, I signed his contract, not even making sure that it specified that I would be prima. I did not know then," she added darkly, "that he had fallen in love with this hussy, and promised her a season. Come." She tapped the music smartly with the backs of her polished nails. "Let us now return to this other pig of a lover Almaviva, and run him to confusion."

"I saw the Devil last night," put in Madame Bontemps from her chair opposite the windows.

"Did you?" Madame Montero tweaked a curl back into place. "No doubt he was looking for a fiacre—why are they never about when you need them? So. The finale. This time I will try a little fioritura, just to show these people what true singing is."

For the next two hours they concentrated on the Count Almaviva's efforts to exercise *le droit du seigneur* on his barber's bride, Susanna's efforts to elude him, the Countess's struggle to win back her husband's love, and the page Cherubino's double dilemma of achieving puberty and evading conscription. Only when January was handing the soprano into a hack at the end of the rehearsal was he able to return to the subject of Incantobelli. It was just after noon by then, and he had been hard put to keep his mind on the music, wondering whether he would find Marguerite conscious or even alive when he returned to Olympe's. *If anything had happened, they'd have sent for me,* he told himself.

But his heart felt sick.

It came back to his mind that in the dark of the alley, his fist had connected with a chin not very much lower than his own; he remembered the bulk and weight of his attacker, throwing him against the wall. As he led Madame Montero through the French door to the Rue des Ursulines, he asked, "You say Incantobelli made threats against Belaggio for stealing his opera and passing it off as his own? Threats of murder?"

"Of a certainty." She tilted her head to look up at him through the dusky cloud of her mantilla. Draped over a comb nearly a foot high, it rose above the mountain of love-knots, bows, gems, and ringlets on her head. "I myself heard him."

"So it might very well have been Incantobelli who hired the men who attacked Belaggio." Many castrati, January knew, grew to be enormously tall—which did not seem to be the case with Incantobelli, so far as he'd been able to glimpse him last night—but it was no eunuch whose beard had scraped his knuckles in the dark.

"Never." Montero shook her head decidedly. "He may have taken a warm bath in his youth, Incantobelli. . . ." She switched casually to Italian with the old phrase that described the operation by which boys were castrated. "But he is a Neapolitan, when all is said. Hire louts to administer a beating for such a thing? Pah! It is not like the seduction of a man's wife, who after all is but a wife. It is the rape of his daughter, his child. One does not delegate chastisement for such a deed. Ah! Behold the fine *caballero*—I trust you will not speak of seeing me here?" She extended a round little hand for Hannibal to kiss as the fiddler came up the banquette. "That back-alley drabtail d'Isola carries tales enough to Lorenzo as it is. All we need is that she should say I am plotting against her, that it is my doing if greenstuff is thrown at her after she sings Tuesday night."

"If she sings." Hannibal removed his shabby high-crowned beaver and saluted the hand as if it were a holy relic. "If there's a performance at all. I took the liberty of calling on Mr. Caldwell to tell him he needs to find a new ballet mistress and the man's in near hysterics, sending messages to Belaggio at his hotel and Marsan at his town house—though neither of them, apparently, can be reached. I thought Caldwell would give birth. He's procured the services of Herr Smith, by the way. . . ."

"Smith?" January groaned. Madame Montero, whose hand remained in Hannibal's, raised an eyebrow. "Smith—who was certainly called something else in

Dresden, before he left for I think political reasons—is probably one of the finest instructors and arrangers of opera ballet that the reign of Louis the Fourteenth ever produced. Unfortunately, Louis the Fourteenth has been dead for about a hundred and twenty years and we do things a little differently these days."

"If you want a strict regulation of passepieds in every opera prologue, musettes in the first act, and tambourins in the second, with every dancer doing his or her specialty turn no matter how it fits into the story," explained Hannibal, "Smith's your man. Though he'll fight like a maddened butterfly to get more allegorical costumes for the rats."

Montero paused in the door of the fiacre. "Allegorical—as what? The spirits of Love and Duty in *Figaro?* Of Hearth and Home?"

"If he can manage," said January, "he'll do it."

"Smith was at liberty." Hannibal shrugged. "What more need I say? *Difficilis, querulus, laudator temporis acti se puero.* . . . I overheard Knight complaining that Davis raised the pay of his own dance-master rather than let Caldwell hire him away—about half the Opera Society was at Caldwell's, running around like the fourth act of a bad opéra bouffe trying to figure out a way to stop the duel over cakes and tea, not that they offered me so much as a bite. Kentucky Williams tells me Kate the Gouger may know something about Belaggio's friends in the alley, by the way," he added as they shut the fiacre door and the jarvey whipped up his horse. "Kate runs a bath-house on Tchoupitoulas Street near the cattle-market. Occasionally one can even get a bath there. The lovely Mistress Williams remembers there was a pair of brothers renting a room from her, spending money she's pretty sure they shouldn't have had."

"Were they indeed?" The thought of dealing with any friend of Kentucky Williams—a cigar-smoking harpy who ran a combination grog-shop and bordello on Perdidio Street in the part of town referred to by one and all as the Swamp—made January wince. The prospect was not sweetened by contemplation of the swinish rabble of filibusters, gun-runners, mercenaries, and river-rats native to Tchoupitoulas Street, which skirted the levee upriver like a dirty rampart of cotton-presses and baracoons. Under ordinary circumstances January would cheerfully have consigned Belaggio to Hell and his stolen opera with him, no matter how beautiful its music, rather than venture into territory so perilous.

But the circumstances were not ordinary. So after a brief and frustrating visit to Olympe's house, long enough to ascertain that Marguerite had neither wakened nor stirred in the night, January and Hannibal made their way across Canal Street in the sharp, heatless brightness of noon, and as far as they could along Magazine, which was at least in daylight hours marginally more genteel. Here among the white-painted board houses, the brick shops and liveries of the American section of town, an approximation of Sabbath quiet could be detected: a number of stores were closed and slaves weren't lined up on the wooden sidewalks outside the salesrooms as they were on other days of the week. But winter was the time when business got done in New Orleans. It was the end of the *roulaison*—the sugar-grinding season—and the beginning of the cotton harvest. Factors, planters, brokers, steamboat companies, all made their money in the months between November and March; and on their coattails, the owners of refineries and cotton-presses, livery stables, salesrooms, bordellos, saloons. To lose one day in seven was more than ridiculous. It was impossible, irresponsible, absurd.

You can sleep during Lent.

More than buying and selling was going on, too. Men strolled from barroom to barroom along the mud street, whiskery savages who came down from Kentucky and Tennessee with the keelboats, in their homespun shirts and heavy boots, pistols and knives at their belts. River traders, some of them—or the thieves and pirates who adopted that name—indistinguishable from the ruffians who made up the occasional wildcat military expeditions organized to help South American guerrilleros or dictators in the rebellion-torn nations of the south for a price. Slave-smugglers, some of them, bringing in Africans against the laws of the United States and the vows of the British Royal Navy, and trappers from the wild lands of northern Mexico, in their buckskin shirts and leggins with their squaws walking silent at their heels. Here and there Indians from those lands could be seen as well, black-haired and watchful-eyed, or staggering drunk and debased; Mexicans with silver conchos on their low-crowned hats. Every second building along Tchoupitoulas Street seemed to be a tavern, doors and windows gaping and the sickish-sweet stink of tobacco—smoked or spit—vying with the smoke of the steamboats, the stench of untended privies, the fetor of spilled or vomited whiskey and beer.

As January and Hannibal proceeded upriver, the reek of the cattle-market and the slaughterhouses overwhelmed these other smells, and black buzzards hunched watchfully on eaves or fenceposts. "I wish they wouldn't look at me that way," complained Hannibal, and coughed. "Like creditors, or one's family after someone's blabbed about the contents of one's will. At least one can disinherit one's family."

"I'm not sure," said January, and pointed to a big bald-headed bird on the limb of an oak—the buildings hereabouts were thinning, and becoming progressively more rude as they left the town behind. "That one looks like a lawyer to me."

"*Tu as veritas, amicus meus.*" The fiddler bent to pick an empty bottle from the sedge-choked ditch and flung it at the bird, which swayed back a little on its perch, wings spread like a witch's cloak. Then hopped from its place and pecked at the black glass. "Now that you mention it, he does indeed bear a startling resemblance to my father's solicitor—Droudge, his name was. If he swallows the bottle, I'll know for sure he's the very man, garbed in a clever disguise."

To their right, inland from the river, a man shouted. January had been aware for some minutes of the sullen rumble of voices, the occasional hoarse oath. The vacant lots here had blurred into stretches of marshy woodland, and it was hard to see exactly what was taking place, but January guessed. He felt he'd been born knowing, and his stomach clenched. He'd been aware, too, that he and Hannibal were not the only pair of men—one white, one black—to be making its way into this seedy neighborhood. At least two or three other couples of like composition waded through the weeds along the edges of the muddy streets, and in every case the black member of the pair was younger, taller, and fitter than his companion.

The sound of yelling spiked, with wild howls of encouragement.

January knew exactly what was going on.

Neither Kate the Gouger nor any of her boarders were at the filthy collection of sheds that comprised her

establishment. Hannibal poked his head through the door
of the ramshackle bath-house—which more resembled a
woodshed, with a couple of crusted tin tubs on the bare
earth and an open firepit in a shed at the back—then re-
emerged with a shrug. Behind the main building a sort of
cabinet did duty as Kate's bedroom, with a kitchen, a
privy, a huge pile of cut wood, a murky-looking cistern,
and another long dormitory shed grouped a few yards off.
Nothing moved except a skinny cat sneaking along the
roof of the dormitory, her purposeful air boding ill for
any who might nourish hopes for a rodent-free night.
Since the mob gathered around the fight was only a hundred yards or so up a nameless muddy street, in a clearing
past a line of tupelo trees, it was obvious where everybody was.

January felt as if everything in him had shrunk to a
cold knot of iron.

In Paris, during the tumults that had led up to the ex-
pulsion of the last Bourbon king, his friends used to say,
It's only a riot, and they'd joke at his unwillingness to go
along and see the fun.

The snarling anger of mobs always made him shiver,
like the scent of smoke on the wind. If you were raised
black in New Orleans, it was second nature to turn
around and walk the other way. Fast.

The fights were being held under the auspices of the
Eagle of Victory saloon, one of the last buildings of the
town on this side. One of the first, indeed, to be built on
what had been the fields of a sugar plantation: through
the stringers of cypress and loblolly pine, where other lots
had been cleared, January could see piles of lumber or
stacks of bricks marking someone's good intentions. This
section of the Faubourg St. Mary was a wasteland of old
fields cut across and across with new streets—sodden

tracks for the most part—and overgrown with elephant-ear and the skinny remnants of degenerate cane. Just past the Eagle of Victory's unpainted walls, men shoved each other for a view, a solid wall of backs: greasy buckskin sewn with porcupine-quills, blue or gray or black broadcloth and superfine. Slouch hats, fur hats, tall hats of silk or fine beaver. Most of the yelling was in English, with the hoarse inflection of Americans. "Kill him! Kill him, goddammit!" "Get up, you black fool!"

Against the saloon's rear wall a man lay on a blanket on the ground. Bruises stood out even against the dark mahogany of his skin. A barechested and shivering boy in his early teens knelt beside him, sponging away blood from chest, arms, thighs with his own shirt. As January and Hannibal passed the boy looked around desperately, as if seeking help or advice or merely the permission to seek it, and January walked over and knelt beside him. "May I?"

The boy nodded, offered him the shirt, and smeared the tears from his face.

The man's eye had been gouged nearly out of its socket, his left ear bitten half away. His breath was shallow; when January pinched his fingernail, the nailbed stayed pale.

"He be all right?" the boy asked, watching fearfully as January gently massaged and kneaded the engorged flesh of the eye back to something resembling its proper position. "He got blood in his piss." He handed January a gore-smudged bandanna when he held out his hand; January made a pad of Hannibal's handkerchief and tied it over the eye.

"Much?"

The boy shook his head. "Michie Marsan's Lou kicked him in the nuts. Kicked him like a mule." He looked around as someone roared with rage in the thick of the crowd. A moment later a savage storm-gust of cheering made January's skin creep. The boy said, "He done as best as he could. Just Big Lou was bigger. Lots bigger."

And probably didn't want to end up lying on the ground leaking blood any more than this man did. January carefully manipulated the bruised and swollen genitals, ascertained that the swelling was minimal, that there didn't seem to be hematomas deeper in the groin. The downed man was clearly a fighter, with scars on his cheeks and belly-muscles like a double row of fry-pans.

"Get him under a blanket." He fished in the pocket of his shabby corduroy jacket for a half-dollar. "One of the whores should have one to sell you. He needs to be kept warm. Get rum or brandy to clean that ear. Get him out of here as soon as you can."

The boy nodded, wiped his eyes and his nose again on the back of his bare arm. "We got to wait on Michie Napier. He got Charlie in there fightin' Big Lou now."

Lucky Charlie.

"Do what you can." January stood, and patted the boy's bony shoulder.

Behind him a man said, "You're behind the fair, friend. You want to get your boy ready if you're going to get him in against Big Lou." January turned. The man was an American, dressed like a tradesman in a rough wool jacket and pants and a calico shirt. He spoke to Hannibal with a friendly matter-of-factness, sized January up with polite approval, and added, "What's your boy's name?"

January opened his mouth to express a sentiment both unwise and inappropriate for a man of color, be he ever so free, along Tchoupitoulas Street, and Hannibal cut in with "Plantagenet. Hal Plantagenet. *A bawcock and a heart of gold.* Let's go, Hal."

January went. The frenzy of shouting died abruptly into a sated growl and the tight-clotted wall of backs opened abruptly into a myriad of little groups. Men counted money into each other's hands, men joyfully re-lived each hold and throw and bludgeon, here and there men cursed furiously. *(And how much would people lay on* YOU, *fat man, if you and that scrofulous weasel you're screaming at started hammering each other naked?)* January glimpsed Vincent Marsan, towering in his tobacco-brown coat, gloves, and waistcoat all en suite, illuminating the finer points of the match to Harry Fry with explanatory jabs of a sardonyx-headed gold toothpick. A few feet away, an older slave, a tough little man who was clearly a trainer, kneaded Big Lou's shoulders while the fighter slumped on a broken crate with his forehead on his knees. Blood glistened on a shaven scalp. He looked exhausted, uncaring; an iron mountain of a man with strips of pick-led leather wrapped around his enormous hands. January glanced at the angle of the sun above the curtain of trees and wondered how many more men Big Lou would have to fight before he could go home.

Other men crowded around, obscuring the scene. Hannibal said, "Ah! *A lovely being, scarcely formed or molded / A rose with all its sweetest leaves yet folded,*" and wove his way to Kate the Gouger, a nondescript, hard-faced girl with red hair skinned back into a dirty knot on the back of her head. She was handing around a brown glass bottle, saying ". . . better at my place over yonder past the trees." She shot a swift glance toward the Eagle, wary of its owner's prior claims to customers on his prop-erty. "Pussy's better, too."

"Yeah?" demanded a squat cut-throat whose long

brown hair crept visibly with lice. He spit—there was enough tobacco underfoot to send up a smell that rivaled the piss-stink of the bushes all around the clearing.

"Sure enough." Kate blew a cloud of cigar-smoke in the man's face. " 'Cause it's *me!* I'll take on the lot of you and have you beggin' for mercy!"

The men whooped and laughed and slapped her narrow buttocks, and said, "Well, we'll just come along and see who begs for mercy!" Then there was a shout as the milling crowd coalesced. Heads turned, and the men crowded back to where Big Lou was squaring off again, leaving the Gouger momentarily alone. She looked after them with contempt and weary calculation in her hard brown eyes.

"Poor bastards," remarked Hannibal, and she glanced over at him and grinned, broken-toothed, like a wolf. "Don't know what they're getting into."

"Thought you was playin' for the op-ree." She stuck a black-nailed brown hand down her uncorseted bosom to scratch one shallow breast. Most of the small-time madams of her sort in town usually wore cheap Mother Hubbards—good-time dresses, the free colored of the lower sort called them—but Kate had rigged herself out for the fights in a faded frock of red calico rotting away under the armpits, and a skinning-knife the length of January's forearm sheathed at her belt. She was probably, January guessed, not more than twenty. "You missed good fightin' this afternoon."

"Well, and so I am playing for the opera." Hannibal bent to kiss Kate's hand with the same reverent attentiveness he'd lavished on Consuela Montero's. "But I couldn't forgo a few moments of your delightful company." Kate made a simper and pushed him, like a schoolboy shoving a mate, but for one instant January saw the look in her eyes: shy pleasure that someone had called her delightful. That someone cared.

"You gonna get yourself in trouble one day," she said, and under its hoarseness her voice was the voice of a girl. "You come around sweet-talkin' every girl."

"Then I'll rely on you to rescue me." Hannibal pressed his hand to his side, fighting a cough. "Kentucky Williams tells me you had a couple of heroes staying at your place who might have been hired for an alley job last Thursday."

"Gower boys." The Gouger nodded briskly, once. "Buck an' Bart. Sounds like a couple hounds, don' it? Came down on a flatboat with a load of corn, spent all they daddy's money on forty-rod an' quim, you know how it is. Hangin' around my place, tryin' to make five hundred dollars choppin' wood. Then all of a sudden Bart comes in, pays me what they owe—this is Wednesday around supper-time. They pack up their plunder. Stuff's still in my attic. I ain't no thief. 'Sides, it's just a couple shirts an' a powder-horn. Bart come in Friday mornin', begs me for some medicine an' bandages an' sech truck. Looked like he been in a fight, cheek all bust to hell an' swole up, mud an' blood on his shirt. Last I saw him."

"And his brother?" Hannibal produced a bottle from his coat pocket, took a sip, and offered it to her.

She shrugged, and drank like a thirsty sailor.

"How tall is Bart, m'am?" asked January.

She glanced up at him.

"You see, m'am, we both play for the opera, and it looks like somebody might have hired Bart and his brother to go after different people in the company. Go after 'em and kill 'em." January carefully graded his English to the same roughness as hers. He had long ago learned that nothing intimidates and alienates so much as elegant speech. His English was, most of the time, as excellent as his French, but the music of speech was a hobby of his: fortissimo to pianissimo, Paris-perfect to the "mo kiri mo vini" of the cane-patch. "We don't know who they'll go after next"—he glanced worriedly at Hannibal—"nor who hired 'em nor why. We ain't gonna get Bart an' his brother in trouble, m'am. We just need to know."

Mollified, the girl said, "Bart's about six foot. Buck's bigger, near your height."

"They both got beards?"

She looked surprised at the question—a clean-shaven man on this part of Tchoupitoulas Street was usually either a pimp or a gambler—then nodded. "They's both kinda blondy. Not real blond, but like Kentucky," meaning, since the remark was addressed to Hannibal, Kentucky Williams, their mutual acquaintance. "Bart asked me to listen around for somebody takin' a boat up-river next week. I said I would."

Hannibal and January traded a glance. Then January said, "If we was to leave a note with you, m'am, to give Bart when he comes in, would you do that?"

She thought about it, glanced at Hannibal again, and nodded. "I'll do that."

"Thank you." Hannibal kissed her hand again. *"If the heart of a man is deprest with cares / The mist is dispelled when a woman appears.* We shall be deeply in your debt."

Madame Bontemps was still sitting in the parlor when January returned from the levee. It was now late afternoon—nearly five—and the harsh rays of the sinking sun showed up the chips and stains in the stucco of the house, the cracks where resurrection fern had taken greedy root. As January started to go down the passway to the yard, his landlady's flat voice grated out at him from the street window: "That woman with the spectacles was here." In six weeks of residence, January had yet to hear Madame Bontemps refer to Rose by her name. "I told her not to wear them. They bring bad luck. That woman in the veil this morning, she doesn't wear spectacles, and you see the kind of luck she's had."

"That's true," agreed January, coming back to the parlor's French door. It was far easier to agree with Madame Bontemps than to disagree and continue any conversation, and he wanted to have at least a short nap before meeting Rose for supper. "Did she leave a message? A note?"

The woman thought about that, rocking her body in her chair, lips pushing in and out like dry kisses. She had a tea-cup on her knee. The saucer covered its mouth and her hand pressed down the saucer. January didn't want to think about what she might have trapped inside.

"It isn't right that women should write," she declared at last. Which meant, January knew, that he'd have to search the privy for the scraps of whatever Rose had slipped under his door. "I told her that. I told her I saw the Devil, too. She didn't believe me. But he was here last night. He waited beside the house until it started to get light."

January, who had nodded agreement again and started to walk away, stopped. Cold stillness gripped his chest. "Beside the house? In the passway, you mean?"

Madame Bontemps nodded, still rocking. In his mind, January heard the crack and rustle of a stealthy foot, first in the wet, leafy dark of the labyrinth, then in the shadows along the Bayou Road. Saw Marguerite lying beneath an oak-tree, blood dotting the strawflowers tangled in her hair.

"What did he look like?" he asked, and the unguessable reverie in Madame's dark eyes sharpened to scorn.

"He was invisible," she said, as if explaining the obvious to a stupid child. "He looked like the Devil."

Meaning it had been pitch-black along the side of the house. Meaning there might not have been anyone at all waiting there for him to come home by himself.

Seeing that nothing else would be gotten out of the landlady, January turned to go. Too much to hope, he thought, that the visitor—if there had been one—had left a scrape on the moldy bricks that paved the passway and the yard, or had dropped a glove or a signet-ring or a letter bearing his seal.

He wasn't sure which of the American town's numerous heretical Protestant establishments counted Shaw as a member, or what he could tell the policeman if he went to him. *I think we were followed after the Trulove reception last night? I think Madame Scie was attacked in the woods by someone who may or may not have been at Bichet's illegal gathering?*

You got her, Philippe had said.

Even if Shaw didn't believe January had tried to kill a white woman—a woman he was known to have bedded—it was no guarantee the crime wouldn't be fastened on him anyway. Or on someone else who'd been at Bichet's, Paul or Mohammed or any of a dozen others, by who knew what vagaries of *blankitte* reasoning.

Once you called on the whites, and the white man's law, everything was out of your hands.

Behind him, Madame Bontemps's voice called out, "He had a knife."

EIGHT

❦

"If Madame Bontemps objects that much to a woman knowing how to read," remarked Rose, gravely stirring the fist-sized clot of rice provided into the rest of the gumbo that had been brought to their table at the Buttonhole Café, "I shudder to contemplate what she'd say if she knew I'd been hired to put together pyrotechnics for Mr. Davis's production of *La Muette de Portici* on the thirty-first."

As the landlady had not torn Rose's note into thumbnail-size fragments and dropped them into the privy—something she had done often enough in the past for Rose to be resigned about it—but had merely ripped it several times neatly across and added it to the box of old newspapers left there for the convenience of the occupants, January had been able to meet Rose without trouble. The Buttonhole was a small establishment on Rue St. Anne that catered to free colored musicians and artisans, and served up in its tiny plank-walled front parlor the best gumbo and jambalaya in town. Cora Chouteau, who owned the place, further enlivened the room by pasting up every playbill she could lay hands on—advertisements for both Caldwell's and Davis's rival productions of *La Muette* smeared the wall behind Rose's head.

"Caldwell may have bought up all the red silk and ready-made fireworks in town," Rose added, seeing January's start of surprise. "But colored fire is fairly simple to manufacture. It's surprising what you can make people think they're seeing, with a little red glass and forced perspective."

"I'll take your word for it." The scant sleep January had managed to achieve that afternoon had refreshed him somewhat, between dreams of Desdemona's song in the darkness, and jolting awake every few minutes at the fancied creak of a foot on the gallery. Outside the café's open windows, Rue St. Anne was already noisy with carriages full of maskers, with gaudily-costumed women calling out to men, and the racket of someone playing "When Darkness Brooded O'er the Deep" very, very badly on a cornet.

It would be, reflected January wearily, a very long night.

Rose took off her spectacles and rubbed her eyes. There were few ways by which the quadroon daughter of a plaçée could earn her living in New Orleans at the best of times, were she unwilling to place herself under the protection of a man. If Carnival was the harvest of January's year, it was the starving winter of hers. Poverty was beginning to tell on her—he could see where her gloves had been mended, and where the sleeve of her blue merino dress was shiny with wear. He was glad she'd been able to find the work with Davis, particularly since it might well lead to more, and to work better paid than she was generally able to find.

Since her involvement in the same scandal of lies and libel that had robbed January of most of his living the previous winter, she had been unable to teach. January was daily astonished that this bookish, brilliant woman had survived the destruction of the school that had been her life's work. He knew she eked out a desperate living these days with her translations, but he'd never heard her repine, or speak of might-have-beens or if-onlies. She was jealous of her liberty, of her solitude and her work, and the treatment one man had given her had left its terrible mark on her spirit. One day, he hoped, he'd have sufficient money saved to be able to ask her to be his wife, but hadn't the faintest idea of what she would say when he did.

And he knew it was not a question he would be able to ask twice.

"Do you think he followed you?" She replaced her spectacles on her nose and devoted herself to the gumbo. "Incantobelli?"

"He was at Trulove's. And if, as Madame Montero says, Belaggio stole his opera, I can see him being angry enough—hating enough—to want to destroy not only Belaggio, but the entire opera season as well. So I can almost understand coshing the ballet mistress. Certainly Marguerite's replacement by Herr Smith isn't going to help the performance. But surely Incantobelli can't intend to murder the orchestra piecemeal."

"He can intend to murder the one member of the orchestra who held sufficient conversation with the ballet mistress to be a witness. That's always assuming Incantobelli to be sane," she went on thoughtfully. "Though why he would bother to go after Belaggio is beyond me. Belaggio seems to be running toward his own doom swiftly enough to outdistance the most vindictive of foes."

Playing schottisches and waltzes, marches and cotillions a few hours later in the tasteful ivory-paneled confines of the Salle d'Orleans, January understood the schoolmistress's point. As usual, one of the Carnival subscription balls of white society—the French Creole St.

Margaret's Society—was taking place in the Théâtre d'Orleans next door, and there was much discreet coming and going through the olive-colored velvet curtain that masked the passageway between the Théâtre and the Salle. January watched some of the most socially prominent white gentlemen of the town as they danced with their mistresses, or the women they hoped to make their mistresses, and shook his head. *The custom of the country,* he'd heard people say—he himself had said it, many times, as if that somehow made it acceptable. At the other end of the passageway, where a floor had been set up over the Théâtre's parterre and other musicians played, the wives and sisters, fiancées and mothers of these selfsame gentlemen sipped lemonade and chatted, and pretended mutual bafflement about where their menfolk had slipped away to.

The gambling-rooms downstairs, they all said. *That's where they've gone.*

January recognized Lorenzo Belaggio despite the mask of bronze leather that hid his face. The impresario, clad in bronze armor, kept as far from Vincent Marsan as possible: by the way he kept drifting toward the olive-curtained windows, January guessed he was suffocating in the costume never designed for dancing. Marsan was all in crimson satin, a full-skirted coat and breeches, long waistcoat, and crimson stockings and shoes, topped off with an old-fashioned periwig the size of a sheep. Watching him flirt with the café-crème princesses, Columbines, shepherdesses, and odalisques, January wondered if the drab Madame Marsan had been left *bredouillée,* as they called it, in the Théâtre, "making a tapestry" with the other women along the walls.

Hubert Granville's wife certainly had. January glimpsed the banker tripping through a sprightly cotillion with Eulalie Figes, a former plaçée and the mother of a hopeful young damsel. The banker's motley rags and exaggerated back-hump made January wonder for a dizzying moment if the squabbish Mrs. Granville in the next room was really clad in gypsy-dancer garb and accompanied by a stuffed goat. Hannibal's evaluation of the upcoming duel as material for a bad opéra bouffe seemed amply justified: every time Marsan left the Salle, Granville would stride over to Belaggio, take him by the bronze vambrace, and expostulate furiously, clearly trying to talk him out of the duel. At the reappearance of that tall crimson figure, Quasimodo would hop back into the cotillion to catch Eulalie Figes's hand as if nothing had happened.

Had Marguerite not been lying at Olympe's house unconscious—had January not heard, over and over again in his mind, his landlady's flat, harsh voice saying *He had a knife*—he would have been hard-put not to laugh.

Belaggio wasn't the only one being worked on. During the course of the evening Jed Burton, James Caldwell, the prim little Mr. Knight—his immaculately anonymous evening-dress scorning the fantasies of the other men—and his lumbering clerk, all made it their business to corner Marsan with varying degrees of vehemence. "The Widow Redfern and Mrs. Trulove have been at him across the way," remarked Hannibal, strolling through the velvet curtains and over to the buffet table when supper was announced at the Théâtre. About half the men in the Salle rather sheepishly made their excuses to their ladyfriends and retreated to rejoin their wives: "I can't imagine why they bother," remarked the fiddler, who'd been hired to play at the Society Ball rather than this one. "La Redfern was in charge of the refreshments over there. I never saw so much bread and butter in my life. They water the champagne, too." He'd helped himself to a bottle of Mr.

Davis's, and a vol-au-vent, and leaned against January's piano, chalky and shaking with fatigue.

Around them, the men who'd lingered moved from woman to woman, chatting with the young ladies, gazing into dark eyes or more discreetly down the tender-shadowed creases of half-exposed breasts. They talked more easily with the mothers, who hovered smiling, waving their painted silk fans, graceful and gracious and sharply cognizant of the value of money, aware—as their daughters were not—of the transitory nature of male passion, of the precarious position of any free woman of color in New Orleans. January's eye picked them out, too: Dominique's friends and neighbors, his mother's friends and their daughters. Marie-Anne Pellicot, shy and lovely on the arm of her young protector, a wealthy planter's son. Catherine Clisson, darker than most of the other plaçées, almost African-black, and striking in a Renaissance gown of yellow silk, whose plaçage with a rich planter twenty-five years ago had nearly broken January's very youthful heart. Dominique's friend Iphigénie Picard, laughing as she teased the discomfited Yves Valcour about having to return to his mother and sisters next door. . . .

White men and young ladies of color—for of course the only men of color in the room were the musicians, and the waiters who brought in the food. Not all of the girls, January knew, were entirely willing, legally free though they might be. It is easy to persuade the young, who are aware of how limited their options are; easy to play upon family obligations, to convince a girl to become what her mother was. Obligations to their mothers: obligations, too, to their white fathers, invisible in the background but capable of using these left-handed children as pawns, as they used everything else. *Be my mistress and I'll give you a house, you who will have nothing without help. Be my friend's mistress or I'll cancel your mother's pension, or speak a bad word of her at the bank next time she wants to borrow a little money to enlarge her business, or educate your brother.*

The white men all knew one another. And they were strong.

And behind them all lurked the shadow of Kate the Gouger, a terrible reminder of what happened to a girl who had no protection, and nothing to sell.

"Is Henri there?" Dominique rustled over to the musicians' dais, gorgeous in the pink-and-gold panniered Court gown that January had seen on Iphigénie last year.

Hannibal hesitated. The exhaustion of the long walk to Tchoupitoulas Street had taken its toll—he was weaving a little on his feet and the soft Anglo-Irish accent that mostly disappeared when he was sober was much to the fore. Then he shrugged, and said, "With *La Mère Terrible* playing monster to his Andromeda, O Queen. The lot of Viellards—Henri and his sisters—are done up as, I think, the Kingdom of the Ocean—in any case it more nearly resembles a school of whales than anything I've recently. . . ."

"And is she?"

There was no need to ask of whom Dominique spoke.

"You might as well tell me," said January's sister, when Hannibal did not reply. "It can't be worse than what I'm imagining."

"He doesn't look happy, if that's what you fear." He'd acquired a nosegay of small yellow roses from somewhere, and used it to tie up his long, graying hair. "She's a well-looking girl. Pale and skinny, but nothing to—"

"I've seen her," interrupted Dominique. "One does, you know, on the streets and in church. I know Chloë St.

Chinian is beautiful. And I know she's cold as stone. And no, I don't imagine . . ."

Her breath snagged. January followed her gaze. Henri Viellard, ridiculous in fish-scale green-and-silver, stood before the passageway curtain. He had a trident tucked under one chubby arm and was in the act of carefully putting his spectacles back on after pushing up his mask. That done, he looked around for Dominique, met her eyes . . .

She held his gaze for a long moment, then turned her head, flipped open her gold lace fan, and went on as if she hadn't seen him, "I don't imagine Henri will want for anything in the way of a dowry from her. Good heavens, is that Babette Figes over there, dressed up like a sultana? I must find out where she got those silks—darling, how gorgeous . . ." And she rustled off just as Viellard came lumbering across the ballroom toward her, his hand held out and misery on his round face.

"Is she beautiful?" January asked softly, watching his sister retreat, chattering nineteen to the dozen with her friends about the newest shape in sleeves and why Marie-Toussainte Valcour had been obliged to cut off most of her hair.

Hannibal polished off the champagne. *"Like the night / of cloudless climes and starry skies. . . .* A little blond thing like a china doll and not more than sixteen. In that costume she really does look like a mermaid—not the sweet ones sailors dream about, but the other kind, the ones that have no hearts."

"It's not that I'm jealous, p'tit," sighed Dominique, returning to January's side later in the evening, after Hannibal had gone back to work on his side of the passageway and most of the men had drifted in again for the *tableaux vivantes* that were a feature of quadroon balls during

Carnival. Having played the other side of the passageway in his time, January was familiar with the hemming and hawing, the muttered avowals of it being time for a smoke or the assurances that they had to go meet a man down in the gambling-rooms—*No, I'll just be a few moments, my sweet.* . . .

Mr. Knight had cornered Vincent Marsan at the buffet beside the musicians and jabbed at him with a tiny finger: "You're asking too much of me!" shouted Marsan, and Knight made a gesture for silence, with coldly blazing eyes. And then, more quietly, Marsan said, "In any case, it's all arranged."

Not, thought January, what any of the Opera Society wanted to hear.

Henri Viellard had not returned. January was aware of his sister's glance, flickering from the passageway to the triple arch that led through to the broad vestibule and the grand staircase of white marble and black. "It's just that I'm afraid poor Henri's going to be made absolutely wretched by that girl, and of course he hasn't the least notion how to defend himself." She tossed her head, making the miniature windmill and its tiny grove of trees tremble in her enormous powdered wig. *"Bleu,"* she cursed. Behind a curtain in an alcove, the first of the *tableaux vivantes* was assembling—the inevitable Maidens of Camelot. The *tableaux vivantes* hadn't changed much since January had first started playing at the quadroon balls in 1808: the Ladies of Camelot. The Sultan's Harem. (His wife, Ayasha, had been a Berber. Her accounts of what life was really like in her father's harîm made January wince at these tableaux, as he winced at the Duchesse du Durras's romanticized novels of slavery.) A Garden of Living Flowers.

"But at least I have no intention of making a fool of

myself, like the white ladies who sneak over here in masks. . . ."

"Do they often?"

"Let me remind you that ten years ago, you faced ruin," Knight was telling Marsan angrily. "Certainly for saving you from that, if for no other reason, you owe it to me. . . ."

"Darling, of *course* they do!" Dominique flourished her fan. "That girl there, you see? In the pink domino cloak? You can always tell the white girls, because they never talk to anybody, and their dresses aren't nearly as smart—and they *stare* so. Like they've never seen men before in their lives."

Certainly the maiden in the pink domino was keeping herself well to the back of the big room, lingering in corners while other chatting groups teased and flirted with the men. When Belaggio approached her, creaking in his leather armor, she made a hasty excuse and fled through the vestibule doors. . . .

"They can't *abide* the thought of their precious husbands and fiancés and brothers coming over here to be wicked with us," Dominique went on with bright artificial cheer. The old-fashioned flat-fronted corset gave her an air of curious dignity, the exaggerated white wig making her face at once older and more serene. "I quite expect Madame Chloë will be here eventually with the best of them, looking absolutely silly, of course, because they all do. . . . Darling, what a lovely idea!" She whirled and skipped away to greet Phlosine Seurat, her other bosom-bow, entering the Salle late on her protector's arm and leaving a trail of detached silk flower-petals in her wake.

You only hope, thought January sadly, *that Madame Chloë will be here with the best of them, spying on her husband.*

Rather than that she succeed in forbidding him to come at all.

Rather than forcing Henri—through money, through family, through sheer strength of will against his luxury-loving softness—to give you up.

"You know not what you ask of me," intoned Belaggio a little later, when Caldwell—ridiculously got up in the blue velvet robe of a mystical adept and a false beard like a horse's tail—stopped him between dances. "There are things a man cannot be seen to accept from another man. Am I to wear horns before the whole of the town?" He pushed up his mask and peeped cautiously around.

"It isn't as if she were your wife," replied the theater owner, and he picked a tendril of beard out of his mouth. "Or even as if you'd been with her more than a month or so. I understand you—er—encountered her only at Christmastime. . . ."

"You have been speaking to that Mexican Messalina," Belaggio said. "Consuela is jealous of my beautiful one, and spiteful as a cat. She would say anything to her disadvantage. And surely you know, Signor, that when one finds the woman of one's dreams, length of time is nothing. When souls love for a thousand years . . ."

He froze, eyes bulging. January, floating effortlessly on the opening bars of the Sylph Cotillion, followed his gaze to the vestibule doors. The man who stood framed in the triple archway was costumed in close-fitting black trousers and jacket accentuated by crimson bucket-topped boots, a crimson hat with a white plume, a crimson baldric on which hung a very businesslike sword. A long velvet rope attached to the back of the trousers did duty as a tail; the black velvet mask that covered the beardless face bore whiskers of silver wire; and around it, long silver hair swept in a gleaming mane. Without another word, Belaggio yanked his mask back into place and bolted for the passageway, the renowned feline trickster striding in his wake.

"Did he catch him?" asked January nearly two hours later when next Hannibal made his appearance. It was now past two. The St. Margaret's Ball had broken up, and several of the musicians drifted across to play a few more songs and chat with friends as the tail-end of the Blue Ribbon proceedings grew more relaxed.

In the street the rattle of carriages could still be heard, women's voices calling farewells and invitations to future dinners and danceables. The male population of the room, thinned by the necessity of last dances with wives and fiancées, burgeoned again: *Just going to have a drink with old Granville before coming on home, my dear. Won't be a half-hour, I assure you.*

All around the Salle d'Orleans couples stood quietly talking in the shadows of curtains and pillars. Masks were lifted, kisses stolen.

"Puss in Boots?" Hannibal grinned. "I take it that was the famous Incantobelli?" He made his violin embroider a little ornament on the dreamy waltz January and the others were playing, a counterpoint comment plucked from *Don Giovanni*—he could quote phrases of music the way he quoted fragments from his omnivorous reading. "I've never seen a statue move that fast. He nearly ran down Marsan in the doorway."

Marsan had returned to the Salle d'Orleans an hour previously, much the worse for drink. He stood now in the corner with his mistress, a ripe-figured woman with the almost-straight bronze-dark hair so prized by whites. His head was bent down over hers, forcing her to drink a cup of punch. She kept shaking her head, trying to push him away, and January saw possessiveness transform that

Adonis face as rage had transformed it last night. Saw the blue eyes grow paler with malice, the carven lips wrinkle like a beast's. Marsan seized her roughly by the back of the neck and pushed the cut-glass rim to her lips. The liquid spilled down her chin, splashed the soft, heavy breasts, and wet the gold-stitched ruby velvet of her gown.

"There's another one." Dominique strolled back to them as January surrendered his piano to Ramesses Ramilles, who broke into a far livelier jig than had been permissible at the St. Margaret's Ball. Minou had lost a few more roses from her coiffure, and under the edge of her mask her mouth had an ashy paleness. She'd flirted most of the evening, with no man more than another, but, January had observed, she'd spent the bulk of her time between dances talking with her female friends.

The woman she nodded toward now moved lightly from group to group but never spoke to anyone. She kept to the rear of the room, and always managed to be just turning away when any man approached.

"They sneak dominoes in with them because they're easier to bundle up in a dress-box than a completely different costume," Dominique went on, sketching with her gesture the billowing cloak of black velvet that hid the slender figure, the ruffled hood that covered the hair. "Not that a man would ever recognize what a woman had on, of course. And even if two of them happened to have the same idea and ran into one another here, they'd cut their own throats before they'd admit it."

"They might sneak dominoes into the cloak-room," remarked Hannibal. "But they'd be smarter to smuggle in a change of shoes as well. Because those particular pink-and-yellow slippers belong to the American Theater's costume for Roxalana, the Sultan's Bride, and I last saw them earlier this evening, at the St. Margaret's Ball, being worn by Drusilla d'Isola."

"But I love him." La d'Isola pressed her lips with one pink-gloved hand, and tears filled her eyes. "God help me."

January thought of Belaggio in his bronze armor, coming and going between the two balls. Of the woman in crimson shaking her head at the champagne punch, and how the spilled liquid splattered on her heavy breasts as Marsan forced her to drink. Of the ugly glitter in those cerulean eyes. "God help you indeed," he murmured.

Every table around the coffee-stands in the market was crowded with imitation Ivanhoes and masked counterfeits of Raleigh and Essex. Turkish beauties, classical goddesses, hennaed princesses laughed too loudly at their jests and leaned too close to their shoulders. Respectable women had taken to their beds long ago. Cressets stitched the bare branches of the sycamores around the Place d'Armes with gold and made every word a puff of luminous fire. From the steamboats on the levee—and the levee was a rampart of them, like floating barns—rolled the tinny jangle of a dozen conflicting tunes. A man with a bottle in either hand and a ragged Boston accent staggered along trying to sing to all of them.

"Do you hope he'll make you his mistress?" asked January. Drusilla's dress was pink and yellow—he found himself reflecting irrelevantly that in such colors Marsan would never let her near his somber crimson splendor. "You saw him with his plaçée tonight. Do you think he'll put her aside?"

"Vincent's said he loves me." She looked pleadingly

from January's face to Hannibal's, begging them to make all things well.

"Darling," said Dominique, "I understand how it is to love. But he's not going to abandon Liane for you."

"You don't know that."

Dominique's mouth tightened. A breeze from the river caught the sails of the tiny windmill that crowned her wig, making them turn; rustled in the miniature grove of Lilliputian trees. "Believe me, *chère*, I know that. M'sieu Marsan isn't a man to let *anything*—certainly not a woman—go, once it has been his. He's not a good man, Mademoiselle. Not good for you, or for anyone."

The dark eyes lifted to hers, sulky and frightened with a fear unacknowledged—furious, too. "You're only jealous," Drusilla said in her stumbling French. "Jealous because Vincent's so handsome, so wealthy—jealous that he loves me. You want him for yourself, don't you?"

Dominique slapped her fan down onto the table. "*Marsan?* I'd sooner bed the crazy old man who sells gumbo on the corner! Darling, Vincent Marsan—"

"I will not hear this!" The girl turned her face away. Dominique reached out as if to grasp her wrist, to shake her, pulling her hand back only at the last moment, remembering that this dusky girl, in her fancy-dress and her gaily-striped mask pushed up to her tumbled dark hair, was white, and not to be casually touched. "I do not have to listen! Yes, it was wrong of me to seek Vincent in that place! But the heart is stronger than the head! From the moment I saw him, I knew we were one heart, one soul! You do not understand, you who *sell* your love!"

Flouncing to her feet, d'Isola plunged away between the brick pillars, and a moment later her bright dress flashed in the jumble of torchlight and darkness in the square. January started to rise but then sank down again in his chair, and glanced sidelong at Dominique: his sister's mouth was open in shocked indignation, but if there was anger in her great brown eyes at d'Isola's remark about *you who sell your love,* at least there were not tears.

"Well," remarked Hannibal, edging his way back to the table with four cups of coffee in his hands and a plate of beignets balanced on one forearm like a waiter, "I can see it wouldn't take more than a few pennyweights of heart to be stronger than whatever she's got in *her* head. *God is thy law, thou mine: to know no more / Is woman's happiest knowledge and her praise.* More beignets for us."

"I'd better go after her," sighed January. He picked up the satchel she'd left behind her, in which she'd stowed her cloak at the Théâtre—nearly new, lined with green silk and expensive. Belaggio's gift, beyond a doubt. "She doesn't know much French and no English at all, and this isn't the time of night for a young woman to be roving about the streets alone. I'm not sure she even knows the way back to her hotel."

"If she's so purblind foolish as to fall in love with Vincent Marsan," retorted Dominique acidly, "it's quite obvious she shouldn't be abroad without a keeper in the first place. Not that it wouldn't serve her right . . ."

But by the time January had crossed the jostling darkness of the Place d'Armes, he glimpsed that daffodil headdress again in the light of the torches on the Cabildo arcade, bobbing as d'Isola negotiated in her laborious French with a cab-driver. January watched from the shadows until she got into the fiacre, then made his way back across to the market, satchel still in hand, with little detours to avoid a shouting-and-shoving match of drunk keelboatmen and what sounded like a furious argument among seven or eight equally inebriated French Creoles over the putative parentage of France's Citizen King.

When he reached the torchlit market arcade again, Hannibal was kissing Dominique's wrist and quoting Petrarch to her—a marvelous antidote, thought January, to whatever reflections she might have entertained about Henri Viellard's absence from the ballroom. "No wonder you were obliged to leave Ireland, if you carry on with ladies like this." She tapped the fiddler's cheek with her folded fan. "The cloud you left under must have covered the earth and the sky."

"No greater than the darkness that will devour me should you turn your eyes away. Οιον το γλυκύμαγον εγεύρεται ακρό επ υσδό. . . . Find her?"

"She got a cab." January removed the saucer Hannibal had set over his coffee-cup, to keep it warm. River mist blurred the torches—the sounds of festival seemed to grow distant as well, retreating like voices in a dream. "Minou, you say Marsan never lets go of anything, particularly women. Might he have been the one who hired those bullies to beat up Belaggio? Is Marsan the jealous type?"

"Jealous?" Dominique stared at him as if he'd idly put himself forward as a prospective husband for Andrew Jackson's sister. "P'tit, don't you *know*? Vincent Marsan *killed* a plaçée of his just for speaking with another man."

"Killed her?"

"Slashed her to death with his sword-cane."

"A free woman?" January stared at her, stunned. He had, in two years, reaccustomed himself to the yawning chasm between the rights of the whites and the ever-diminishing legal position of the free colored; still, this was more than he'd expected or feared. "Do they know this?" He remembered the hardness of those blue eyes, the way Marsan had lunged for Belaggio at Trulove's; saw that powerful pale-blue figure retreating down Rue St. Louis in casual chat with Trulove. Saw him dancing with Anne Trulove, with Henrietta Granville, while their husbands looked on.

When Knight had said, *You faced ruin,* January thought the man spoke of money.

"Was it proven?"

"*Yes!* There was a terrific scandal over it. They found his gloves on the scene, and his cane, or anyway rose-colored gloves that were like the pair he'd bought the week before and a cane with a big rose-colored stone in its head, though of course Marsan said they weren't his. Even ten years ago, near-bankrupt as he was then with only that wretched little plantation, he always had things that matched. He has them made specially, to his orders, by Dumetz in the Rue Chartres—who charged Iphigénie's friend Yves Valcour *five dollars* to make a coat, out of ivy-green superfine, but it was so beautiful, I went to him to have a jacket made—out of that clay-colored silk-satin, you remember? He made a big show in court of trying to get the gloves on his hands—M'sieu Marsan, I mean—and swearing they were too small. . . ."

"If I were on trial for murder, I'd make sure I couldn't get the gloves on, either." Hannibal bit into a beignet in a snowfall of powdered sugar.

"It came to *trial*?"

"Of *course*, p'tit," said Dominique patiently. She leaned forward, the diamond clusters at her ears swinging like chandeliers. "Her family made sure of that. But of course the jury were all white men. Even the ones who weren't related to Marsan or his wife—and just about half the Creoles in town are—do business with him, or his family, or his wife's family. Hiring men to kill Signor Belaggio because he was jealous over Mademoiselle d'Isola would be *nothing* to him."

"And he could get away with it," said January slowly, "because Belaggio is a foreigner." There was a sour taste in his mouth. "The Austrians don't even have a consul in town to look after the affairs of their subjects here. No one would inquire."

He thought again about Marsan's striking beauty that so dazzled La d'Isola; of how cold that marble-fine countenance was, until rage or jealousy transformed it. D'Isola's sweet, desperate voice came back to his mind, and the doomed Desdemona's words, *Sing willow, willow, sing willow. . . . His stubbornness and frowns, these I embrace. . . .*

But I love him. As if that would somehow change what Marsan was.

Rising, he picked up his music-satchel, and that which Belaggio had given La d'Isola. "I'll walk you home," he told Dominique.

"Will you be all right?" he asked as the three of them made their way up Rue Du Maine away from the torch-light and music of the square. The fog was thinner away from the river, but the light that suffused the mist failed quickly. The clouded glare of the iron lanterns on their chains above the intersections failed to do more than guide pedestrians from one street to the next. January kept glancing at the dark mouths of the passways between the houses, listening behind him for the wet step of other boots on the banquette.

He had a knife, Madame Bontemps had said.

And he knew where January lived.

If he existed at all.

The dark air breathed of dampness, of chimney-smoke and sewage. Dominique's pattens scraped metalli-cally on the brick underfoot, and her enormous white wig made a bobbing splotch, like an overfed ghost in the dark.

"I think so." She drew a deep breath and pulled her bronze silk cloak closer about her shoulders. "Yes, of course I'll be all right, p'tit. Even if the worst happens and Henri—decides to sever our friendship, I know he'll be generous." The brittle note was back in her voice. The artificial airiness of a woman pretending not to care. Pretending not to hurt.

"The question is," put in Hannibal, his breath laboring as he walked, "how generous will Mama Viellard and Mademoiselle Chloë allow him to be? This is a girl who had her own nurse and half-sister sold at auction when her father died."

"I think we can trust Mama," said January grimly, "to make sure your rights, at least, are protected."

"Oh, yes," replied Minou in a tiny voice. "Yes."

"She may have her faults," mused Hannibal, "but give your mother a dollar to fight for and there will be blood in the gutters." He stopped, leaning against the wall, and tucked his violin case beneath his arm to press one hand to his side. "Shall I continue on with you to your doorstep, *amicus meus?* Not that I'll be a great deal of help to you against such hearties as *La Gougière* described to us this afternoon, but if one of them's asking for water transport out of town next week, it's a sporting bet the other one's wounded. Since Davis paid us, I can get a cab home."

"Thank you," January said. "I'd appreciate that." If the presence of Madame Bontemps—unnerving but certainly not threatening—had been enough to put last night's "devil" to flight, it was a good chance the attacker was more worried about an alarm being spread than about the physical might of a second opponent. "Hannibal's right," he added in a low voice as he climbed the two brick steps that led up to Dominique's bedroom door. A lamp burned within. Through the gauze curtains January could see his sister's maid, Thérèse, dozing in a chair beside the tall half-tester bed, waiting up to unlace her, make her some cocoa, brush out her hair. "I certainly wouldn't want to try to get around Mother on a contract. Whatever happens with Viellard, I don't think you need be afraid of poverty—or of having to return to living under Mother's roof."

Dominique mimed a great, exaggerated shudder. "P'tit, you know I love our *maman very* much, but when you were living there, my heart absolutely *bled* for you. I'll be all right. It's just that . . ."

She hesitated, twisting a curl of her wig, and glanced past January to where Hannibal waited out of earshot.

"For what it's worth," January told her, "I'm pretty sure Henri loves you."

"I know he does, poor lamb," whispered Minou. "But you know, Madame Viellard controls all the family money. It's how she forced him to offer for that *dreadful* girl in the first place. And poor Henri has never done anything in his life except read Rousseau and press flowers and do the accounts when they grind the sugar. He can't go against them. Not his mother and a wife both. And I'm afraid." A tear crept down her lashes, and she touched it away, mindful of her rouge even on the threshold of her own bedroom.

January thought again of his landlady, eking out a living by taking in boarders, spending hours a day on her hands and knees scrubbing floors, scrubbing steps. Keeping up the only thing that remained to her from her days of plaçage. True, she hadn't had Minou's quick wit or Minou's ferocious mother. Still . . .

He put his big hands gently on his sister's arms, the silk crinkling with a sigh like dry leaves. "I know you don't think this now," he told her, "but there are other men." As the words came out of his mouth, he remembered his wife sitting in the window of their little room in Paris, combing out the black bewitching midnight of her hair. Smiling at him under her long, straight lashes, like a desert sprite masquerading in her proper Parisian dress.

Would he have understood, in the horrible days following her death, that there were other women in the world?

That Rose Vitrac existed in Louisiana, scholarly and bespectacled, thumbing through Lyell's *Principles of Geology* with her ink-smudged fingers and then looking up with that fugitive sunshaft smile?

"I know," answered Dominique in a beaten voice. "Only I've just recently discovered I'm with child. And I don't know what to do."

NINE

Rehearsal Monday was marked by the same eddies of activity that had characterized the Salle d'Orleans the previous night. During the dance rehearsal—long before any of the principals put in an appearance—James Caldwell prowled the backstage, severely discomposing the new ballet master and causing the latter to trip over the silk-leaved rose-bushes of Count Almaviva's garden. Throughout endless repetitions of the fandango in Act Three and the Act Four ballet, January heard the staccato chatter from behind the flats: had Signor Belaggio been heard from yet? Had Monsieur Marsan sent a note? "What are we going to do?" wailed Mr. Trulove's voice as Herr Smith attempted for a fifth time to instruct Oona Flaherty in the execution of a simple pirouette that did not hopelessly entangle her in her own supporting wires. "Can we get someone else to manage these performances?"

Toe-dancing—usually with the assistance of wires—had been the rage at the Odéon and the Paris Opera for years, but it was new here. Only Tiberio—and January, thanks to Marguerite—had the slightest idea how the system of pulleys and counterweights operated, but Trulove was adamant. Oona Flaherty would be the "Queen of the Milkmaids," and she would dance on her toes.

"Cafone," muttered the little prop-master as he and January adjusted the sandbags for La Flaherty's not-inconsiderable weight, and she bounced delightedly, testingly, up and down on her wool-stuffed toes. *"Pezzu di carne cu l'occhi.* It isn't enough to have these candles and trellises and summerhouses to keep track of? Now I have to make this *butana* fly. And by the beautiful Mother and verily, *now* must he go sell those who were to help me, *ptui!"*

Tiberio spit with Levantine eloquence. On-stage, Herr Smith fluttered his hands and cried, "No, and *no,* Fräulein—I mean, Mademoiselle—*Miss*—do *not* lift the skirts! I don't *care* if no one can see your toes, you will *not* transform the classical beauty of the dance into a peepshow for every lust-ridden savage from the riverbanks!"

Eyeing the wires, January guessed that even with the borderlights concealed in the proscenium arch burning at full, the light wouldn't be strong enough to show up the support.

"Irish, he says, I will hire you Irish. *Malòcchio* on his Irish! *Cornutu e cornutu abbiveratu,* with more horns to him than a basket of *babaluci....* "

Whatever, reflected January, losing the thread of the little man's Sicilian, *babaluci are—*

"Hideputa!" shrieked Consuela Montero's rich voice from backstage. "What do you mean, he has sold Nina? Who will dress my wig? What are the rest of us to do for dressers tomorrow night, eh? Are we chambermaids? Peasants?"

January sighed, gathered his music into his satchel again, and made his way from the stage into the wings. Most of the principals were having their lunch in the green room: Signora Chiavari gravely discussing the length of Susanna's skirts with Madame Rossi, while Cavallo and Ponte shared the hard Italian sausage and

wine in the rose-shadowed lattices of the dissected sum-
merhouse. Caldwell had cornered Belaggio near the steps
up to the gallery, gesturing persuasively around him at the
growing clusters of singers and ancillaries, to which entreaty the impresario only shook his head. At the same
time, Mr. Knight's clerk was trying to explain something
to Mr. Rowe—Caldwell's manager for the American
Theater—and the Austrian bass Cepovan sat at the
Contessa's white-and-gold writing-desk explaining to
Cochon Gardinier and the Valada brothers that during
his Act Three solo they were to take their cues from *him*,
not from Belaggio on the conductor's stand.

January took bread and cheese from his satchel, and
the bottle of lemonade he'd left stashed in the prop-room,
and settled himself on the lower slopes of Vesuvius to eat.
Cochon joined him, and Jacques, and Ramesses Ramilles.
"M'am Scie all right?" asked Bichet in an undervoice, and
January shook his head.

"Still unconscious," he replied. "I was there this
morning, before the dance rehearsal. She hasn't stirred.
Mr. Caldwell gave me a bank-draft to pay Olympe for her
care." It grieved him that Marguerite would be stricken
like this in a foreign country, where she knew no one and
was without family or friends. According to Olympe,
none of the company had come to the cottage on Rue
Douane to ask after her. He supposed this was as well.
When he had examined her again early this morning, he
had seen how livid the marks of huge fingers stood out
against the waxy skin of her throat.

Whatever else Incantobelli might have done, the
hands that went with those neat, narrow boot-prints in
Trulove's garden-maze, with that trim figure in Puss in
Boots garb, would not have made those.

"You were in the kitchen when the lights went out,

weren't you, Jacques?" he asked. "Was there anybody at your place that evening who could have been mistaken for me in the dark?"

"Ben, the side of the *house* could have been mistaken for you in the dark," retorted the flautist. "But I don't know who else. There's damn few niggers your size in this town, and that's a fact."

"And who says it was a nigger?" argued Cochon reasonably. He settled his three hundred-plus pounds on the rim of the volcano's lowest caldera, a deep bowl in which wet clay would be packed to avoid, if possible, setting the entire theater alight. A few feet away, Caldwell and Knight intercepted Mademoiselle d'Isola: Knight gripped the young girl's hand desperately. "You cannot allow our season to end before it begins, Signorina! Not after all the work we have done to bring proper opera to this city!" He sounded on the verge of tears. January couldn't imagine that the girl's intercession between the two men would do anything but fan the flames.

"Once people started blowin' out those candles," Cochon went on, "the King of England could have walked into that kitchen and grabbed Madame's hand. Didn't Hannibal say one of the men you pulled off Michie Belaggio in the alley was darn near your size?"

"Maybe," January agreed doubtfully. But a little later he sought out old Tiberio again, where the Sicilian sat glumly, connecting what appeared to be miles of hosepipe with young Ponte's good-natured aid, and asked him, "Did you know Incantobelli? Was he mad enough to—to attack, or have attacked, the other members of the company as well as Belaggio? To destroy the opera season as well as the man who wronged him?"

Tiberio cocked his head a little sideways. Something about the way he stood reminded January of the buzzards near the stock-pens, angry black eyes glinting among the heavy folds of skin. "You don't know Sicilians, do you, Signor?" he said. "Sicilians and Neapolitans. Even the Milanese, and the stuck-up Florentines, even the block-headed Romans, they don't know us. We're a poor people, Signor. We scratch in the dirt to raise a little food for our-selves and our children, and we see the nobles, *i padroni,* who sell us the very water we need to survive, take it away from us. We pray and do penance and we see the *parrinu*—priests, you understand—get fat on the tithe we pay."

Ponte set down a coil of thick leather tubing and said, "This is true, Signor."

"So the thing that is truly important," the prop-mas-ter went on in dialect so thick that January had to bend all his attention to understanding, "the thing that makes a man a man and not a beast—this thing men call Honor—that we hold to, for it is all we have. And the man who takes that away, or tries to take it away—that man will suffer. And he must be made to suffer so that all that see, understand."

January was quiet for a time, thinking about that. Be-hind him he heard Belaggio say, "What is between Signor Marsan and myself is a thing of honor, but for the other, I could not agree with you more, Signor Caldwell. . . ." And a little farther off, Cepovan shouted at someone, "Young Italy! Don't talk to me of Young Italy! Traitors, and cut-throats, Carbonari! Looking only to stir up dis-content and bring back the horror and bloodshed of Napoleon's time!" And Hannibal's light, hoarse voice added, *"Video meliora, proboque,* as the poet says—not that there's a superabundance of *meliora* about Perdidio Street. . . ."

"So you think Incantobelli would value his honor above an innocent woman's life?"

"What woman is truly innocent, Signor?" asked Tiberio. "Or what man? Sometimes honor demands more."

Cavallo appeared in the door of the little hallway that led back to the prop-room, looking around the backstage as usual for his friend. Ponte set aside his hoses and rose to go. "Myself," he said, "I would not have thought it in Incantobelli to do such. But neither would I have thought it in Signor Davis, who has as much reason as any to wish that Milanese *cornutu* ill."

"Incantobelli was castrated as a young boy so that his voice would remain beautiful forever," said Tiberio as the chorus-boy walked away. "There are men who accept the knife as a gift, and men in whom the theft of their manhood burns like a secret canker throughout their lives, so that they think of nothing but evil and revenge. And it is not always possible to know which man is which."

Dress rehearsal proceeded uneventfully enough. The only interruption came from James Caldwell's suggestion that since the American audience was unfamiliar with both Mozart and the Italian language, the talents of the lovely Miss d'Isola and the equally lovely Mrs. Chiavari might be better showcased were certain more popular— and more familiar—American songs inserted at key points into *Le Nozze di Figaro*.

"What?" said Cavallo, shocked.

"You're joking," said Hannibal.

January knew better than to state any opinion of his own to a white man in the State of Louisiana, but he did ask himself whether he'd assisted the wrong parties in the alley last Thursday night.

And the lovely Mademoiselle d'Isola turned wide eyes to Cavallo and whispered, *"Qual'? Di cos' sta parlan'?"*

"I've marked in the libretto where these should go," Caldwell continued. "Here—you see?—in Act Two, we have the Countess singing 'Soft as the Falling Dews of Night' when we first see her, and then 'Blest Were the Hours.' Both very pretty songs, I'm sure you'll agree."

"Are you *crazy?*" demanded Hannibal, lowering his music to stare at the theater owner. "You want to put 'Soft as the Falling Dews of Night' into *Mozart?*"

"Well, that's precisely our point," explained Trulove, his pink oval face beaming with satisfaction at his own cleverness. "It's a little too much Mozart, if you take my meaning. . . ."

"I agree," chimed in Belaggio, "I agree completely."

January found himself wondering what Anne Trulove would have to say on the subject, if anything. Or did she content herself with operating the plantation, the sawmills, the brick-yard, and the cotton-press, and leave her husband to pursue his hobbies as he pleased?

"Now, we have the dance number in Act Three, which I think would go just as well with the John Quincy Adams Grand March and Quick-Step—"

Herr Smith opened his mouth, but no sound came out.

"—and then Susanna in Act Four can sing 'Look Out Upon the Stars, My Love,' when she's in the garden at the beginning, and follow it up with 'Cherry-Cheeked Patty.'"

Hannibal repeated soundlessly, *Cherry-Cheeked Patty?* while Belaggio nodded and approved, "Yes, of course— just the songs for my beautiful d'Isola, are they not?"

"I will have to learn them in English?" Drusilla

looked as discomposed as if the lyrics had been in Mandarin.

"A few run-throughs merely," declared the impresario. "I'm sure the musicians won't mind staying a bit later after rehearsal."

"You'll see," said the theater owner encouragingly. "It'll bring the American audiences back shouting for more."

"And add immeasurably to *our* reputation as musicians," muttered Hannibal under his breath as Caldwell, Trulove, and Belaggio—hugely pleased with themselves—turned away. He reached beneath his chair and brought out his hat, a shaggy, flat-brimmed chimneypot that hadn't been fashionable since Napoleon's day, and turned it over like a beggar's bowl. "Anyone want to start a fund," he inquired, "to purchase bullets for M'sieu Marsan?"

January sighed, and dropped a couple of silver half-reales into the hat. Cavallo threw in a franc; stout Herr Pleck left his double-bass and made a contribution, remarking in German to the ballet master, "I cannot approve of violence, you understand, Herr Faber, but under the circumstances . . ."

"It is Smith," corrected the ballet master stiffly, "in this country—and has been since Messires Talleyrand and Metternich between them chose to give most of my country to the Prussians to thank them very much for Waterloo."

"Naturally this facetiousness must be displeasing to any man of pretension to taste," remarked Mr. Knight. Disapproval radiated visibly from his prim, pale face. A silver English shilling clinked into the hat. "And yet . . . 'Cherry-Cheeked Patty.' " He shuddered, and went to follow Belaggio and the others to the stage.

. . .

Whether through the tearful pleadings of La d'Isola, or the more monetary objurgations of Mr. Knight, the following morning's *Louisiana Gazette* carried the following letter from Vincent Marsan:

> *In the words of the great gentleman Lord Chesterfield, Si fueris Romae, Romano vivito more—When in Rome, live in the Roman way—*January winced at the misquote—*the true gentleman does not place the same expectations upon men of foreign extraction as upon those with whose ways he is familiar. In view of the representations made to me by those more familiar with the Italian customs and sensibilities, I have come to accept as bona fide the assurances that no insult was intended in the words spoken by Signor Lorenzo Belaggio to me at an entertainment given by Monsieur Fitzhugh Trulove on the 24ᵗʰ inst.—fortunately, before fatal shots could be fired in anger. May this incident be an example and a warning. . . .*

January glanced up from the smudged pages and blinked in the pale morning sunlight that fell through the French windows and into the rear bedroom of Olympe's cottage on Rue Douane. "I'm at a loss to decide how one man may call another a *stronzolo* without intending insult."

"Possibly he meant an aromatic and socially useful *stronzolo.*" Hannibal, who had brought him the paper at Olympe's after not finding him *chez* Bontemps, sat on the smaller of the little room's two beds, which in ordinary circumstances was shared by Olympe's daughter, Chouchou—aged five—and her two-year-old brother, Ti-Paul. A low fire burned in the room's small hearth, welcome after the morning's chill, and he held out his hands to it like one who never expected to be warm again. "Care to hear Belaggio's apology?"

"What does it amount to?"

"That everyone in the ballroom mis-heard him, presumably including his second. At no time did he ever intend etc. etc." Hannibal stood and took the paper from January's hand. In the yard beyond the French doors, fourteen-year-old Zizi-Marie helped her father stretch and fit stiff black horsehair over the framework of a curve-legged chair, amid neat piles of the dark, wiry moss that made such excellent upholstery. Taller already than most boys of twelve, young Gabriel emerged from the kitchen, the ladle in his hand giving off steam like a banner in the cold, and asked something of Chouchou, who was stirring alum into a big clay jar of rainwater to purify it for drinking; little Ti-Paul gravely lined up fragments of kindling in order of size on the bricks by the kitchen door. Looking worriedly down at the chalk-white face of the woman on the bed, Hannibal said, "She hasn't wakened, has she?"

"Olympe tells me she came around enough last night to be taken to the privy." January sighed, and gently touched Marguerite Scie's hand. "She tried to get her to drink a little water, but she doesn't think she actually swallowed any. She hasn't stirred since." The ballet mistress's hands were cold. Her breath was barely sufficient to lift the clean starched linen that covered her breast. The eyelids, beginning to wrinkle like an old woman's, did not move.

January wondered if she dreamed, and of what. "No word from the Gouger about the Gower boys?"

"Not yet." Hannibal sounded worn to thread-paper, but January knew he was playing at one of the taverns that afternoon, for reales and dimes—the girls at Kentucky Williams's as often as not would get him drunk and go through his pockets for whatever he'd earned the night before. "Can I get you anything?"

Out in the Rue Douane a woman's voice sang, "Berry pies, cherry pies, mince and quince and peary pies!" and farther off was answered by the wailing, dreary singsong of the charcoal man. On the house opposite, posters had gone up, enormous letters proclaiming THE MARRIAGE OF FIGARO above stylized figures in powdered wigs and skirted coats, gesturing alarm, adoration, delight. AN OPERA BY MR. W. A. MOZART. There were at least six posters in a line, covering over the earlier poster, which had advertised:

LA MUETTE DE PORTICI
Musical Spectacle and Excitement
PRODUCTION BY JOHN DAVIS, FRENCH OPERA HOUSE

"Nothing," said January. He looked down again at Marguerite's sunken face, wondering what the police would say about the marks on her throat, were she to die.

"I'll be here all day, if you hear. If you'd care to return for supper, I'm sure Olympe would put another plate on the table before the performance."

"Thank you." Hannibal shrugged a worn plaid shawl around his shoulders and put on his hat. The bullet-fund for Marsan had actually been spent on beer for the musicians after the rehearsal; Trulove assured everyone that following the performance, a collation would await the cast backstage, courtesy of the St. Mary Opera Society. "I must say I'm astonished that we've made it as far as the premiere performance of the season, and confess to a certain degree of curiosity about what will happen tonight."

"Tonight?"

"Of course." Hannibal paused in the doorway to the front bedroom—no good Creole entered or left a house through the parlor—and regarded January with raised brows. "You don't think Incantobelli's going to let his enemy get away with an uneventful show, do you? I'm only hoping that the assault takes the form of a direct attack on Belaggio—say, a garrote in one of the corridors outside the boxes—instead of a bullet fired from the gallery, which could hit anyone in the orchestra. Or maybe something simpler, like burning down the theater."

January shut his eyes and leaned his head back against the wall, and hoped that in the event of mayhem, John Davis would have a good alibi for his own whereabouts. "*O Sable-vested Night, eldest of things,*" he said. "I can hardly wait."

"She's locked in her dressing-room." Julie, the dresser's assistant whose exclusive assignment to La d'Isola had caused such heart-burning among the rest of the female cast, twisted her hands in distress and cast a frantic eye at the box-clock. "The door's bolted from the inside, but I heard her moan."

"*Mille diavoli!*" Cavallo strode toward the gallery steps, tearing off hat and greatcoat. "Drusilla! Drusilla . . . !"

"What is it?" January sprang up the last three steps from the prop-vault in time to see the tenor's hasty ascent. "What's happened?"

"Drusilla is ill." Emerging from his own office, Belaggio looked ill himself, far more shaken than even the sudden indisposition of his beloved might warrant. "She was perfectly well, gay and happy, when we parted this afternoon. . . ."

"Has she had anything to eat?" In his days as surgeon,

half of January's patients had turned out to be ill from spoiled food. Though not, it was true, at this time of year.

"We lunched with Signor Trulove, but like a true *artista,* she ate no more than a light omelette, a little fruit. . . ."

"I took the Signorina up a bowl of soup just after she came in," provided Madame Rossi. She looked harried and put out—as well she might, thought January, eyeing the half-dozen milkmaid's gowns piled in her arms. "She told me earlier to have one ready. . . ."

"Why did she lock herself in?" From the gallery above, January could hear Cavallo rattling the door of the big corner dressing-room, calling La d'Isola's name.

Belaggio shook his head and looked around him helplessly. Everyone was milling about incompletely costumed in the midst of the Contessa's gilt-trimmed bedroom furniture and segments of Mount Vesuvius. Sable-vested Night was well and truly on its way, and patrons were lined up already outside all three of the theater's doors. "Perhaps," offered Hannibal, coming up the steps in January's wake, "she wished to take a nap and feared some ill-intentioned person might slip into her dressing-room and put a piece of glass in her shoe, or a roach in her wig."

"Who would do such a thing?" cried Madame Montero. She was wearing, January noticed, the Countess's pink-and-gold gown from Act Two, considerably too tight in the bodice, as it was made to fit d'Isola's slimmer form.

"Signor." January pulled his notebook from his jacket pocket and began to scribble on a blank page. "Might one of the stage-hands be sent to this number in the Rue Douane? It's a gold-colored cottage. My sister Olympe is a midwife; she understands local fevers." There seemed no point in saying that Olympe was a voodoo who knew all about poisons; Tiberio snatched the note from Belaggio's hand as he beckoned one of the two stage-hands who had been hired that afternoon.

"Unless you wish to set the stage yourself you send Julie."

"Julie!" Oona Flaherty, who had been following the criss-cross of French and Italian with difficulty, grasped at least the name and yanked the paper from the little man's fingers. "And the lot of us standin' about in our corsets with our faces hangin' out bare as eggs?" It was not specifically her face that was hanging out bare as eggs, mused January, though she was, indeed, in her corset. . . .

"I'll go." Bruno Ponte, still in street trousers and a shirt, took the note, scooped up his rough tweed jacket, and departed.

"Lorenzo"—January heard Montero's voice behind him as he climbed the gallery steps—"if, God forbid, Drusilla is unable to sing, I could do the part. You know I am able to do it. . . ."

And you just happen to have been through it recently. . . .

Cavallo still stood by the dressing-room door. "Is there another key?" asked January, and the young tenor shook his head.

The smell of vomit crept nauseatingly from the room. Three smaller dressing-chambers opened straight off the gallery, the rest being cramped cubicles partitioned from the long rooms devoted to the female and male cast members at large. The corner room, January knew, in addition to its palatial appointments, possessed a stout door to ensure quiet, and, it appeared, a lock to safeguard both privacy and security for whatever the most favored cast member might have in the way of necklaces or stick-pins.

"I looked. It would have been in Caldwell's office."
His dark curls rumpled, his face drawn with concern,
Cavallo had a boyish air, like a worried student. "But the
door is bolted from within. Could it be broken?"

"No!" Caldwell wailed, struggling up a stair jammed
with cast, chorus, and curious musicians. "Don't break it!"

"She can't be left there." January fished in his music-
satchel for his stethoscope, which he generally carried,
along with a scalpel and narrow-nosed forceps, just in
case. He put the end of the boxwood tube to the panels
and listened as well as he could—everyone who'd pushed
up onto the gallery seemed to have advice to give or anec-
dotes to relate concerning personal experiences of a similar nature. Above the level of the backstage gasolier, the
dim air was suffocating.

"No, of course not." Caldwell slithered and wriggled
to January's side. "But breaking the door won't be necessary. When the theater was built we'd already gotten
William Pelby—nobody remembers him now, but ten
years ago he was one of the greatest tragedians in
America—"

"I remember Pelby," declared the bass Cepovan, his
face already embellished with old Antonio the gardener's
whiskers and wrinkles. "I never thought him above average."

"Heymann was better," added Chiavari's husband,
Trevi.

"Not as Rolla in *Pizarro*!" protested Mademoiselle
Rutigliano, the company's mezzo—whose name was actually Lucy Schlegdt, from Basle. "In Philadelphia two years
ago—"

"Pelby was to perform *Macbeth* at the theater's opening," Caldwell went on, ignoring the argument about the
two men's relative merits, which quickly spread down the

stairs. "The dressing-room was built with him in mind. He was—er—something of a ladies' man. One of his stipulations was a private entrance. A private stairway."

"Leading from where?" January mentally tried to orient the rooms of the theater's rear. "The stable yard of the Promenade Hotel?"

"Oh, the hotel wasn't built until 'twenty-nine," said Caldwell. "There was just a vacant lot on St. Charles Avenue. You could still get in that way if we can find the key. It should be on a nail with the others in my office."

Of course it wasn't.

"Hannibal . . ."

In addition to his talents on the violin, Hannibal Sefton was a reasonably gifted forger. He had, January gathered, studied antique orthography at Balliol College, Oxford, and put the knowledge to use producing various unauthorized documents, most frequently freedom papers for the runaway slaves who drifted into New Orleans by the hundreds every year. One of these individuals had repaid the favor by instructing him in the techniques of lock-picking, a skill January gathered he was passing along to the ever-inquiring Rose.

It was a tight squeeze between the moss-grown, filthy bricks of the stable-yard wall and the grubby and peeling planks of the theater. The stable yard drained into the slit between the two walls, and it was quite clear that whatever garbage and offal the hotel servants didn't particularly want to haul down the alley to Camp Street found a final resting-place there as well. Cavallo and Caldwell followed January and Hannibal in, oil-lamps upraised to illuminate Hannibal's assault on the private door's lock with a bent bullet probe and long-snouted forceps from January's bag, and a buttonhook borrowed from Madame Montero.

"The Lord looseth men out of prison," coaxed Hannibal, angling his head to avoid his own shadow. "Why so recalcitrant, my love? 'Had we but world enough and time, / This coyness, Lady, were no crime. . . .' "

"If Drusilla comes to harm," growled Cavallo, "I'll personally thrash that Mexican bitch. . . ."

"Now, we don't know that she had anything to do with this!" pleaded Caldwell, unnerved at the prospect of both Countesses being put out of commission an hour before curtain-time.

"Got it," said Hannibal.

The four men clambered up the narrow steps that wormed between two dressing-rooms and a closet, lamplight splashing around them on a stuffy universe of mouse-droppings and cobweb. The narrow door at the top was painted incongruously bright yellow and green, to match the decor of the room into which it opened.

The smell of vomit hit January even in the stairway, infinitely stronger as he thrust on the door. The inflowing lamp-gleam showed him the screen that hid the chamberpot knocked down, a chair lying on its side, and a crumpled form curled up on the floor between the chamberpot and the daybed. No candles burned. She'd been lying there since before dusk.

"Drusilla!" Cavallo fell to his knees at her side, almost dropping his lamp. *All we'd need,* thought January, catching it up—he had a lifelong performer's dread of theater fires. At the brassy brightness on her eyelids the soprano moaned, then gagged and reached for the overflowing chamberpot again.

Cavallo held the young woman steady as she retched, unable to come up with more than a little saliva. "Get water." January set the lamp on the marble-topped dressing-table. Hannibal shoved back the door-bolt and sprinted straight into the entire cast of *Le Nozze di Figaro*.

"Oh, the unfortunate creature!" Consuela Montero clasped her hands before her brutally-corseted bosom. "I am sure she cannot go on! How fortunate that I—"

"Get that woman out of here!" Cavallo surged to his feet like an indignant Apollo. "Get her out or I shall strip that dress from her worthless back and—"

Montero backed a step, colliding with Olympe and nearly taking the both of them over the gallery rail.

"She been poisoned, all right." Olympia Snakebones sniffed at the remains of the soup. "Indian tobacco, smells like, and not much of it, thank God." She took the water-pitcher from Hannibal and poured some into the spirit-kettle to heat. While she added herbs to the kettle, January took the rest of the water, added clean charcoal to it, and worked at getting it down d'Isola's throat.

"Get out of here now," Belaggio was saying to the rest of the cast, who showed signs of crowding into the dressing-room to further add to the confusion. "Good God, it's already past six! Consuela . . ."

"I can go on," d'Isola whispered. She raised her head, pushed back the sweat-black strings of hair from around her face. Her rouge stood out against skin gone ashen with shock and she groped for Cavallo's hand.

"My dearest . . ." pleaded Belaggio.

"Don't be silly," said January.

"I can go on," she insisted. "Signora . . ." She looked up at Olympe, panting with the effort not to be sick again. "There must be something that you can give me, that I can sing."

"*Cara,* you must see it is impossible. . . ."

"If that Montero whore goes on in place of Drusilla,"

said Cavallo quietly, "you'll have to look for another Basilio as well."

"And another leader for the chorus," added Ponte.

"Bastardos!" hissed Belaggio. *"Froscios!"*

The two men regarded him stonily, and d'Isola struggled to sit up in January's arms.

"It's all right." Her brown eyes were heavy with exhaustion, but she cleared her throat, forced her voice to calm sweetness. "Thank you, my dear friends. I'll be able to go on." She turned to Olympe, asked in her broken French, "Will I not so?"

The voodooienne's dark eyes held hers for a long time; then Olympe smiled. "Oh, I think so." And in the coarse patois of the cane-fields, the mostly-African French of slaves, she added, "You do got the bristles, girl. You keep your belly tied up and you be fine."

TEN

⸺⸺

From his place in the orchestra—what seemed like only minutes later—January searched the audience for Incantobelli's silvery mane. The pit was lively, the rougher spirits of the American sector shoving and jostling good-naturedly, ready to be pleased by anything. In the boxes—divided only by partitions and not the separate curtained rooms they were in Europe—he picked out the Widow Redfern, resplendent in black velvet and diamonds and as usual in the center of her little court of hopeful bachelors. In the next box Fitzhugh Trulove danced anxious attendance on his wife, dispatching footmen right and left to fetch lemonade, negus, and coffee from the concessionaire for her and for their shy, curly-haired daughter. Dressed *en jeune fille,* her hair still down and her skirts schoolgirl-short, the girl looked all of fifteen, an age when Creole girls were all out and frequently wed: gossip said she would be sent to a finishing-school in England soon. In the meantime the sons of the great French Creole families hovered around the back of the box, proffering nosegays and sweets under Trulove's paternal glare. Vincent Marsan, another box over, also had his daughter with him, this girl a few years younger and very much a schoolgirl. She and her mother both wore white, quite clearly to complement Marsan's nip-waisted black coat, his three waistcoats of black, white, black again, with their diamond buttons. The narrow-skirted, skimpy-sleeved dresses were clearly old and the white suited neither of them; January saw, on the girl's bare arm, a dark bruise just above the elbow.

"You don't think the poor girl took the poison on purpose, do you?" Dominique appeared in the curtained demi-porte behind the orchestra in a whisper of yolk-gold silk and creamy lace. "I met Olympe on the way out—she says the girl will be quite all right. Darling, what happened? You know Liane—Marsan's *plaçée*—tried to kill herself last year—not the one he murdered, but the one he has now. She begged us all not to let him know."

January saw again the big girl's gentle face as she fought to turn her lips from the punch Marsan forced on her. *The heart is stronger than the head. . . .*

His stubbornness and frowns, these I embrace. . . .

Golden hair shimmering in the house-lights, Vincent Marsan turned abruptly to speak to his wife, and her unthinking flinch said more than any words January had ever heard.

"I don't think so," he told Dominique. "I don't think it was even intended to kill her. There was very little poison in that soup, just enough to make her thoroughly sick. Which leads me to think—"

He broke off, seeing his sister's eyes flick to another box, then dart away.

Henri Viellard entered, like a mammoth plum in his damson coat and pale-green waistcoat, with Chloë St. Chinian small and delicate in ivory satin on his arm.

"Darling, I must be off." Dominique tapped January on the shoulder with her fan and gave him her most sparkling of smiles. "I have to see to the champagne up in my box—I'm right up there." She pointed to the third tier of boxes above and behind them. About half of them were latticed discreetly, that the plaçées might receive their protectors between acts while everyone in the theater kept up the pretense of not knowing. Gaslight danced behind those gilded grilles as wall-jets were kindled. Shadows passed back and forth. Soft soprano laughter floated down like a dropped blossom into the noisier roar of the pit.

"I've ordered *dragées,*" she added conspiratorially. "Henri can't resist them. *If* he can wrench himself away from his mother." She did not speak Mademoiselle St. Chinian's name. In the Viellard box, Madame Viellard was holding forth on some subject to her four daughters—who looked absurdly like one another and more absurdly like their only brother—the half-dozen ostrich-plumes in her ash-hued hair quivering like lilac-tinted palm-trees in a hurricane. "Shall I send you down some? Play well!"

And Dominique swirled away to join the ranks of the demimonde in their stuffily hot upper boxes, their world of laughter and bonbons and lamplight and feather fans. A number of the girls would be with their protectors—protectors who would, during the course of the show, circulate between the boxes of their mistresses and those of their wives in much the same fashion they skulked back and forth along the passageway between the Théâtre and the Salle. A moment later, if he listened hard, January heard his sister's gay voice calling out greetings, laughing over the quality of the champagne available, and wailing in exaggerated apprehension over an American production of *anything.* . . .

I'm with child, Dominique had said. *And I don't know what to do.*

Chloë St. Chinian flipped open her fan—the elaborate mother-of-pearl engagement-fan presented by young Creole gentlemen to the damsels who would be their brides—and spoke to Henri, who moved his chair a little closer to hers and gave an order to the liveried valet who had followed them into the box. The valet departed, probably in quest of the coffee and sweets being sold in the lobby. Mademoiselle St. Chinian put her tiny white-gloved hand on Henri's wrist and blinked out over the parterre with her huge pale-blue eyes.

I'm with child. And I don't know what to do.

Nor would she, thought January, arranging the candles on the piano's music-rack, until it was far too late to do anything except birth the child of a man who had put her aside. For a young lady of color in quest of a new protector, a dangerous encumbrance.

For a young woman of color without a protector, a heartbreaking expense.

Every box of the three tiers was full. Candles gleamed behind those moving shadows as servants brought up chairs for people to visit during the performance. In Milan and other Italian cities, they played cards and chatted, stopping to listen only to favorite arias. Parisian audiences, January had found, were more attentive, but any performance in Paris was bound to be interrupted by the hissing, or booing, or cheering of a claque, regardless of the quality of the singing. He'd even known fashionable preachers to hire claques to murmur approvingly and nod their heads during their sermons.

So perhaps the Parisians hadn't so much to boast of after all.

The pit, by contrast, was a shoulder-to-shoulder mob, men and women both, the smell of them thick in the air: wool too seldom washed, bear-grease pomade,

sweat, spit tobacco. Trappers in buckskin elbowed trades-
men in corduroy and shopgirls in flowered calicoes.
Women edged among them, selling pralines, oranges, gingerbread, lemonade. Above the third tier of boxes, where
the rising heat from the gasoliers collected under the ceiling, the gallery was aswim with faces, pale on the right
side, dark on the left, and spotted with bright tignons like
blossoms lost in shadow. An occasional, broken pea-nut
hull would drift down, catching the gaslight like errant
snow. The rougher patois of slaves mingled with rough
English, rough Spanish, rough French. Happy voices, an-
ticipatory laughter.

They were here to be pleased, thought January. And
why not? Beauty like this was like walking in a garden of
roses. If the songs had been sung in French, or in English
for that matter, half these people would still only follow
the action, marvel at the beauty of the sets and the ballet
between acts. They came to hear music, to see love and
kisses. . . .

A black man's kisses, on a white woman's lips?

Was that it? he wondered. Whoever wrote that heart-
shaking music, it was Belaggio who was insisting on having *Othello* performed next month. Was it really
Incantobelli, maddened with this final insult, who was
taking out his fury and spite on the company, on the production itself?

Or was there someone in one of those boxes—or in
the gloom at the back of the gallery, where the white flicker
of the auditorium's gasoliers didn't reach—or somewhere
in the maze of catwalks among the flats and flies and the
corridors and stairs leading to boxes, galleries, dressing-
rooms, prop-vaults—waiting with a rifle? It wouldn't be
difficult to smuggle such a thing into the theater, despite
James Caldwell's stricture on the inhabitants of the pit

leaving their weaponry at the door. *If I wanted to stop Othello being performed,* thought January, *it's what I'd do.*

Shoot Belaggio in the one place—the conductor's stand—where he can't run away.

Or, if I didn't want to chance being convicted of shooting a white man, warn him: shoot one of the orchestra, with the implication, *You're next.*

Not a comforting thought.

"Ladies and gentlemen!" The flames on the gasoliers dimmed, the footlights brightened behind their wall of tin reflectors as Mr. Russell worked the valves of the gastable in the wings. Resplendent in evening dress, James Caldwell stepped through the curtain with uplifted hands. "Welcome to the first season of the New Orleans Opera at the American Theater."

Someone spit tobacco against the dark drapery that concealed the orchestra from the pit. Someone else, by the smell of it, started peeling an orange. Here near the footlights the stink of the burning gas nearly drowned out other odors, and the heat was like being trapped in a crowded room too near the hearth. Around him, January heard the rustle of music being ranged on desks, the scrape of chairs. Candles like stars. Hannibal's stifled cough.

Murder and mayhem, and Marguerite cold and still—maybe dying . . . Hate like a malevolent ghost watching from the shadows . . .

Still, there was no moment quite like this.

"I believe we can promise you the finest performances, the most beautiful spectacles, the best and greatest singers this city has ever seen. Tonight the season will open with Mozart's *The Marriage of Figaro.* . . ."

"I wanna kiss the bride!" trumpeted a voice from the pit.

"Friday night we will present *The Mute Girl of Portici*, a stirring drama of love and liberty. . . ."

Fitzhugh Trulove leapt to his feet and applauded madly, nearly falling over the rail of his stage-side box. To judge by her expression, Anne Trulove was considering pushing him. Caldwell beamed. January thought about John Davis opening the same opera on the following night at his own theater to half-filled boxes and a pocketful of debts.

". . . *La Dame Blanche*, followed by Rossini's masterpiece *Cinderella*. Then we will have a new opera, the United States premiere of Lorenzo Belaggio's *Othello*, a most masterful tragedy based upon the work of Mr. William Shakespeare, and the season will conclude with von Weber's astounding work *The Magical Marksman.*"

More applause. *Just what we need*, thought January: *someone on-stage with a rifle.* In the Viellard box, Chloë St. Chinian fanned herself, looking bored. Henri cast a glance up at the latticed boxes opposite and above, reflected footlights making hard gold squares of the lenses of his spectacles, a fireburst of the stickpin in his cravat.

"And now, ladies and gentlemen, the moment you've all been waiting for: *The Marriage of Figaro!*"

"Betcha Figaro's been waitin' harder'n us!"

Had Drusilla d'Isola not spent most of the afternoon vomiting, January supposed she might have sung better—but probably not very much. He'd heard her in rehearsal.

Still, she was on-stage, chalky beneath her make-up and operating, as many artists can, strictly on learned technique: a gesture, an angle of the head, a flourish on the end of a cabaletta, an ornamental trill. Automatic responses, like a well-bred hostess trading commonplaces with morning-visitors while planning the menu for next week's dinner for twelve. The simpler popular songs, if somewhat mispronounced, required nothing in the way of skill and were easily within her range.

At least she didn't forget her lines, though she came close to doing so in the third act. She opened the desk-drawer to get out paper and pen for the Letter Duet—January's favorite piece of the show—and gagged, stammered, jerked her hand back. . . .

Somebody put something in the drawer, thought January, between annoyance and resignation. The favorite was a dead rat, though in other performances of *Nozze* he'd also encountered a live rat, the biggest spider obtainable by the diva's rival, and any number of obscene drawings designed to reduce the heroine to blushes, giggles, or aphasia at the start of this critical piece. At the Paris Odéon once, a rival had tried to introduce a turd into the drawer, but the smell had tipped off the stage-hands, resulting in a great deal of ribald speculation backstage.

Whatever was in the drawer, d'Isola simply closed it, took a much smaller scrap from the top of the desk, and settled down with her pen. She certainly sang no worse for it. Though it would be difficult, reflected January sadly, for her to sing worse than she already was.

Montero would have been ten times better.

But it didn't matter. D'Isola was exquisite, the music was beautiful, and though the wealthy patrons in the boxes (and quite a few of the slaves in the gallery, who had seen enough opera to tell good from mediocre) might sniff, the pit was ravished. Thunderous applause greeted Susanna's musical duels with Almaviva and his scheming minions; whoops and hollers encouraged Cherubino's leap from the balcony; boos and hisses excoriated the lustful Count's advances. The scantly-draped ballet performed between acts and, in greater strength, in Acts Three and Four to yells of approval and delight—

"Cherry-Cheeked Patty" notwithstanding—and everyone had a marvelous time.

Only afterward did January learn what was in the drawer.

Mr. Trulove had spoken no more than the truth about the promised feast. Cold ham, champagne, *foie gras,* and pastries loaded down the trestle table that had been set up in the green room. Early strawberries and hot-house grapes blazed like jewels. A second table provided cakes and lemonade for the musicians. It was an arrangement January had encountered in Europe on those occasions at which the boxholders' associations deigned to include the musicians at all. The difference in America was that a third table, pushed up against the footslopes of Vesuvius, provided *gaufres,* fruit, and oysters for the white members of the stage crew, and for the little rats, most of whom had access to the green room anyway at the invitation of various gentlemen whose friendships they'd secured in their days in town.

Not that it mattered, of course. The green room was so small, and the Members and Cast collation so ostentatiously splendid, the principals' table filled most of the limited space and those who had sought to preserve their exclusivity were quickly driven out into the backstage among the riffraff in order to eat without crashing elbows.

". . . A splendid choice," Trulove enthused, extricating himself from the press and casting an ardent glance at Oona Flaherty, her mouth full of strawberries and pâté. "Since dance is truly the universal language, freed of all concerns about French or Italian, I cannot imagine a better or more expressive work to perform. . . ."

"But surely controversial?" Trulove's wife, holding close to his side, raised her pale brows. "There were riots when *La Muette* was first performed in Brussels. . . ."

"Oh, I don't think we need worry ourselves over that." Caldwell cleared his throat uncomfortably, aware of being on equivocal ground. "America is a democracy, after all. The sentiments expressed—Masaniello's courageous battle for liberty from the Spanish oppressors—should strike a chord of sympathy. If you look at the struggles for liberty in New Grenada, in Bolivia and Brazil and in Mexico, to free themselves from the tyranny of Spain . . ."

"As if the average American even knows of Mexico's liberty," muttered Cavallo—fortunately in Italian—to Herr Smith.

Marsan, who appeared to have sent away his women-folk as soon as the final curtain rang down, stood beside the green-room door until the press had eased somewhat and the danger of spilling something on his sable waistcoat had receded. Only then did he fetch lemonade, a vol-au-vent, and a morsel of pâté to carry to La d'Isola, who still looked waxy and ill. Belaggio, rather than abandon his position in Madame Redfern's orbit, merely steered the soprano around so that he stood between her and Marsan.

"You look pale, *querida,*" crooned Madame Montero, gowned—or almost gowned—in a dress strongly reminiscent of the décolleté in Paris in the days of the Directorate. "Perhaps you'd feel better if you sat down?" She indicated the Almavivas' drawing-room sofa, about thirty feet away in the shadows.

"She's well where she is," snapped Belaggio, tightening his grip on d'Isola's elbow and glaring at the hovering Marsan.

And La d'Isola whispered, "I'm well where I am."

"If women dueled, I'd put my money on them rather than into the pool for a Davis-Belaggio match." Hannibal propped himself discreetly at January's side and poured laudanum into his punch. *"Yet surely Cassio, I believe, re-*

ceived / From him that fled some strange indignity / Which patience could not pass. . . ."

"I think we've seen the opening round." During the romping in the Almaviva garden in Act Four, the villainess Marcellina had showed a distressing tendency to trip and fall whenever she got anywhere near the chorus of shepherds and milkmaids, once executing a full-out pratfall on her posterior and another time plunging headlong into the shrubbery, to the joyful howls and whistles of the pit. If looks could maim, Bruno Ponte would have been carried off the stage on a plank. "If that's what's going on."

Twice during the performance January had glimpsed the lanky shadow of Abishag Shaw, once at the rail of one of the empty boxes, looking down into the pit, and once in the demi-porte that led from the orchestra to the backstage. Olympe had told him earlier that Shaw had visited her house on Rue Douane but had not questioned the dressings wrapped close around Marguerite's bruised throat. It was as possible, January supposed, that a potential killer could have deliberately run a woman down in a carriage as it was that he'd lured her into the dark of the *cipriere* and strangled her. In any case, Shaw seemed disposed to take seriously the threat of further mayhem.

". . . so much prettier," Mrs. Redfern declared in her hard, over-loud voice, and sipped her negus. In the white-touched black of second mourning she resembled nothing so much as a jeweler's display stand, the little square red hands in their lace mitts flashing with diamond fire. "Of course I can't understand a word they're singing either way. Why, I never knew Mr. Mozart wrote, 'Soft as the Falling Dews of Night'! It's my favorite tune! Is there any chance Miss d'Isola could sing it again in the next opera?"

"But of course! The very thing!" Belaggio smiled warmly down at the widow. He'd resumed his black silk arm-sling for the performance, and winced in agony whenever he moved his arm and remembered to do so. "If I may say so, I have always been struck by your keen judgment of artistic matters. Davis—well, I will not say anything of his jealousy, nor his malice toward me. I am large-minded enough to deal with whatever small peril there may be. But I think his hatred stems from his realization that the Italian style is so much more beautiful than the French." He gestured grandly with his glass of champagne. "Mr. Caldwell and I can present what is new, what is fresh. . . ."

"New is one thing." Mrs. Redfern nodded judiciously, her little square mouth pursed. "And yet, I feel I must speak to you tonight, sir, regarding this new opera you announced—this *Othello*?" And she held out her hand, into which Caldwell hastily placed the green-bound libretto. "I hardly like to speak of the matter, sir, but I feel in all honesty that I must. Surely you are not going to put *this* on the stage?"

Dr. Ker, the slim, gray-haired Head Surgeon at Charity Hospital, opened his mouth in protest, but young Harry Fry hastened to step in with "I couldn't agree more. *Othello* is a most unsuitable choice. Not a subject at all that is pleasant for the fair sex." And he bowed deeply to Mrs. Redfern as if she were the only woman in the room, and the only one he'd ever seen in his life.

Mrs. Redfern drew herself up with the air of one prepared to fight for her prejudices, but without a breath or a blink, Belaggio cried as one suddenly enlightened, *"È vero,* you are right! I said myself to Signor Caldwell, I said, *I have my doubts about this opera. . . ."* He took the libretto, held it folded against his chest. "Did I not, Signor Caldwell? Most unsuitable to present to ladies?"

"Eh?" Caldwell caught one glance from the Widow

Redfern and nodded vigorously. "And I agreed with you on that, sir." He took charge of the offending text. Tapping the green leather binding with one forefinger, he went on oratorically. "What is right for a European audience is sometimes lost on—or completely inappropriate for—the new-forged civilization of America. It is exactly what I was considering myself, only do you know, I never put it as succinctly as you have, Madame."

"That's ridiculous!" exclaimed Dr. Ker. "What on earth is wrong with *Othello*? It's one of the great tragedies of literature, one of the great tales of love and jealousy—"

"I did not find it so," replied Mrs. Redfern. "Merely an unpleasant tale of a savage behaving disgracefully. Now, if Mr. Othello were perhaps—well—made to be a European gentleman, it would not only be more realistic, but more tolerable."

"It is *Shakespeare*!" cried Ker, horrified, as Belaggio opened his mouth to consent to this last-minute revision. "You can't rewrite Shakespeare!"

"Might I suggest Mr. Bellini's *The Sleepwalker*?" Caldwell plucked another glass of negus from the table to replace the empty one in Mrs. Redfern's hand. "Much simpler, don't you agree, Signor Belaggio?"

"It would not be difficult to re-write," argued Belaggio, at the same time shifting Drusilla d'Isola around so that she was on the inside of the group rather than the outside, where Marsan was idling over toward them. "Since the *bella* Signora wishes it, I could do it in a matter of a few days merely. . . ."

But as a former actor, Caldwell had his limits. "Best we simply substitute the one for the other, don't you think?" he said, and Ker, exasperated, flung up his hands. "The other is, as you said, Madame, of an unpleasant nature. . . ."

"*The Sleepwalker* is new," agreed Belaggio. "I believe Signor Cavallo has sung Elvino before. My lovely d'Isola"—here he tugged her gently to the fore, her face gray and strained in the harsh light—"can learn the part of the lovely Amina to perfection, can you not, *bellissima*?"

The girl tore her gaze from Marsan's, smiled tremulously as Belaggio repeated the question in Italian, replied, "Of course. Of a certainty." She tried to tug away in the direction of the couch, but Belaggio's grip was relentless.

". . . *Sleepwalker* might not be quite right." Ludmilla Burton detached herself from the lively discussion of servants with the Granvilles and came over with her ears almost visibly pricked like a gun-dog's. "It just struck me that another of Mr. Bellini's excellent works might be performed, that wonderful Roman opera, *Norma*? The one about the two druidesses in love with the Roman soldier? I realize you don't have children in your company, Mr. Belaggio, but it so happens that my niece Ursula—a more beautiful child you'll never see—has the most exquisite voice. She and her sister Violet have both been praised for their adorable ways in the private theatricals we hold every Christmas. I'm sure that they would be perfect as the two little girls. . . ."

"I'll bet they can sing 'Cherry-Cheeked Patty,' too," murmured Hannibal, as Mrs. Redfern loudly proclaimed her desire to see druidesses and Belaggio began eager inquiries as to how many of his principals had appeared in provincial performances of one of the most staggering operas ever written. "So much for a man risking death for the sake of his art." He added another dollop of laudanum to the dregs of his punch-cup. "Rather like seeing Esmeralda hop into Claude Frollo's bed for the price of a glass of beer, isn't it?"

"I give up." January set down his empty plate. He felt suddenly drained, exhausted by the events of the past six hours and as disgusted with his own earlier emotions as a man who discovers his love-poems being used for curling-papers. "Let Belaggio be murdered. Let them put on whatever they want and stick as many Grand Marches and choruses of 'Bonny Dundee' as they want into it. Beauty and integrity and courage and liberty are obviously none of my business. I'm going home. I'll see you tomorrow at rehearsal."

"Signor Janvier?" Drusilla d'Isola stood behind them.

Like all the women of the company, she had taken off the heavy stage make-up, but even under the delicate rice-powder and rouge with which she'd replaced it, she looked like a dead woman. The gorgeous knots and swags of blond lace and point d'esprit that framed her shoulders only served to accentuate her pallor; January sprang to his feet. "You should be lying down, Signorina," he protested. "Please, sit—or, better still, allow my friend and myself to walk you back to your hotel. That was a heroic performance, but you must rest."

"It had to be done." She shook her head at the offer of a gilt-trimmed chair, glanced over her shoulder at Belaggio, still surrounded by well-wishers and soaking up praise like a camel at a water-hole. "Once they begin to replace you— once people hear another's name rather than yours . . ." She took a deep breath. "Thank you, so much, for sending for your sister to help me. She is a strong woman, your sister. A—a *strega*, such as we have in the villages. She was very good to me." She crossed herself.

Tired as she was, beaten and struggling to stay on her feet, she seemed very different from the fluttery, sweet child who clung so calculatingly to Belaggio's arm; who followed Marsan with such adoring eyes. Maybe, thought

January, because this was the first he'd seen Drusilla away from either of her lovers, operating on her own.

"Silvio—Signor Cavallo—tells me that you are . . . are concerned in the matter of the strange events that have taken place here. Are concerned to find out who assaulted Lorenzo, and who may have tried to poison me."

"I *was* concerned about who assaulted Signor Belaggio," said January. "I am a friend of Signor Davis's, whom Belaggio has all but accused of the crime. And since I find it unlikely that two violent attackers are pursuing members of the same opera company, I think the same person is responsible for the injury to Madame Scie. Which means that others may be in danger as well."

D'Isola paled still more, if that was possible, and crossed herself again. "I know," she whispered, and reached like a child to pluck at his sleeve. "That's what I have to show you."

She went to the end of the musicians' table and fetched a candlestick—"At first I thought it was just that bitch Montero, trying to force me aside. . . ."

"I think it was," said January. "The day before yesterday she hired me to take her through the Countess's part. In case, she said, you and Signor Belaggio had a falling-out. It would be hard to prove. . ."

D'Isola stopped in her tracks, lips hardening and eyes snapping fire. "Did she so?" She stamped her foot. "Cow! Slut!" Her hand clenched the gaudy brass as if she meant to brain her rival. "I would never have . . . oh! As if putting poison in my soup weren't enough . . ."

"You mean something else happened?" January saw again how she'd flinched as she opened the desk-drawer on-stage.

"That scorpion! That . . . but of course, Signor Janvier. During the Letter Duet."

She led the way down the short corridor beside the rehearsal-room, to the little prop-room originally reserved for the variously colored glass filters that changed the color of the gas-jets, and now promiscuously crammed with rolled-up scrims, stacked chairs, and the hats, coats, and instrument-cases of the musicians. The Contessa Almaviva's white-and-gilt writing-desk had been thrust into a corner: "Signor Caldwell insisted, Signore. He— and Lorenzo—ordered me to tell no one. He said it would not do for *i padroni* to know there had been more trouble."

The desk was old and French and rather delicate, cabriole-legged and tricked out in overemphatic gilding that looked gaudy by daylight, but by the glow of candles or gaslight on-stage merely seemed rich. The small scrap of paper on which she'd scribbled still lay atop it, with pen, standish, Cherubino's military papers, and the pins and combs that had been in one of the ballet dancers' hair.

"Elizabetta—Signora Chiavari—says it's *Malòcchio*— the Evil Eye—but I never have believed in the Evil Eye." She gazed up at January in the candle's single flare, grave as a child. "Neither does Concha, I know. That's why . . . I can understand that she'd poison me, so she could be the Countess." She pulled open the drawer. "But I don't think she'd have done this."

Everything in the drawer—papers, quills, a stray hair-ribbon and the lambswool that had escaped from some long-ago dancer's slipper-toe—was saturated with blood.

ELEVEN

—◦◦◦—

Naturally, no one had the slightest idea who had last been near the writing-desk before it was taken on-stage. Even the new stage-hands, Paddy and Liam—each of whom insisted the other had carried the desk—were prepared to swear that the blood hadn't been in the drawer at that time, until they realized Caldwell wasn't accusing either of them of putting it there. "I thought I'd smelt somethin' amiss, y'see," confessed Liam at last. "But there was sich a helter-skelter an' all this plunder to be got onto the stage . . ." He took the long-nine cigar from his mouth and gestured around him at the Gothic archways, carven-legged tables, and bundles of banners bearing the arms of Spain and the emblems of the Duke of Arcos that jumbled the backstage together with Roman columns and classical statues brought up for the melodrama *Brutus* the following night.

"I understand," said Caldwell. It was nearly midnight, the tired cold stinks of greasepaint and gas-lamps mingling sourly with the smell of the man's cigar. The remains of the food had been taken away by the Marsan and Trulove servants; the voices of those few who remained in the theater—January, Hannibal, Caldwell, Tiberio and his two helpers, Belaggio—echoed eerily in the cavernous night of the ceiling. Wrapped in Comte Almaviva's purple velvet cloak, La d'Isola sat on a well-head belonging to the town of Portici, Cavallo and Ponte hovering behind her like a pair of watchful brothers. "Perhaps," said Caldwell helpfully, "if we reconstructed where the desk was, we might be able to determine who came near it. . . ."

As if, thought January, looking around him at the maze of flats, ropes, shadows, and segments of papier-mâché boiserie, *anyone couldn't have slipped through unseen to dump . . . to dump what?* The blood had been fresh. *Chicken, cat, rat . . . ?*

He took up again the brass candelabrum that d'Isola had earlier carried—it would reappear Friday night in the Duke of Arcos's palace hall and probably adorn Caesar's palace in between—re-lit three of its guttered tapers from the nearest gas-jet, and carried it down the steps and so out to the alley. Cloud had moved in to blot the stars, warming the air but filling it with the thick promise of rain. In the passway between the stable-yard wall and the theater, he found a cheap metal rattrap of the cage type, still containing three rats—the prop-vault stank of them—and a little dish of ground-nuts. All three rats had had their throats cut. A second dish, of half-spilled sugar-water that reeked of laudanum, explained why the rodents hadn't put up much of a fight.

A few minutes' more search in the garbage of the passway yielded the tightly-corked gourd that had held the blood.

January couldn't be positive—cage and gourd were set to the left of the door, farther from the alley end of the passway—but he didn't think he'd seen them at seven, when he'd come this way to force the lock.

But his mind had been full of fear for d'Isola then, and the passway already dark.

In any case, thought January, cage, gourd, laudanum, were cheap. They could have been purchased easily and anonymously in the marketplace. He'd already guessed that the perpetrator was connected with the theater. Anyone could have slipped into the prop-vault, or up to the repair-shops in the attic, or to any of a dozen other nooks and corners in that crowded building, to kill and drain the rats during the dinner-hour between rehearsal and the performance. Hell, thought January, you could have butchered a cow in the cluttered back corners of the prop-vault, hidden the remains for a week, and no one would be the wiser. The confusion resulting from d'Isola's poisoning would have made that doubly simple.

Voices in the alley. The bang of the stage door. Cavallo's: "Drusilla, *cara mia*, truly the place for you is at the hotel, in bed. After all you've been through . . ."

"Oh, Silvio, what evil is going on here! Signor Janvier told me he believes this same person who attacked Lorenzo was also the one who tried to kill poor Signora Scie. And he will try again, maybe to kill you, or me, or . . ."

"What befell Belaggio in the alley has nothing to do with you, little bird. How could it? It was that sow Montero . . ."

"But why would she have put the blood in the drawer if she intended to sing the Countess herself? Or if she put the blood, why would she have poisoned me? Silvio, no, it is a plot, an evil plot! You know this Incantobelli. Could he be so wicked? So mad?"

"Signor Janvier asked that also." Young Ponte's slow, countryman's voice. "Honor demands vengeance, yes, but not vengeance on harmless women. This Signor Davis . . ." Their voices faded as they moved toward the street and were lost in the general clamor of Carnival. A few moments later the door banged again. Caldwell's vel-

vety baritone echoed against the brick of the alley walls—
". . . need hardly tell you that none of this is to be spoken
of to anyone. The last thing this theater needs is a rumor
that a madman is out to do murder during a performance." Keys jangled. A bolt scraped.

"As for myself, I walk abroad o'nights," quoted Hannibal in the gloating accents of Kean playing the Jew of
Malta, *"and kill sick people groaning under walls: / Sometimes I go about and poison wells. . . ."*

"People believe it, my friend," admonished Caldwell
grimly. "People believe it." Footfalls squished, diminu-
endo. Then the clop of hooves and the American's voice
dimly telling the driver of a fiacre where to take him. *I'm
the last one here.* January reflected uneasily on the empty
darkness of Rue des Ursulines, and his landlady's voice:
He had a knife.

More footfalls, then a cough.

"O blood, Iago, blood." Hannibal leaned a shoulder
against the corner of the tiny passway in which January
crouched. "Find anything of interest?"

"How now? A rat," returned January gravely. *"Dead
for a ducat, too."* Edging carefully between the stable wall
and that of the theater—the space was barely as wide as
his shoulders—he carried cage, rats, and blood-stinking
gourd up to the door of the secret back-stair and set them
in the little three-by-four space just inside, to keep them
safe for the remainder of the night. "I take it it's too late
for Shaw to be here still."

"It's too late for *God* to be here." The fiddler coughed
again, and fished a handkerchief from his pocket to hold
to his lips—January saw a fleck of blood in the wavery
gleam of his candles. "I'll see you home."

January blew out the tapers and left the holder there,
too, carefully closing the door. "You don't have to." By the

rasp of his breathing Hannibal wasn't well enough to see himself home.

"I have money." They felt their way down the passway and along the alley in the dark. "All we have to do is get you to your doorstep—I doubt the invisible Devil's going to brave another meeting with Madame Bontemps. I wouldn't."

But the driver of the fiacre they hailed from the theater's front steps bluntly refused to drive January anywhere. "I could get in trouble, me," said the man. Under the slouched brim of his hat his eyes glinted in the glare of the gaslights. "Me, I don't care who I drive, but there's a law in this town, eh? They don't want me to drive no colored, I won't drive no colored."

"I'm only seeing my friend home," began January, one arm around Hannibal's shoulders, and the driver shook his head.

"Then I see your friend home, me."

"Idiotes!" High heels tapping sharply on the boards of the sidewalk, Consuela Montero strode over to them from the City Hotel across the street. Plumes and bows nodded in her black hair as she pulled the velvet ruffles of her cloak about her. *"Imbeciles,* with your silly pride . . . Get on the box." She gestured January imperiously to the seat beside the driver, the traditional place for servants to ride.

"Yes, m'am." January bowed with every appearance of deep respect. "I was just wanting to get Michie Hannibal—"

"Señor Hannibal is sober, at least enough to see to himself," retorted Madame Montero as the driver flipped open the carriage door with his long whip. As January crossed behind the hack and around to the driver's perch, Hannibal handed the soprano up the step: *"Es verdad,* the pride of men! What does your man think, that this driver has never seen one who had to be helped home by a footman? Rue des Ursulines. Then you will take my friend here back to Perdidio Street."

"Bounteous madam," quoted Hannibal, removing his shabby hat, *"whatever shall become of Michael Cassio / He's never anything but your true servant."*

As the fiacre passed before the lights of the City Hotel, January saw Montero glance sidelong at Hannibal, amused speculation in her dark eyes. "And is this the same Michael Cassio of the play, that has but a poor and unhappy brain for drinking?"

"Drunk?" protested Hannibal floridly. *"And speak parrot? And squabble? Swagger? Swear? And discourse fustian with one's own shadow?"*

"*Basta!* I think maybe if, as I hear, there is evil about . . ." She switched to Italian, in case the driver spoke Spanish as well as French. "I, as well as some others I might name of this company, might find myself in need of a true servant or two."

"And was there," asked Rose the following morning when January stopped by the backstage of the Théâtre d'Orleans with coffee and *callas,* "an invisible devil with a knife concealed somewhere in the Rue des Ursulines awaiting your arrival?"

"There was someone." January poured her out some coffee from the stoppered gourd and perched on the foot-slopes of Mount Vesuvius. This Vesuvius was smaller than the American version—an American would have said that was only to be expected—and instead of a long trackway where red and gold silk would be rippled in counterfeit for lava, it had a sort of metal-lined ditch. But like its American counterpart, it was studded with caldera, into which basins of wet clay or sand could be set, to control the flares of its eruption. Leather hosepipes trailed across the backstage floor and vanished among the flats, to be hooked to the gas-jets in the proscenium when it came time for poor mute Fenella to leap off the balcony into the blazing lava.

January took a bite of the sticky, egg-sized rice-ball he held, getting powdered sugar all over his trousers, jacket-sleeves, and the front of his yellow calico shirt. Rose was having the same problem, with the result that Vesuvius looked as if it had experienced a light fall of unseasonable snow.

"As I was getting off the box, I saw someone step out of a passway between two houses and stand for a moment on the banquette. He was too far off for me to be sure—but I think he was tall. The streetlamp over the intersection was out and I didn't have more than a moment to look before Madame Montero ordered me to go inside and tell a fictitious maid that she wouldn't be coming in after all. If I hadn't ridden the fiacre as her servant," he added quietly, "I would have walked past that passway, coming home on foot."

Rose patted the fine white dust from her hands as she slipped down from her own seat on the mountain's flank. "Have you any idea why?" she asked, eschewing exclamations of horror or concern—she'd have been useless as the heroine of a melodrama, January reflected, amused. "Why you? Why not the other musicians?" Over her plain blue frock she wore a smock of worn pink calico, which, being Rose, she'd disdained to match with a pink tignon: the headscarves she wore were almost invariably white, suiting well her plain, neat dresses. The smock's pockets bulged with pens, small notebooks, bits of chalk, and pestles, giving her the air of an apothecary.

January followed her into the napkin-sized proproom. Space had been cleared on a little table for half a dozen boxes labeled with the names of various importers in New Orleans who brought in chemicals from New York, London, and Hamburg for use in sugar refining, paint manufacture, and the apothecary trade. *Nitrate of Strontia,* said the label on one large jar of needle-like white crystals. Another jar contained sulfur, and a small cask set carefully to one side was simply labeled *Gunpowder.* A wicker-wrapped carboy, by its smell, held alum.

Various sieves, of fine hair or bolting-cloth, which January recognized as Rose's own property rather than that of the theater, were stacked neatly on a rear corner of the table—a row of wide-mouthed porcelain jars offered powders, which she proceeded to measure and mix with a small bone knife on a sheet of white paper. More paper, rolled into cylinders and gummed, lay ready to hand.

"I have to get as much of this done in advance as possible," explained Rose. "One can't mix the chlorate of potassa or the gunpowder in until the very last moment, of course, and even with the ballet, there isn't long between acts. Did Madame Montero say how she happened to be in front of the City Hotel at midnight?"

"I did not have the opportunity to ask. But she's staying at the Hotel, and midnight is not so very late, so it could have been chance. I trust," added January grimly, "that this room is kept firmly locked when you're absent." As a surgeon, he had been called once to the scene of a theater fire. Paper flowers, masses of curtains, jumbles of stored props and flats—too few doors and too many people all crammed together on benches and chairs . . .

The minute he'd heard *La Muette* was going to be

performed at the American Theater, he'd made sure he knew the quickest route from the orchestra pit to the nearest window.

"Well, I don't think there's enough of anything here to blow up the theater," said Rose reasonably as she gently spooned gunpowder into a marble mortar and began—carefully—to grind it. Above her head, rain drummed gently on the gray window-glass. "But yes, Mr. Davis has given me the key and has moved out all the other props into the main backstage. And the whole of the mountain's going to be wet down with jugs of water just before the curtain goes up on Act Three. With luck it won't dry out before the eruption. And you haven't answered my first question."

"Why me?" From the doorway where he leaned—there wasn't space for two of them in the room—January picked out with his eye the clay water-jar that stood in the corner, mentally estimating how long it would take him to reach it and dump it over Rose and the contents of the mortar before the whole theater shot up in flames. "If I knew that . . ." He frowned. "I was going to say, *If I knew that, I'd be closer to knowing who's doing this,* but I'm not sure that's true. I suspect—I assume—that whoever followed us to Jacques's house Saturday night was following Marguerite. He was hiding in the woods when he heard me say she wasn't dead; he believes she regained consciousness at some point and told me who attacked her, or believes that she will regain consciousness and tell me."

"In other words," said Rose, "Signor Belaggio's decision not to produce *Othello* after all doesn't end the possibility of an attack on you. Or on Madame Scie."

"No," said January quietly. "If in fact the production of *Othello* is the target at all. It might not be, you know.

Or if it was, I'm not sure that Incantobelli—if it is he behind these acts—will know of Belaggio's decision that *Othello* is 'unsuitable' "—his voice twisted sardonically on the word—"for presentation before chaste American widows."

"And if he does," remarked Rose, turning back to empty the mortar of fine-ground powder onto a sheet of white paper, "I'm not sure he wouldn't feel even more mortally dishonored in the withdrawal than in the presentation. And I can't say that I blame him." She began to scoop the powder into the coarser of two sieves, shaking it gently onto a second sheet of paper, working matter-of-factly, like January's nephew Gabriel making a roux.

"It's a thought." January folded his big arms, watching her with a sensation of his hair standing on end, wondering if she'd ever seen the victims of gunpowder burns. He wanted to pull her from the room, wrest the bone knife, the sieve, and the scoop from her hand, shout at her never to tinker with such deadly things again. . . .

As if she were a child. As if she were *his* child, and not a woman grown and free, who had trained in the handling of such deadly chemicals. Who gained what joy she had in life in making experiments of this kind, in seeing how fire and air and earth related to one another.

He took a deep breath, and let the impulse dissolve. Pushed aside the pain of Ayasha's death, and the fear of losing this second treasure. *That's my Rose,* he thought. Or the woman he hoped would one day be his Rose.

"In a way," he said, "I hope the attacker does strike again, and soon. Because unless he does, we won't be able to catch him. Yet he'll still be there, waiting for me. Waiting for Marguerite, if she lives. And if she does not live," he finished quietly, thinking about the wasted hands lying on the coverlet, the bruised eyelids closed and already beginning to grow hollow with hunger and dehydration, "I will see that man hanged."

Marguerite was still unconscious when January reached Olympe's house later in the morning. "I tried most of the night to get her to drink," said his sister, haggard-looking herself as she poured him out some of Gabriel's semi-ambrosial coffee. "I kept her lips moist, a drop at a time; maybe she drank a little of it, I can't tell." Like Rose, Olympe, too, sat at a table with pestle and mortar before her, with clean newspaper spread and little jars and gourds and dishes of ingredients to mix. But instead of alum and stearine, sulfuret of antimony and nitrate of soda, dried herbs were heaped on pottery dishes: jessamine and jack honeysuckle, willow bark and sassafras. There was a little pile of brick-dust in a saucer, and another of salt. A bright tin box such as candies were shipped in from England contained mouse-bones; on a piece of clean white paper lay the dried and wrinkled skins of two toads and a ground-puppy.

Juju. Gris-gris. Ouanga. The smell of the honeysuckle, of the gunpowder that she mixed with some of them and the dried dog-shit she mixed with others, came to January like a whisper out of the past, a breath of darkness. The side of his life he'd forsaken when he took ship for Paris to learn about medicine and music and reason and light. *I do confess the vices of my blood,* Othello says. The past from which no man can flee. The soil that nurtures whatever fruit will grow.

"I asked around the market this morning," said Olympe. Through the open rear doors the smell of the rain blew through, soft and gray and like no other, and from the kitchen, Gabriel's cheery song. "And yes, they say a woman bought Indian tobacco of Queen Régine. They say she was a dark-haired woman with red jewels, that spoke like a foreigner, and she asked specially that it be not enough to kill, but only to lay out that other woman good."

"I thought as much."

Olympe's long fingers sifted together the gunpowder and sulfur, the salt and the fragments of bone. As she bound them up in a scrap of red flannel, he saw her lips move, invoking the spirits of power, of malice or love. Then she glanced up at him again. "Might this be the same? This woman—had she enemies of her own back in France? Those who'd want her dead, and have nothing to do with these Italians, with their operas and their money and all their *ja* over who gonna run things? Just 'cause you keep soap in the kitchen doesn't make it food, you know."

"No," agreed January thoughtfully. "But Marguerite is a poor woman. Her family was noble before the Revolution, but she's the only one of them who survived the killing. She's danced all her life, and cares for nothing else. And I never yet met one of her old lovers—and they are legion, believe me—who did not speak well of her, and remain her friend."

"Then she's a special woman indeed." Olympe set aside her little gris-gris bundle and folded her strong, callused hands. "I've prayed for her to Loco, who puts the strength of healing into medicines, and hung tobacco for him in a straw basket on a tree in the square. If the gods listen, she'll come back to us."

January drew his breath to protest this piece of superstition, then reflected that hanging tobacco in a straw basket for the *loa* of the trees wasn't so very different from burning a candle in front of a statue in a church. God's Mother wasn't a statue and didn't have any actual use for a penny's worth of wax. So he merely laid a hand on his sister's shoulder and said, "Thank you. That's good of you." Five years ago he wouldn't have said it—he'd burned candles for Olympe's soul for years—but five years ago his sister would never have petitioned Loco for a white woman's life. "I'll be back tonight. And I'll be at the theater most of the day, should there be any change."

For the remainder of the day he concentrated on Monsieur Auber's impassioned tale of the brave Neapolitan fisherman's revolt against his country's oppressors, groaning inwardly every time La d'Isola sang, wincing at Oona Flaherty's efforts to toe-dance even with the assistance of wires and counterweights, and flinching whenever a whoosh and flash of flame backstage reminded him that Tiberio and his Hibernian myrmidons were still experimenting with Vesuvius's fiery bowels. Cavallo sang a fine impassioned Masaniello, but between the volcano's misfiring and Fenella's laboriously-expressed emotions ("Triumph is denoted with the hand open and raised above the head," instructed Herr Smith from among the dangling sandbags at stage right. "To express Entreaty you must stretch out the hands downward toward the knees. . . .") January's hopes for the opera were not high.

And, of course, whether it was bad or good, no one would want to see John Davis's production of it the following night.

Dance rehearsal continued in the rehearsal-room during the evening performance of *Brutus, or, Democracy Betray'd,* and did not end until past midnight. Cochon, Jacques, and the Valada brothers escorted January home through the rain, and if an invisible devil lurked with a knife anywhere on Rue des Ursulines—getting soaked, he hoped—he saw no sign of it.

Waking late the following morning, he found a note thrust under his door.

Signor Janvier,

I knocked but could not wake you. I cannot stay.
Yet I learned the truth about the plot. I go now to
find who Lorenzo's conspirator is. I beg you, follow
me to the place called La Cornouiller. I need your
help.

D'Isola

The house called La Cornouiller had been built forty
years previously, when more efficient refining and hardier
strains of cane had suddenly made it easier to get rich as a
sugar planter. Unable to afford the already prohibitive
price of land along the river, many English, Irish, and
Germans had tried their hand at planting sugar on the
banks of those few bayous large enough to support water-
craft, wherever the high ground was sufficiently wide to
lay out fields before it sloped into palmetto thickets, cypress swamp, and finally the flat, reedy wilderness of open
marsh.

In general these small plantations had not prospered.
When January had come through that part of the west
bank with the militia just prior to the Battle of Chalmette
in 1814, his impression of the little plantations along
Bayou des Familles had been one of shabby houses little
better than the cabins of slaves. Lately, he had heard that
many of these places had gone over to lumbering, cutting
the huge cypresses of the swamp and floating them down
to sawmills. Those that hadn't had largely sunk back into
being small poor farms, their cracker owners raising a little cotton and corn, or vegetables for the city market, with
a slave or two; living like patriarchs of old on the increase
of their herds of cattle and swine.

It was slave-stealer country. Captain Chamoflet, whose thin, dark face January recalled from the New Exchange, had connections even this far north of the great swampy maze of the Barataria marshes, as had Jean Lafitte before him. Trotting his rented horse from the ferry-landing at Point Algiers, January felt pricklingly conscious of the hush of those dark-green monotonous woods. He kept glancing around him, as if among the oaks and loblolly pines, the palmettos where the riverbank's cane-fields faded into the *cipriere,* invisible eyes watched him. Jean Lafitte had had a regular route up Bayou des Familles in the old days, transporting whole cargoes of pirated goods and selling them openly in town. When the Navy—and the British Royal Navy's anti-slave-trade crusade—had run Lafitte out of the Gulf in 1821, a constant small traffic in roguery persisted, slaves being stolen and sold to dealers who sold them in turn to the new territories to the north and west, or travelers robbed when the swift-falling tropical nights dropped on the marshlands. January had a spare copy of his freedom papers stuck in his boot—one of Hannibal's best forgeries, since the originals never left January's room—besides the usual copy he carried in his jacket pocket, and a completely illegal knife in his other boot, plus a pistol in his saddlebag. He'd sent messages to Hannibal, Olympe, and Rose, telling them where he was going and when he expected to be back, and had tried to find Shaw at the Cabildo, leaving a message for him when he could not.

And none of it would do him a particle of good, he thought, if Chamoflet and his gang should catch him.

And d'Isola had come out here alone.

Idiot! he thought for the hundredth time, leaning from the saddle to look at the sharp prints of the gig's wheels in the fresh mud. The man who ran the ferry remembered her well, had described her hesitant French

and her yellow sprig-muslin dress. A rented gig—
"Pinçon's livery, I seen that gig come acrost and back on
this ferry of mine a hundred times,"—and a dapple horse:
"Thunderbolt, old Pinçon call that horse, and anything
less like a thunderbolt you'd have to go far to find. Why,
three weeks ago this Boston feller—had one of them silly
beards they wear, with no mustache, looked like an ape,
he did—had German Sally with him, you know German
Sally? Runs the Green Lizard saloon on Gallatin Street,
but she'll get herself dressed up and her hair slicked and
you couldn't tell Sally from a lady at two paces, till you get
her likkered up. . . ."

I will box that silly girl's ears. Where had she been
raised, that she would drive out into the countryside
alone? *And dress rehearsal this evening, too,* he thought, trying to see more than a few yards into the dappled, silvery
stillness of the *cipriere.* Ahead of him he could glimpse the
too-bright-green of the upper end of Bayou des Familles,
like potage St.-Germain with duckweed; the glint of sunlight on the open tangle of second-growth where a plantation or farm had once lain. The clamshell road from Point
Algiers back to Bayou des Familles was in fairly good re-
pair, and the wet shells crunched under his gelding's
hooves as he nudged the animal to a trot again.

I learned the truth about the plot.

A note found in Belaggio's room? A conversation
overheard? In what language and with whom?

La Cornouiller. Named for the tree the locals called
Bois-de-Flèches. The old plantation's site on Bayou des
Familles, that link with the bandits of the Barataria, was
telling. It was hard to imagine even a rage-maddened operatic castrato trying to murder Marguerite to disrupt a performance: what operatic castrato wouldn't know how easily
dancing-mistresses were replaced? But from everything

January had heard about Captain Chamoflet, it was all too easy to believe that an order to dispose of someone had been given and executed without a moment's thought.

DAMN the girl. Would she have the sense to hide the gig?

Creole plantations were built pretty much to a plan. As narrow as the high ground was along this part of Bayou des Familles, there was really only one logical way to lay out buildings and fields. January came into view of the overgrown fields, the crumbling and dilapidated sugar-house, an hour or so past noon, and approached the place with caution, circling back through the fields and the *cipriere*. The house had been burned some ten years back—he remembered his mother telling him about the noisy and entangled lawsuit that still bound Jed Burton to the contending branches of his first wife's family—and he saw the tall brick foundation before him as he worked his way through the trees. Like most Creole houses, La Cornouiller had been built on a six-foot brick foundation, the ground-floor area used in some houses as storage, in others as dining-room and offices. January left the horse tied in the ruin of a slave-cabin, and hoped he'd find it when he returned.

The pistol and powder-flask he slipped into the pocket of his jacket.

He heard their voices, careless as the play-songs of children in the breathless silence.

"Niente," proclaimed the clear, strong tenor of Silvio Cavallo. "No tracks, no marks—nothing."

Damn it, thought January in irritation. *You might have told me you got Young Italy to accompany you, instead of bringing me out here into slave-stealer heaven.*

"But the note said this was to be their meeting-place," argued La d'Isola. "It said, 'Beneath the old house at La Cornouiller.' " She pronounced the French with difficulty, and gestured helplessly toward the ruin as January emerged around the corner of the old kitchen. The lovely soprano looked impossibly stylish, knee-deep in weeds among the puddles in the yard. Her straw-colored ruffles were the last thing anyone would choose to wear while hunting potentially murderous conspirators; her lace-trimmed bonnet was more in keeping with tea in the Ladies Parlor of the City Hotel. Silvio—and his inseparable companion Bruno Ponte—were likewise dressed for town, in checkered trousers, wasp-waisted coats, and a glory of varicolored waistcoats, as if just out for coffee at the Fatted Calf. They swung around as January came into sight, but La d'Isola cried "Signor Janvier!" and gathered up her skirts to run to him through the charred bricks and black timbers, stumbling in her thin satin slippers. "So good of you! I feared you would not come!" She smiled happily up at him. "On my way out of town I met with Silvio and Bruno, you understand, and they made it so much easier. . . ."

"You came horseback?"

Both young men nodded. "We were out riding ourselves upon the levee," explained Cavallo, which accounted for the dandified turnout.

"And I told them about the note," said d'Isola breathlessly. "The note I found slipped beneath Lorenzo's hotel-room door. It said, 'Thursday, beneath the house at La Cornouiller.' It is the plot, you see—the people he intends to meet! It must be they who tried to beat Lorenzo up! I asked the man at the hotel what the place was, and where. And here is the house. . . ."

The door into the brick ground floor stood open, a pitch-black maw like an idiot's yawn. A reasonable place to meet, thought January, studying the stout charred walls. To meet, or to hide something. He knelt to brush with a finger the long, fresh furrow that marked the threshold. The inner wood dry, against the gray damp of that around it. "You saw no one here? This is fresh."

They shook their heads. "We looked around in there for only a moment," said Ponte. "We had just two matches, you understand. . . ."

Of course d'Isola wouldn't have thought to pack candles. January fished in his jacket pockets for the candle-ends he habitually carried, and wondered if there was a lantern in the gig, and if it was worthwhile going to fetch it. He lit candles for himself and the men—La d'Isola had run a few steps to investigate the yellow blossoms of a late-blooming Christmas rose and was trying inexpertly to pluck one—and knelt again to study the gouge that continued from the threshold across the soft local brick of the floor and on into darkness. Something had been dragged inside. Something heavy with corners. The space beneath the house had been partitioned into several rooms, with black damp doorways gaping to the right and the left. The overwhelming, musty smell of moss and wet bricks enfolded January as he stepped inside.

A second tiny room had contained wine-racks, the wood charred and crumbled among the puddles of the floor. A third held a couple of broken oil-jars—everyone in Louisiana emptied the oil out of these and stored water in them—and one or two rat-chewed baskets.

The heavy box that had left the long twin scratches on the floor bricks stood in the middle of the third room, a rude crate weathered by long exposure, filled with bricks and dirt.

Even as Cavallo stepped forward and knelt to toss the debris out of the crate, January thought, *The wood of the crate is damp. And there were no wheel-ruts in the yard. No tracks pressed deep, as there would have been if someone had carried something this heavy. Which means . . .*

"*Che còsa!*" yelled Ponte from the darkness behind them, and at the same moment January heard the outer door slam.

He dodged through the arch again, across the second room, where Ponte was swinging around like a fly-stung bullock, threw himself toward the thin strip of brightness that marked the outer threshold. . . .

And as the door jarred ungivingly, with the clatter of a bolt outside, he heard d'Isola scream.

TWELVE

‹‹‹•›››

"Drusilla!" Candle-light jigged crazily over walls and ceiling-beams as Cavallo blundered through the inner archway. "Drusilla!"

January heaved on the door, and heard the heavy clatter of a lock outside. *"Ibn al-harâm,"* he said, one of Ayasha's favorite oaths.

Both tenors seized the door-handle, threw their weight against the planks, thrust and rattled and slammed while the single flame—still in Cavallo's hand—jerked reeling shadows against the greater dark beneath the house. Both continued to yell the soprano's name as they pounded until January shouted "Be quiet! Let me listen."

He pressed his ear to the door in the ensuing hush.

Nothing. No further screams or cries, no sound of struggle. Somewhere a crow squawked on the bayou.

Then a quick hush-hush-hush of voluminous skirts and slender ankles in long grass, and d'Isola's voice, close on the other side of the planks. "Silvio?"

That started Cavallo and Ponte again. "Drusilla! Drusilla, what happened? Are you all right?"

"I'm all right." She sounded breathless with running, and on the verge of tears. "There were men, three men . . ." More rattling at the door, and the heavy thump of a padlock before she said, "I tripped and broke the heel of my shoe, and my dress is all muddy. I think it may be completely spoilt. There's a lock here, two locks . . ."

January had already ascertained that as the door opened outward, the hinges were on the outside as well. He muttered, *"Ibn al-harâm,"* again, and felt in his pockets for another candle-stub. "Mamzelle, listen," he said over his two companions' energetic cursing at Belaggio. "What happened to the men you saw? Which way did they go?"

Long and panicky silence. Then, "I—I don't know, Signor. I screamed, and ran. . . ."

Then they might still be around.

But if that was the case, there was nothing to be done anyway, so he went on. "Mamzelle, one of those little buildings behind the house is going to be a carpenter's shop. Look around and see if you can find an ax or a chisel or a crowbar, even a screw-driver. . . ." He used the French word for it, *tournevis,* not knowing the Italian, and added—because almost certainly La d'Isola had never seen or heard of such a thing in her life, "It's like a slender chisel, a thin rod with one end flattened and a handle on the other. If you can, bring it. If not, take one of the horses and ride along the bayou until you come to a house. Tell them what happened and ask for help."

"I . . . I don't know how to ride a horse." Her voice snagged on a sob. "I can drive."

"Cara," said Cavallo, crowding close to January to speak. "When you get back to the gig, just put the bit back into the horse's mouth and slip the bridle back up around his head, all right?"

"That metal thing you took out when you tied him up? Will he bite me?"

I'LL bite you if you don't quit wasting time, thought

January, exasperated, though it was quite clear La d'Isola was terrified in a situation far beyond her abilities.

"See if you can find a tool to get us out, Signorina," he said instead.

"All right." Her voice was barely a whisper. "I will be quick."

"*Che culo,* you send her off alone?" Ponte's protest drowned the scampering swish-swish of skirts and weeds. "Those bandits may still be about. . . ."

"If they were about, they've had plenty of time to seize her while we were talking," January pointed out. "And they didn't." He sat on the brick floor, pulled up his trouser-leg, and unsheathed from his boot the skinning-knife that would have gotten him locked in the Cabildo overnight, had the City Guards seen him with such a weapon in his hand. "While we wait, let's see if whoever set this trap thought to search under the house for anything that might be used as a tool."

It quickly became apparent that if there had ever been anything in the various small store-rooms sharp enough to cut wood or strong enough to be used as a lever, it was gone now.

"A trap!" Cavallo smote his palm with his fist. "What fools we were! They have taken everything. . . ."

"Or the neighbors have." Ponte held up his candle high and poked behind the broken oil-jars piled in a corner. "In the *campagna* it is the same, Silvio. Whether it is the lion that dies or the jackal, the ants will pick the carcass. When you are very poor, the tiles off a dead man's roof are treasure. What makes you say it is a trap, Signor?"

"The fresh scratches," said January. "That box of rubble was dragged far enough from the outer door to make sure we were all in here. They must not have seen Mademoiselle d'Isola when they shut it. But it would be the easiest thing in the world to make certain she intercepted some kind of note that would bring her here."

"Austrian pigs," Cavallo gritted through his teeth, "to drag a young girl into this." He strode impetuously through the wine-room and into the chamber of the baskets and the oil-jars, and kicked the side of the box of debris.

"Austrians?" January followed, and knelt to examine the fragments of baskets. They'd been under a roof-leak and were soaked through. "Have you string in your pocket, Signor?"

"String?" Cavallo shook his head with a puzzled frown, and January cursed again. "If this were the work of Incantobelli," Cavallo went on, "or of Signor Davis— someone who simply wishes to disrupt the opera—he would have struck tomorrow. Today only the dress rehearsal is at stake. Attend, Signor." He and Ponte followed January back to the outer door.

"I think Signor Belaggio is being used by the Vienna government to carry messages to its agents in other countries. To do little jobs for them here and there. Nothing of any importance, you understand—"

"Even the Emperor isn't *that* stupid," put in Ponte.

"—but things that put him in touch with the Emperor's agents in Havana, and here."

"Here?" January took his powder-flask from his pocket and shook it. *Idiot,* he told himself. *You should have refilled it, either at Olympe's or in Rose's workshop at the Théâtre.*

Cavallo shrugged. "All of America to the west and south is torn apart now by the struggle for freedom from Spain. All the gold and silver of Mexico, all the coffee and gold and emeralds and sugar of New Grenada and Cuba and the lands to the south . . . You don't think Austria has her agents in those places, sniffing like sharks in the water for blood? The Bourbons of Spain and the Hapsburgs, they are brothers and bedfellows. You think Austria's going to have their paymaster *there*, where one army or another can overrun him before he can flee— What are you doing, Signor?"

He leaned curiously over January's shoulder as January wedged the powder-flask, as well as he could—it was a bulbous copper one and slipped from the bits of wood he was using—against the base of the door. "I'm hoping there's enough powder to at least weaken the timbers." January poured out a thin line of powder. "It's why I asked for string—to fix this up closer to the hinges, and so I wouldn't expend powder on making a fuse."

"Could you not pour the powder onto where the hinges would be?" Ponte nodded diffidently toward the solid slabs of oak. "With it on the floor like that, it cannot weaken the door much."

"Powder itself doesn't explode," said January. "It burns. It's the gases expanding that cause the explosion. The flask is small enough to concentrate the gases from the burning powder into a bomb, but it will most likely simply shoot backward into the room rather than blow up the door. That's what you were doing at the Fatted Calf Thursday night, then? Watching to see whom Belaggio met?"

Cavallo nodded. "It is imperative that we know who these men are."

"So you can tell your friends in Young Italy to beware of them?"

The tenor's dark eyes flicked sidelong at the dry note in January's voice.

January took the candle from his hand, stepped to the door again, and yelled through it, "Mamzelle! Stand clear! Stand well clear!" Then he set light to the powder trail, and he and the two young friends retreated into the farthest of the lightless rooms.

There was a shattering report, the crack of the flask striking the opposite wall, and a huge stink of powder. Coughing in the smoke, January led the way back to the first of the storage-rooms.

The thick planks of the door looked as if they'd been struck by a club, but as he'd feared it would, the force of the explosion had shot the flask back into the room like a bullet rather than expending much force on the door. January threw himself against the door: there was still no give in those solid planks.

"Damn it," he sighed. "We're going to have to do this the hard way."

"You do not approve of Young Italy?" asked Cavallo as January stripped off his jacket and went to break up the drier pieces of the wine-racks in the second room.

"Riots make me nervous," January said. "People who think the justice of their cause excuses the death of people who might or might not be guilty of any legal crime make me nervous."

"And what of the freedom of man?" returned Cavallo quietly. "My brother died in an Austrian prison, Signor; died of jail fever, after five years in a cell, without trial, merely because the Austrian Viceroy of Milan thought that he might be a Carbonaro. What became of his sweet-heart—a girl of the shops, a girl of the people, but honest— I still do not know. The Austrians were given Milan—and Venice, Piedmont, Sardinia—because they sided against Napoleon. To them we are a conquered people, to be taxed, and ruled, and spied upon by their secret police, as the Spanish ruled us before we were liberated."

"And your liberator Napoleon sold *my* country—the

land of my birth, where I had certain liberties as a man—
to the Americans, because he needed the cash," replied
January. "I lived in Paris under the Bourbons, Signor. Can
you tell me that even after the French took over, a man
couldn't be imprisoned without trial in Milan if he offended the wrong person? Couldn't be beaten up in the
streets without recourse? Can you tell me that poor men
are able to bring suit against rich ones in Naples, which
is an independent state, and still is what it was before
Napoleon came?"

Cavallo bit his lip, and January gathered his armload
of broken-up wood from the wine-racks and carried it
back to the outermost room. Cavallo and Ponte followed
him a moment later, each coatless and bearing as many
billets as he could. January had already heaped his burden
on the floor near the black burned smear the exploding
powder-flask had left, and was probing carefully down the
barrel of his pistol to extract the ball and what little powder remained.

"You are right, of course," said Cavallo as he added
his wood to the pile. "And no, I do not imagine that Italy
will be—an earthly paradise—if the Austrians go. Men
are only men."

He turned up his sleeves, and stacked the wood in
such a fashion that any spark kindled would have expired
immediately from suffocation. Ponte knelt beside him
and rearranged the sticks so they would actually burn.
"But suppose a man came to you and said, 'Be my slave,
and I promise you you will never go hungry. You will
never be without a warm place to sleep—I will let you
marry whom you please and raise your children as you
please, so long as they will be my slaves—well-fed and
happy slaves—as well.' What would you say?"

January grinned slowly. *"Viva la Patria,* I suppose."
He pulled off his shirt. "Do you have a flask in your
pocket, Signor?" he asked, going to sop his red-and-blue
calico in the nearest floor puddle. "Dribble the brandy
there, where the hinge will be on the outside of the door.
It's like Mount Vesuvius—we keep the fire where we need
it, and make sure the rest of the place doesn't catch and
cook us before the wood weakens."

Seeing what he was doing, the other two stripped
their shirts and did the same, wetting down the wood
around the place where they wanted the fire to concentrate. With luck, thought January, who'd seen the same
technique used in large when the sugar fields were burned
after harvest, there wouldn't be so much smoke that they'd
all suffocate.

"Keep the shirts ready." He went back to the puddle,
sopped the worn calico in it again. "I have no idea how
long this'll take." He touched the wick of the one remaining candle to the alcohol-soaked cypress of the door, then
to the piled wood beneath. Flame seared up with a strong
smell of burning brandy and powder. "And did Belaggio
meet with agents of Austria Thursday night?"

"He certainly met with someone," said Cavallo. "We
saw Marsan come, at about midnight. . . ."

"Well, we know what *he* was doing there."

Cavallo opened his mouth to snap a rebuke; then he
sighed. "Again you are right," he said. "But please do not
judge her harshly. Drusilla is the daughter of poor people,
almost a child of the streets. She has talent, but she obtained her training—well, in whatever fashion she could,
not having the choices that a girl of better means would
have. If she saw in Belaggio a way to come here to the
New World—to seek a better life—which of us would not

have done the same had we been young, and female, and in such circumstances? Life is not easy for a girl who has no family."

"No." January thought again of Dominique, and of Kate the Gouger standing in the mud and weeds behind the Eagle of Victory saloon, counting up the men she would have to bed. "No. I do not judge her for that."

Smoke was pouring from the wood of the door as the fire licked at the planks. January squeezed his wet shirt like a sponge around the area of the fire, coughing and turning his face aside from the smoke. The other two followed suit, keeping the fire contained, then retreated again to the next room, where they knelt in the doorway in the darkness, watching the progress of the blaze. It was quite clear by this time that La d'Isola had not located— or had failed to recognize—anything resembling a tool, and had gone to seek help.

"There were three others who came after Marsan," said Ponte. "Two big men, bearded, and then a third, who arrived in a cab."

"White men?"

"The bearded men, yes," replied the Sicilian. "Americans, I think. They dressed like Americans. The third one I did not see because I was across the street and the cab blocked my view."

"And he must have been white," said January, "because men of color are forbidden to ride in cabs. And this man came out . . . ?"

"I didn't see him come out, Signor. The outcry started. I ran to fetch Silvio. . . ."

"Whoever it was," said January, "he might have slipped past us in the melee. But I think it likelier he went down the alley and got out through the gate of the Promenade Hotel. I heard it open and slam."

"But there was someone," said Ponte. "To that I can swear."

"And you changed your clothes once you got there . . . ?"

"We saw all the world in the alley," said Cavallo. "That we did not expect. Our hotel is only across the street, but we had told La Montero that we were going back to our rooms, and she at least would guess we hadn't returned there if she saw us still dressed as we were at rehearsal. Madame Scie also, and perhaps Belaggio as well."

"You think this unlikely," added Ponte, tilting his head a little to regard January in the leaping yellow light. "But under the Austrians, men have been hanged on lesser suspicion."

The wood of the door was old, but it was close-grained cypress, and burned slowly. Twice more the three men soaked their shirts and wet down the wood around the blaze. There was nothing to use as kindling to re-start a second blaze were this one quenched. If the men d'Isola had seen were still around, the smoke would draw them.

So at least they won't be lying in wait for us when we emerge.

Odd.

Did they just lock us in here like children locking play-mates in an armoire?

He retreated again, coughing. He'd already guessed they'd miss the dress rehearsal. It was surely well after four. One thin needle of searing light sliced between the massive planks of the floorboards in the third room, its angle marking the lateness of the hour. When another forty minutes or so had passed, he signed to the others, and they raked away the remains of the kindling-fire and beat out the flames. It took the three of them several exhausting minutes, but they finally battered their way through the weakened timbers, twisted the lower hinge free, and crawled forth.

As January had suspected, the hasp and padlock on the door were new. The screws that held it, new, too.

They'd been expected.

This was no spur-of-the-moment lockup, but a deliberate trap, set up well in advance.

For d'Isola? For Cavallo?

For me?

For Belaggio, maybe?

"She should have reached a house long ago, surely?" Cavallo gazed like a young eagle around the wasted fields, the dark line of cypress and the bayou beyond. "We passed several on our way here. She had but to follow the water. She could not have gotten lost."

January kept to himself his reflection on what might have happened to a dusky-skinned young woman, alone in this wilderness of swamp and woodland, and almost certainly on foot. The empty yard, scattered with charred beams, with broken bits of boxes and oil-jars in the sicklied light, seemed filled with sinister silence save for the leathery creak of a tree-branch, like a hinge in the wind.

He said only, "Let's see if we can find her tracks."

All the horses were gone, including the stocking-footed bay gelding January had ridden. The scuff-marks in the dust and weeds of the yard were too unclear, in the failing light, to make out whether d'Isola had taken one of them. Certainly someone had unharnessed the gig. Though there were marks of some kind in the direction of the bayou, it was impossible, in the carpet of elephant-ear and last year's brown oak-leaves, to make out the shape of the foot or whether it was a man's or a woman's, or which way they led.

January cursed. Leatherstocking never had this problem. But then, judging by what he'd read of Cooper's continuing epic, Leatherstocking could evidently see in the dark as well. January wondered if Abishag Shaw had the same abilities.

"I think the best thing we can do," he said, rising from the soft muck of shell and mud at the water's brim, "is to start back to town. I told half a dozen people where I was going this morning. When all four of us fail to appear at rehearsal, they'll send out a search party. With luck we'll meet them on the way to Point Algiers, and we'll be in a better position to look for Drusilla then. Agreed?"

Ponte nodded, but Cavallo strenuously resisted the idea of abandoning their friend in an unknown countryside and growing darkness—darkness that was considerably further advanced by the time January convinced him that the three of them would have far less hope of success if they simply started wandering the *cipriere,* looking for her. With Cavallo's objections, Ponte reversed himself and refused to leave; and when they finally set off, it was nearly full night, and all three were ravenously hungry and thirsty. Both of the house's great wooden cisterns had burned at the time of the original fire.

"According to my mother, the Doughertys and the Burtons are still fighting over the land in the courts," said January, leading the way along the verge of the bayou. "Not that it's worth a great deal—not like land along the river." He glanced back at the blackened ruin disappearing between the trees. "If the families don't get their differences settled soon, it won't be worth the labor it'll cost to bring the place back at all."

"How came they to build it all in the first place," asked Cavallo, "if it was not worth the labor?" He waved irritably at the cloud of gnats that rose around them, ample evidence that the modest levee along the bayou had crevassed in half a dozen places during the years of neglect. January breathed a silent prayer of thanks that it was winter and mosquitoes were few. In summer the place would be unendurable.

"This was all built in the nineties." January skirted a soggy pot-hole, boots crunching on shell—an Indian mound, where once a campsite had stood. Oaks crowned it, and crumbling platforms of brick marked the tombs of the Dougherty family, eroding as this wet land eroded everything in time.

"You could still bring slaves in from Africa then. You could buy a man for three hundred dollars and you didn't care if he died of overwork in two years. You can't do that now." As always, leaving New Orleans and going into the countryside brought him back to his childhood, to the smell of dew-soaked earth and the stink of the cabins, the wailing songs of the men in the fields and the moan of the conch-shell in the dusk. Pain and a deep, sad beauty beyond any words he'd ever known.

"There are men in my village," said Bruno Ponte quietly, "who would sell themselves gladly for three hundred dollars, if they could but find a buyer. This is good land here."

Thin as a nail-paring, the day-moon had slipped away below the trees; as if night had crouched waiting under the trees, the shadows crept forth across the bayou's velvet green waters. A few early frogs peeped, then were still.

Hannibal would surely go to Shaw with word that none of them had been at rehearsal. Or, if Hannibal were unable to leave the battered mattress where he slept in the attic of Kentucky Williams's place, Belaggio would. And Shaw had his note.

It would only be a matter of time.

But what had happened to Drusilla, wandering alone about this countryside in darkness. . . .

"Who-all's that?"

Torchflame and lanterns. Cavallo strode forward, arms outflung, crying *"Molte bene!"* even as January yelled, "Wait . . . !"

"You hold still there!" rasped a nasal American voice, and, when Cavallo didn't stop, added, "Hold up or I'll shoot!" And above the jangle of bridle-bits, the creak of leather in the shadows, January heard the clack of a gunlock.

"Alt!" he shouted, heart sinking like a stone. *"Silvio, no!"* And, in English, "Don't shoot, sirs!" He had to brace himself, first against his impulse to plunge off the road and into the shelter of the swamp, and second against the overwhelming urge to slap Cavallo for pushing ahead so blithely. *Please, God, not Captain Chamoflet and his slave-stealers . . .* "We've had our horses stolen. . . ."

"Well, have you just?" Torches were raised. The silhouettes of slouch hats and horses' ears changed into a gold-and-black mosaic of faces and beasts. The hot light winked on bridle-buckles, on round, shining equine eyes; made dull red slivers along rifle-barrels. The lead rider spit, and nudged his mount forward, the tobacco-stink sweetish-foul on the damp dirt. A tangle of black beard showed under a decrepit hat-brim, and a long, dirty coat hung down over the horse's rump like a rude caparison. "Let's just see some papers on you boys."

January fished one set of his papers from his jacket pocket, watching as he did so the rider's face in the inverted light. *Patrol.* There were a few fat, fair Celtic countenances in the band, which never belonged to swampmen. That didn't mean some of the men weren't smugglers on their nights off, he reminded himself, glancing inconspicuously at the trees and calculating his chances of headlong and immediate flight.

These weren't promising. Three riders moved their horses around to circle them, rifles cradled with careless deftness in the crooks of their arms. The captain bent from the saddle to hand the papers back, and held out his hand to Cavallo.

"We are at Cornouiller," explained Cavallo in his careful English. "My friends and I, and a young lady name Drusilla d'Isola—"

"I don't care if you was picnickin' on Andrew Jackson's front lawn with the Queen of Spain," said the captain. "Let's see some papers, boy."

January thought, *Shit.* "Sir," he said, "please allow me to introduce Signor Silvio Cavallo of Milan, and Bruno Ponte of Naples. They are Italians, engaged to meet Mr. Burton at Cornouiller to—"

"Eye-talians, hunh?" The captain stepped down from his horse, flipping a pistol into his hand as he did so like a magician producing an egg from thin air, and reached to take the lantern from the rider beside him. He held the beam on Cavallo's face, then shifted it to Ponte, who had sprung to his friend's side at the first hint of danger. January saw the mud-streaked, soot-grimed clothing, the swart complexions and close-curled dark hair, and felt his heart plummet. "That's one I ain't heard before, anyways. And I do got to say, you boys sure look like high-yellas to me."

"Ol' Man Ulloa over to Bayou Go-to-Hell had a high-yella boy who'd do that, Mr. Pickney," provided the beardless—and chinless—stripling who'd handed the captain his lantern. "Go on into town tellin' ever'one he's a Eye-talian, and not no nigger at all."

"That so?" Captain Pickney cocked a speculative brown eye back at Cavallo.

"What is it?" demanded the tenor, disconcerted at the lack of response. He fell back a step to January. "What is happening? Who are these men?"

Ponte flung a quick glance toward the woods, and January guessed that had he been alone—or had he been only with January—he'd have run for it. As it was, he moved protectively to his friend's side. Not understanding, maybe, what was going on, but knowing that something was.

"They think you're a slave, an octoroon." January berated himself for not having gone to the Swamp to look for Hannibal before leaving town. Annoyed as he'd been at Madame Montero's rescue the night before last, he knew if an indisputably white man were with them now, they would not be having this trouble.

The custom of the country.

"Perché?" Cavallo turned back to Pickney, horrified bafflement on his face. "Do I look like a Negro? Look-a me . . . do I . . . uh . . ." He fished in his subjunctiveless English vocabulary.

"Silvio, leave it," cautioned Ponte softly.

"Any you boys speak French?" Pickney turned to canvass the posse at large. Though most of the wealthy planters in any given parish were likely to be French, or at least to have learned to speak the language enough to communicate with those who held the majority of wealth and land in the district, once you got away from the choice land on the river, it was a matter of chance who you'd be able to talk to. The men who rode patrol were largely drawn from the smaller farmers, the crackers who tilled—or had a slave or two till—the marshy and less-valuable acres of cotton and corn. Forty miles to the southwest, on the other side of the Bayou des Allemands, there would have been no question—in fact they'd have been hard-put to find a member of the posse who spoke English. But in this part of Jefferson Parish there were as many crackers descended from Welsh and Scots-Irish as there were from the old Acadian stock.

"Vigaud's daughter gettin' married," provided another rider, a heavy-featured man with a dirty red waistcoat under his trailing surtout coat. "That's where him and Clopard and the Nain brothers went. Prob'ly most of the rest of the Frenchies around here, too."

"Well, shit." Pickney chewed for a moment in silence. "And Marsan's up in town."

"His wife might still be at Roseaux." The fat man pronounced it *"Rose-*oh." "He got a li'l gal up in town, so he don't take her nor Miss Jocelyn up more'n he has to."

Pickney sniffed. "You'd think those gals'd have more sense, given what he done to the last one. Well, if'n they ain't there, somebody'll have to ride on up to town, find out what's happenin'. Meantime"—he turned back to January, hefted the pistol that had never at any time been pointed anywhere but at his heart—"looks like the three of you is gonna spend the night in my barn."

THIRTEEN

———⟨∞⟩———

"This is an outrage!" Cavallo stormed as No Chin and Red Waistcoat thrust him and his companions at gunpoint into the farthest stall of Mr. Pickney's barn. "A barbarity!"

"So it is," said January. He wondered if the young man meant the fact that he, a white man, had been mistaken for and treated like a black one, or that anyone had the legal right to treat anyone like this at all.

"This is the United States!" the Milanese went on passionately, falling into French, since none of the Americans was listening anyway. "The land of Washington, of Jefferson! The land that showed all the world the upward road to freedom!"

"Get your boots off, boys." Pickney tossed a length of chain up over one of the low rafters and held out the stout curved shackles attached to either end.

At least, thought January, the stall they were being put into had been mucked out after its last tenancy. That was something. And if the barn was ramshackle in the extreme, like most buildings erected by that semi-indigent, semi-barbaric class of small farmers known as crackers, at least there *was* a barn. Many crackers let their horses and mules make do with rude pens and, at most, unwalled shelters, like the cattle and swine that lived at large in the woods. Pickney's house, dimly glimpsed across the gloom of a dung-littered dooryard, differed from the average slave-cabin only in size, and that not by much. The whole place reeked of woodsmoke and pigs.

Under cover of Cavallo's indignation *("... inspiration for the world of free men, debased by such as you. ...")* January promptly sat on the dirt floor with his back to the single lantern's dim light, slipped the skinning-knife from his boot, and thrust it under the stacks of dirty hay stored in the stall. His skin prickled at the thought of surrendering his last possibility of flight, but to resist, he knew, would have gotten him anything from a beating to a bullet in the back.

Patience, Don Quixote had said, *and shuffle the cards.*

"Rufe!" Pickney shoved the cross-bar of the shackle into place and locked it, thrust a finger in the space behind January's tendon to make sure there was no way he could slip his foot clear. At his call, a small, middle-aged man in the worn osnaburg clothing of a slave appeared from the shadows. "Get these boys a couple blankets and some pone. You." He looked back at Cavallo. "Boots off."

"You go to hell!"

The pistol came up. Ponte moved to throw himself between them and January said in Italian, "Do it, Silvio."

"I will not be chained like a dog. . . ."

"Do it!"

Red Waistcoat started forward and Pickney got to his feet, flipping his pistol around in his hand, club-wise. Neither seemed angry, only resigned to a tedious annoyance.

"What are they going to do?" demanded Cavallo, falling back a step. "Shoot me? Eh?"

"They're going to beat the tar out of you for being uppity," January told him. "Now get your boots off."

Cavallo sat. "This place stinks," he said, pulling his boots off. "You tell this farmer that his barn stinks like a sewer."

"Yeah, I'll tell him that." January watched as Cavallo's ankles were chained. "Mr. Pickney, sir," he said as the farmer stood again. When he spoke, January could see his breath in the lantern-light. "Would you be riding out on patrol again after you leave us here? I ask because there was another member of our party, a young Italian woman, who became separated from us, and who is almost certainly lost in the woods." He spoke his best English—far better than Pickney's, in fact—well aware that for both the French and the Americans, educated speech often proved more telling than freedom papers in establishing one as a free man.

"She speaks no English," he went on, "and very little French. Like Signor Cavallo, she might very easily be taken for a woman of color."

Pickney regarded him steadily for a moment, almost visibly checking behind the words themselves for a plan or ploy, as he would have checked behind a curtain at the sight of a suspicious movement. Then he nodded. "I'll keep a eye out." And spit into the hay. Bruno, whom the chinless youth had chained to the upright at the end of the stall, had said hardly a word through the whole encounter, only watched the guns, and the faces of the men, with the same animal readiness in his dark eyes as he'd had when he watched Shaw.

A peasant, when all was said and done, thought January, taking the word as a definition rather than an insult. A *paysan*. Raised in a world that was far closer to the twelfth century than to the nineteenth. And ready to die, with casual ferocity, for the sake of his friend.

Yellow light lurched drunkenly over the rafters as Red

Waistcoat picked up the lantern, shadows bellying forward to swallow all in blackness. The barn door shut. Cold mist flowed between the warped and shrunken boards of the walls.

"Why the hell did you tell him that?" Cavallo's comprehension of English wasn't good, but he evidently understood "a young Italian woman," and "woods." Hay scrunched and the chain between January's feet jerked as the tenor shifted his seat. "Now they'll be looking for her as well."

"She'll be safer, believe me, if the men think there's a chance she's a European lady instead of a runaway octoroon girl." A mule stamped and snuffled in the darkness. Near-by a savage rustle sounded in the straw, and a rat squeaked in pain. "I only hope if she runs into someone, it will be the patrols and not smugglers from the Barataria."

"And this—this barbarity! To mistake us for Negroes— to treat us in this fashion! Is this a commonplace in this fine country of yours?"

"For black men it is."

"And do you think," said Bruno's soft voice, "that the treatment a *contadino* receives in Sicily at the hands of the *padroni* is any different? There is a great deal of injustice in the world, Signor Janvier. My father was killed when I was fifteen, for striking the man who raped my sister— not just shaming her once, but upon a dozen occasions, whenever he would meet her in the fields or the woods. He was the son of the local lord. His father had my father shot by one of his shepherds. There were no charges brought."

Metal clinked in the raw blackness. "One day I will go back to Sicily and kill Don Remigio, and his son, but then I will die as well. The law lies in the hands of such as they. This is what the *risorgimento* is, Signor. This is what Young Italy is. Not just to cast out the stupid German-heads. Not just to avenge ourselves on the rich. When Italy is one country, and not a dozen little lands, then the lords of those little lands will have someone big who can say to them, *These things you will not do.* Until that time, the wretched of the earth will wear chains as surely as you and I and Silvio wear them tonight."

Slits of yellow light bobbed in the darkness. January heard a man whistling an old song his father used to sing, about the rabbit in the brier, and then the stable-door creaked. "Hello the shop!" called out a husky voice, marred with the telltale roughness of the early stages of consumption, and the slave Rufe appeared around the end of the stall. He had a couple of ragged blankets thrown over one shoulder and a basket in his hand.

"Mr. Pickney really going to get M'am Marsan to come over in the morning?" asked January as the slave hung his lantern on a nail and dropped the blankets to the hay.

"Oh, sure. Don't you worry about that." Actually, a certain number of January's apprehensions had abated with just a look at Rufe in better light. Though a little thin, the man had clearly not been starved or beaten. Nor did he have the hangdog look of one who lives in fear, something that told January at least a few reassuring things about his captor's honesty and intentions. "Last month the patrol catched a woman said she was bound south to meet her husband in New Iberia; said a man up by Big Temple Mound took her freedom papers. Mr. Pickney, he rode all the way up to town, made sure she was who she said she was and that she was free. Though she had to get new papers in town, of course. But he honest, Mr. Pickney."

He set down the basket in front of Cavallo, and with it a big gourd of water. January noticed the man never got within arm-reach of any of the three prisoners. It wasn't the first time by a long chalk, January reflected, that Pickney's Rufe had played jailer.

"Your friends really Eye-talians?" He regarded them curiously. Covered with filth and soot, they could have been anything from bedouins to Chickasaws.

"That they are," said January. "As is the young lady I spoke of to Mr. Pickney—"

"*Cacchio!*" Cavallo, who had drawn the basket to him, sat back with a pone of ash-bread in one hand, a handful of ground-nuts in the other, and a look of disgust on his handsome face. "This is what they give their slaves to live on in this country? Unrisen bread and—what? Pig-food?"

"Ground-nuts." January hunkered beside him, showed him how to break the thin husk and shake out the kernels of meat. "Pea-nuts—*Arachis hypogaea,* and yes, they are used as fodder for pigs, which means they're perfectly edible for human beings. They don't take much looking after, and you can live on them for weeks if you have to—one bush will yield pounds of the things." He popped two into his mouth and Cavallo bit cautiously on one. Rufe laughed at his expression.

"All right," he said, throwing up his hands. "You got me convinced. I never met a nigger yet, no matter how bright, that didn't know what a goober was. They's Italians all right.

"Which is a good thing," he added, "considerin' some of the folk that come to see Mr. Marsan when the moon's dark like tonight, an' the tide's in."

January's glance cut sharply to him, hearing in his voice the stealthy echo of rowlocks in the bayou that led back to the heart of the Barataria country, and the mutter of bargains struck in darkness for human cargo run in from Africa or Cuba in defiance of the law. Shaw had spoken truly when he'd said that as long as the sale of slaves was legal, and the ownership of one man by another was countenanced in any form in the United States, there would be men who'd buy human cattle cheap and bring them in, to charge what the hungry market would bear.

Belaggio had made this delightful discovery: the men, and woman, he'd purchased for three hundred dollars apiece in Havana were salable in New Orleans for four or five times that much. How great a percentage of Belaggio's profit had Marsan charged, January wondered, to act as go-between?

"You mean Captain Chamoflet?" he asked, and Rufe shook his head.

"Ask me no questions an' I tells you no lies. An' believe me, friend, in this part of the country, that's the best advice you'll ever hear."

"You might tell Mr. Pickney," said January carefully, "and anyone else who might need to know it, that in case Madame Marsan isn't at Roseaux, my family in town— and Mr. Belaggio that's the head of the opera company these two gentlemen are in—know we were in this part of the country today and will be looking for us. Or in case Madame Marsan turns out not to speak Italian after all." He stood up as he spoke, his gaze meeting that of the slave, and he saw in those bright, intelligent eyes the understanding of what wasn't asked:

Am I safe?

Is your master to be trusted, with every man in the parish in on smuggling slaves or blood-related to folks who kidnap those they find roving free?

Are YOU to be trusted? Or do you get a percentage for

easing captives' fears with promises that everything will be all right?

Ask me no questions. . . .

Rufe's smile broadened a little, rueful and bemused. "Well, I don't know about M'am Marsan herself," he said, ducking his head. "But Dinah that's housemaid over to Roseaux is the daughter of the cook at Mr. Clopard's place down the bayou, an' *she* says they got a white governess to teach Miss Jocelyn Italian, a little bit anyway, like ladies are supposed to know. So you should be all right."

January spent the remainder of the night trying to plot an escape without knowing how many smugglers he'd have to fight in total blackness, how well they'd be armed, and where exactly Pickney's shabby farm lay in relation to Bayou des Familles. It was a futile exercise and he knew it, but it kept his mind off the lice in the blankets and Cavallo's indignant harangue about leaving La d'Isola to her own devices—*Does he think we'd have stumbled across her by plunging into the woods at random instead of following the bayou back to the river?*—and about what they would or could do to return to New Orleans in time for *La Muette de Portici* the following night.

"This whole affair might well be that whore Montero's doing!" stormed the tenor at one point, yanking on the chain that snaked up over the rafter so that it jerked on January's ankles. "I would not put it past her! It makes more sense than the Austrians locking us up and then doing nothing to us. It is no difficult thing for *her* to hire men to wait here for us, to slip a paper under Belaggio's door for poor Drusilla to find. Montero would do anything to return to center stage—and to that Austrian lickspittle's bed!"

Except, thought January, for the fact that Montero

wouldn't have put the blood in the desk-drawer if she was making arrangements with old Queen Régine to have La d'Isola puking her guts out two hours before the performance.

In his mind he saw again Olympe's strong black hands sorting through the withered little bunches of pennyroyal and St. John's wort, tobacco and mouse-bones, and heard her voice, deep and smoky like their mother's: *Had she enemies of her own? Just 'cause you keep soap in the kitchen doesn't make it food.*

And there was something, he thought suddenly, that didn't fit. That wasn't right. His mind grasped at the mists of half-perceived connections. . . . Something about the poisoning . . .

Something Cavallo had said? Pickney? Someone . . .

"But what of Signora Scie, and Belaggio?" Bruno asked in his quiet voice. "And they waited for you, too, you say, Signor Janvier, in the dark."

He propped himself up on one elbow in the blanket he had spread for himself and his friend: a difference from Americans, January reflected, who would each have appropriated one of the ragged coverings and left the black member of the party to make do with shivering in the hay. "It was to be expected that Drusilla would call on you for help, for you know the countryside. It was only chance that she encountered us on her way out of town. They might have seen us and thought, *Che culo! Now we must kill three men rather than one,* and thought better of it."

"Why would they think that?" demanded Cavallo. "We are alone. They are Austrians. Dead men tell no tales."

The chorus-boy shrugged, and with a peasant's matter-of-fact practicality scooped hay over to cover the two of them like an extra blanket, something January had already done for himself. "If Belaggio is one of them, perhaps he didn't want to have to find someone to sing Masaniello at the last minute."

"Well, if Madame Marsan has gone into town already for the opera," said January in a dry voice, "that's what he's going to have to do."

This led to heated speculation about how well Orlando Partinico—Cavallo's cover for the role—would sing, and just where and how Madame Montero would have found bravos willing to lie in wait for her rival. Just as if, thought January wearily, they did not all stand in danger of losing their liberty and perhaps their lives the following morning. But oddly enough the argument—and its subsequent tangent about the necessity for Italian unification and the formation and composition of a legislature along American lines—proved a distraction from his own fears. On those few occasions on which he did fall asleep, January dreamed he was a supernumerary on-stage in an interminable opera consisting entirely of *récitatif.*

It was nearly noon before the creak of carriage-springs and the slurp of hooves in the muddy yard announced the arrival of Madame Marsan. January and, perforce, Cavallo—the chain over the rafter was barely long enough for both men to stand side by side—went to the outer wall of their stall and peered through the gaping cracks to the misty sunlight of the yard, where a coachman was just climbing down from the box of a plain, scratched, and much-mended green landaulet.

Having seen the smart black phaeton Marsan drove in town, with its matched white team and sparkling brass, January felt a sort of shock of distaste. Not only the carriage was old. The horses, a black and a roan, were both decrepit and thin, and the roan's knees were scarred. Not an animal a dandified seeker after perfection like Marsan would have tolerated in his stables. Certainly the dress worn by the woman Pickney helped down was as unfashionable as the carriage, and as frequently repaired, reminding January of the slightly outdated frocks she and her daughter had worn to the opera. As he watched her with the cracker, he could see fear of men in her rigid stance and the unconscious distance she kept from him, in the way she held her gloved hands folded tight before her breast. Like Rose, when first he'd met her. Wary as a fox scenting a trap.

She glanced in the direction of the barn when Pickney gestured and hesitated, as if she feared Pickney had sent for her only to lure her into that building and ravish her.

She signed to the footman standing on the carriage's rear, an enormous man whose shaven head and massive shoulders were vaguely familiar to January. When he got down, the carriage rocking with his weight, and followed her and Pickney across to the barn, January recognized the rolling stride, the springy animal crouch.

It was the fighter Big Lou.

". . . says they's Italians," Pickney was explaining as they approached. "But I seen octoroons lighter'n them, an' it's best to be sure. I am sorry if I kept you from startin' for town. . . ."

"It is quite all right," Madame Marsan replied in her uncertain English. Her bonnet was old, too, of a wide-brimmed, flat style January hadn't seen in years. It threw a kind of pale shade on her thin face, like a veil that did not obscure the anxiety in her dark eyes. "But you understand I must not stay. My husband expects me. . . ." She didn't turn her head, but January saw in her stance her awareness of Big Lou looming a pace behind her.

"We drives fast, we makes it by four, m'am." There was a kind of careless sullenness in the big man's curiously soft, high voice. "But best we drives fast. You know how Michie Vincent don't like to be kept waitin'."

The woman stiffened, though her slight, noncommittal half-smile didn't alter. "Still," she said, "one cannot refuse to help men in trouble."

"Sounds like they got theirselves in their own trouble, m'am." His words came out as a kind of crumbly mumble, as if no one had ever spoken much to him as a child, or expected words from him in return. "What I wants to know is, what'd a couple of Italians an' a nigger be doin' wanderin' around the old Dougherty place that time of night anyways?"

The open door flung a wan glare into the barn. Madame Marsan hastened forward, wobbling on her iron pattens in the muck. She was, January realized, actually a very pretty woman, dark and slim like an expensive greyhound. But long years of desperate invisibility had told on her, bleached her of anything that might trigger her gorgeous husband's volatile wrath.

Cavallo and January, each guiding his end of the chain with a hand, came together along the path of the beam to the stall's end as Bruno got to his feet and bowed.

"Bellissima madama." Cavallo bent over her hand. "Do you speak Italian? How can I convince you that I am who I say I am—Silvio Cavallo of Milan. . . ."

"Good heavens!" Madame Marsan's free hand flew to her lips. "Oh, my dear sir . . . You're the music master! From the opera Tuesday, the silly music master with the curled wig!"

Cavallo bowed again, still more deeply, kissing the gloved hand again. *"Bellissima madama,* my thanks. My eternal thanks."

She turned to Bruno and asked in careful Italian, "And you are also one of the singers?"

"I am, *bella madonna.*" The young Sicilian likewise saluted her hand. "Bruno Ponte, of the chorus, now and forever at your service and in your debt. And this man is Signor Janvier, of the orchestra, who was good enough to come after us and Signorina d'Isola when we needed guidance and help."

"But I am not Italian," said January gravely in French. For one instant the woman's dark eyes sparkled appreciatively—then wiped themselves clean of humor almost by reflex, as if even in his absence her husband would disapprove if she laughed. January wondered if Big Lou carried tales.

"Monsieur Pickney, these men are—are indeed who they say they are." She turned back to the captain of the patrol with a stiff diffidence, bracing herself slightly, as if she expected anger, a curse or a blow.

And when Pickney immediately replied, "That's good to know, m'am, an' I thank you for troublin' yourself to come here," January saw how the woman's shoulders relaxed. She had learned never to disagree with, or disappoint, a man.

"Best we be goin', m'am," mumbled Big Lou as Pickney knelt to unlock the shackle from January's ankles. "I makes it noon now, an' you know how Michie Vincent gits. . . ."

"Yes," she said quickly, "yes, of course. I hope Mademoiselle Jocelyn has finished the packing and is ready—"

"Anybody to home?"

Big Lou spun, ready as an animal to respond to a threat as a gawky form ambled into the square of the open door's light. At the fighter's reaction, Abishag Shaw stepped back, neatly and unobtrusively, into safer distance: for one instant January was aware of each gauging the other. Then each relaxed just slightly, and Shaw came into the shadows of the barn. "Well, here's where you got to, Maestro!" He pulled his hat off at the sight of Madame Marsan, but went on. "You never heard such a catawumptious conniption, with Belaggio an' yore pal Sefton an' it seemed like beat-all ever'body comin' into the Cabildo durin' the evenin' sayin' as how the four of you been murdered...."

"The *four* of us?" January sat to pull on his boots again, making a play of searching for something among the tousled blankets to cover surreptitiously scooping his knife into his pocket. "Mademoiselle d'Isola didn't return?"

"She ain't with you?" The rain-colored eyes narrowed and cut sidelong to Pickney's face. "Young Italian gal about twenty, wearin' a yeller dress an' white sash? My name's Shaw, by the way, Abishag Shaw of the New Orleans City Guards...."

"Sam Pickney." The white men shook hands. "Mr. January here told us there was a young lady missin'...."

"M'am," interposed Big Lou again, and there was a meaningful edge to his words. "Best we be goin', or Michie Vincent gonna be mad."

"Yes," said Madame Marsan hastily. "Certainly. Monsieur Pickney, if you'll excuse me, I must return and get my daughter so that we ..."

"M'am Marsan?" Shaw put his hat against his chest, looked down at the drab figure before him. "M'am Belle Marsan?"

"This here M'am Marsan." Big Lou interposed himself between the woman and Shaw, watchful contempt in eyes like small black beads. Like his French, his English was slurred and crumpled, and there was neither fear nor diffidence in his voice. He was sure of his ground and apparently feared no white man's retaliation. "Michie Vincent told me bring her on safe into town."

Told you to keep Americans from her, too, thought January, observing the tilt of the scarred bullet head, the compacting of the breast and belly muscles beneath the neat muslin shirt, the blue fustian coat. Instinctively readying himself to lash out.

Shaw met the big man's eyes. "They's time," he said in English. After a long moment Big Lou dropped his gaze—far longer than any white man would have expected a black one to hold his eyes—and Shaw shifted his glance back to the woman. In execrable French he went on. "At Roseaux they told me as how you was comin' here," and a beat of silence followed the words, like the small deadly breath of wind that precedes the driving storm-rains. "Best you have a seat, m'am."

She pulled her hand from Shaw's—and Pickney's—attempts to guide her to the nearest seat, which was in fact the top of a firkin outside the barn door. January could see in Pickney's eyes, and Rufe's, what he himself knew: *Best you have a seat, m'am* always translated to *I have bad news for you. The worst of bad news.* She stiffened like a child bracing for a whipping. "Tell me."

Shaw folded his big hands before him, respecting her choice of time and place. "Vincent Marsan was found dead early this mornin'," he said. "In the alley beside the American Theater."

FOURTEEN

─────◦◦◦─────

January recognized the plantation of Les Roseaux immediately as one he'd visited on the same scouting mission in 1814 that had taken him to Cornouiller. On seeing the place from the back of Sam Pickney's light wagon, however, he felt the same jolt of distaste he'd experienced at the sight of the carriage itself. Marsan's finicking wardrobe, his mistress, and his lavish town equipage had all given January the unconscious expectation that at Les Roseaux he would see reflected the same prosperity.

Instead, he saw fields nearly as overgrown and neglected as those at La Cornouiller, run-down slave-cabins, a house in need of paint and patching. In all things, not just in women, Marsan was a man who would not share. He'd rather match his sapphire cuff-buttons than pay for a new dress for his wife. Even the sawmill, ostensibly the source of the plantation's profits, had a dilapidated air. Only a few dozen cypress trunks lay outside it, and the piles of lumber stacked behind it were small.

"Far's we can tell," said Shaw quietly in French as much to include Cavallo as to exclude Rufe on the driver's seat, "Marsan died sometime between midnight—which is when the last wagon came through that alley to the Promenade Hotel—and six, when the first couple horses went out." He glanced ahead of them at the landaulet, but satisfied himself that there was no chance that Madame Marsan could possibly overhear. She sat like a wooden thing in the middle of its seat, tearlessly telling over her rosary with fingers that shook.

Nevertheless he edged his bony chestnut horse closer to the wagon—Big Lou had expressed the same sentiments about free colored riding in Michie Vincent's carriage that the cabmen of New Orleans did—and kept his voice low. "Nobody heard nuthin', nor saw nuthin' from the street, an' maskers goin' back an' forth along Camp Street most of the night. He was carved up bad. Face, chest, belly . . ."

"Hands?" asked January, and one of Shaw's pale brows tilted.

"No," he said. "No, he didn't fight. He took one deep stab straight under the left shoulder-blade from behind, then all the rest in the front, like as if he'd fallen down an' the man what did it knelt on top of him an' cut. Somebody wanted to make damn sure Belaggio was dead this time."

"Or somebody was damn mad."

"If somebody was damn mad, he was damn careless, too." Shaw turned his head aside and spit. "If'n you're gonna kill somebody like that, you should at least take the trouble to make sure of your man."

In his mind, January saw the two men together, framed in the lion-gold curtains of the Trulove ballroom. Saw how both towered over the cowering girl, almost obscuring her from sight. Of course an attacker would mistake the one for the other.

"Maybe he thought he had." January remembered also the note that drew La d'Isola to this half-deserted countryside, d'Isola, who would naturally have been with

Belaggio at that hour. After her unexplained absence from the dress rehearsal that afternoon, her name might have been enough to ensure Belaggio's appearance at the theater after midnight. "What does Belaggio say?"

"Not much," said the policeman. "Looked sick as a cat when I talked to him this mornin', jumpin' whenever one of them fireworks went off in the back. Say, they really gonna have a volcano erupt on-stage?"

"Such is the intention," said January. "I feel certain that even if Mademoiselle d'Isola isn't found—or isn't well enough to perform when she *is* found—Madame Montero will be more than ready to step into the role." And he outlined to Shaw the tale of the "opera lesson" and its sequel, continuing with La d'Isola's discovery of the "note" that had brought her to Bayou des Familles. "As Signor Cavallo said yesterday, it would make a good deal more sense to have set the trap today—the night of the performance itself—if the intention was to disrupt the opera, or substitute Madame Montero for d'Isola on-stage. Obviously," he added grimly, "it wasn't. I take it this isn't a simple case of robbery."

"Marsan had a hundred and fifty dollars in the inside pocket of his coat, not to mention his watch an' a ring an' a stickpin with a topaz in it the size of your fingernail. Caldwell says the dress rehearsal finished at six—barely time for Mr. Russell's stage crew to set up for that night's performance of *The Forty Thieves*—an' when he mentioned Belaggio came back to the theater after it was done, Belaggio remembered as how yes, he'd come back to fetch a couple of them liber-ettos he'd left in his office. He didn't stay, though, he says."

"He does, does he?" The house at Roseaux came into view around the cluster of bayou oaks, and on the steps stood Mr. Knight, looking even more prim and disapproving than usual, his hand on the shoulder of the young Mademoiselle Jocelyn Marsan.

"My dear Madame . . ." The business manager hastened down the steps.

"Is it true, Mama?" Mademoiselle Marsan's voice had a dead quality to it, all emotion boned tight as her straight-fronted schoolgirl corset. Her frock had been cut down from a woman's, with too little fabric in the skirt, and telltale lines where seams had been picked out and pieces skillfully joined. Her black hair hung in braids, fine as silk.

"This gentleman says that it is." Isabella Marsan drew a deep breath, steadying herself on Mr. Knight's arm as she descended. "If you'll go around to the back gallery, Messires, one of the men will take your horse and bring you . . . bring you coffee and sandwiches." Her glance encompassed Cavallo and Ponte, settling instinctively the conundrum of the logistics of Creole hospitality by which Europeans—even Europeans in muddied boots with soot crusted on their shirts—rated an invitation to the parlor while Kaintucks would be relegated to the back gallery, if that. "Monsieur Knight, if you would be so good . . ."

"Of course, Madame." The factor led her up the steps to the house, where a tall, thin man in a butler's livery waited just within the French door that led to the women's side of the house.

By the time Rufe had let Cavallo and Ponte off by the brick piazza at the rear of the house, and a servant came to take Shaw's horse, most of the housemaids, the plantation laundress and carpenter, the sawmill boss, Big Lou's trainer, and the cook were clustered behind the kitchen, just out of the line of sight from the back gallery. Rufe drew rein and January sprang down as the butler came down the gallery steps and crossed the yard—

"It true?" asked the sawmill boss, glancing from Rufe to January to the butler as all three came around the corner of the little building, with that instinctive sense of where those places were that the white folks couldn't see. "Jules?"

In English, Rufe replied, "It's what the man say," and Jules the butler nodded. January felt the ripple of exhaled breath among the assembled men and women. Saw how shoulders relaxed, bodies loosened. Eyes shut in brief prayers of thanks. Given the near-certainty of sale that would result in the death of the Master, the breaking of communities and families—given the fact that the devil one knew was nearly always less terrifying than the unknown darkness of the future—it was a devastating indictment of the man as a master.

He's gone. He's dead.

Whatever's going to happen now, it surely can't be worse.

Since Rufe didn't speak more than a few words of French, January filled in what details he knew: that Marsan had been stabbed to death, his body found in an alley in town; that he had not been robbed. "Was it the family of that girl?" asked Jules, speaking better French than January commonly heard even among house servants. Speaking, too, as if even here he feared to be overheard. "That girl he killed?"

"They don't know who it was." January stepped aside from the servants around Rufe. He was about to say, *He was killed by accident, in mistake for someone else,* but instead, he asked, thinking of Dominique, "What was the girl's name?"

"Sidonie Lalage." The butler was a few years younger than January, though his hair was grayer and he'd lost quite a few teeth. Two small fresh scabs marked the left side of his face: *riding-whip,* January identified them at once. Similar, slightly older marks welted the cheekbones of one laundress and the cook. "I always said no good would come of that, for all that white jury let him off. No proof he done it, they said. Of course there was proof. An' it wasn't the first time he beat her for speakin' to another man." He shook his head. "I always knew there'd be trouble from the girl."

"Could this have been the smugglers?" asked January even more softly. *Ask me no questions . . .*

Maybe Belaggio had asked more questions than he should have. Maybe Captain Chamoflet had simply resented someone moving in on the illicit importing of slaves.

"I don't know anything about that." The butler lowered his dark eyes. "It's better, hereabouts, not to know."

January glanced toward the house. Shaw and the two Italians sat on wicker chairs on the rear gallery, talking to Mr. Knight, who sat as far from the Kaintuck as was possible within the same group. The plump cook emerged from the kitchen, bearing a tray that contained sandwiches and lemonade. As she handed this to Jules, she looked up at January and said, "As if everyone in this countryside doesn't know about Captain Chamoflet. Don't you listen to Jules, sir. But if you're thinking it was the captain, or any of his boys, that's ridiculous. Michie Vincent always kept on the good side of the captain when they dealt together, and how not? He wasn't stupid, Michie Vincent, except about that temper of his."

"And even there," said the trainer in a quiet voice, "I did notice that he never gets real mad, killin' mad, at anyone who can fight back, or hurt him later."

"Besides," the cook went on, "Captain Chamoflet, he

doesn't go up to town much. Why kill a man there with the police all around, when you know he'll have to come riding down here some night?"

January watched Jules cross the yard with the tray, mount the steps of the rear gallery. Shaw was sketching out directions with his big, lumpy-knuckled hands, gesturing toward the bayou, toward the town. A search party for d'Isola, almost certainly. By the shadow of the kitchen's sagging roof on the dirt of the yard, it was nearly two. January's silver watch had stopped—he'd forgotten to wind it last night, sitting awake listening for the tread of slave-stealers in the damp dark of the barn.

The curtain would go up on *La Muette de Portici* at seven, d'Isola or no d'Isola.

Did that make a difference? he wondered. Had someone sent a note to Belaggio last night, telling him to be at the theater?

Or had he gone there to meet Marsan? Marsan, who had acted as go-between for his slave-dealing? Who less than a week ago had challenged him to a duel? Marsan, who had a furious temper, and the devil of jealousy in his heart?

Conversely, had Marsan gone there, arriving after Belaggio's departure, and seen something—or someone— at the theater? Tinkering, maybe, with Mount Vesuvius in order to guarantee a disaster at the performance tonight?

The blood in the drawer. The milky sunlight on the burned house at La Cornouiller. A voice whispering "nigger" in the alley's darkness, and Marguerite lying in Olympe's house, sinking deeper and deeper into cold and silence. . . .

Where did that nagging sensation come from in his mind, the feeling that he'd heard something recently that didn't fit?

". . . duels over the damnedest stupid things!" The cook's voice brought him back to the present. "He killed a fellow named Brouillard 'cause of the color of his necktie— his *necktie!* 'Cause Brouillard said it didn't match his waist-coat or some fool thing like that. Poor M'am Marsan lost a night's sleep weeping till she was near sick over it with fear, for, of course, if Michie Vincent were to die, she'd never keep this place, and her with a young daughter and no son, and the whole crop borrowed against before the cane stood three feet tall."

January looked back toward the house. The coachman was leading out the carriage again with a new team—as mismatched and sorry as the former—preparatory to tak-ing the widow to town to claim her husband's body at the Charity Hospital morgue. One of the maids emerged from the cabinet that housed the attic stairs, her arms full of mourning dresses, and with the girl Jocelyn at her heels crossed to the door into Madame Marsan's bedroom.

Absurd to think that even with the money from smuggling slaves, Marsan hadn't been in debt. Having been married for ten years to a dressmaker, January had a good idea of what it cost to be a dandy: to indulge the ob-session with clothing to that meticulous degree.

Shaw's horse was hitched to the footman's dickey, the scar-kneed roan saddled beside it on a lead. More logistics of hospitality, thought January wryly. Cavallo and Ponte would of course be invited to ride in the landaulet. They were, after all, Europeans, and civilized men. The Kain-tuck would ride behind. Under ordinary circumstances January would be left to walk, but his inclusion in the party with those Madame Marsan considered his betters required some means of transportation be found for him as well.

"Did he fight?"

"That he did, sir, and was brought back here three-quarters dead on a plank. Michie Knight was fit to split his corset-lacings, he was so mad, and you could hear M'am Marsan weeping clear out to the quarters."

On the gallery Cavallo sprang to his feet, hammered one fist into his palm. *L'Italiana in Algeri*. January remembered ironically the opera of that name, and tried to imagine the lovely soprano tricking her way out of a lustful Pasha's harem and escaping to a convenient ship with her own true love.

But her own true love was dead, he thought, in the place of the lover she'd sought to escape. And d'Isola herself . . .

If worse came to worst, he supposed Captain Chamoflet could be traced through one of Hannibal's disreputable connections in the Swamp, and the girl ransomed. If Belaggio's jealousy—or avarice—proved unequal to the task, they could probably apply to the Sicilian consul, whose jurisdiction also covered Neapolitans.

That was always assuming that Drusilla hadn't met the man who'd smashed Marguerite's skull. The man who'd doused the contents of that drawer with blood.

As the other slaves dispersed to spread the news to the stables, the laundry, the quarters, January looked around him at the run-down kitchen, the unpainted stucco of the shabby house. Only a few men moved around the sawmill, and there was little evidence of industry there.

In the other direction, past the kitchen, he could just glimpse a long, low brick building set behind a line of trees. Though it lay close to the bayou, the trees would screen it from either the water or the road: it was the only building in all of the dilapidated plantation that looked new and well-maintained. And even more curiously—on a plantation whose depth back from the bayou was severely limited by the narrowness of the high ground—the ground for a hundred feet around it was open, cleared not only of the chicken-runs and pig-yards that January vaguely recalled occupying that space in the spring of 1814, but of weeds, sapling pines, and trash.

The cook had gone to trade speculations with Rufe, leaving January momentarily alone. Quietly, he moved off, around the corner of the kitchen and thence behind the plantation shops, working his way toward that low, stout structure. He paused to glance around him to confirm his suspicions about the relationship of that building to the trees, to the bayou, to the quarters.

Long before he reached it, he knew exactly what that building was.

There were sixteen cells, tiny as the nuns' cells in a convent. January counted eight low doors on each side, the judas-hole in each providing the only light or ventilation the occupant of each cell would have. Every door had two bolts, with hasps and staples for padlocks. All were shut, though only one was locked. January peered through the judas in that locked door: he saw only a cell a little cleaner than the others, with a shelf set high above the floor. He wondered if he might find somewhere the store of padlocks, to compare them to that which had fastened the door on Cornouiller's store-room. Opening one of the other doors, he found rings set into the brick of the wall, strung through with shackles and chains.

Sixteen. He drew back in sickened anger. No slave-jail on any plantation he'd ever encountered had sixteen cells. Most had only one or two.

Sixteen cells wasn't a jail. It was a baracoon.

No wonder Vincent Marsan had stepped so easily into the role of Belaggio's go-between. No wonder he had so easily found clandestine buyers for his slaves.

Clearer still was the rescue of the plantation from debt and ruin, a resurrection that had nothing to do with the sawmill, or with Mr. Knight's financial expertise, and everything to do with the position of Les Roseaux on Bayou des Familles, gateway to the marshes of the Barataria, and through them to the sea.

Bastard, he thought. *You dirty, slave-smuggling bastard.*

He walked around the rear of the building, observing anew how close it lay to the water. A plank wharf poked out among the cypress-knees, almost hidden by reeds. The trace that led to it twisted sharply between the thick grove of cypress and tupelo that utterly masked the building from passers-by. Once smuggled past the Navy ships in the Gulf, slaves could be brought up through the marshes in Captain Chamoflet's pirogues: Cubans, or Africans brought in from Cuba. The very men, in fact, whom Shaw had been looking for last week at the New Exchange.

This was where they were being brought in.

Or one of the places, anyway. The smell of human waste in the cells told him they'd been used within the past month, though it was hard to be sure those one or two hadn't held plantation hands whom Marsan wanted to punish. That was the point of working through a planter. To have a point of origin in the United States.

Standing in the open doorway of one of the cells, looking in at the chains on the wall, January wondered if it was Big Lou who Marsan got to help him in all this, as it was Big Lou who controlled Marsan's wife.

If it hadn't been for Marguerite—and for the half-glimpsed shape on the banquette the other night—January didn't think he'd have heard the whisper of a naked foot on

the packed earth behind him. He whirled without thinking, flung himself aside from the open cell door just as an
immense hand closed around the back of his neck. The
strength that hurled his two-hundred-plus pounds forward
smashed him into the wall rather than pitching him into
the tiny prison. By instinct, he brought up his shoulder,
tucked his head, taking the stunning impact on the meat of
his biceps rather than on his skull, and turned with both
forearms up and both hands locked in a double fist before
he even identified Big Lou.

He hunched, whipped his head to one side past a
punch like a hammer, and turned his hip: the crippling
wallop of Lou's kick was like being struck on the thigh by
a steel beam, and he didn't even want to think about what
it would have done to his balls. He lunged down and in,
using the wall to lever his shoulder into the bigger man's
solar plexus, fighting to get clear. Lou slammed him back,
elbowed him brutally: trained jabbing blows. It was like
fighting a steamboat. January had never been a fighter—
for most of his life his size alone had been protection—he
felt like a flailing child as he tried to defend himself and
get clear.

Keep moving, he told himself, *whatever you do.* But it
was hard to even think. January tried to thrust himself off
the wall—he knew he was trapped there—and was shoved
back into it, twice and thrice, dizzy and unable to breathe.
The blows he did manage to land seemed like punches
thrown in a dream, though he felt his knuckles crunch on
the iron skull, the shoulders like leather-shod rock. He
felt himself going over and tried to twist out from under
on the way down and didn't manage it, caught a smashing
blow on the face, and then heard a girl's voice shouting
"Lou! Lou! Stop it! Stop it right now!"

A knee ground in January's belly and a fist caught the side of his head like a mule's kick and he thought, *You heard the lady, Lou. You stop it right now. . . .*

The shadow reared back off him; Lou's head turned. Mademoiselle Jocelyn had run in close to the two men and whacked Lou over the back with a cane-stalk, and January seized advantage of the fighter's distracted attention to roll and twist with all the strength in his body. Taken unawares, Lou pitched off his balance and fell like a tree.

"Lou, stop it!" screamed the girl again as January rolled to his feet. The fighter bounded up with terrifying lightness, but Mademoiselle Jocelyn stepped in front of him, huge dark eyes blazing in that too-pointy white face. For one instant January thought—looking at Lou's face, at those small eyes like the cunning, hate-hot eyes of a wild pig—that Lou was going to swat his master's daughter aside like a barking bitch-puppy to get at him.

"He's dead, Lou," said January, and Lou stopped.

And January thought, *That made a difference.*

And loathed Vincent Marsan anew for what that knowledge told him.

Lou wiped the blood from his lip. In that soft, mumbly voice he said, "Your daddy don't want nobody near that barn."

"Go back to the house," said Jocelyn. She was shaking like a sapling in a gale. *Lou would have hit her,* thought January, almost disbelieving the enormity of it. Not that a black man would strike a white girl—that an adult so huge would strike a child.

And almost by instinct, he knew Marsan wouldn't have punished Lou in any way that mattered.

"He lookin' around the barn," reiterated Lou stubbornly. "Your daddy say—"

"My father is dead." Jocelyn's cold, small voice was like broken china. She still held the cane-stalk in both hands, not much less in diameter than her bruised, skinny arm. "Go back to the house."

The small, dark eyes turned to January. Studying him. Regarding him with absolute chilling impersonality. A job to be done. A task unfinished.

January stood where he was, breathing hard, hands hurting, thigh hurting, belly hurting, face hurting, blood hot on his own flesh and every muscle trembling as Lou turned and walked away back toward the house, wiping the blood off his chin with his white muslin sleeve.

Only when Lou was out of earshot did January say, "Thank you, Mamzelle." He wiped at the blood running down the side of his face. His head felt bloated with air, his knuckles as if someone had brought a flat-iron down on them.

"Are you M'sieu Janvier?" Closer, Jocelyn's pale face had a sharp prettiness to it, though her eyes—brown like her mother's in her mother's fine-boned face—were smudged underneath, as if she did not sleep well. Under the torn flounce of her schoolgirl dress her black-stockinged ankles were like sticks. They would get her mourning clothes in town, January found himself thinking, when they went to claim her father's body.

"You want to be careful what you say to Lou, M'sieu." She held out her handkerchief to him. January waved it aside, knowing how badly blood would stain white linen and not wanting to make work for the laundress. He pulled his own blue bandanna from his pocket to stanch the cut on his cheek. "He's a bad man."

"Thank you," said January. Many white girls—white adults, too—would have said, *a bad nigger:* meaning he was useless for the purpose God intended, which was to serve the whites. *A bad man* meant something different, bad by anyone's standards. "I noticed that." He flexed his right hand.

Good thing it wasn't Mozart tonight, he thought. Amid the hair-tearing hysterics of Auber's score, any deficiencies in his speed and deftness of touch should be adequately covered by the eruption of Mount Vesuvius.

The girl met his eye for one instant, and for one instant January saw in it a bright, sardonic glint, the same humor that had almost been killed in her mother, tempered by a cynical awareness of too many things. Then she glanced aside.

"The American animal back at the house asked to find you," she went on, falling into step beside him as he headed—cautiously—across the open ground toward the yard. She pronounced *American animal* exactly the way his mother did, as one word, as if the noun could not take another adjective or do without that particular one. "He says that they've found the young lady that was lost."

FIFTEEN

"My dress is all ruined." Drusilla d'Isola wiped the tears that streaked the mud and dust on her face, and gazed up pleadingly from the brocaded satin study couch where Sam Pickney had carried her. "I don't know who they were, or what they wanted, but they tied me up. They put a blindfold on me, spoke to me of I don't know what!" Tears welled again, and she clung to Cavallo's hands with bruised fingers scored by dirty cuts.

"My dear child!" Madame Marsan knelt to tuck a thick woolen shawl around her shoulders, voice soothing as if to her own daughter. "How could anyone have . . . ?" She looked around her, at Shaw, January, and the others gathered in Marsan's study. "Jules, please have Dinah fetch this young lady down some dry clothing. She's of a size with Mademoiselle DuClos, I think."

"This dress cost twenty-five dollars!" sobbed the girl, touching the tattered and mudstained organdy, "and now it is all torn, and my shoes, too, and they took my pearls and my locket! I have never been treated so, never!"

Mademoiselle DuClos—Jocelyn's governess—hastened back to the attic stairs. Jocelyn went after her, but returned only moments later with a nearly-empty bottle of lavender-water and a handkerchief. Cavallo took this with a murmured *"Grazie,"* to massage d'Isola's welted wrists. "Are you hurt?" he asked—meaning, January guessed by his tone, *Were you raped?*—but d'Isola had her face buried in her hands and only shook her head, and repeated that her dress was ruined and her shoes, too.

"Those smugglers are a disgrace!" Isabella Marsan took the basin of warm water that Jules brought in and gently began to wash d'Isola's bare, scratched, and bleeding feet. "The entire country knows about them—including Sheriff Arbitage and M'sieu Pickney—yet no one will do a thing!"

Mr. Knight, who could not have been ignorant as to the source of his employer's wealth, cleared his throat and said, "Very true."

"Only look at my hands!" wailed Drusilla. "What is the matter with everyone in this country?"

Cavallo took her hands again between his own, and Bruno, who'd been sitting on a corner of Marsan's cypresswood desk, came to press his big peasant palms against the girl's shoulders in silent reassurance. Madame Marsan, wearing now the mourning black that every adult woman owned in that land of large families and tropical diseases, rose and went out to the gallery for one of the glasses of lemonade that had been left on the tray there.

"Was they the same men as you saw lock your friends under the house?" asked Shaw after January had translated.

D'Isola blew her nose on one of Madame Marsan's handkerchiefs and raised red eyes to the policeman. "I do not know, Signor. They would have to be, wouldn't they? I couldn't make the horse go, and I got Cavallo's horse and tried to get on it, but I fell off, and then these men came out of the woods and grabbed me, and they talked and I didn't know what they were saying! They had beards and slouch hats and they spit tobacco and stank—beg pardon, Signor. . . ." Because Shaw had just at that moment leaned out the window and spit onto the gallery. "But I'd never seen them before and I don't know who they were or what they wanted."

She wiped her eyes. Cavallo relaxed a little, evidently taking all this to mean that if her attackers wanted sex, even she couldn't have failed to deduce it. But whether they were Americans speaking English, or Chamoflet's slave-stealers speaking swamp-rat *argot* beyond La d'Isola's limited capabilities in French, was still undetermined.

"They put me in a boat," she went on. "But there was a razor, left down between the seats among their coats and bags. Signora, *grazie*. . . ." She took the lemonade Madame Marsan offered and drank it gratefully. "I pretended to faint while they were rowing, and cut myself free, look." She held up her hands. "And now I have ruined my hands, and torn my best yellow dress. . . . They struck a floating log, and were cursing—it was nearly night—and I rolled overboard, and swam and swam, and lost my shoes in the water, and I could hear them shouting behind me, and saying I don't know what. . . ."

"Was they white men," asked Shaw, "or black?"

"Oh, white," replied d'Isola the moment January had translated. "With beards, and their hair all curly. Swarthy men, like Spanish."

Which could mean, thought January, white or black—or any of the myriad divisions and combinations in between. It certainly described any number of the inhabitants of the Barataria, third-generation Acadians out of Canada or the mixture of French, Mexican, Spanish, and Levantines that had made up Lafitte's crews and their children. As Madame Marsan and Jules helped La d'Isola to her feet, January backed to let them pass. On the shelves beside him he noted among the plantation ledgers a couple of books about sugar and cotton—a very few of these—and over a dozen volumes of racing-stud records. There were, surprisingly, novels, too: *The Sorrows of Young Werther,* in German, by Goethe. *Die Elixiere des Teufels,* by Hoffmann. Musäus's *Volksmärchen der Deutschen.* Kant's *Kritik der Urteilskraft.* As everyone filed from the office, he glanced at the desk, and saw the green-bound libretto of *Othello* lying open. So Marsan evidently did read. It was the best thing he'd learned of the man so far.

He wondered briefly if Madame would be willing to part with the Hoffmann, and discarded the thought of asking her. *A pity.* It was one thing to be civilized enough not to intrude on grief, but it was the only copy of *Die Elixiere des Teufels* he'd seen in America, and one couldn't ever count on what books would show up in the job-lots sent from Paris and New York.

Only as they were helping Mademoiselle d'Isola into the landaulet—attired now in Mademoiselle DuClos's starched gray muslin—did January say to her softly, "Do you realize who this woman is, and to what house you have been brought, Signorina? That is Madame Marsan. . . ." He nodded to the black-draped form on the back gallery, giving final instructions to Jules, Jocelyn, Dinah, and Mademoiselle DuClos, and readied himself to clap his hand over d'Isola's mouth, white woman or no white woman, if she should scream.

"And she wears mourning because Vincent Marsan was killed last night."

The heart is stronger than the head. . . .

La d'Isola's eyes flared, huge within the delicate bones of her face. But she glanced toward the widow who had been kind to her, and pressed her own hands to her mouth. *"O Dio mio."* Then she inhaled hard and let it out, and averted her face, pressing her forehead into Cavallo's filthy shoulder to conceal her tears. "His wife. O my beautiful one, my adored."

Cavallo clasped her close. On her other side, Bruno rubbed her shoulders as one would comfort a child. Jules descended the gallery steps with a small portmanteau and strapped it on the dickey, and Shaw came loafing around the corner of the house and stepped into the saddle of his horse. January mounted his own borrowed animal, and heard Cavallo explain to Madame Marsan as Mr. Knight helped her into the carriage, "The Mademoiselle is tired, so tired, from all she have go through."

Knight cast at Cavallo a glance of infinite gratitude that he'd been spared a very complicated scene, and Isabella Marsan stroked La d'Isola's trembling back and murmured, "Of course. Of course, poor child."

Buttoning his all-encompassing buff surtout to his chin, Mr. Knight climbed into his own smart gig, bestowed his briefcase of papers beneath its seat. As he removed the yellow kid gloves he had worn in the house and with fussy care put on driving-gloves of York tan, January was reminded that the man was French, whatever he was passing for now. What thoughts did he have, if any, about the whole sordid business of working with Vincent Marsan?

Or had he, too, succumbed to that miasma Hannibal had described, and now thought of nothing beyond the plantation's profits?

The shabby house, the overgrown yard, vanished behind the little caravan as they rounded the curve of the bayou. *What will they do now,* January wondered: this crushed-looking woman, that too-thin girl-child. He couldn't imagine Madame Marsan taking up her husband's connections with Captain Chamoflet's men. He supposed the enterprising Baratarian would find another planter along the bayou to act as go-between instead.

Or would Knight coerce Marsan's widow to maintain the commerce? Had the factor been taking a cut? Looking at the prim, secretive face, he couldn't tell. One way or the other, without that clandestine trade—with no crop, few slaves, and little viable machinery—a woman had few choices, her daughter fewer still. No dowry meant few prospects of marriage. Most convents wouldn't even take a girl without guarantee of support. They wouldn't starve— January had overheard her mention to Shaw something about her Dreuze relatives, and he knew the Dreuzes were rich. But Madame and her daughter would dwindle to poor relations, companions to richer cousins or governesses to children, consuming the bread of charity and required to pretend they enjoyed it.

That, too, thought January, was the custom of this country.

The carriage swung out onto the shell road along the bayou, and January looked back to catch a glimpse of the baracoon, barely visible behind its sheltering line of tupelos. In the shadows of the trees, Big Lou stood, massive arms folded, watching the carriage away. For one second, January met those cold, steel-black eyes.

It was a silent ride back to Point Algiers.

"I will go on," d'Isola said as simply as a child. "Of course I will go on."

"Mi brava!" Belaggio surged forward, enfolded the young woman in his meaty arms, and planted kisses on her cheeks and throat. *"Mi bellissima! Mi cara! Mi prima!"*

"Get me out of here," muttered Madame Montero to Hannibal. "I think I may be sick."

D'Isola looked fairly ill herself.

"It would have been more than I could endure, *mi fiora,* if you could not take the stage tonight!" By the gaslight glare, Belaggio's cheeks had a blotchy look, as if the man were still pale with the shock of the morning's news. When Liam tangled a swatch of fish-net on the side of Masaniello's humble cottage and brought the whole thing down with a crash, the impresario leapt like a startled deer.

Moreover, he seemed to have shared January's apprehension that someone might have tinkered with Vesuvius. "Already done it, Signor," said Tiberio when January suggested—as he did immediately upon arriving backstage—that Marsan may have recognized someone who had no business about the theater last night. "Signor Belaggio had me check every hosepipe, every chemical— nay, had me examine the very gas-jets, and in his office and the dressing-rooms and the proscenium as well. A man who keeps his eye not only on the scorpion and the serpent, but on the millipede, too."

"But it is Marsan himself," protested Cavallo, coming to January's side as the Sicilian vanished like a gnome into the mountain's hollow core, "who had no business about the theater at that hour of the night. What would he have been doing here? Had Drusilla been in town, perhaps I would understand, but . . ."

"He may have thought she *was* in town." January sank down onto the rustic bench that would shortly grace the Portici village square. Hannibal reappeared through the jumble of flats, a couple of lumpy parcels balanced in one hand and a cup of coffee in the other.

"The folks at the Promenade Hotel kitchen said they're coming to see Vesuvius erupt and don't want the spectacle destroyed by poor piano-playing. The coffee they threw in as lagniappe." The fiddler laid one of the parcels on January's swollen knuckles—it was ice, done up in a rather grubby green bandanna. "They're taking their places even now in the left-hand gallery, *en bloc* and set on seeing the volcano."

The ice was agonizing, but January spread his hands wide and laid it over his knuckles. "They may have agreed on a rendezvous days ago," he went on to Cavallo. "It may be why Belaggio was at the theater to begin with. If he got wind of it . . ."

"But it seems he did not." The young man had washed the soot and grime from his face and put on the buckskin breeches, boots, and shirt of the doomed and heroic fisherman. His damp hair he'd slicked back from his face, preparatory to donning the wig for the role, and it put the fine bones into prominence, the wide, clear brow and deep-set eyes. "On the gallery at Les Roseaux, Signor Knight"—he called him *Notte,* and January didn't feel up to explaining that *Notte* and *Cavaliere* sounded alike in English—"said to your policeman that he'd encountered Belaggio at about eleven, at the barroom of the City Hotel. The man had just come from the theater and was inquiring again whether Drusilla had returned. They were together some time, Knight said, before Belaggio went up to his room."

And the last carriage went up the alley to the Promenade at midnight, thought January. Eleven would have been just after the conclusion of *The Forty Thieves,* when cast and crew still milled about and the sweepers were clearing up. "Knight didn't happen to mention whether Belaggio had his libretti with him, did he?"

"He said at the end of their conversation Belaggio 'picked up his books' and went to his room. If . . ."

Belaggio appeared at the top of the gallery stairs with

arms outspread and cried in triumph to the backstage at large, "She will sing! She will sing!"

"But *can* she sing?" asked Caldwell from the floor below, caught up in the drama of the moment.

"Of course she cannot sing." Madame Montero flounced over to Hannibal's side. January observed that she wore Princess Elvira's flower-bedecked wedding-dress from Act One, which fit her no better than had the Countess's. "She never *could* sing. *And* she has taken all the dressers, the worthless *puta,* and there is no one to unlace me. . . ."

As the Mexican soprano strode off in the direction of her dressing-room, she passed Bruno Ponte, bearing bowls of cheap jambalaya in either hand. "She's the one," he remarked quietly, "I would be asking after, where *she* was last night. This is not bad," he added, handing January one of the bowls. "Better than the *brodaglia* that Rufe gave us this morning, anyway. Silvio, you'd best come if you're going to get your make-up on and lie down before you go on. If you want your voice in its best heart . . ."

"You can't seriously believe Consuela stabbed Marsan in mistake for Belaggio," said Hannibal in a pained voice as the young Sicilian urged his friend away. "Not that she couldn't undertake a very competent murder, you understand. But dark or not, in that alley it's not a mistake she would make. Besides, I happen to know Madame Montero—er—couldn't have murdered anyone last night."

"*Querida . . .*" Madame paused on the stairs, looking back expectantly at Hannibal.

Hannibal said, "Excuse me," with dignity, and went to join her. *Presumably,* thought January as they ascended the stair together and the dressing-room door shut behind them, *to unlace her. . . .*

That's all we need to complicate matters.

"Myself," declared Tiberio, popping through one of the volcano's craters again and resting an elbow on a garishly painted lava-flow, "I do not think anything was touched because I was here until all were gone. They are thieves, you understand, these *schifui Americanese.* They would run off with the gunpowder, and the silk to make the effects of fire and lava and smoke. So I make it my business to remain until all are gone, and then to check where everything is before I leave. And it is all as it was, believe me."

"No, no, my dear," wailed Herr Smith's despairing voice from the rehearsal-room door. "One applies the hand passionately to the forehead, then step back on the right foot, with the body quite backward. Both hands up denotes Astonishment rather than Anguish. . . ."

"So you saw Belaggio leave?" January bent and stretched each finger of his swollen hands.

"I did, Signor. It was just before eleven. He said he had been back and forth many times to the hotel in search of the *bella signorina;* he would return there, he said, to await her."

"Was he angry?" asked January. "Jealous?"

"No, Signor. Only afraid that things would become complicated for the opera, you understand." The Sicilian cocked a dark, knowing eye at him, like a parrot. "Whatever she told him after this nonsense of the duel, he believed. She is good, La *bella* d'Isola."

"I brought your things, Uncle Ben." Gabriel appeared beside him, panting from his dash through the streets. He had January's black longtailed woolen coat over his arm, a shirt of clean linen, cream-colored waistcoat, trousers, and a neck-cloth. "Are you all right? Mama says you were in some kind of trouble last night."

"I'll be fine." January got to his feet. In spite of a night spent in a mule barn and a day of riding around the countryside with little to eat—in spite of Big Lou and all the patrollers in the world—the quick, controlled bustle of the backstage preparations was beginning to have its usual effect on him. A sort of electric humming tingled behind his breastbone. A kind of anxiety mingled with delight, like a child in a very good dream, in that moment just before the fairies appear.

Like the far-off drumming of hooves, the murmur of the crowd in front began to wash over him, cleansing away any consideration beyond that of the music: the joy of doing a wonderful thing wonderfully.

He scrubbed his hand playfully over Gabriel's close-cropped hair, and went to change his clothes.

Filing into the orchestra pit behind the Bratizant brothers and a rather rumpled Hannibal, January scanned the boxes as usual, wondering whether Incantobelli would be there. He saw Henri Viellard immediately, solicitous in handing his mother into her chair before turning his attention to that porcelain doll at his side. Was Dominique, January wondered, in the latticed loges of the plaçées, waiting as all the ladies of Rampart Street learned to wait?

The heart is stronger than the head . . . He saw d'Isola's eyes in the light of the flaring cressets of the market-place, heard the passion in her voice as she turned her face away. *I do not want to listen to this.* . . .

O my beautiful one, my adored . . .

What about the woman Liane? Had anyone thought to tell her? Or was she still waiting for Marsan to arrive, looking across at the gaping black square of his empty box? *She tried to kill herself last year,* Dominique had said.

And like a dim echo behind his sister's voice, the butler Jules: *I always knew there'd be trouble.* . . .

And what else? January's tired mind groped at the other words someone had said, somewhere—he thought—on the Bayou des Familles. Something that had alerted him, or would have alerted him if he hadn't been worried about slave-stealers and patrols and d'Isola. . . .

Alerted him to what?

He shifted the rag around his hand, wrung out this time in hot water begged from the coffee-makers in the lobby.

Three women tonight, he thought, who must seek another protector. Four, if you counted the girl Jocelyn.

Madame Viellard leaned across to ask her son a question, gestured with her moss-colored satin fan at the empty box. Turned to Madame Mayerling in the box on the other side, passing the gossip along. Candles flared in the second-tier box above the Mayerlings: a servant kindling girandoles on the partition. A small, stout form took the chair by the rail, solitary and anonymous in dark evening-dress and the black domino mask of Carnival. But January recognized at once, even at the distance, the grizzled curly hair, the double watch-chain with its three gold fobs.

"What's Davis doing here?" whispered Hannibal.

January shook his head.

Then Belaggio's solid black shape blocked his view, stepping up to the conductor's box. January's mind grabbed for the opening onslaught and dropped into the blood-and-thunder pyrotechnics of the overture as if he'd fallen overboard from a steamboat, to be carried away on the Mississippi's implacable tide.

By the time Act One concluded, January's hands felt like he'd caught them in a cotton-press. He bribed Hannibal to take the piano during the entr'acte ballet, and retreated to the wings and his half-melted packets of ice. It was there that one of the boys who hawked candy along the boxes found him, with a note—"From the gentleman in Box Twenty-six, sir."

Meet me, it said.

Of course, from the boxes John Davis would have seen him leave.

A catwalk ran above the backstage and through the flies to the demi-porte that led to the corridor behind the second-tier boxes. Davis met him there above the tangle of arbors and statuary, bollards and nets and cottage-fronts coming and going. Half covered by the music of the ballet, the backstage clamor rose up with the gasolier heat around them: hidalgos and grand ladies scrambling to shed ruffs and farthingales and don the coarse skirts and leather jerkins of the fishing population. Higher still, the third-tier boxes and the galleries would be worse.

The black and white of Davis's clothing was barely to be made out in the swaying shadows of suspended rope and canvas, sandbags and pulleys and wires. On the other side of the door, the voices of the boxholders could be dimly heard, instructing footmen or maids to fetch this or that from the lobby: coffee, champagne, ices, fresh decks of cards.

"What happened last night?" In such upside-down light as filtered from between the flies, the theater owner looked terrible, his face sunken and lined and at the same time puffy around the eyes.

January said, "Sir, are you all right?" and Davis gestured him impatiently back.

"It's nothing. Is it true what I've heard? That Marsan was murdered in mistake for Belaggio?"

"That's what it looks like, sir, yes. Were you . . . ?"

"One of my dealers told me late this afternoon that someone was in the gambling-rooms asking the servants about where I was last night. Later that City Guard, that American Shaw, came by, and asked me the same thing. What have you found out?"

"Not a great deal, sir. Someone set a trap yesterday, I think, for Drusilla d'Isola—to keep her from performing tonight. . . ."

"And here I thought there were no true opera-lovers in this town! My God, my Princess Elvira can sing rings around that girl! And of course no one's going to be there to see her do it."

"I got here too late to have a look at the alley where the body was found. And of course with all the carriages and horses going back and forth all morning, there wouldn't have been much to see. Hannibal's still trying to find information about the two men who attacked Belaggio before, but if they were the ones who did the murder, my guess is they're already out of town. Weren't you in your gambling-rooms last night?"

"Not after eleven," Davis said. "I wasn't well—I haven't been, you know. . . . Damn!" he added, shaking his head like a goaded bull. "It's enough to turn you into a debauchee! You go home quietly and go to bed like a Christian, and how can you prove that?"

"Do you have a man?" Davis's wife had died the previous year; though January had heard he had a mistress, or had had one, Davis's concern now told him the woman—if there was one these days—hadn't been with him last night.

If he were feeling poorly, she wouldn't have been, of course.

"It's Carnival, Ben. My valet knows I'm usually not

home until two or three. God only knows where he was—not where he was supposed to be, that's for sure. And in any case," he added, a wry expression twisting his tired mouth, "you know his testimony wouldn't be admissible, if it came to that."

"Testimony?" January shied from the word. "You don't think . . . ? It's ridiculous. That you'd actually murder a man, or contemplate murdering him, because he robbed you of a *premiere*?"

"Ben." The stray glow of the gaslight showed up how deep the lines were in Davis's face, how dark the liverspots on cheek and jaw against the unhealthy pallor of the skin. "Men kill each other every day in this town over whores' smiles. Over two-dollar poker pots. Over the personal habits of Napoleon Bonaparte and Louis the Eighteenth, and both of them have been dead for years! Lorenzo Belaggio insulted my theater, called me mediocre in public newspapers, cut me publicly in front of half the Americans in New Orleans at Trulove's party, and suggested—also publicly—that I'm jealous enough to hire men to beat him up in an alley. Do you think there are twelve men in this town who'll believe that isn't grounds for assassination?"

January was silent. He could hear the ballet—a saucy Mozart piece—winding to its final movement. It was time to go.

"Ben, they're asking. That means the obvious people—like Belaggio himself—have already been eliminated." Davis reached into the front of his coat, brought out a small leather bag that clinked softly of silver as he held it out. "Use this to find out what you can," he said. "And keep the rest." He clapped January lightly on the arm. "Do what you can for me, all right?"

Following the mute Fenella's laboriously coy Act Two recapitulation of her rape, her brother Masaniello's outrage, the vows of comradeship, rebellion, and revenge and a few preliminary rumbles and sputters from Mount Vesuvius, January re-emerged from the score to look up at Box Twenty-six. John Davis was still there, though he had moved his chair back into the shadows. Too many people on the City Council, thought January, would be in the other boxes, for him to jeopardize his chances at a building contract by appearing weary or ill. It was at parties, at the gambling-rooms and barrooms after parties that such business truly got done. A man had to have stamina to keep in the running.

Alone of the boxes, with their chattering trickles of guests—Creoles to Creoles, Americans to Americans—Davis's had no company, no guests.

More ballet, while Liam and Paddy raced to transform the beach at Portici into Princess Elvira's drawing-room and Tiberio manipulated the counterweights in the wings, and everybody prayed that Mademoiselle Flaherty wouldn't tangle the gauze bows of her topknot in the wires. Caldwell had picked this entr'acte—a Pleyel rondo—which January could probably have played backwards, he knew it so well; he was halfway through the rondo when La d'Isola slipped through the demi-porte and sat on the piano-bench at his side.

"I never thanked you," she whispered, setting between them a hot towel and one of the half-melted packets of ice. The firefly candles of the orchestra all around them showed up the gold lace mitts she'd added to her costume to cover the rope-welts on her wrists, and gave to her face the illusion of color that the less forgiving gaslight parched away. Against the immense white platter of her ruff, her head had a guillotined look, like the main course at a feast dressed in its hair and its pearls.

"It was good of you to ride out after me the way you did. You must have known what a—what a foolish thing it was for me to go into the countryside, where men like that roam about. I feel such a fool. I was so sure I'd found a deadly plot."

"I think you did." January took advantage of a violin passage to wrap the warm towel around his aching hand. "Though whether against you, or Belaggio, or Italian liberty, I'm not sure. Did Belaggio ever see the note, by the way?"

"I don't know. I left it where I found it, on the floor just inside the door. He'd gone out to breakfast, you see, with Mr. Caldwell and Signora Redfern."

She swallowed hard; January could see her eyes were swollen with weeping, under their layer of Princess Elvira's paint.

"Were you going to meet Marsan after the dress rehearsal?" he asked gently.

"We . . . I . . ." Her small, scabbed finger darted quickly to intercept a tear before it tracked her make-up. "He would have known I wasn't at rehearsal. He always did come to watch from one of the boxes."

"But if he didn't for some reason, he wouldn't know?"

She shook her head.

She had three acts yet to get through, thought January as he resumed his playing and she slipped away. And after that, Belaggio's amorous demands. And she could not even weep.

Foolish or not, as Olympe would say, she did have the bristles.

It struck him, not for the first time, how desperately

unfair the life of the demimonde was to the women who led it. To be always beautiful, to be always cheerful, to be always ready to leap into bed and perform. Or to risk that soured comparison, *You're just like my wife. . . .*

And if the man was rich, there were always women younger and less worn-down waiting to tell him how delighted they were, to be at the beck and call of a man as handsome and virile as he.

Oh, Dominique, thought January again as the corps de ballet—those little apprentice demimondaines—scampered back to the wings and the principals took their places on the dim stage. He saw her again in his mind as she whispered, *I don't know what I'm going to do.*

Princess Elvira confronted Alfonso in anger, then fell into his arms. The ballet displayed bosom and ankle in the market-place of Naples, followed by a rush of armed supernumeraries who began the rebellion with such spirit that a number of them emerged with bloodied noses and bruised arms when the field was won. Masaniello repented in horror of the much greater quantity of stage blood that had been shed, helped Elvira and Alfonso escape, went mad, and perished in a rousing chorus of "Courons à la vengeance," after which Fenella, with a good deal of twirling and spinning that threatened to hopelessly entangle her in her own supporting wires, flung herself from the balcony into the flaming stream of Mount Vesuvius's red silk lava.

One more chorus of "Amour sacré de la patrie" and *The End,* the volcano belching mightily center stage and La Flaherty huddling gamely behind the balustrade that hid her from view while yards of scarlet and yellow silk writhed on the gleaming wet sides of the mountain and gas-jets flared and dimmed and bathed the stage in fiery light. Roman candles and pots of colored flame burst and spurted from the main crater and a dozen lesser caldera, and smoke poured from the volcano's every orifice, stinking to heaven of sulfur and coal.

This was what everyone had come to the theater to see, and the applause was roof-rattling. Every Kaintuck in the pit sprang to his feet, stamped, hollered approval, and contributed wolf-like howls to the general din. Belaggio, exalted, wildly signaled for more finale, so orchestra and chorus vamped passages from "Amour sacré de la patrie" for another five minutes and Tiberio continued to roar on the thunder-drums and Mr. Russell to work the gas-jets full-cock, with Paddy and Liam surreptitiously dumping water on everything they could reach without being seen from the front. To the last, January was convinced that the whole theater would ignite, disproving, perhaps, Shaw's theory that Davis was behind all the murder and mayhem—the man was still there in his box—but at rather high cost.

Only when the curtain finally closed—and he heard the reassuring hiss of vast quantities of steam—did he relax. The lights went up. The orchestra rose to go. As he did so, remembering Davis's look of drawn exhaustion, January craned his neck for a last look into Box Twenty-six to make sure the man did get up to go, in time to see the gangly shadow of Abishag Shaw step into the light, and lay a hand on John Davis's shoulder.

Rose was waiting for him backstage, with Gabriel, bearing a note from Olympe.

It said, *Your friend is awake.*

SIXTEEN

⸺∞⸺

"Your sister asked me already." Madame Scie stretched a hand to touch January's, then sank back into the worn clean linen of the pillows. "I suppose she feared I was going to be like one of those tiresome women in novels who open their eyes, gasp 'It was . . . It was . . . the black periwinkle . . .' and die leaving the hero to scratch his head for another four hundred pages. And I shall disappoint you, Ben, as I disappointed her. The last thing I remember is Nina lacing me up in my gold silk, which it would be too much to hope survived an assault on my person. . . ."

"It survived," said Olympe with her tight, close-mouthed grin, and Madame Scie sighed.

"A spar salvaged from the wreck of an evening. Will I regret the memories I've lost?"

"I fear so," said Hannibal, who had insisted on accompanying January to Olympe's house in spite of the fact that the performance had left him chalky and shivering. "It was opera itself. Belaggio challenged Marsan to a duel in a scatological cabaletta that rivaled Villon. Trulove had a secret assignation with the mute dancer. Lots of chorus work, lots of gorgeous supernumeraries, and one very lovely aria. You know there's been murder done."

She murmured, "I know."

"Well, comfort yourself with the fact that you probably haven't lost anything." January pulled a chair up to the side of Zizi-Marie's bed and held the bedside candle a few inches from Marguerite's face. The pupils of her eyes were still of unequal size; she blinked and pulled away. "Most people lose memories when they suffer a concussion, and mostly they come back. How many fingers am I holding up?"

"I'm trying to decide how many *hands* you're holding up."

"Does your head hurt?"

"Like sin." She coughed, and tried to clear her throat, as if puzzled that it should be sore. The marks there were still livid, yellow and green around the edges as they healed. They would be a long time fading. "Though in most cases I've found it has been virtue that's given me the real headaches."

January took the spouted cup of water Olympe handed him and held it to Marguerite's lips. She sighed and seemed to sink deeper into the bed linen, bruised eyelids sinking shut.

"Can we get you anything," asked Rose from the other side of the bed, "before you sleep? Benjamin brought your bags from the hotel."

"Yes, I see." Her thin fingers moved again on the worn lace of her night-dress. "Thank you. I cannot repay you, Benjamin, or your kind sister. . . ."

"Mr. Caldwell's taken care of that." January knew that a lifetime of living hand-to-mouth had given Marguerite a horror of being in debt. "Is there anyone we should write to? Anyone who should know of this?"

He thought of those she had told him of: the airy, scholarly dilettante father, the pretty stepmother she'd adored. The brothers: Clovis, Claude, Octave . . . All swept away in the Terror, and with them sister, uncles, cousins, aunts. Some publicly beheaded while the unemployed scum of the Paris streets spit on their faces, a number cut to pieces alive in one of the hysterical massacres when the Paris mob was swept by rumors that the prisoners awaiting trial were in communication with "enemies of the Republic." For as long as he'd known Marguerite, she'd lived in two rooms in the Rue de la Petite Truanderie, had walked to the Odéon for rehearsals, performances, instruction of the little rats who were the whole of her life, and to Les Halles for bread and vegetables and scrap meat for her cats. Nothing that the Terror had taken away had she replaced: not family, not possessions, not wealth. Who Monsieur Scie had been, and when he had crossed her path, she had never said. Her rooms had been spare and clean as a nun's cell.

She'd lived on air and light, and the laughter of her friends.

Looking down, he saw she was asleep again.

"I'll sit with her," said Olympe. "Paul will walk you home if you'd like."

"Thank you. They've arrested John Davis, of all people. . . ."

"T'cha!"

"Have you heard anything? Or has Mamzelle Marie?" Most secrets, January knew, came to Marie Laveau in the end. The voodooienne was the queen of secrets, the center of a web of information, rumor, and blackmail that stretched far up and down the river, a web that touched the slaves who cleaned the gutters and the planters who bought and sold those slaves.

Like his mother—like Olympe, or any woman of color—Mamzelle Marie kept her ears open for gossip and tales and speculation. But what for others was entertainment, she pursued as a vocation and a livelihood. She fit pieces together that others merely noted in passing, assembled facts with the patience of one of those Florentine artists who form mosaics so intricate, they cannot be distinguished from paintings. People said she could look in your eyes and read your dreams.

Sometimes January thought she could.

Other times, he guessed that all she really needed was to have your housemaid owe her a favor.

"I'll go to her tomorrow," Olympe told him, "and see what she has heard. There's always someone who knows something." She shrugged. "But it's like waiting for a branch to come down-stream. It sometimes takes a while."

January leaned down and kissed Marguerite's lips. They felt cold under his own, like silk left outside on a dry winter night.

Rehearsals for *Robert le Diable* began the following day at noon.

Since the little rats would assemble at ten—to receive Herr Smith's instructions in transforming themselves into the mad ghosts of dancing nuns—January rose early, and reached the Cabildo before eight. As he walked through the chill gray of dawn, he noticed that the city official in charge of such matters had stripped all posters of *La Muette de Portici*, Davis's as well as Caldwell's, though Davis's production of the opera was to take place that night. Posters for *Robert* were already pasted to every wall and corner in town.

In the big stone-floored watchroom of the Cabildo, Shaw slouched at his desk, explaining something to a little man who looked as Irish as a pot of bubble-and-squeak:

"This here's Mr. LeMoyne," the policeman introduced them as January hung back, and gestured for January to join them. "Mr. Davis's lawyer."

"Pleased." The lawyer held out his hand. "I know you. You're the piano master, Mr. Davis spoke of you." LeMoyne spoke French with the accent of Normandy and called January *vous*, not *tu*. "I've been telling this—this American"—he might just as well have said *sbirro*—"that it's not only ridiculous to hold Mr. Davis here on these absurd charges, but it's clearly detrimental to his health. He's not a well man."

"That's true, sir," agreed January, looking at Shaw. "He's sixty-two years old and his heart isn't strong. You know yourself that jail is a pest-hole. . . ."

"I know that," replied Shaw. The patience in his voice let January know that the overcrowded cells with their stink of filth and disease—with convicted thieves and murderers cheek-by-jowl beside suspects awaiting trial, drunks sobering up, runaway slaves being held for their Masters' arrival, and madmen with whom nobody quite knew what to do—had already been a topic of discussion between himself and the attorney. "An' as I told Mr. LeMoyne here, in cases of murder, there ain't no provision to let the culprit go walkin' around the public streets on bail."

"Any number of men in this town," said January dryly, "can reassure you as to the unlikelihood that Mr. Davis, if released, will run wildly through the streets, stabbing strangers at random. Sir."

"They's welcome to come to the arraignment Monday an' do so." Shaw folded his big, clumsy hands, the knuckles of which were as swollen and bruised as January's own. Carnival was not a good time, thought January, looking down at them, then up at the Kaintuck's black eye and cut cheek, to be responsible for peace and good order in New Orleans.

"I'm sorry," January said. "That was rude of me. But you know John Davis."

"I do," said Shaw. At the watch sergeant's desk an extremely inebriated Texian in soiled buckskins expostulated at length on how his scheme to send a force of armed American warriors to aid the rebels in New Grenada had necessitated a shooting-match in the middle of Gallatin Street at four in the morning.

"An' I know Mr. Davis ain't likely to go around killin' nobody else—nor probably that he won't high-tail it, neither. But there's folks in this town that have sort of remarked as to how them that's friends of the Prieurs an' the de McCartys an' the Bringiers an' all them other old French families don't spend near so much time under hatches as Americans do, an' have made kind of a issue of it in the last City Council meetin'. An' I must say, they do got a point."

"A point," said LeMoyne, "seems hardly grounds on which to keep a sick man locked in a cell where he'll be lucky if he has a cot to sleep on. It's the strongest who get them up there, not the sick. As you know."

Shaw's lips tightened. It couldn't be easy, thought January, for him to maintain his position, since he guessed Shaw agreed with LeMoyne. He guessed, too, that someone on the City Council had spoken to Shaw—and to Shaw's superior—about the need to administer justice even to the friends of the Creole planters whose money ran the town.

"Problem is"—Shaw focused his attention on trapping a flea on his frayed calico shirt-cuff and crushed it beneath a thumb-nail—"that at quarter to one, when Mr. Davis claims he was home in bed, he was seen in the

barroom of the City Hotel, which, as you know, is across
the street from where Marsan's body was found. He was
masked an' armed with a small-sword an' a knife, an' the
witness said as how he appeared to be keepin' a watch
out on the street, like as if he was waitin' for someone to
come past."

"What?" LeMoyne jerked to his feet and smote the
corner of the desk with his palm. "Mr. Davis was home in
bed . . . !"

"What witness?" asked January more mildly. "How
do they know it was Mr. Davis if he was masked?"

"Feller name of Tillich." Shaw consulted a rumpled
wad of illegible notes. "Described him pretty good: short
an' gray-haired with a round chin, wearin' a dark-blue
waistcoat—which folks at the gamblin' parlor at the Salle
d'Orleans say Davis was wearin' earlier that evenin'—an'
two watch-chains acrost it, one with fobs of hearts, diamonds, an' spades. It does sound like Davis."

"It does not," said LeMoyne stubbornly, "sound like
anything Mr. Davis would do. There are other fobs of
card-pips—I've seen them—or Mr. Davis's could have
been stolen—"

"But they wasn't," said Shaw. "They was on his
watch-chain when he was arrested. An' you can't deny Mr.
Davis has been in duels." Shaw spit—inaccurately—toward the sandbox in the corner. "I understand there was a
shootin'-match in 'twenty-nine, with an American feller
name of Burstin. . . ."

"Mr. Davis is the proprietor of a gaming establishment," said LeMoyne. "On that occasion the American
had not only been cheating, but impugned the honesty of
the house. Mr. Davis had no choice, under the circumstances, but to issue a challenge."

"Oh, I understand." Shaw folded his notes together

and stuffed them under the pile of newspapers, summonses, legal notices, and dog-eared ledgers that heaped the corners of his battered desk. "What I'm sayin' is, the law has to take all this into account. Now, far as I could find out just askin' around yesterday, this Mr. Tillich don't know John Davis from Davy Crockett, 'ceptin' as he's played in his gamblin'-rooms now an' then. He ain't a personal enemy an' has nuthin' to gain through lyin'. An' even if he was an' did, we'd still have to indict on the strength of it, an' the threats Mr. Davis made, in public, the day he heard about this opera they's both puttin' on. An' the day the law starts pickin' an' choosin' who it's gonna jail," he added, raising his eyes to January's face, "is the day I'd say we's all in trouble."

There was a moment's uncomfortable silence.

"What about Incantobelli?" asked January. "If anyone would have murdered Belaggio . . ."

"If'n anyone woulda murdered Belaggio," said Shaw, and spit again, "it woulda been Marsan. I'd'a picked Incantobelli to come in second myself, but Incantobelli *was* in Mr. Davis's gamblin'-rooms, till close on to four in the mornin', got up like a Roman emperor in this sort of purple-an'-gold tablecloth with about a peck of gold-painted spinach on his head. A hundred people saw him. You couldn't hardly not. An', I might add, no matter how dark that alley was, I'd have thought Incantobelli knowed Belaggio well enough to know that wasn't him."

"Damn this town," muttered LeMoyne as he and January made their way out into the flagstoned arcade that ran across the Cabildo's stuccoed face. Morning had stirred the Place d'Armes into full life before them: sellers of fruit and chocolate cried their wares beneath the plane-trees, a bright fringe around the confusion of market and levee, cotton-bales and hogsheads of sugar, carriages and market women and pigs. "It would only need that if the Americans on the City Council take it into their thick heads to push for a conviction just because of Mr. Davis's connections with so many of the French."

"Would they?" January glanced uneasily down at the little man. "What business is it of theirs . . . ?"

"What business?" LeMoyne's hazel eyes glinted cynically. "You talk like a damned Englishman, sir! What business is it of anyone's if a man is French or Creole or American or Chinese, for that matter? Except that most of the Americans in this town have tried to borrow money from French-owned banks—and have been turned down—and every Frenchman will tell you how the Americans are upstarts and have to be kept out of any positions that matter before they marry everyone's daughters." He shrugged. "What I'm afraid of—other than Mr. Davis suffering a stroke in that Bastille back there—is that if the case comes to trial, Mr. Davis will get caught in a political crossfire that's none of his doing. That he will be tried, not for his own crime, but for his jury's grievances against his friends. And don't think it doesn't happen all the time."

The doors behind them opened, and a man in the blue uniform of a city lamplighter escorted forth a chained group of prisoners armed with buckets and shovels, to clean the garbage from the municipal gutters. Since there were many miles of these, and guards to supervise the prisoners in the task were frequently in short supply, it was a job often pungently in arrears. January watched the sullen, bearded faces of the men, white and black and colored. All filthy, all bestial, all angry.

He wondered what they would make of the sick man in those overcrowded cells. The man in whose gambling-rooms they had almost certainly lost money.

"You're employed at the American Theater for the opera now, aren't you?" The Frenchman's voice broke into January's troubled reverie. "Mr. Davis told me he'd asked you to find out what was going on there."

"I've kept my eyes and ears open," replied January. "So far I haven't learned much. But Belaggio isn't the only one to be attacked."

"So I've heard. The ballet mistress, I understand. I may be able to make something of that in court." LeMoyne stepped aside as Shaw and two Guards slammed through the Cabildo doors with the air of firefighters scenting smoke, and strode away in the direction of Canal Street.

"Except she remembers nothing." January wondered what sort of violence anyone would have the energy to commit at not quite eight-thirty on a Saturday morning. "It isn't uncommon, in cases of concussion. She may remember later." And if she didn't, he thought, at least the incriminating bruises on her throat would have time to fade. "Yesterday what appeared to be a trap was laid out at Bayou des Familles, though it isn't clear whether it was for Belaggio or for the prima soprano. . . ."

"The one who can't sing?" LeMoyne made a face, leading January to deduce that the lawyer had been disloyal enough to his employer to attend either *Nozze* or *Muette*. "There was trouble between Belaggio and Marsan over her, wasn't there? Pity someone saw Belaggio." He shook his head, and as the Cathedral clock struck the half-hour, pulled out a steel watch-chain jangling with fobs, as if to confirm the time.

"Would you do something for me?" he asked, shoving the whole mess back into his pocket as well as he could. "I understand you have your living to make—pupils as well as rehearsals—but as you have time, could you write out for me everything you've learned so far? Send it here. . . ." He checked two or three pockets before producing a steel card-case, through which he searched for a time for a card that didn't have notes—or other people's addresses—scribbled on the back. The address was on the Rue Chartres: it had been altered in pencil twice. "In the meantime, I'll see if I can at least make sure the case comes before a French judge, and try to get as many Frenchmen on the jury as possible."

January watched the attorney out of sight, the last of the thinning mists waning away and sunlight sparkling over the confusion of the Place d'Armes. "Peas, peas, goober-peas," sang a tiny woman in an astonishing purple-and-yellow skirt, the basket of ground-nuts on her tignoned head huge as an oak-tree's crown. Another woman's voice lifted, wailed, trailed up and down strange African scales in praise of the flowers she bore; the fragrance of jack honeysuckle and verbena smote his nostrils like a brimming cup of mead.

Just 'cause you keep soap in the kitchen—January heard Olympe's smoky voice in his mind, hard on the heels of that familiar sweet scent—*don't make it food.*

Thoughtfully, he glanced at his own watch and turned his steps, not toward the gumbo-stand in the market for breakfast, but downriver, toward Dominique's house in the Rue Du Maine.

SEVENTEEN

Iphigénie Picard was just leaving the rose-colored stucco cottage Henri Viellard had given Dominique. Dominique's bosom friend, she was a year or two older and a little taller, her willowy height still further increased on this occasion by the intricate folds of a spectacular blue-and-yellow silk tignon, several blue-dyed ostrich-tips, and pattens strapped to her blue kid shoes to protect against the mud. *"Chère,* I know it hurts," she was saying as she drew on her gloves, fluffed the enormous Montespan sleeves of her jacket. "But I tell you, if you bear this child, it still won't hold him. Not with that mother—and not with that girl as his wife. They'll only say you conceived on purpose to get extra money out of him."

Dominique looked aside, lips like stone.

"Pretend it never happened. That way if he does stay your friend—and maybe he can lie to her about you— you'll have lost nothing."

"Except Henri's child." January's sister straightened her back, smiled her bright, sweet smile, and clasped her friend's hands. "Darling, thank you for caring. Thank you for coming this morning. . . ."

"Just think about what I've said. Please." Iphigénie looked over at January, standing a few yards off on the banquette to give the girls privacy, and beckoned. "Ben, you tell her. She's almost three months now. Whatever she's going to do, she has to do it soon. If she waits till after the wedding . . ."

Dominique's head lifted. "I'm not going to kill Henri's child until I know. . . ." She looked from her friend to her brother, eyes filling with tears. Very quietly, she said, "I'm not going to kill Henri's child."

"Dearest . . ."

Dominique held up her hand against Iphigénie's words. The older girl stood for a moment regarding her with exasperation and tenderness, then tiptoed awkwardly—Dominique still stood on the high brick step of the French door of her bedroom—and kissed her.

Then she walked away up Rue Du Maine, pattens clacking on the soft brick.

January walked around to the passway at the side of the house—it went without saying that no plaçée would admit even her brother through the doors a white man would use—and Dominique met him in the dining-room doorway. She looked up at him with her chin raised, as if she expected another argument of the kind she'd clearly just finished with Iphigénie; January bent his tall height and kissed her cheek.

"Did you know Sidonie Lalage?" he asked, and she regarded him for one blank, startled moment, then relaxed and smiled.

"Iphigénie told me Marsan was dead," she said, correctly bridging the reference. She glanced back into the parlor behind her, lifted her voice. "Thérèse, darling, would you bring another cup and some cocoa for my brother? Do you have time, p'tit?"

Past her, January could see the cocoa-cups on the parlor table beside the hearth, the warm amber glow of the fire reflected in simple vases of Venice glass, on yellow and white winter roses like the skirts of the little rats, on the sugar-bowl's plump custard-colored cheek.

"Was he going to see that poor silly singer who loved him so much? He was killed near the theater, Thérèse said." She seemed glad to put aside the topic of Henri and the decision she must make. Glad to be reminded that there were other griefs in the world not her own, and worse things that a man could do than marry a porcelain-pale girl with a mermaid's diamond heart.

January settled in the chair by the hearth that Iphigénie had vacated and related everything Shaw had told him about the manner of Marsan's murder and the condition of the body. "As it happened, Drusilla d'Isola was having her own adventures with slave-stealers down in the Bayou des Familles Thursday night. She says Marsan would have gone to the rehearsal and seen she was absent. But if he didn't, he might have returned to the theater to keep an assignation, particularly if he didn't believe whatever Belaggio might have told him about Drusilla not being there. You said Sidonie's family made trouble in court."

Dominique's forehead puckered. "Her mother did, yes. But even if it was Sidonie's brothers after all these years—and they might very well have attacked M'sieu Belaggio by mistake that first night, because he is a big man like M'sieu Marsan—I can't imagine them harming the rest of the company. That will be all, Thérèse, dearest, thank you. . . . Why would they lie in wait for you? Why hurt poor Madame Scie? Or leave that ghastly warning for Mademoiselle d'Isola? It doesn't make sense."

"It might," said January, spreading jam on the roll

Thérèse had brought him and hearing, from the rear bedroom, the stealthy creak of floorboard that told him the maid was eavesdropping again. He lowered his voice. "If whoever killed Marsan knew about the attacks on the opera company, and decided now was a good time to strike."

The roll was hot and fresh, the butter new from the market, garish with the dye of marigolds or carrots that covered the pallor of the winter season.

"At Roseaux the slaves immediately assumed that Marsan was the intended victim. And Olympe reminded me when Marguerite was hurt, that any one of these crimes may not, in fact, be connected to the others. Certainly the attempt to poison La d'Isola was part of another conflict entirely. Now, Marsan's own sins may in fact have nothing to do with his death, but I'm just a little curious as to where Sidonie Lalage's brothers were at the time of Marsan's death."

Dominique sighed, and stroked the plump white cat, Voltaire, who had come padding into the room and jumped onto her lap, kneading at her skirts with enormous soft paws. She was dressed in a gown of pink-striped jaconet, but Iphigénie had evidently arrived before she'd put up her hair—it lay over her back and shoulders in silky waves, catching mahogany gleams in the cool sunlight from the street. Her eyes looked suddenly older than her twenty-two years, and tired. Eyes that had seen too much, and understood too thoroughly how it was, between white men and the ladies of color they took unto themselves. "Yes," she said softly. "Yes, it was Vincent Marsan who deserved to die."

"Tell me about Sidonie."

"I didn't know her, you understand." Dominique

sighed, and in that sigh was the accumulated pattern of everything she had heard and knew from her mother, from her mother's friends, from the gossiping Thérèse. From other women who, like Sidonie Lalage, had stayed with men who struck them because they had contracted to do so, because they had nowhere to go except down. Women who had seen the men who claimed to love them walk away arm-in-arm with white girls of fortune, sending maybe a bouquet of flowers, maybe a strand of pearls: *pour prendre congé.* "I was twelve when Sidonie died, and still in school. But later I got to know her sister. And Cresside Morisset's aunt Marie-Pucelle was one of the witnesses at the trial. And of course Mama followed the case in the papers, and I heard about it every morning at breakfast for weeks."

She folded her hands on Voltaire's fluffy back. Collected her thoughts.

"According to Delia—Sidonie's sister—and to my friend Phlosine, who's Liane's cousin, Vincent Marsan was one of those men who didn't like his plaçée to see her family or her friends. He'd fly into blind rages if he came to the house when Phlosine or Liane's sister was there; I gather he did the same with Sidonie's friends. Even if they left before he came, he used to look around the house for signs that they'd been there, or come by at odd times during the day. You know how most people are very good about not visiting in the evening, when Henri's likely to be here—except poor Clemence Drouet, who has *no* tact—and of course I'd never *dream* of visiting Iphigénie or Phlosine, for instance, after dinner, because of course Yves or Philippe might be there. You know how it is."

January knew how it was. In the Paris demimonde it was the same. Daytimes belonged to one's friends, unless one's lover had sent word he'd be there for a drive in the Bois or an excursion to the shops of the Palais Royale. Nighttimes, women spent alone. Waiting. Jeweled and bathed, powdered and smiling, reading yellow-bound novels or thinking pleasant thoughts as they waited for a man who might or might not arrive, and might or might not be sober when he did.

Generally, January knew, men and women reached their little agreements. There were men like Henri Viellard, who scrupulously sent their mistresses notes when they might—or could not—be expected. Men who understood that these young ladies might like a night out with their friends now and then, or an evening to visit their families, mothers and sisters who were often in "the life" themselves. But even those men expected that when they came by the little houses at the back of the French town—the cottages along Rue des Ramparts and Rue Burgundy that they had purchased as part of the contract of plaçage—that they'd find their ladyfriends at home.

Waiting with a smile, just for them.

Get you to bed on the instant, Othello commands. *I will be returned forthwith.*

The women for their part knew that this was expected. And all except the queens of the demimonde understood that this was something they must accept. This was part of what it was to be a plaçée. They knew, too, what they themselves might expect if the man who supported them arrived, at any time of the day or evening, and found them gone.

"It's funny"—Dominique ran her fingers gently over Voltaire's apple-domed skull—"but men get so *angry* when you say they're like that. Jealous, I mean, and wanting their ladyfriend to be right there every minute. As if you said they had smelly feet or didn't clean their teeth. As if every woman in town can't tell what's going on when one of their friends suddenly just drops out of sight. Doucette's friend M'sieu Bouille is like that, and nobody sees Doucette anymore— Oh, I mean you'll see her in the market, and at the Blue Ribbon Balls with M'sieu Bouille, but she never comes to tea, or goes strolling in the Place d'Armes just because it's a lovely day. She never goes to see her mama and sisters, and always goes to the very earliest Mass on Sundays, and leaves before the end. When you see her she's always in a hurry, to get done what she has to do and then run home in case he comes. Liane is like that. And Sidonie was like that."

"Is Liane all right, by the way? Did someone tell her Marsan was killed?"

"Oh, yes. She's stunned, I think—Catherine Clisson told her, she heard it from an uncle of hers who works at Charity Hospital in the morgue. He said he knew right away who it was, because no one else in town would wear a coat of buff-colored velvet like that. Liane cried, Phlosine said, and said she felt hideously guilty about feeling so relieved. And fortunately she has family. Her sister Daphne is Prosper Livaudais's placée, because, of course, M'sieu Marsan won't have left Liane a penny, if he made a will at all."

Liane—the woman in red at the Blue Ribbon Ball— had tried to commit suicide last year, January recalled. He thought of Isabella Marsan, stiff as a doll in that shabby carriage, telling over her beads. Had she wept, he wondered, when she saw her husband's mutilated body in the morgue? Had she said, *O my beautiful one . . . ?*

"What happened the night Sidonie died?"

"I don't remember the details exactly." Dominique sank back in his chair, slim hands folded with an unconsciously protective gesture over his belly. January rose, and knelt by the hearth to add another few billets of pine to the flickering blaze. The nostalgic whiff of the smoke mingled with that of bread and cocoa and flowers, a kind of sweet sadness, like the songs he remembered his father whistling on the way to the fields. By the time he turned back to his chair, Voltaire was curled up in the center of the seat with every appearance of settling in for the day.

"There was a Blue Ribbon Ball that night, and Marsan challenged a man to a duel because he'd talked to Sidonie," Dominique went on as January lifted the cat's hefty weight and sat down again, Voltaire protesting in his pitiful kittenish voice. "Flirted with her, Marsan said, but the man—a French wine-merchant or something—swore he'd only spoken commonplaces with her, as any man will with a pretty girl."

Puta, January heard Belaggio scream, *putana,* and the icy splintering of the dish, spinning from d'Isola's hands to shatter on the beeswaxed floor.

"Marsan fought him later, too, days after Sidonie was dead. The surgeons had to stop the fight because the other man was so badly injured.

"In any case, Marsan took Sidonie away from the ball early and stayed with her for an hour or so at her house. Then he left, but he came back—Aunt Marie-Pucelle had the cottage across the street, and she was just about the only person who hadn't gone to the ball, because she had a cold that night. Except for everybody's servants, of course, but they all sleep back from the street and couldn't hear as well. Aunt Marie-Pucelle couldn't sleep and she saw a man she swears was Marsan let himself into the house with a key. A few minutes later she heard Sidonie screaming, screaming over and over. . . ."

"And she didn't investigate."

Dominique's mouth tightened like a furled rose. "Sidonie had screamed earlier that night, just after she and Marsan went into the house that first time," she replied, carefully devoid of expression. "Aunt Marie-Pucelle saw Sidonie let Marsan out a few minutes later and kiss him on the doorstep."

January said, "Ah."

"And she'd heard her scream on other nights. The slave-girl who lived in the room next to the kitchen—Sidonie's kitchen, I mean—said the same thing. Said she just put the pillow over her head. When you deal with someone like Marsan, that's all you can do, really. When the slave-girl—her name was Marthe—came out in the morning, she found a cab-driver who lived near there dead in the yard, stabbed through from the side, and Sidonie in the house. Her throat was cut. . . ." Dominique's gaze remained fixed on the leaping yellow silk of the new fire. "She had cuts on her hands and chest, and across her back, as if Marsan had chased her around the house. There was blood in every room, and furniture knocked over. The door from the house into the yard was open, and just inside they found a rose-colored kid glove that was supposed to be Marsan's, though at the trial he said it wasn't."

"And of course Marthe couldn't testify."

"No," said Dominique. "Cresside's aunt did. But the jury was all white men. So I'm not sure how much good it would have done if a slave like Marthe *could* testify. The jury ruled Sidonie had been killed by 'person or persons unknown,' but there was the most awful scandal, and M'sieu Marsan was in all sorts of financial trouble, because no one would back bills for him or extend him credit. Then later Mr. Knight came to town and took over running his plantation for him, and all of a sudden he had lots of friends again—"

If he was smuggling in slaves and selling them cheap, I just bet he did.

"—and new carriages and things. But Mama says there are still people who won't ask him to dinner."

He was carved up bad, Shaw had said. *Face, chest, belly . . . He didn't fight.*

A massive jade-green form squared off against the bull-like Belaggio. A sky-blue dandy in the courtyard of the New Exchange, golden hair gleaming in the morning light. The curve of a dusky purple arm, lifting d'Isola and bearing her up the stairs, and the way the girl Liane turned her head aside from the cup of negus, the bright liquid spilling on her crimson dress. . . .

Like as if he'd fallen down an' the man what did it knelt on top of him an' cut.

"How many brothers did she have?" asked January.

"Three. Delia died three or four years ago—her protector paid her off when he . . . when he married"— Dominique's voice stuck a little on the words—"and later she married a man who worked in the iron foundry. She died in childbed." Again that expressionlessness; again the protective touch on the smooth curve of pink-and-turquoise jaconet, the sleeping life inside. "If it was her brothers, wouldn't they have to have been connected with the theater in some way? To know about the attacks on the rest of the company? Though, of course, the way everyone in this town talks—I swear Thérèse was telling me the other day about why Mayor Prieur wants to sell off his matched bay carriage team! Because her sister is walking out with M'sieu Prieur's groom's friend . . . Why would they have waited till now? Sidonie's brothers, I mean. Why not when it happened?"

"I don't know." January shook his head, baffled. "This is all just—just thoughts. Questions I have. When I was out in Bayou des Familles, I thought there was something amiss with all this: that a slave, or a free colored, had to be involved."

Dimly the clock of the Cathedral sounded the three-quarters past nine, and January knew it was time for him to go. He'd promised to meet Rose for an early dinner that night, and to assist her backstage with Mount Vesuvius. It was the least he could do, he reflected, to make sure John Davis's theater didn't burn down or blow up while its master was incarcerated.

"Will you be all right?" he asked as he rose.

"Oh, yes," She stood, too, and walked with him through the little double parlor to the rear door. The small dining-table there was set already for lunch à deux: French china, exquisitely simple. Linen napkins freshly pressed. January recalled the chipped china on Madame Bontemps's table, the mended sheets worn nearly transparent. Faded curtains, and empty servants' rooms rented out to strangers.

Would Dominique come to that?

He couldn't imagine that chill-faced doll of a girl sanctioning a stipend that anyone could live on.

He paused in the door, aware of Thérèse somewhere in the house listening, and of the cook shelling peas at the table in front of the kitchen. "Can I do anything for you?"

The sweet mouth curved in a sudden wry smile that reminded him she was Olympe's sister, too. "You should see your face, p'tit," she said. "Can I—er—DO"—she pulled down the corners of her mouth in an expression of somber and significant discretion, at the same time mimed a grasping motion, like a surgeon's hand, toward her belly— "...uh... ANYTHING...for you? Not that we'll say what." She was laughing at him, but tears sparkled in her eyes.

And January laughed at his own euphemisms. "All right," he said, keeping his voice low. "But Iphigénie was right, you know. You'll have to make up your mind soon. And you probably won't know what Henri is going to do until after his wedding."

"I know." Dominique sighed. "And I'll speak to you when I... When I decide." She brushed back the tendrils of hair that surrounded her face, re-settled her tortoise-shell combs.

Had Sidonie Lalage's hair been up or down, January wondered as he walked away, that morning ten years ago when her slave-girl had found her soaked in her own blood?

When he reached the theater, it was to find James Caldwell in the midst of replacing Princess Isabella's second act aria with "Look Out Upon the Stars, My Love," and Tiberio grumbling about the decision to incorporate all the smoke and fire effects of Vesuvius into the cave of the doomed Robert's infernal parent, while Belaggio in his office re-counted his narrow escape to Hector Blodgett, a journalist who worked for the New Orleans *Bee*.

"The man is insane!" Belaggio's voice boomed forth as January came up the steps to the backstage. "Obsessed! I have heard him myself, blaming the failure of his opera season this year on me—blaming me for the losses in his gaming-rooms, even! Envy..." He shook his head gravely, and Blodgett, sloppy and bewhiskered and more than half drunk, nodded and scribbled something in his notebook. "Envy is at all times and places the greatest foe of art. . . ."

"Ah-ha!" Herr Smith came bustling out of the rehearsal-room and caught January's arm. *"It is in good time! I feared Herr Sefton would have to play for the rehearsal alone. . . ."*

Madame Rossi and Madame Montero emerged from the prop-room, arms filled with brown peasant skirts and tags of lace.

". . . simply too plain," La Montero was saying. "It's ridiculous that I should be required to look like a farm-girl. . . ."

"But, Madame, Alice *is* a farm-girl. . . ."

"Fire, he says." Tiberio perched grumblingly on one of the net-draped bollards that had so lately decorated the shore of Portici village and was soon to do duty as medieval Sicily. "More fire. One ovation and now he must have fire everywhere. . . ."

"They have a witness who claims he saw Davis at the City Hotel just before the murder," said January softly as he took his place beside Hannibal in the rehearsal-room. Several little rats were warming up at the barre with exercises January recognized as Marguerite's. Miss Flaherty had cornered Caldwell and was trying to convince him to enlarge the mad, ghostly dancing abbess's role to include a song, and possibly a romantic interlude with the hero as well.

"Sure, and Mr. Trulove thinks I'm good enough—"

"The fact that Davis is an honest and clean-living person doesn't mean he wouldn't have assassinated Belaggio." Hannibal coughed, and tightened the pegs on his violin. "Quite the contrary, in fact. *One may smile, and smile, and still be a villain. . . .* Not that I'd wish a stay in the Cabildo on even the dishonest and filthy-hearted. But at the moment it's a fairly moot point." He tightened another peg, drew the bow experimentally across the strings, and then played a fragment of "The Lost Sheep," like a stray butterfly in the dingy room. "I've located the Gower boys."

EIGHTEEN

⬥⬥⬥⬥⬥

"I wouldn't let you anywheres near him." Kentucky Williams looked January up and down with hard blue lashless eyes in a face like five pounds of veal. " 'Ceptin' he needs a doctor bad, and ol' Doc Furness been drunk a week."

At this hour—rehearsals hadn't ended until nearly five—her front room, and indeed most of the surrounding Swamp, was fairly quiet. Men drifted in from the levee or the canal, joshed with friends, lit up long-nines, and cracked jokes with the few women who worked the place. When the damp river breeze bellied the sheet of osnaburg that did duty as a door, January could see the physician in question, snoring soddenly on a bench in the corner. From here he could smell the man, too, which given the general atmosphere of woodsmoke and sewage that typified the Swamp argued for a fair degree of pungency closer up.

"What's wrong with him? Gower, I mean, not Furness."

"Cut up." Kate the Gouger, sitting tailor-fashion on Williams's unsheeted bed beside Hannibal, paused in the act of braiding her rufous hair. A half-barrel near-by did duty as a nightstand, bearing two candles and a battalion of half-finished liquor-bottles. January wondered that mere proximity to the spilled dregs didn't ignite the place. "Took a cut in that alley rumpus, and it's all swole up an' fever. Furness bled him four-five times—puked him real good, too—but he just gets worse. Reckon if they put him in the Calaboose, he'd die."

Him and Davis, thought January.

Williams was pulling on a man's buckskin jacket over her grease-spotted calico. "You bring your bag?"

January nodded. He'd paid the son of the Fatted Calf's proprietor to fetch it, but the boy had been turned away by Madame Bontemps, who'd insisted that January's note to her had been forged by King Louis's spies. He wasn't sure whether she meant Louis the Sixteenth or the Eighteenth—it could have been the Eleventh, for all he knew. In the end, January had walked back to his lodgings, fetched the bag, then rendezvoused with Hannibal at Williams's. It was after six, and he'd given up all hope of supper with Rose. He only hoped Rose would still speak to him, at whatever hour he finally managed to present himself at the Théâtre d'Orleans.

Williams whistled through her teeth, and a couple of men pushed through the curtain, Kaintucks, filibusters, or keelboatmen, bearded and filthy like most of their breed. As they blindfolded January, he heard Kate say, "I went and heard that operee last night, that you give me tickets to? I never heard anything so pretty in all my life. It ain't right, somebody tryin' to do them nice folks a harm. . . ."

Heavy hands took January's arms, pushed him out into the drizzly chill of the early-falling night.

He didn't think they led him far. The smell of the Swamp lessened around him, the stink of tobacco and woodsmoke and untended privies gave way to the thick green odor of standing water. He felt the wet slash of weeds on his trouser-legs, the soggy give of the uneven ground, and nearly broke his shin on what had to be a cypress-knee. Then the tufts of grass underfoot gave way to the slither of bare mud and the stink of civilization again, and he heard the knock of wood on wood, the faint plash of water.

Near the canal, then.

Hannibal coughed. One of his escorts spit.

"Here we are."

Leather hinges creaked. The muggy atmosphere of a shut-up room and the overpowering stink of sickness: rotting flesh, latrine bucket, blood, and the foul sweat of illness soaked into bedding unwashed. A tallow candle and greasy sausage. Rats. January heard water splat from a wrung-out rag, and a man said softly in coarse English, "You gonna be all right, Buck. Don't you give up on me now."

"Pull that curtain over the window," instructed Williams. "You want the whole town to see us?" And then, "Here's the doctor we talked about."

The blindfold was removed. "They's nigger doctors?" asked a big blond bearded man in surprise, straightening up from where he knelt by the dirty pallet on the floor.

January opened his mouth to snap that if he was so damn nice in his taste, he could go to the Cabildo and ask for a physician there, then met the man's eyes. And saw he was young, probably under twenty, the blond beard like the loose, soft stringy fuzz of a puppy's coat. Saw that there was no malice in his words or his eyes, only genuine brute ignorance. Saw that he'd been crying.

The young man's gaze went to Kate as the Gouger

unblindfolded Hannibal, then to Kentucky. He looked
back at January and swallowed hard. "You ain't—you ain't
gonna bleed him again, are you? I don't know if he can
take it."

"Don't worry, sir," said January. "Nigger doctors don't
bleed 'em like white ones do." He glanced at Williams,
said in the deliberately sloppy English copied from Shaw,
"Might you get your boys to boil me some water, m'am?
Clean the wound up a little so's I can see what we got?"

He could already tell what they had: raging infection
by the smell of it, the fever-ravaged body weakened
steadily by bleeding, purging, and probably dosing with
calomel as well while the slash wound on the right biceps
probably hadn't even been washed. He took half a dozen
candles from his bag and drew the packing-box close to
support them.

Buck Gower was delirious, but so debilitated by fever
that Williams and one of her boys could hold him easily
as January first irrigated the wound, then with deft speed
carved out the decaying tissue. Behind him, he heard the
murmur of Kate's voice, explaining things to the sick
man's brother. He heard the word "operee" and later,
". . . want to know who hired you. . . ."

"They ain't gonna tell the Guards?" asked Bart anx-
iously. "I said, *no Guards*. . . ."

" 'Course Ben ain't gonna tell the Guards. What's he
gonna tell 'em? Sassafras is bringin' his boat down tonight
an' you'll be out of town an' gone come mornin'."

Once the arm was clean, January inspected it
minutely, holding the candles close. Though horribly
swollen and oozing, the surrounding flesh and the arm
below it showed no sign of the dark lividity of
mortification, and the sweetish, nauseating whiff of gan-
grene was absent from the wound itself. When January

had trained at the Hôtel Dieu, there had been two or three surgeons there who had insisted on fanatical cleanliness of their persons, their tools, and the wounds on which they worked, and though these men had been roundly scorned by most of their colleagues, January had observed that they seemed to lose fewer patients. And keeping everything clean, he reflected as he packed and bound the yawning mess with fresh lint, was such a simple thing to do, and no sillier than putting slices of onion under the patient's bed to chase away the vapors of contagion. . . .

If it *was* silly. Some people in the plague hospitals during last summer's outbreak of yellow fever had recovered after such onion-slices had been placed. January personally didn't think the onions did anything but vary the diet of the local rats—dozens more patients had perished than had survived—but then, he didn't think bleeding helped, either.

Another reason, he thought, that he probably would never be able to make his living as a surgeon, even should he somehow and miraculously become as white as a Swede.

Good thing I can play the piano.

"You gonna give him medicine?" Bart Gower edged his way back to January's side, and snuffled, wincing as he did so. His left cheek was discolored and swollen where January's fist had connected with it in the alley beside the theater, and that side of his mustache was slick and glistening with a permanent leakage of watery mucus from the break. "Katie tells me you said you'd help him if'n I told you about bein' hired to kill this operee dago. That you wouldn't help Buck if'n I didn't."

January glanced back at Kate. With her snarly hair and her uncorseted frock, she looked dirty and sinister, tamping smoking-tobacco into the bowl of a clay pipe with her thumb, her tongue thrust out a little between her teeth in concentration. She'd probably lain with both of Kentucky's bearded henchmen—possibly with the Gower boys as well—with as little thought as she'd have given to drinking coffee with them in the market-place: what's another man, more or less? And if any of those four men were to decide to cut her throat as an accompaniment to coupling, they would almost certainly never be caught or punished.

This is the fruit of whoring, they would say with Iago. A woman who lets a man have her is admitting that he is permitted to do with her what he pleases.

January's jaw tightened, and he looked back at the young man kneeling beside him. "The lady mis-heard me, sir," he said. He settled back on his heels. "If you'd tell me who hired you, I'd appreciate it, because it might save the lives of myself and my friends. But I don't hold back from helping a man because he can't pay, or can't help me in return."

Bart Gower looked around indecisively, then picked up a bottle from the several on the packing-box and held it out to him. January accepted it, and took a drink—fiery and vile. Handing it back, he said, "I better not take more of that. The man who hired you may be waiting for me the minute I start back for home alone, and I'll need my wits."

Bart took a brief swig, winced, snuffled again, and stood to hand the bottle along to Kentucky. "Buck gonna be all right?" he asked again, his eyes pleading. "That other doctor—Lordy, it give me the creeps to see him, with his knife all waverin' around in his hand. We got a feller gonna take us out of here tomorrow, get us back to Ohio. We thought we was some punkins, but we was sure wrong." He wiped his mustache gingerly, as if his whole face still hurt on that side, and held his other hand down to help January to his feet. "We just wanted the money to get home on, see."

January nodded. "It's a bad town, sir," he said, "to those who come to it for the first time." He went to the bucket, where what was left of the boiled water still steamed gently in the candle-spotted gloom. Bart followed him, and watched with puppy-like curiosity as he washed his hands again, as if he'd never seen a man perform this same act so many times in the same night— maybe the same year.

"You said a mouthful," the boy agreed. "Buck gonna be all right?"

"I don't know." January dried his fingers as well as he could on the bandanna from his pocket. "It would be best if you could let him rest a few more days before you try to travel. . . ."

"We can't." Bart shook his head vigorously. "Not if some other fella got hisself killed by that theater. We didn't do that, I swear it to God, but I been here nursin' Buck here by myself, an' who's gonna believe me? We been waitin' to get Buck better all this time, an' all he got was worse."

"Then take this." January held out the little packet of powdered willow-bark that was Olympe's favored febrifuge, and wrote on it, with the stub of pencil, F, for fever. "Boil it in water, like tea—about this much"—he sketched a few tablespoonfuls in his palm—"at a time. It will bring his fever down some. And wash the wound with this, boiled up in water"—he wrote W, for wash, on a packet of comfrey root—"and change the bandage every day for as clean a one as you can get."

The boy nodded earnestly, marking the instructions

down in his mind. In a gang of men, thought January, he'd probably have beaten January up on the street if that was the entertainment going that night. Now he was alone, and confused, in pain himself and scared for his brother, and wanted only to go home. Where his mother and sisters probably loved him.

January wondered why he continued to strive to understand humankind. How much simpler to hate and be done.

"Thank you." The boy snuffled, and shoved one packet into each of his trouser pockets. He took another drink from his bottle. "Well, I can't tell you the name of who hired us, 'cause I don't know it, but it was a lady, not a man. A woman, anyway . . ."

He hesitated, trying to sort out remembered distinctions of dress and speech in his mind, and January, startled, said, "A woman?"

Bart nodded. "She come right into the Blackleg, where Buck was dealin' cards—we made a kind of deal with ol' Shotwell that owns the place for a cut of Buck's winnin's. Tryin' to make back some of what we lost so we could go home again, see. An' she says, 'You Bart Gower? I hear you're lookin' for a way to make some money.' "

"This woman knew your names?"

"Well . . ." He made a little embarrassed shrug. "Just about ever'body round the Swamp knew by that time we was lookin'. We did a little stealin', see, on the levee. But the Levee Boys let Buck and me know it was their territory, an' took most of it off us."

"I see." January reflected that between the City Guards and the various gangs that regularly worked robberies on the levees and such hellholes as Girod and Gallatin streets, it probably wasn't easy to make money in

New Orleans even as a freelance thief. Bart and Buck were lucky to make it home with no worse than a broken cheekbone and a useless arm. Many simply ended up in the river or the morgue. "What day was this? The day you made the hit?"

"Day before." Bart wiped his nose again.

Wednesday, then. "What did she look like? Was she white or black?"

"Oh, white. They don't let no black girls into the gamblin'-room at the Blackleg. She had on this veil over her hat"—his fingers sketched something that looked like Spanish moss over his face—"but I could see through it she was white." He fished around in what was probably a rather limited vocabulary for something to illustrate his memory of the encounter. "I think her hair was brown."

"Brown eyes?" asked January, since the dark scrim of a veil would have obscured whether her complexion was pink or olive, and in any case he doubted the boy would make the distinction. Bart nodded. "Or blue?" Bart thought about it and nodded again. "Was she tall? Short?"

"I dunno. All girls is kinda short, ain't they?"

To Bart they would be, of course. Bart was only an inch or so shorter than January's six-feet-three.

"Young or old?"

"Young, I guess. I mean, she weren't bent over like a old lady or nuthin', an' she talked like she had all her teeth. She talked to us over in a corner of the gamblin'-room, away from the lights, so it was kinda hard to see. Mr. Shotwell, he don't spend too much on lamp-oil. But she had this kind of accent, like folks around here do."

"But she spoke English?"

"Well, yeah." He looked surprised that January would have to ask.

"And she offered you money to—what? Beat up a man in the theater alley?"

"Kill him," replied Bart somberly. "She said, *I want him corpsed. I want him cold stiff for the dirty bastard he is.* That's what she said. An' she give Buck a hundred dollars an' said there'd be a hundred more when she seen the body. Said to wait in the alley by the American Theater an' he'd be along about midnight. Which he wasn't—it was close on to three in the mornin', an' we'd waited there for hours, with other people comin' in and out an' all."

"In?"

"There was this fella got down from a cab an' went in, right after we got there. He had on a mask, an' a big hat, an' a pistol, too—we seen it by the light over the door we's s'posed to watch."

"Was he tall?" January asked. "Short?"

"Yeah. Shorter'n us, anyway." Bart's forehead squinched with concentration, trying to summon back a recollection of a shadow glimpsed in shadow. "I only saw him good from the back, when he went up the steps into the door."

Belaggio's Austrian contact. And of course any white man could walk around New Orleans on a Carnival night masked and cloaked and bristling with weaponry. No wonder Shaw didn't look like he'd slept since Twelfth Night.

"You called him an opera dago a few minutes ago," said January. "Is that what she called him?"

"No. That's just what Kate said just now. This woman—lady—said as how he'd be big, big as us. A big white man. *Take him,* she said, *an' snuff him. Cut him up bad.* An' her voice got mean when she said it, like he done somethin' to her. An' later Buck said to me, *Let that be a*

lesson not to rile up a woman in THIS town, little brother.
An' we laughed."

He looked down at his brother, sunk into sleep now,
his breathing light and slow. Under matted, lousy hair his
face was haggard and thin. Bart reached down and
touched the unswollen hand. Snot dripped off his mustache, and he wiped it again, as January suspected he'd be
wiping it for the remainder of his life. "God, I hope he's
gonna be well."

A woman, thought January as he, Hannibal, and Kate the
Gouger made their way back toward the Place d'Armes. It
was something he hadn't expected to hear.

Grimy light filtered from the windows of the bars and
saloons, glinted on the criss-crossed lines and X's of
wheel-ruts like some indecipherable, muddy map. Along
the building-fronts, where tufts of filthy grass made the
ground firmer, men jostled along in their high boots,
homespun shirts, and rough flannels; eyes gleamed in the
shadows as they passed. Music scratched and razzled. A
woman in a calico dress staggered out of the Turkey-Buzzard, fell on her knees in the gutter before January, and
whimpered, her hair hanging down over her face. In the
saloon the men roared with laughter.

When January stooped to help her to her feet, she
spit on him, pulled her arm free of his steadying hand,
and staggered away.

A woman.

"You have any insight into what Madame Montero
was doing Wednesday afternoon?" he asked as he and his
companions resumed their walk.

"May I see your watch?" Hannibal answered, and

paused in the bar of ochre light from the door of the Ripsnorter Saloon to look at the time. "Half past nine. I wondered how long it would take you to ask me that question."

"Admittedly, it doesn't sound very much like her."

"It doesn't sound anything like her." The fiddler snapped the watch-case closed and handed it back. "I can't see Concha depriving herself of the pleasure of stabbing Lorenzo Belaggio in the back herself—that carving-up of the corpse does sound like a woman, doesn't it?"

Kate shoved him in not-quite-mock annoyance and said, "I'll carve *you* up, pard."

"But in fact Consuela did what any sane woman would do upon arrival in a foreign city: she went shopping. With Madame Chiavari and her husband, I gather to devastating effect."

"Just asking."

"Wednesday is a trifle early for it to have been any of the ladies of the St. Mary Opera Society," Hannibal went on, hopping across the ankle-deep slough where Tchoupitoulas crossed Gravier Street, and offering a gallant hand to Kate. "The company arrived from Havana only Tuesday, and if the motive for mayhem had anything to do with the subject matter of *Othello,* while I can't say *no one* would have had time to become murderously offended, it does sound rather quick. Particularly if one had bullyboys to locate and hire. It argues for familiarity with the town."

As he made his way toward the Théâtre d'Orleans after parting company with Kate and Hannibal, January had to admit that the fiddler's point was a good one. Everyone in the Swamp knew the Gower boys were for hire. But someone from out of town would need a local informant.

January arrived at the Théâtre barely in time to help

Rose set flares in the sides of Mount Vesuvius for the Act Five finale and to crouch beneath the stage to work the steam-cocks that generated what appeared to be volcanic smoke. Though he was far less fond of the forced, barking style of singing favored by the French opera, it was still plain that both the Princess Elvira's singing and Fenella's dancing were considerably superior to those displayed by their alter-egos on the previous night.

Sparse applause echoed discouragingly in the half-empty theater. January hoped that if Monsieur LeMoyne were present, he'd make as good a story of it as he could when he reported to Davis in the jail. The owner of the Théâtre had enough problems without hearing his show had failed.

Afterward January walked home with Rose in the chilly mists, Rose with her tignon and dress smelling of sulfur and paraffin and smuts of ash on her cheek. They drank coffee in the market arcade and ate beignets and ginger-cake, and watched maskers driving their carriages full of Ivanhoes and Greek gods and Indians and Turks through the square, the steamboats on the levee all lit up like jewel-boxes and music pouring out of saloon doors and houses. They giggled and groaned about Vesuvius's shortcomings, and re-wrote the ending of the opera with the heroic fisherman and his loyal companions being locked in a barn on the far side of Herculaneum and missing the revolution entirely. When January walked Rose up to the gallery of her little rented room, he put his hands on her slim waist and kissed her gently; felt her stiffen for one instant at old memories, old hurts. Then her hands slid swift and light around his shoulders and her mouth grew warm under his, tasting at first, hesitant, then crushing, devouring, and yielding to be devoured.

January walked home feeling curiously breathless and

light, as if he'd found a note from God under his pillow, saying, *Everything will be all right.*

Everything will be all right.

He went to Mass early the following morning. At a guess, the man he hoped to see at the Cathedral wouldn't attend until later—if he attended at all—and January knew he might have to wait, and watch, a good part of the day. The early Mass was mostly market-women, black and white and colored, though January recognized Dominique's friend Doucette LaBayadère, hurrying in early that she might the sooner hurry home. Home to wait for her protector, in case he should chance to come . . .

He lit a candle before the Virgin's statue after the Mass was done. Told over his beads in prayer as the priests' voice rose: *Adorate Deum, omnes Angeli ejus. . . .*

For Marguerite, he thought. *Blessed Mary ever-Virgin, hold her hand.*

And another one, in gratitude, for his own sake and that of Rose.

Everything will be all right.

Emerging from the sanctuary's dimness, January saw silhouetted before him in the doorway the tignon of a tall woman just going out—a tignon tied in seven points, like a halo of flame. Only one woman in New Orleans wore such a style—she who wore it would permit no imitators. "Mamzelle Marie," he called, and Marie Laveau turned back to him and smiled.

Unlike Olympe, the voodooienne was a devout Christian, worshipping the God whose light she saw through the different-colored lenses of both *loa* and saints. "Will you have coffee with me?" he asked her, and they settled themselves on a bench near the fruit-sellers and cafés that ranged the upstream side of the square, where he could watch those who came and went through the Cathedral doors. After Mamzelle Marie had asked his judgment of Marguerite's condition, and they exchanged opinions on Philippe duCoudreau's discretion about where January had been when Marguerite was attacked ("He'll keep his lip tight, never fear that," she said), he asked her, "Did you know Sidonie Lalage?"

"That I did," said the voodoo queen. She was dressed quietly, in accord with the surroundings, her dark wool frock the dress of a well-off carpenter's widow, which was what she was. Like his mother, and the more prosperous *libre* women both respectable and plaçée, she wore corsets, the whalebone giving her clothing and posture a straight, queenly dignity. Only her tignon, blue-and-violet madras that framed a face in which the high cheekbones of an Indian joined strong, clear features of both African and white, showed what she truly was: none but the reigning voodoo queen could wear a tignon wrapped into seven points.

"Sidonie'd come to me many nights, for *ouanga* to make him love her, for powders to make him care. She'd ask me for little charms and gris-gris, too, to bring him luck in gambling, to make the saints send him money. This was back in the days when he had little. *He'll be happier when he worries less about money,* she'd say. *He'll treat me better when things are better for him.*"

She shook her head, in her Indian-dark eyes the wisdom one acquires when one is queen of secrets; patience and tolerance learned only by peering into the ugliest of shadows. "I couldn't convince her it doesn't work so."

January said nothing. Had Isabella Marsan, he wondered, gone to Mamzelle Marie with one of her husband's colored gloves, for a mix of steel dust, sugar, and honey to

draw him back to her? Had Dominique at least thought
of asking Olympe to make her a packet of gunpowder,
flaxseed, wasp-mud, and filé to cast across Chloë St.
Chinian's doorstep?

They both watched Liane Troyes as she emerged from
the Cathedral, her opulent figure sheathed in mourning,
her soft brown-sugar face framed by the darkness of a veil.
Would she seek another protector? January wondered. Or
had her experience with Marsan turned her against the
life of a plaçée?

One thing was certain. Even behind a veil, and in the
smoky gloom of the Blackleg Saloon, there was no way
that woman could have been mistaken for white.

"She's lucky, that one," said Mamzelle Marie quietly.
"Lucky Marsan did not turn on her as he turned on
Sidonie. For such men as he, no matter how careful a
woman is, no matter how still she sits, he'll always find a
reason to be angry."

"What else do you know," he asked, "about Vincent
Marsan?"

But at that moment he saw, coming around the corner of the Cabildo, the man he sought. After Shaw's description of the purple toga and gilded wreath, he'd
insensibly been expecting everyday garb of equal flamboy-
ance. In fact, Incantobelli wore a plain coat of drab gray
wool, and his silver hair was brushed back under a dilapidated beaver hat. He slouched along almost shyly, with
none of the swashbuckling verve he'd displayed as Puss in
Boots. January could conclude only that there was something about a costume that released the artist in the man.

Like those engravings one saw of Shakespeare, he
thought: balding, demure, and howlingly middle-class.

January excused himself to Mamzelle Marie and re-entered the Cathedral, taking his place in that portion of the side aisle reserved for the free colored, but where he could watch the castrato during the ensuing Mass. Though the nave was far more crowded now than it had been, he was still close enough to confirm his earlier impressions of lithe slimness and medium height. The swarthy face, without a mask, was puckish with a thousand lines and dominated by a nose like the beak of a Roman warship; two dandyish waistcoats of cream and charcoal-gray revealed a glimpse of theatricality under the nondescript coat.

After the Mass, January followed him out, to where he paused to buy a bunch of violets from a girl on the step, and called out, "Signor Incantobelli!"

The singer turned, took one look at him, gasped in horror, and bolted into the crowds of the Place d'Armes.

It was the last thing January had expected. "Signor, wait . . . !"

Incantobelli veered to head for the line of fruit-stands set up under the sycamore trees along the square's edge, where the crowd was thickest. January, moving to cut him off, edged and dodged through the market-women, idlers, well-dressed ladies on their way to the Fashion Show Mass. Incantobelli darted up to a gentleman just emerging from Bernadette Metoyer's chocolate-shop, caught the man's shoulders with the light strength of a waltzer on the dance-floor, shouted "Thief! He has stolen your watch, sir!" and thrust him into January's arms.

Too startled—and too close—to dodge, January found himself tangled in the gentleman's arms and legs, being elbowed and belabored with a mahogany cane: "Ah, will you, you wretch!" When he struggled to free himself, the man seized him, and three others—two merchant types and a steamboat pilot in a blue coat—hung on to him like staghounds as Incantobelli darted away into the crowd.

"Damned thieves are all over this city!"

"Had my wallet lifted the other day . . . !"

"Right in front of the goddamn Calaboose . . . !"

"Sir!" January knew better than to lift a finger in his own defense, merely ducked his head into his raised arms and stood still. At least, he thought, he wasn't in the Swamp, so it was unlikely he'd be knocked down and kicked. "Sir, I didn't take your watch! I didn't take your watch, sir!" he kept repeating. "It was an accident, sir!"

"Don't you lie to me, boy!"

"Thievin' nigger . . ."

"Put him in the stocks. . . ."

It wasn't until they dragged him into the Cabildo and thrust him before the sergeant at the desk that January was able to say, "Sir, look in your pocket, sir. Your watch is still there, sir," and be heard.

The man brought out his watch—flashy Dutch-gold that probably cost a quarter of what January's had—and reddened. "Got you before you brought it off!" he trumpeted, his white sidewhiskers fairly bristling with fury.

January didn't dare roll his eyes. "Sir, you're very lucky you were the one he picked to shove," he replied, wondering if DeMezières—the desk sergeant—would recognize him as a friend of Shaw's, or whether he was going to spend the night comparing notes about *La Muette de Portici* with John Davis. "It's an old game, sir. One man starts a fight that way between two completely innocent strangers, and during the scuffle his accomplices go around and pick the pockets of everyone who stops to watch."

He glanced around him. Of course Shaw was absent, on a Sunday.

"You know damn-all about it," growled the white-whiskered man.

"I should," said January in his best English, and manufactured a rueful grin. "I got taken that way about six months ago, stopping to watch an affray just like it on the levee. It cost me a silk handkerchief and a week's pay."

And if the three rescuers start to laugh at him for being taken in, he thought, *I'm doomed.*

But one of them—a ginger-haired man in coarse tweed—only remarked, "Deuced clever," and the steamboat pilot spit in a contemplative fashion on the floor.

"You were right to react the way you did," added January, not mentioning that if the white-whiskered gentleman had gone after another white man with his cane on so little provocation, he'd have ended up taking an unexpected bath in the nearest municipal gutter. "And very quick, too." He wondered the next moment if that was a little too fulsome, but the man only made a harrumphing noise, like a dog brought to heel and consenting to be patted.

But of course he and his three rescuers and newfound friends had to recount the whole affair to Sergeant De-Mezières from beginning to end, and minutely examine January's papers. When the Sergeant identified January as a well-known and respectable musician—"as honest as the day is long"—the third man, a stringy Westerner of the kind January had seen picking through the New Exchange for bargains, demanded, "And how do we know that?"—not of DeMezières, but of the other three. "Goddamn Frenchmen stand behind their friends no matter what they do."

The Sergeant stiffened. "You're talking of the law in this city, my friend. . . ."

"I'm no friend of no Frenchman and I'm talkin' about the dam' police, not the law." The Westerner's pale eyes blazed. "And I know dam' well you'd let a man pick pockets right here in this here dam' room if he give you a cut, because that's what the banks in this damn Frenchified town do. . . ."

Altogether, it was some hours before January emerged from the Cabildo, nursing the half-dozen fresh bruises from the white-whiskered gentleman's cane and wondering what the hell had caused that expression of utter, panicky terror he'd glimpsed in Incantobelli's eyes.

NINETEEN

⸺

"I had no idea you were so formidable, Benjamin." Hannibal worked the yellow chunk of rosin along his bowstring, touching it now and then with a finger to judge the texture. "I see I need to give myself greater credit for daring to be in your company."

"A daring that Incantobelli clearly doesn't share," replied January. "Since I cannot imagine an operatic soprano of forty years' standing being seized with such shyness, I can only guess he was afraid of who might see him talking to me."

Hannibal ran a sinister trill of descending minor notes on his violin, to test the bow, and glanced at January under raised brows. "The gentleman who tried to strangle Marguerite? One can scarcely blame him. When it comes to protecting themselves the people who shoved Davis into the arms of the police the way Incantobelli shoved your friend with the white whiskers into yours yesterday don't seem to know what scruples are. If Incantobelli hadn't been wearing that—er—unmistakable garb in a public place the night of Marsan's murder, they'd have found someone who saw *him* masked and cloaked and wearing a small-sword at the City Hotel, instead of Davis. Remind me to purchase a crimson coat with gold braid

on the sleeves or something equally memorable. . . .
Costly thy habit as thy purse can buy. . . ."

"*Rich, not gaudy,*" agreed January, and he bit into the
juicy sweetness of an apple taken from his music-satchel.

Deeper in the bowels of the cavern, Tiberio muttered
in Sicilian, "More flame, he says. Let us have the show."
He adjusted the red glass filters that would color and
magnify the eerie, flickering gas-jet's light. "They will do
Barber of Seville and have Figaro make his entrance
through a trap-door in a blaze of fire. . . ."

"Did you see Davis?" Hannibal asked.

"I was lucky I didn't spend the night with him." January pitched the apple-core into the nearest sandbox. "I
spoke with LeMoyne and offered to cancel my pupils this
morning to testify at the arraignment as to the state of
Davis's health, but LeMoyne said it wasn't necessary. They
got Ker from the hospital," he added, trying not to let the
annoyance he felt carry into his voice. It was childish—
and, his confessor would have said, prideful: Dr. Ker had
been asked because he was the head of Charity Hospital,
not because he was white and January was black. Moreover, January knew it.

He shook his head at himself. Hannibal had been
right when he'd said there was a miasma in this land of
slavery, like the red light of illusion, that tainted all
things.

"LeMoyne says Davis is holding up—he's been running a faro-bank in his cell since Friday. . . ."

"Sounds like him." Hannibal poked with his bow at
one of the theater cats who'd leapt up to investigate the
uneaten dish of jambalaya he'd bought from one of the
street vendors for lunch. All around them, chorus-boys
and musicians were filtering in, joking and calling to one

another; Caldwell rapped at the door of Belaggio's office, then rapped again. It occurred to January that he'd seen little of the impresario in the three days since Marsan's murder. He'd kept to his office as much as he could during rehearsals Friday and Saturday, arriving late and departing early.

And, January realized, never alone.

Had Belaggio, too, seen the Devil with a knife, waiting on a banquette in the dark?

". . . assumed Drusilla would go to the Young Italians of her acquaintance when she found the note," Hannibal was saying—January pulled his attention back with an effort—"but not that she'd invite you to the picnic. Certainly not that she'd have the bottom to rent a gig herself. Were the horses ever found, by the way?"

"Oddly enough, yes. Desdunes from the livery returned my deposit money to me yesterday, and told me that white-stockinged bay I rented had been found about a mile from Big Temple—on Bayou des Familles—" he added, seeing his friend's eyebrows lift at this curious piece of nomenclature, "and brought back to town by Sam Pickney. And just now Cavallo said that Thunderbolt and the two horses he and Bruno rented were found grazing by the river near English Turn."

"Meaning whoever took them didn't want to be seen with them in town." Hannibal drew up his feet to let Mr. Rowe, the theater manager, pass, frantically giving instructions to Paddy about bringing up the flats for tonight's performance of *The Soldier's Daughter*. "Has it occurred to you, by the way, that if Incantobelli's a soprano, and slight of build, he could easily have passed himself off as a woman. . . ."

"Theoretically," agreed January. "Have you had a

close look at our Neapolitan nightingale? His nose is on
the botanical order—somewhere between a large yam and
a cypress-knee—and he has more lines on his face than a
linen shirt straight out of the mangle. Unless that veil was
thicker than a trade-goods blanket, even so unobservant a
witness as Bart Gower must have commented that their
employer was the ugliest woman he'd ever seen."

"Hmn." Hannibal shifted again as Claud Cepovan
edged closer to watch Tiberio place his firepots. He had a
measuring-stick with him, of the kind undertakers used
to mark the height of corpses: the cave-mouth was narrow
and he'd be lucky, January thought, to make his entrance
into Act Three without igniting his own cloak. "And I
take it Monsieur LeMoyne didn't think much of your tale
of clandestine interviews with vanishing assassins in the
wilds of the *cipriere* by night?"

"He appreciated the information that he may be
looking for a woman," said January. Belaggio emerged
from his office and cast a nervous glance around the backstage before emerging from beneath the gallery; when
Herr Smith herded the giggling, chattering corps de ballet
abruptly from the rehearsal-room, he shied as if at a gun-
shot.

"He may subpoena Harry Shotwell from the Blackleg
to testify to the woman's conference with Person or Persons Unknown on the day before the original assault,
which would be more useful than attempting to catch up
with the Gower boys on the Natchez Trace—they'd only
refuse to testify. As would Incantobelli, I suppose." He
sighed. "Danton, Robespierre, and Mirabeau did the
world a great disservice—maybe Franklin and Jefferson
before them. They made an ideal—be it the Restoration
of Proper Order or the Rights of Man—justification for
killing another human being. So we have now not only to

worry about protecting ourselves from evil men, but also from good ones."

"Man, proud man," sighed Hannibal, rising from his chair as the rest of the orchestra filed past toward the stage. *"Drest in a little brief authority . . . like an angry ape / Plays such fantastic tricks before high heaven / As make the angels weep."*

"This is ridiculous!" Consuela stormed past, brandishing her copy of the score. Behind her, a hollow-eyed d'Isola nodded, smiling agreement to Belaggio's account of which songs she must sing at the reception at the town house of Senator Soames tonight. "What do you mean, you can't find the muskets?" wailed Mr. Rowe. "We can't have *The Soldier's Daughter* without muskets!" "Melodrama!" sneered Tiberio, and d'Isola tried not to shed a tear as the impresario kissed her hands.

Navita de ventis, January recalled the words of the Roman Propertius: *The seaman tells stories of winds, the ploughman of bulls. . . .* And the soprano of the indignities of being prima or the injustices of not.

He wondered whether there would be time between the end of rehearsal and that reception—which he was also playing at—to go to the Cabildo and speak to Davis, or to LeMoyne's office, or to Olympe's to see how Marguerite did.

"Even in that," pursued Hannibal as they took their places behind the drape of the pit, "Peter the Hermit and St. Augustine—and Mohammed, of course—are there before you. It's one thing to die for the Rights of Man, and quite another to be hanged because someone doesn't want the police asking questions about what Lorenzo Belaggio might have been doing at ten-thirty Thursday night. One wonders," he added as Belaggio gave La d'Isola one final wet kiss and stepped to the podium as if he expected it to drop from beneath him like a scaffold trap, "just what the Austrians thought Marguerite knew, and might have passed along to you."

According to Olympe—who like most voodoos made it her business to know everything about everyone in town—Theodore Lalage, although an attorney-at-law, had refused to have anything to do with the prosecution of his sister's murder in 1825. He had concentrated instead on the purchase of two male slaves whom he rented out by the week to the various cotton-presses in the American section of town, and the acquisition and rental of a number of houses in the Faubourg Tremé. In the ten years since the trial, this course of action had proven so profitable that Lalage had been able to sell the cottage that had belonged to their mother on Rampart Street and buy a roomier dwelling on the fashionable Rue Esplanade.

"Which he should have taken shame on himself for doing," declared Olympe as she cleared away the supper dishes by the light of several branches of tallow candles on the sideboards of the rear parlor. It had been a quiet meal, though January suspected ordinary conversation wouldn't have waked Marguerite through the back bedroom's shut door. When he'd arrived for supper, she'd greeted him drowsily, eating with good grace the blancmange and soup Gabriel had made for her, and asking about the rehearsal. She'd fallen asleep soon after, and January guessed she wouldn't recall the conversation at all when—if—she woke.

He followed Olympe across the darkening yard to the kitchen, carrying dishes. "He cheated his brothers and sister out of the price of the house, which Laurent, the youngest, could have stayed in after their mama's death.

The boy's a common laborer, without the brains to make his way like the older boys. These days I'm told Theo Lalage pretends his mother wasn't plaçée, nor his sisters, either. He tells his daughters they were dressmakers."

January nodded, and tried to look as if the matter were only of casual interest. His sister had her own views of justice, and would not have brought Sidonie's brother to the notice of the white police, only to save a white man's skin.

Still, he had learned what he needed to know. The following morning, before his pupils arrived, he dressed in his roughest trousers and his red-and-blue calico shirt and loitered among the trees along Rue Esplanade until he saw Theo Lalage send off his slaves to their hired work. He took note of how the sturdy, gray-haired gentleman stood, in his blue coat and high-crowned beaver hat, when he talked to his bondsmen in a cold, clipped matter-of-fact voice: *Don't linger in the market on the way home. Don't let me come past Camp Street this afternoon and see you chatting to the orange-sellers. Your labor reflects on me.*

Yes, sir. Yes, sir.

The man himself January recognized, as he was coming to recognize most of the prominent men of the free colored community, from playing at the balls of the Faubourg Tremé Militia and Burial Society. Not a man, January guessed, who after ten years would avenge a sister he had winced to acknowledge in her life. He went home, conscious of how he now watched all the shadows of the trees behind him, and took a circuitous route. It was going to be a busy day.

There was a final dress rehearsal for *Robert le Diable* at noon, added for the benefit of the dancers. Since Princess Isabella was essentially Princess Elvira in a houppelande instead of a farthingale, La d'Isola had only her usual problems with the role and Consuela Montero was well content with a role that would allow her to display her own formidable coloratura. The eponymous Robert's agonies concerning salvation and damnation were not notably different from Masaniello's agonies concerning honor and liberty. The cavortings of the ghostly Abbess before the tomb of Ste. Rosalie were highly reminiscent of the cavortings of Fenella on the Portici beach. Claud Cepovan shied like a spooked virgin every time he had to spring out of the demonic cave in his seven or eight yards of flowing demonic cloak.

And well he should, thought January. Belaggio fairly chortled over the amount of flame and smoke the cavern would generate, but January remembered the blood-soaked papers in the drawer, and the veiled woman who had said *I want him corpsed.* Despite Cavallo's assurances, there was something more here than Austrian politics.

January felt it in his bones.

In the event, the opera went well. La d'Isola sang "Look Out Upon the Stars, My Love" and "Softly Fall the Dews of Night" as badly as she would have sung anything Monsieur Meyerbeer ever penned. During these English interludes, Madame Montero moved casually around upstage, taking the combs out of her dark hair, wrapping herself in the Princess's shawl, and, finally, lifting her skirts to adjust a garter on her knee in a way that completely distracted d'Isola, to say nothing of its effect on the Kaintucks in the pit. Half the time the prima soprano's back was to the audience as she sang. In Act Five the smoke-bombs misfired and instead of vanishing in a cloud of infernal fumes, the Devil Bertram was clearly seen to drop through a trap-door, which snapped closed on a corner of his cloak, leaving eighteen inches of unexplained fabric at the feet of the united lovers during their final duet.

But at least nobody dropped dead on-stage, thought January. No one's cloak or skirts caught fire. No wires were crossed to strangle the ghost of the dancing Abbess mid-pirouette, and no one took a shot at anyone from the gallery.

Only at the end of the performance did January groan, when Belaggio stood on-stage and announced that "Friday's performance of the mystical Hibernian opera, *La Dame Blanche,* will be conducted by the newest member of our opera season, Monsieur Arnaud Bucher."

Arnaud Bucher was—or had been—John Davis's conductor. *Just what Davis needs,* thought January. *Yet another reason to have murdered Lorenzo Belaggio in an alley. I wonder when that was arranged, and if the State Prosecutor will bring it up at the trial.* After the near-donnybrook in the prison watchroom two days previously, he'd lost what little hope he had ever had of any jury trying a Frenchman without politics entering in.

". . . *Cinderella* on Tuesday, and the incomparable Roman tragedy *Norma* by Bellini on Friday, which will bring us to the final opera of the season," Belaggio continued over the surge of polite applause, "*Orfeo ed Euridice,* for which I promise you, with my hand upon my heart, the most unsurpassed and dazzling spectacle of all."

"*Orfeo ed Euridice?*" said Hannibal, startled, as the gaslights in the house went up. "What happened to *Der Freischütz?*"

"*Orfeo ed Euridice?*" January pinched out his candle and got to his feet, gathered his gloves and music. "GLUCK's *Orfeo ed Euridice?* He's going to put that on for *Americans?*"

"You think Americans won't appreciate the Dance of the Blessed Spirits?" Hannibal's eyebrows quirked. "The most beautiful piece of music Gluck—or almost anyone else—ever wrote?"

"I think Americans won't sit still for two hours of people singing arias about Love at each other without anything resembling a duel, or a riot, or even a kiss . . . Sir." He hastened to overtake Belaggio as the impresario strode backstage, almost running to the shelter of the green room.

"Sir, are you sure *Orfeo* is a good choice? Please excuse me for speaking, but—"

At January's first word, Belaggio slewed around, the blank terror of startlement on his face changing swiftly to pugnacity. "What is a bad choice about it?" His jaw thrust forward, as it had when January had raised the subject of *Othello.* "It is Gluck!"

"It is absolutely static. Sir. The music is beautiful, but absolutely nothing happens on-stage. Nothing. It's like trying to stage Dante's *Paradiso.* Two people stand and sing at each other, then two more people come and sing at each other—"

"Nonsense!" The big man waved January back as Anne Trulove and Caldwell, champagne and *foie gras* in hand on plates of gold-rimmed china, looked at one another uncertainly: January had spoken, not in Italian, but in English. "You are thinking of another *Orfeo,* my friend. We will have fire, *varoosh!*" He swept his arm in the direction of the satanic cave, still faintly wreathed in smoke, on which several of the Sicilians in the chorus were perched with their plates of bread-and-butter. "We will have writhing choruses of devils—ba*run* da-da *dum!* We will have angels floating down from the heavens—"

"Dancing angels!" cried Mr. Trulove ecstatically,

clasping white-gloved hands before his breast and casting a lovelorn eye at Oona Flaherty.

"We will have an audience that falls asleep in its chairs," muttered Hannibal, fortunately in German, which no one but January—and the Herren Smith and Pleck, currently out of earshot—understood.

"Fire always makes a spectacle on-stage," approved Caldwell, who probably couldn't have distinguished Gluck from Goosey-Goosey-Gander. "And it's the spectacle that puts bums on seats, you know. That's where we've been ahead of Davis all the way along. We've got the French Opera House licked—absolutely licked!" he added, throwing a triumphant glance back at the patrons of the Opera Society. Jed Burton and Hubert Granville raised their glasses to him; their wives nodded in a forest of plumes. "Of course, I'm sorry about Mr. Davis—it's ridiculous to think he'd have had anything to do with poor Marsan's being killed that way—but it'll come to nothing in court, you mark my words."

He put a hand on Belaggio's massive shoulder, steered him away in the direction of the overcrowded green room, and January knew better than to follow. "Now, how, exactly, do you propose we dress the ballet for this Dance of the Blessed Spirits? Could we have them *all* come down from the flies on wires? And if we used 'The Last Rose of Summer' . . ."

"Cheer up." Hannibal handed January a plate of pound-cake. "Austrian agents may murder the lot of us before we have to participate in a debacle of this scope."

"If they don't," retorted January glumly, "I can guarantee you the American audience will."

TWENTY

❧

"Have you learned anything?" Cyril LeMoyne lifted a stack of ledgers, newspapers, and two volumes of Blackstone's Commentaries from the spare chair in his office, looked around seeking another place to set them, and finally settled for moving a half-empty cup of coffee aside to balance them on a towering column of similar composition on the corner of his desk. "Anything at all?" January would have shifted his chair sideways to get a better view past it of the little attorney's face, but a couple of deedboxes and another stack of books—the Code Napoleon and most of the Law Code of the State of Louisiana—wedged him immovably into place.

He leaned sideways to talk.

"No more than I told you Monday morning," he said. "No further odd occurrences, unless you count Caldwell's plans to replace the 'Dance of the Blessed Spirits' with 'The Last Rose of Summer.' No threats or attacks on me or anyone else. Marguerite seems a little better—she's conscious for a few minutes at a time—but still doesn't remember what happened." He had just come from breakfast with Olympe and her family, and though his friend's listlessness still troubled him, he was beginning to feel hope.

"I made the time before last night's performance to

speak to the stable-hands at the Promenade Hotel," he
went on. "One of them—Scipion—heard the attack on
Belaggio in the alley and went to open the gate; he says a
man in a cloak and a mask thrust it open moments before
he got there, shoved him aside, and darted across the yard
and into the hotel. He thinks the man was short. The
yard was dark by the gate, though there was some light
closer to the hotel. Scipion's not a tall man himself."

"Telling us exactly nothing," responded LeMoyne
gloomily. "The number of not-very-tall men walking
around New Orleans masked, armed, cloaked, and in
evening-dress on any night during Carnival rivals the
mise-en-scène of the average Venetian melodrama. The
prosecution would point out that the description fits
Davis as well as Incantobelli—or myself, for that matter."

"Or a woman," said January. "Breeched or not—
cloaked and in darkness, it would be difficult to tell.
What happened at the arraignment?"

LeMoyne flung up an ink-smudged, despairing hand.
"What didn't happen? Tillich positively identified John
Davis as the man he saw at the City Hotel the night of
the murder—waistcoat, watch-chains, voice.... Davis
swore he was at home in bed. Wasn't this a peculiar place
for the owner of a gaming-house during Carnival? Davis
said he hadn't felt well, hadn't been well for some weeks.
Did he have a physician who could attest to that? Well,
no, he hadn't gone to a physician. . . ."

"If a man's trying to convince the City Council to
award his contracting company the rights to build a steam
railway," said January, "he isn't about to let anyone think
he might be ill. Not that Mr. Davis would admit he was
unwell for anything short of a broken leg—and I've seen
him run the Théâtre with that, or a broken foot, anyway.
Nothing slows him down."

"I should introduce him to my sister." LeMoyne scratched around in the mounds of papers, all dribbled with pooled tallow and interspersed with candles stuck at random on shelves and corners. January shuddered at the thought of one of them being knocked over some night. "I would, too, except she's busy running a tile factory, a dress-shop, a printing business in Le Havre, and our sister's marriage. She even plays dominoes fast. Can you see a blue-bound notebook anywhere? He'd have done better to look a little feebler—God knows his color was as bad as ever I've seen a man's—but he was head-up and scrappy, and seemed perfectly capable of taking on a man Belaggio's size who'd insulted him. Then, of course, everyone had to get into the act, putting themselves forward as character witnesses, Pitot and Freret and Blanc and Dizon and half the Creole aldermen . . ."

"Pouring oil onto the blaze for those who think Davis is being protected by 'rich friends in high places.' "

"For those Americans who have bids in on that lake-front railway, anyhow. Jed Burton got up and testified that he'd heard Davis threaten to murder Belaggio, and that Belaggio had 'drawn back in alarm' from him at some gala the other night. Belaggio apparently said on that occasion that Davis was hiring assassins. . . ."

January rolled his eyes.

"I've located Incantobelli, by the way. He's staying at the Hotel Toulouse, on Rue Toulouse, under the name of Castorini. . . ."

"Which probably is his actual name," said January. "A lot of the castrati took stage names—not that they're the only ones to do so," he added, thinking of Lucy Schlegdt, alias Rutigliano, the company's diminutive Swiss mezzo.

"Surely Incantobelli would be able to testify that Belaggio was mixed up with things he shouldn't have

been, at least to the extent of 'reasonable doubt.' That's all
we need, really. Greenaway—he's the prosecutor on this
case—will say your friend Cavallo is Belaggio's enemy because he thought he was stealing, but Incantobelli was his
partner. . . ."

"Whose opera he stole."

"Doesn't the man have *anyone* who doesn't hate him?"

"Not that I've heard." January leaned back in his
chair, then had to lean forward again as LeMoyne vanished behind the dizzily piled papers and books. "But
Incantobelli ran like a rabbit the moment I called his
name. Since there's nothing to connect me with the City
Guards, I can only assume he's jumping at shadows. Having spent the past week looking over my own shoulder, I
can understand how he feels. I'll take a note to his hotel
and see if I can arrange a meeting in a private place, but
my guess is, he won't testify publicly."

"Maybe not." The lawyer sighed, and picked a cup at
random from among the several tucked like swallows'
nests in the insane jumble of papers. "But like the Gower
boys, he may point us in a useful direction." He took a
sip, and made a face. In the front office a bell rang, and a
moment later an emaciated and disapproving clerk appeared in the connecting doorway.

"M'sieu La Ronde to see you, sir."

LeMoyne looked around for someplace to set the cup
and finally wedged it between two deed-boxes on a shelf.
"Thank you, M'sieu Janvier. The trial's the second of
March; needless to say, I couldn't get bail. Dr. Ker testified
as to Mr. Davis's poor health and was pretty much
shouted down by the Americans. A good deal depends on
the jury, of course." He walked January out through the
scrupulously neat outer office. "But we need to come up
with something. When you start mixing in the quarrel

between the Americans and the French, mere innocence is not going to be enough."

Rehearsals for *La Dame Blanche* lasted until nearly five in the afternoon. In addition to the ghosts, hidden treasure, and missing heirs provided by Monsieur Boieldieu, Mr. Caldwell introduced a duel between the evil Gaveston and the noble George Brown in the third act ("To liven things up, you understand"), and added several choruses of "Bonny Dundee" to the baptism scene in the first. When January and the other musicians took their leave, in quest of supper before the Faubourg Tremé Militia and Burial Society Masked Ball, Belaggio was trying to convince Tiberio to find a way of making the White Lady appear out of a column of "unearthly flame."

"What's this I hear about you taking the night off, Ben?" demanded Cochon as the group of them jostled onto the worn benches at the Buttonhole and Cora's husband, Gervase, limped across from the kitchen with the first dishes of a feast of étouffé, grillades, oysters, and dirty rice. "Stealing away for a little walk on the levee while the rest of us sweat?" His wife, Susan, who'd come with several of the other wives and ladyfriends—including Rose—elbowed him sharply and Rose, sitting beside January, laughed and blushed.

"Listening to Herr Smith every morning has left me feeling poorly," January said gravely, which got more laughs.

"Oh, I just *know* it's to hear Herr Smith he takes those dance rehearsals," joshed Cora, batting her eyelashes.

In fact, it was the knowledge that the Militia and Burial Society was having its Carnival ball that night that had caused January, on his way from LeMoyne's office to the American Theater that morning, to stop at a slop-shop on Race Street near the levee and expend fifty cents of Mr. Davis's money on a much-worn sailor's blouse of blue wool, and a pair of wide-legged canvas pants. Changing into these in the kitchen of the Buttonhole after supper, he wrote out a note asking Incantobelli to meet him and LeMoyne in the back room of the Café Venise the following morning. The other musicians had gone, but Rose remained, and they took coffee together in the corner, and talked of matters that had nothing to do with Davis, or opera, or Incantobelli. It was nearly dark by the time he made his way to the Hotel Toulouse.

At this hour of the evening he had no expectation whatsoever of finding Incantobelli at his hotel, and in that he was not disappointed. When he handed the note to the clerk at the desk, however, the man glanced at the envelope and shook his head. " 'Fraid he's left."

"Left, sir?" January felt no surprise, only a kind of dismay. He couldn't even feel anger. Not after the way he himself had watched the shadows of gathering twilight in the Buttonhole's yard. Not after he'd found himself staying to the crowded streets, the busy parts of town.

Incantobelli knew these people.

"Cleared out Sunday night." The young man leaned a companionable elbow on the wooden counter and shook his head knowingly. Being several shades lighter than January, he quite clearly assumed the roughly-garbed January to be someone's slave, and addressed him as *tu* rather than *vous*. He may have been a slave himself. "Bill-collectors, if you ask me."

"You can spot 'em just like that?" The clerk had the air of one who thinks himself admired, so January put admiration into his voice.

"Pshaw!" The clerk waved a kid-gloved hand. "After three years behind this counter, my friend, I can tell just about everything about a man the minute he walks through those front doors." Though waiters and gamblers and men in various stages of Carnival dress came and went around the glass doors of the gentlemen's parlor just off the lobby, the lobby itself was quiet. A white-jacketed waiter was turning up the gas-jets under their fancy glass shades. "Sunday afternoon we had a couple of men coming in to ask, did the Italian gentleman have a room here—not that I told them a word, that's not my way—but I thought: all those fancy clothes and la-di-da airs, and who's paying for it all?"

"And you could tell these men were bill-collectors just lookin' at them?"

It was like scratching Voltaire the cat under his chin. The clerk almost purred. " 'Course. The tall one had a notebook and a brief with him, wrapped up with string, but he was a tough. You could tell by the way he looked around. The short one with the winkers"—he touched his own spectacles self-consciously—"sort of looked past me to see which rooms had mail in their slots." He imitated the action of a man trying not to appear too obvious about inspecting what wasn't his business. "Only bill-collectors or lawyers do that, and these wasn't lawyers, for all the one was a gentleman. A lawyer wouldn't bring his clerk just to hold his brief for him. Got to be bill-collectors."

Short and tall, thought January, loafing out after another fifteen minutes of superfluous detail about Incantobelli's hasty packing and departure, and about what a model of discretion the clerk had been in letting him know he'd been asked for, and how he'd made sure he got the singer's bill paid in cash rather than a draft. Or one shorter than the other, and the shorter one maybe wore spectacles, though there were few forms of disguise simpler to assume. Since it was a French hotel, and the clerk had clearly, like January, been raised in the French Creole world, January guessed that the visitors had spoken French rather than English: as observant as the clerk was, and as proud of showing off his observations, he guessed as well that they'd spoken Creole rather than European French, and had spoken it without accent.

Brains and brawn.

No mention of a woman.

Were they trying to protect Belaggio? he wondered. Or themselves?

Had they assured the impresario that no, no, he wasn't a target, when in fact they were preparing to dispose of a man whose connection with a flagrant slave-smuggler was endangering their whole operation?

I want him corpsed. Cut him up bad.

Had in fact Marsan been the intended victim, as a warning to Belaggio? Or Belaggio, as a warning to Marsan?

Just 'cause you keep soap in the kitchen . . .

When January reached the Rue Esplanade, it was gaudy with floats and carriages, costumed maskers reeling along the torchlit banquette, and tinsel-bright music flowing out—in various degrees of quality—from town houses and saloons.

As January had suspected, the Lalage servants—including the three he'd watched Lalage send off to work Tuesday morning—had been left with strict orders to remain at home and behave themselves. Naturally, then, the moment the family had disappeared for the Militia and Burial Society Ball, the cook had brought in a few friends for a game of dominoes in the kitchen, and the butler had made an assignation with a woman servant from three streets over. . . .

"But he tell *us* not to make no trouble," said the stevedore who came out to the yard when January opened the gate at the house's side and came hesitantly through. "Can we help you?"

"I hope so." January glanced at the number of the house, which he'd written in large, unsteady figures on the note originally inscribed to Incantobelli. "This here the house of Michie Theodore Lalage? My name Gilles Blancheville. I'm a friend of Michie Lalage's sister Mamzelle Sidonie. 'Least I *was* her friend 'fore I shipped out to serve on the *Dorchester* back in 'twenty-three. This the first I been back in town since I left, and I'm tryin' to look up old friends. Woman at the market told me I could find Michie Theo here."

"He live here, all right," said the slave. "Zerline?" He called back over his shoulder to the lighted kitchen. "Zerline, fella here say he lookin' for Michie Lalage's sister. . . . Michie Lalage have a sister?"

The cook came out, a small, trim woman in her sixties, her face puckered with concern. January repeated his tale. "Oh, my dear sir," she said, sympathy in her soft voice. "I am so sorry. Yes," she added, glancing at the other slave, "Michie Lalage did have a sister—two sisters, in fact. Were you good friends with Mamzelle Sidonie?"

January nodded. And because the cook was a friendly soul—and readily believed his veiled implication that he and Sidonie had been childhood sweethearts—and also because the domino game had had time to pall a little, he was treated to slightly bitter coffee ("M'am Lalage lock up the fresh beans, but these grounds only been run through once") and bread-pudding fresh out of the oven, and everything he could possibly have wanted to know about the family.

"I will say this for the other boys—Laurent and Jean—they didn't turn their back on their mama and sisters the way Michie Theodore did," said Zerline after she'd confirmed Olympe's remarks about the lawyer's disdain for his antecedents. "And where does Michie Theodore think his mama would have got the money for him to go to school, and to read for the law, if she hadn't been friends with Michie Jean-Pierre Lalage the way she was? When Michie Theodore wanted to set up his own office, he was quick enough to go to Michie Jean-Pierre for a loan, for all he talk about his mama—his own mama!—not bein' *no better than she should be*—and you tell me how a woman *should* be, when she's got the chance to have a better life—and not speakin' to Sidonie at Mass. Nor lettin' poor little Delia cross his threshold until after her Michie Gesvres parted company from her, and she married Joseph Listolier and became respectable."

January exclaimed in shock and in grief, and the cook's two friends—the laundress from the house next door, which belonged to a well-off house carpenter of color, and her sister, who was lady's maid to a plaçée—clucked their tongues, and added tales from their own experience with the sons or cousins of plaçées who, upon attainment of position in the *libre* community, ceased inviting their sisters or cousins to dinner on the same days when they entertained their more legitimate friends.

"And he wouldn't have nothing to do with the trial, and him a lawyer?" January brought the conversation back with the air of a man who has been ruminating over some shocking fact for several minutes while the words of others flowed on around him. He looked from face to face of those around the kitchen's worn pine table as if still numbed by shock, and felt obscurely guilty at the sympathy, friendliness, and pity he saw in their eyes.

One of the three slave laborers sniffed, and said, "What you think she was, a member of his family or somethin'?" and the others laughed ironically.

"Michie Jean—that was the oldest of Selene Lalage's five children—asked him that." Zerline shook her head with regret. "Spoke quiet, for Michie Jean's a quiet-spoken man, but with a hardness in his voice that we could hear clear out here in the kitchen. He say, *You a lawyer, Theo. You going to let him get free with what he did?* He's not a big man, Michie Jean—they're none of that family very big—but he got a big anger in him. And Michie Theo says, *It's none of our look-out. We don't know but what Sidonie asked for it. And anyway there's nothing we can do.*

"And there isn't," added the cook sadly, going to the kettle of water that hung steaming on its hook above the fire. "That jury, they wouldn't listen to a woman of color—who was, like that lawyer say, *no better than she should be* herself." Though her voice had up to that time been gentle, the wormwood bitterness showed through on the phrase.

She brought the bowl to the table and gathered the used coffee-cups to wash; her laundress friend got a clean towel to lay them on, and another to dry them with as they came out of the bowl. Like all the Lalage slaves, Zerline looked decently fed, and her simple calico clothing, though faded, was whole and clean, unlike her laundress friend, whose worn frock had been repeatedly patched.

"Maybe I'm unjust," Zerline went on after a moment. "Folks do what they have to do. And Jean went back to Natchez, where he has a cartin' business, full of anger at his brother, and hasn't spoke to him since. Nor has poor Michie Laurent that lost his leg in 'twenty-nine, cuttin' cypress logs across the lake, and him and his family so poor now, it'd break your heart. And I do see Michie Theo's point: Why get the men who hire you to do their legal papers for them mad at you, by stirrin' up trouble against their cousin or their friend? But it's just not the way I was taught you behaved to your own family."

Footsteps creaked on the outside stair and the cook said, "Oh, Lordy, here he comes," and her friends got to their feet. The three male slaves headed for the door but weren't nimble enough; a tubby man in a butler's dark livery appeared in the kitchen door, a frown of permanent peevishness stamped between his brows.

"Zerline," he began, "I believe Michie Lalage has spoken to you before this on the subject of visitors. . . ."

"We'd just stopped by to return the eggs Zerline borrowed last week when there wasn't any at the market," said the laundress with the adept promptness of one used since girlhood to improvisation. "My brother Gilles happened to be visiting us"—she gestured to January—"and he offered to walk us, the streets bein' so noisy and all."

The butler glared at the little bowl of wash-water and the drying coffee-cups, but said nothing. Zerline said, "I'll walk you to the gate, Lucy, Kitta—Gilles. . . ."

Behind them as they crossed the yard they could hear the butler lecturing the three laborers. January guessed, from the silence of the men, that the words originated as much from Lalage as from his servant.

"I thank you for telling me all this, m'am," he said to the cook as she opened the gate for him and her friends. "I don't know why, but it kind of rests me to hear how it came about, an' to know someone at least tried to get her justice. Poor Sidonie! I came by here last Thursday night, when first I came into port, but didn't see no lights in the house. . . ."

"They was home," said Zerline doubtfully. "What time you come by?"

January frowned a little, cogitating. "Close on to midnight, it must have been. Maybe they'd gone to bed already. We rotate the watch on board ship, so sometimes I'm up and don't rightly remember how late it is."

"They'll have just gone up to bed," smiled the cook. "Thursday nights is when M'am Annette—that's Michie Theodore's wife—has her family over to dinner. They stay up in the parlor playin' speculation sometimes, or listenin' to young Miss Netta play the pianoforte with her cousins. What beautiful voices those girls have! I tiptoe over sometimes from the kitchen, after I've done with the washing-up, just to listen. You must have come by just after they put out the candles and went up to bed."

January walked back along the Esplanade, turning what he had learned over in his mind. Trying to sort what he had learned into some kind of logical order. Wondering why, with Cavallo's certainty and Incantobelli's fear, his own mind kept sliding back to the ghost of a woman ten years dead. A woman whose surviving relatives, moreover, were either in no mood or no position to make her cause their own.

He supposed word could be sent to Natchez to inquire if Jean Lalage had left his business at its most thriving time of year on a rumor—transmitted how?—that Marsan was connected with an opera company whose members were being spectacularly threatened. . . .

Was his growing conviction that Marsan was the target simply his disgust with the man? His desire that he be punished for Sidonie's murder, for the baracoon behind the trees, for the look in his wife's eyes and the bruises on his daughter's arm? Marsan was smuggling slaves, acting as the contact-point between the rogue Chamoflet down in the Barataria and his own circle of friends in New Orleans. He'd gotten in touch with Belaggio about selling his Cuban slaves pretty early, if Belaggio had arrived Tuesday and by Saturday night had arranged the sale of Pedro, Louis, and Nina.

Whoever Belaggio's Austrian contact was—presumably the maybe-bespectacled Mr. Tillich—he must have been livid when he heard his messenger was hooked up with a slave-smuggler under the very noses of the City Guards.

I want him corpsed. Cut him up bad.

And yet, thought January . . . and yet. Something someone had said, amid that smoky confusion of plots and banditti and adventures out in Bayou des Familles . . . Maybe just the way the servants on Les Roseaux had looked at one another when they'd heard Vincent Marsan was dead.

He stopped on the corner of Rue Dauphin, where it turned upriver from the Esplanade. This was a part of the French town only recently divided up into lots when the Ursulines sold it before moving their convent downriver. A quiet district, where town lots still stood empty, filled with darkness, timber, and bricks. No streetlamps burned here as of yet, and the yellow glow of windows was few.

You're acting like a child, he chided himself, looking down the empty street into darkness. Somewhere a late-walking vendor sang "Ha'angerchiffs, red-blue-yellow-green ha'angerchiffs . . ." with as much flourish and delight in the climb and fall of the notes as any prima donna showing off her coloratura on the La Scala stage.

But the street's blackness was nearly impenetrable. The waxing moon slipped from sight behind a smother of sooty cloud. *You can't spend your life running away from someone who might or might not be there.*

A big man and a little man, he heard the clerk of the Hotel Toulouse say. A tough. *Brains and brawn.* A man big enough to be mistaken for him in the inky confusion of a blacked-out kitchen in Tremé?

He had a knife. . . .

January felt the hair prickle on his scalp. *If I go on,* he thought, *and am attacked, there's a chance I can overpower him. Find out who he is, and who sent him and why.*

And what makes you think he's alone? whispered a voice in the back of his mind. *What makes you think a knife is all he has?*

In the darkness of the passway from Rue des Ursulines back to the garçonnière behind Madame Bontemps's cottage, a man wouldn't have to be much of a marksman to kill, even in the dark.

Maybe the same voice whispered that to him that kept tugging him to ask questions about Sidonie Lalage. Olympe would have said it was the spirit that lived in the cowrie-shell that hung around her neck on a red ribbon, or the one in the black-painted bottle she kept on a shelf in her parlor. Maybe it was gray-eyed Athène, who came down to the beach at Ithaca in the shape of a child and plucked at Odysseus's ragged tunic. In either case, January retraced his steps along the Esplanade to Rue des Ramparts, and made his way through the crowds of maskers there upriver to Rue Douane, where he begged a bed for the night in the crowded cabinet-room with Gabriel, Chouchou, and little Ti-Paul.

He never found out whether anyone was waiting for him in the dark street near Madame Bontemps's house that night or not.

Two nights later, during the performance of *La Dame Blanche,* Lorenzo Belaggio slipped away in secret and took ship for Havana.

TWENTY·ONE

*"City Hotel
New Orleans
6 febbraio 1835*

*Signor Caldwell,
    Travel arrangements having failed for the
additional cast members necessary to make the
final performance of the season the true and
breathtaking spectacle that the people of this city
have come to expect of Lorenzo Belaggio and the
American Theater—"*

"What additional cast members?" Caldwell turned plain-
tively to the Truloves and the Widow Redfern, standing
beside him in the door of the green room with heaping
plates of Westphalian ham in hand. "I knew nothing of
additional cast members! I knew nothing of this at all!"

"Let me see that." Trulove was far too polite to snatch
the page from Caldwell's hand, but edged himself around
to read over the theater owner's shoulder. The crowd of
singers, musicians, chorus-men, and little rats maneu-
vered closer, glancing at one another in the unsteady crystalline pallor of the gas-jets overhead, and January, sitting

on a Gothic bench of plaster and wood, glanced sideways at Arnaud Bucher. The new conductor, bald and paunchy in his carefully-cut black evening costume, looked as shocked and baffled as anyone.

"—*people of this city . . . Belaggio and the American Theater*"—Trulove took up the reading in the plummy upper-class accents that thirty years in America had not erased—"*I have been obliged to return to Havana and see to matters myself.*"

"Skipped!" Jed Burton just stopped himself from spitting. "I tell you, it's that Frenchman Davis's doing! He has powerful friends in this city. I've said it all along! The police may have jailed him good, but that don't mean a man who's crossed him is safe from the French that run things around here."

"Good heavens, man," protested Hubert Granville, "a Creole will challenge a man to a duel if he's angry at him, not pay bullies to beat him up in an alley!"

"It's how it's done in Europe," attested young Harry Fry, who'd never been to Europe in his life. He poured another glass of champagne for his dusky-skinned Felina, and January fought back the ludicrous mental image of the buxom Madame Viellard creeping, veiled and stealthy, into the Blackleg Saloon to hire the Gower boys on Davis's behalf.

"Under the *ancien régime*, perhaps." Trulove held up a hand to still further discussion and continued. "*Rest assured that by the terms of our contract, neither the American Theater nor the St. Mary Opera Society is liable for the unexpected or additional costs of such cast or their travel. I apologize for the inconvenience which my absence will incur, though I have taken what steps I can. . . .*"

"Like hiring away Davis's conductor?" inquired Hannibal, but January's gaze had gone from Bucher to La d'Isola, standing just beyond him, still clothed in Lady Anna's old-fashioned, ghostly shroud, her dark hair cascading thickly over her shoulders. Her red mouth rounded into a startled little O, and her eyes were wide with shock.

She hadn't known.

Beside Hannibal, Madame Montero smiled with a kind of blazing triumph, one small, round hand bunched into a fist. And January, with an inward sigh, made a mental note to ask Hannibal to do what he could to make sure that in the absence of her protector, the younger woman would at least not come to any physical harm.

> "... trust that the result will be a spectacle such as your fair city has never before witnessed upon its stages, well worth whatever small inconvenience my absence will cause.
>
> Yours sincerely,
> Lorenzo Belaggio."

"Extraordinary," marveled Caldwell as Trulove lowered the note. "Most unexpected. This is the first I've heard of additional cast for *Orfeo*. And surely whatever supernumeraries were needed could have been hired here. Mr. Knight, you're familiar with the opera. . . ."

"I agree that this is an opera that demands spectacle. . . ." The little business agent, pleased to have his expertise recognized, pondered deeply. "But how many ladies of the chorus can the man need?"

"I admit I shall be pleased to see the work done properly," put in Herr Smith. "I recall when the opera was presented in Dresden for the French consul's visit, they had a hundred and thirty dancers to personate the Blessed

Spirits, forty of them descending on ropes from the clouds, and over a hundred in the Devils' Chorus. Truly a veritable army of Hell . . ."

"He left nothing in his office that might indicate trouble." Cavallo emerged from the little cubbyhole beneath the upstairs gallery, an expression on his face of mild righteousness. As if, thought January, he had every right to search his employer's office at the first unguarded moment. "No money seems to be missing. Yet why should he leave in this fashion, without a word to anyone?"

January collected pound-cake and a praline from the musicians' buffet, and with the plate in hand threaded through the shadowy maze of flats and curtains to the stage. The gaslights were still up in the house, for the cleaners who moved among the benches of the pit, sweeping up soiled sawdust and a rubbish of hulls and stubs. A man's slouch hat had been left on the front-row bench, a woman's green glove lay like a battle-casualty in the aisle. The air smelled of spilt beer and lemonade. January shaded his eyes against the glare of the gasolier. "Lieutenant Shaw?"

A gangly shadow disengaged itself from the blackness at the back of the Viellard box, signed to him to remain where he was. Though January had seen little of Shaw, owing to the doubled and quadrupled lawlessness of New Orleans during the Carnival season, the Guardsman had continued to patrol the American Theater during the performances of *Robert* and *Dame*. Sometimes before the performance January had glimpsed him at the rear of the slaves' gallery up under the stamped-copper garlands of the ceiling, sometimes during the entr'actes on the catwalk above the stage among the flies. Public Prosecutor

Greenaway, an American, might believe in John Davis's guilt, but Shaw did not. He'd listened to January's account of his attempted interview with Incantobelli and its sequel at the Hotel Toulouse as he'd listened to the earlier possibility that the attack had been connected with *Othello:* quietly weighing up the likelihood of each, comparing the evidence in his mind.

The Guardsman emerged a few moments later from the lobby door at the back of the pit and loafed up the aisle, hands in pockets, greasy hair hanging down over his shoulders like dirty weeds. "Belaggio's gone," said January when Shaw sprang up onto the stage. "Havana, he says." And he related what the letter had said, that Caldwell had discovered posted prominently in the middle of Anne Trulove's silver epergne among the hothouse fruits and confits of the green-room table.

"Not that there's any guarantee that he's actually gone to Havana," he finished. "The clerk at the Hotel Toulouse said Incantobelli decamped Sunday night, after two men came inquiring for him Sunday afternoon. According to Bucher, Belaggio came to him Monday with an offer of work. Eight dollars a performance for the remainder of the season, whether he conducts or not—he claimed the reason was his health."

"His *health?*" Fingers and chin-stubble full of crumbling yellow cake, Shaw raised his brows.

"He may have meant it," said January grimly. "Belaggio's running scared. What interests me is that he doesn't seem to have helped himself to the exchequer in departing. Yet he chose *La Cenerentola* pretty much so they could use the same sets from *Robert* and *La Dame Blanche*. I'm a little surprised he had fifty dollars to hire Bucher, much less these 'additional cast members' he talks about."

"*If* he actually paid him." Shaw licked the last crumbs from his fingers, then dug in his coat pocket for a twist of lint-flecked tobacco.

"He did," said January. "Eight dollars for tonight—Belaggio was here during the first act and said he'd watch from backstage, but I don't recall seeing him after that—and eight apiece for *Cenerentola* and *Norma* next week. Whether—and with what—he means to hire 'additional cast members' in Havana—or go to Havana at all—and whether or when he'll be back, I don't know. Meanwhile, Incantobelli takes fright and flees Sunday; Belaggio hires a substitute Monday afternoon, and vanishes Friday night."

"An' Incantobelli dies sometime Monday, close as we can reckon it." Shaw bit off a hunk of tobacco with strong, brown-stained teeth. "Couple stevedores haulin' moss to town along the canal found his body this afternoon."

The New Orleans City Morgue was a long room at the back of Charity Hospital on Common Street, whitewashed and reeking of decay and the turpentine they brushed along the base of the walls to discourage ants. The plank-walled barrelhouses and tent-roofed bordellos of the Swamp lay not many streets away. Convenient, one might say. Many of the men and women occupying the line of tables down the center of the room had met their ends there—knifed, shot, drowned drunk in the puddles of the unpaved streets. Coming in behind Shaw the following morning, January glanced down at the corpse of a girl no more than fifteen, her braided, nappy hair and open mouth filled with mud.

Incantobelli lay on the next table. His throat had been cut.

Like every other body of water in southern Louisiana, Bayou St. John teemed with crawfish. After nearly a week's immersion, the soprano was identifiable chiefly by his long white hair, and, naked on the morgue table, by the scars where his manhood had been taken away fifty years before, for the sake of that throat, when such voices were the fashion. January remembered going with Marguerite to the Théâtre des Italiens to hear Velluti in *L'Incoronazione di Poppea:* remembered the eerie beauty of those sweet alto voices. Chillingly bodiless, like angels might sound, cold and perfect and nothing like the voices of women, or of children, to which those who had never heard them invariably compared them. Like the stars, which Plato contended were of an element that did not exist on earth.

His clothing lay in the line of little heaps along the upstream wall of the room. January could imagine the jokes of the morgue attendants when they'd stripped him. It was the same nondescript twill coat, the waistcoats of cream and gray, that he'd worn to church. In the buttonhole clung the stems of the violets he'd bought from the girl on the steps.

"Little bruisin' on the upper arms," said Shaw laconically. "Some on the back of the head an' shoulders. Looks like someone might have grabbed him an' slung him back against a wall someplace, cut his throat 'fore he knew what was happenin'."

At a table farther down the room, a man cried out in disgust and rage: the body of the woman he'd come to claim had had her hair cut off almost to the scalp by some attendant or other in the night. He was lucky, reflected January. Sometimes they took the teeth as well—there was a dentist on the Rue St. Louis who paid cash for them, no questions asked.

"They's bloodstains all down the front of his clothes, though they's pretty much washed out. They musta tipped him into the canal right as soon as it was done."

"Tidy of them."

The man who'd written *Othello.* Who'd woven that music from who knew what love, what bitterness? What knowledge of what it was like, to be jeered at and denied love not for who he was, but for what he was.

January wished with all his heart that he could have spoken to him. And not about John Davis or Lorenzo Belaggio.

"Tell the Coroner I'll claim the body," he told Shaw. "Tell him the musicians, and the singers, of the opera will arrange for burial. I'll speak to them about it at rehearsal, which is where I'm going now. He isn't to lie in a pauper's grave."

"Did he have family?" asked Rose late that night when rehearsal was done and they sat together beside Marguerite's bed. Across the yard, the firelight from the kitchen made a sort of friendly Hell-mouth. The damp air magnified the smells of wet yard-bricks and mud, and intensified the dim clamor of maskers in the street.

"I'm gratified every time I wake to hear it," Marguerite had confessed earlier. "Sometimes I'm afraid I'll wake and be told I've slept like Rip Van Winkle, on into the next century."

The children had gone to bed already in the cabinet behind the bedroom; Paul was moving about the parlor, ready to walk January back to Rue des Ursulines. Rose had spent the evening at Olympe's, nursing Marguerite or reading to her between translating Anacreon for a book-seller on Rue Royale.

"Consuela says no," said January. "People in the theater make their own families, you know. His friends in Naples and Palermo and Rome, they'll be glad to hear that he was properly buried. That friends came to put flowers on his grave."

He shivered as he said the words, looking down at Marguerite.

She slept now, the sudden, heavy sleep that would fall on her sometimes between one word and the next. She'd always been full of laughter and mockery at her family: this uncle had claimed that daily thrashing made his peasants more intelligent ("I should introduce him to M'sieu Burton"), and that aunt had put so many children out to nurse in the villages of her estate that she lost track of two or three. . . . But Rose had told him that in her sleep, the dancing-mistress still sometimes called her father's name.

"It was good of you to see to it, Ben," said Rose, and she poured out a cup of tepid tea for him from the pot that shared the bedside table with an invalid's cup, three books, a branch of yellow candles burned nearly to the sockets, and a French watch marked in those bizarre hundred-minute hours that the Committees for Public Safety had tried to impose during the Revolution. Packets of medicines crowded the top of the small cypress dresser between the bed—usually Zizi-Marie's—and Chouchou's smaller cot; the light burning there under the china veilleuse added its distorted shadows to the candles' wobbling glow. "With your lessons and rehearsals . . ."

"Someone had to," said January. "And I felt I owed it to him. If I hadn't spoken to him in front of the Cathedral, they might have left him alone."

Rose glanced up at him, though he would have sworn he'd kept his voice light; she set down the teapot and crossed to where he stood beside the parlor door. "They wouldn't have," she said.

January only shook his head, and turned his face aside.

"They wouldn't have," Rose repeated. The insistence in her voice drew his eyes back to meet hers. "You had nothing to do with his death."

"I know that."

And he did. Or a part of him knew, anyway.

Rose took his hands. "If anything, if he'd stayed to talk to you, you might have learned something that would let you protect him," she said. "You might have convinced him to put his trust in you, gotten him out of the Hotel Toulouse, hidden him somewhere. He was already afraid," she reminded him. "He knew they were already after him. Look at the times he went out, always masked: Puss in Boots, Julius Caesar. Only to church . . ."

"And to Trulove's reception," said January. "He must have heard about the attack on Marguerite the following morning, and realized he was in danger."

"And still he stayed in New Orleans." Hooves clattered furiously in the street. It was the hour of night when rich young men tended to leave parties afire with the impulse to race their phaetons like chariots through the streets. Rose's strong hands tightened over his own, and she shook his arms gently, as if to make sure he heard her, to make sure he believed. "He could have left. But he wanted his revenge. His honor."

"If I had written that music," said January, "and had it stolen, I'm not sure I wouldn't have done the same."

"And you would have met the same fate," said Rose. "He chose it, Benjamin. He knew these people, remember. Not who they were in New Orleans, but the kind of people they were, and what they would do. I suspect that's why he left Belaggio. Because he didn't want to have anything further to do with them."

She put her hands on his shoulders and tiptoed to brush his lips with hers. "You didn't cause his death. And you may not have been able to save him."

"But I can avenge him."

"You seen what happened," said Olympe, coming quietly into the room with a half-dozen fresh candles, "when he tried to avenge himself, brother. It's a dangerous thing to go playin' around with, vengeance. A long chalk more dangerous than them chemicals and gunpowder you get so twitchy about Rose playin' with. You be here tomorrow to sit with her, Ben?"

"In the afternoon, yes." He pinched out the burned-down bedside candles one by one. "There's no regular rehearsal, though M'sieu Bucher's asked me to spend a few hours taking La d'Isola through Euridice's part. Belaggio's had her reading the part, and practicing with him, since she came back from La Cornouiller."

"God knows what that silly Italian was thinking," said Rose to Olympe. "*Orfeo* is what they used to call a court opera: masques, pageants, dancing, but not much in the way of a real plot. It's just people standing around, singing. . . ."

"Oh, I'll wait in line all night for a ticket to that," commented Olympe, taking the faintly sheep-smelling tallow stumps from her brother's hand.

"Don't listen to her, Olympe, she's a complete barbarian," said January. "*Orfeo ed Euridice* is one of the most beautiful pieces of music ever composed. But it's an old-style piece, and it was certainly not composed with Americans in mind. And with our friend Smith in charge of the divertissements, God help us, all the Hell-fire Tiberio can conjure won't change the fact that—"

He'd heard, while Paul laughed, the clatter of hooves far down the street. And he'd thought, *Dumb damn Kaintucks running races....*

All this he remembered later.

As the words "all the Hell-fire Tiberio can conjure" came out of his mouth, as if in fact naming Hell-fire was a conjuration, there was flame, and smoke, and shattering glass, spraying into the parlor from the broken windows. Fire skated across the beeswaxed parlor floor, burst from the woven rugs. Paul shouted, plunged into the dining-room for another rug; January grabbed Rose aside, struck at her skirts, which were beginning to catch. Smoke, footfalls, Olympe's voice shouting for water—people running, and more flame spilling from the lamp as Paul knocked it over in his haste....

Someone pressed towels into his hand; January dunked them in a water-bucket (who'd brought that in? In the smoke he couldn't see) and slapped at the flames, eyes burning. Someone stumbled into him, nearly knocking him over; a door opened and wind swept through the parlor, fanning the flame. January cursed and realized it must be Zizi-Marie or Gabriel, getting their tiny brother out of the house. Shouting in the darkness.

Then, from somewhere, a child's scream.

Marguerite's room. January turned to the door through the front bedroom to the back, and a shape loomed at him in the dark. Collided with him, struggling in the smoke, coughing—he thrust past, and into the rear bedroom, where a single candle still burned blurred with smoke, and Chouchou, Olympe's five-year-old daughter, crouched in a corner, staring with huge eyes at the door.

She screamed again as January came in, and hid her eyes, but January—who would ordinarily have beaten half to death any man who frightened her—plunged instead straight to the bed.

The bed where Marguerite lay, a pillow covering her face.

"She says she came in and saw a man there," said Olympe quietly. The fire in the parlor was out. January, Rose, Paul, and Gabriel gathered again in the smoke-stinking dining-room as Olympe emerged with her daughter in her arms. The French door from the front bedroom to the street had been standing open. Through the open door between the rear bedroom and the rear parlor, dim candle-light showed January Marguerite's still face. He kept looking at her breast, where the white sheet lay over it, watching each slow, shallow breath she took with sick dread in his heart.

Nothing he'd tried—not water, nor light slaps on her hand, nor burnt feathers, nor the ammonia stink of hartshorn—had waked her.

She was breathing. That was all.

Olympe rocked Chouchou in her arms, leaned her head down to listen to the girl's whispered communication. Now and then she nodded. "That's right. That's my brave child." She looked up again. "He had the pillow over M'am Scie's face, holding it down. A Devil, Chouchou said, in a big black cloak and a mask, with a kerchief over his head."

"Maybe the one who looked like a tough," said January. "Maybe Mr. Winkers—the one who ran out of the alley—has more than one bullyboy. Either he or another rode the horse and threw the torch." For they'd found the torch that had been thrown, butt-first like a flaming javelin, through the French door of the parlor. In spite of the heavy curtain drawn over the broken panes, a draft came through, chilling the room and making the curtain itself quiver and flop with sickening life.

Beside Marguerite's bed lay the shattered remains of the teapot. Little streaks of blood skimmed the puddles of cold tea. Part of the handle had lain on the sheets near the ballet mistress's hand, the broken edge wet and red, and blood had spotted the bedclothes, the floor, and the night-dress Marguerite wore.

She had fought.

"Was it chance, do you think"—Rose twisted back her soft walnut-colored curls where they'd fallen over her shoulders in the confusion of beating and dousing—"that all this happened the night after Signor Belaggio fled town?"

It was close to dawn. Neighbors had come crowding over to help put out the flames (which had been out within minutes in any case) and offer other unspecified assistance. In not many hours, January was aware, he was due at the theater again. Coffee and breakfast seemed to make more sense than sleep.

"I don't think anything is chance, these days."

He sent his nephew, as soon as it was light, to Madame Bontemps's for clean clothes, for his music-satchel, and his own shaving-things. "What a spook!" said the boy, coming back when January was shaving with Paul's borrowed razor in the cabinet behind the dining-room. The cabinet opened onto the yard as well; smoke from the kitchen where Olympe was making breakfast scented the air, coffee-smells, syrup, and grits. In the front parlor Paul was already neatly cutting out the two or three floor-boards that had been badly burned, preparatory to planing and fitting new.

"I told her I had to get your things because you hadn't been able to come home last night, and she just looked at me and said, *But why didn't he get them last night when he was here?* Like she didn't even hear me."

Or like someone came to the garçonnière late last night, thought January. *And waited for me to come home.*

Shaw came, but could find little, and the accounts given by the neighbors were not much help. They confirmed what January had guessed, that there were at least two men, one of whom had ridden down Rue Douane at full gallop and thrown a torch through the window to bring everyone into the front parlor, but beyond that there was little to learn. In Carnival time, masked men careering down the streets at full gallop were not uncommon. At that late hour, most of the neighbors—free colored artisans, for the most part—had been asleep in bed.

Shaw examined the broken teapot, the blood, the fading bruises on Marguerite's throat. The blackened prints of fingers had diffused into a general greenish-yellow mass of discoloration. January still didn't know if he'd done well or ill to conceal them—he knew only that he'd done what he had to, to keep his friends and himself from the grip of the white man's law.

He went to Mass—the Fashion Show rather than his usual early Mass—and lit a candle for Marguerite before the statue of the Virgin, as he had every day that week, and another for Incantobelli. But even that brought him no comfort. A week ago he had come here to lie in wait for the singer, and now the man was dead.

Blessed Mary ever-Virgin, he prayed, *help me to find these men. Put the clue of thread into my hand, and give me the strength to follow it wherever it leads.*

He was to reflect, later, that he really needed to be more careful about what he prayed for.

Thou hast delivered us, O Lord, from them that afflict us, said the priest as January slipped quietly out through the great Cathedral doors, and made his way upriver to the American Theater to deal with Euridice's journey to the Underworld and back.

La Cenerentola being written for a mezzo, and it being unthinkable that Drusilla d'Isola would play an Evil Sister, the prima donna was able to concentrate on learning Euridice's role. She had more opportunity for this than even she had counted on, it transpired, because on Wednesday, the day of the first general rehearsal for *Norma,* she overslept, waking at last with a splitting headache that January at least recognized as one of the symptoms of being dosed with opium. He had little worry that the Emperor Francis's minions were to blame for this, however. One of the bottles of laudanum that Hannibal habitually carried in his pockets was missing, and most of the cast had seen Madame Montero, who had been surreptitiously taking sessions with Hannibal in the role, talking with the soprano when she came backstage to congratulate little Signorina Rutigliano, after watching the opera from Mr. Caldwell's private box.

The upshot of it all was that Madame Montero took the rehearsal. Even compared to the florid, if interchangeable, Princesses of previous operas, Norma is a gruellingly demanding role. What was merely a difference of ornamentation between one soprano and another in the case of *La Muette* and *Robert* became a painfully evident gulf. James Caldwell, a little to everyone's surprise, put his foot down at Thursday's rehearsal and politely requested that Madame Montero continue to sing Norma to Rutigliano's Adalgisa.

"And I'm not sure," the theater owner confessed, taking January aside into Belaggio's office between the dance rehearsal and the beginning of dress rehearsal, "whether I shouldn't replace Miss d'Isola in the Gluck piece as well."

As the player whose work formed the base-line of the small orchestra—and one of the two most musically knowledgeable men in the ensemble—January was often treated as spokesman by both Caldwell and Davis. Caldwell, who genuinely loved opera, had come to rely more and more on January's technical advice, particularly after Belaggio's unexpected departure. "Would you very much mind—and I know you're certainly stretched thin as it is—taking an extra, private rehearsal Sunday with Madame Montero for the part of Euridice? I know how fond Signor Belaggio is of Miss d'Isola, but . . ."

Caldwell hesitated, stroking his trim, dark mustache. Outside the office, Tiberio could be heard calling upon Heaven to witness that he could do nothing with the final act if Norma and her boneheaded lover refused to show a little courage about the flames of the pyre. What was a little fire, after all?

"In spite of the—the quite dramatic pyrotechnics in Act Two, and the beauty of the music, *Orfeo* is a very . . . a very—"

"Static?" suggested January.

Caldwell nodded eagerly, relieved to be so tactfully seconded. "A very *static* work. Oh, I realize that much of its appeal lies in the stage direction. And Signor Belaggio was most insistent that it be performed." Despite his best efforts, an edge crept into his voice. "And of course Mr. Trulove backed him in that. . . ."

Had Mr. Caldwell not been a white American gentleman talking to a black musician, January felt he would have expressed himself more fully on the subject of the special dance that Trulove was paying Herr Smith to evolve for Oona Flaherty—utilizing the tune of the Martin Van Buren Quick-Step—to be grafted on to the Dance of the Blessed Spirits.

"But looking over the libretto itself, I must admit that there doesn't seem to be much activity. Except for the dancing, of course. I fear poor Madame Scie's talents are greatly missed. How is Madame Scie?"

"The same." After days of stillness, she had drifted back to a sort of clouded consciousness late the previous night, enough to drink a little broth, which had given January hope. But that morning she could not be wakened, and he had gone to the theater with chill fear riding his shoulder like a vulture.

There has to be some way of finding the man who did this, he thought, desperation returning to his heart. He'd gone to see Davis that morning in the Cabildo, and the entrepreneur had had to be helped to the door of his cell to speak to him. "Just a little tired," Davis had said. "I've had worse accommodations, believe me, and running a faro-bank here has done wonders for my popularity. . . ." He'd lowered his voice conspiratorially. "Particularly since I know when to start losing." He had ordered LeMoyne to draw a draft on his bank for money to give Olympe, for Marguerite's care, he'd said, and for a contribution to Incantobelli's tomb in the New Cemetery on Claiborne Street. "We can't let an artist go off without a show," he'd said.

A clamor of voices drew Caldwell to the door— Blessed Spirits having a violent disagreement about who danced in front of whom, with Herr Smith's voice pecking ineffectually at the general din like a gull-chick flapping against a storm. "My dear young ladies," said Caldwell. "Remember that variety is the key to a pleasing performance. . . ."

January crossed the little office to the bookshelf, pulled down the ledger—as he'd already done three times previously, whenever he could steal an unobserved moment—and scanned back another page. It told him nothing. There didn't seem to be appreciable skimming, and there was no record of where Belaggio had gotten the money to pay Bucher to take his place.

Certainly there was no budget for "additional cast" in *Orfeo.*

A footfall beside the open door made him shove the book back among the other ledgers—which he'd also had a look at—and the dozens of bound copies of libretti, stacks of sheet music, and half a dozen German and Italian novels that shared the shelf. He turned quickly, but it was only Cavallo, already moving away from the door, looking embarrassed, like Lover No. 1 encountering Lover No. 2 in the soubrette's bedroom door in a rather low-class farce.

Exasperated, January took one last quick look at the shelf as he turned away, but there was nothing else of interest, nothing he hadn't looked at before. A small stack remained of *OTHELLO, Tragedia Lyrica in two acts by Lorenzo Belaggio,* bound in the familiar green with stampings of inexpensive Dutch gilt. Opening the top one, January found no papers, no notes, within.

There's a clue in all this somewhere, thought January, replacing the libretto on the shelf. *What is that one piece of information that struck me like a sour note?*

That told me . . . what?

Marsan dead. Incantobelli murdered. Marguerite attacked. Davis in the Cabildo, facing the fiasco of a trial that could go in any direction . . .

Bayou des Familles. I got a glimpse of it at Bayou des Familles. . . .

He fished in his memories of that run-down plantation, of the long brick jail-house hidden by the trees, the servants clustering around the kitchen. *Was it the family of that girl?* Jules had asked.

Evidently not.

And Sidonie's successor certainly wasn't the woman who had told Buck Gower, *Cut him up bad.* She was too dark of skin to be mistaken for a white woman, even behind a veil.

And why would the Austrians, who'd shown themselves willing to kill to protect their secrecy, have brought down an investigation on their heads by the nearly-public murder of a man so prominent and so closely connected with their messenger? Particularly when waylaying him on his next trip to Les Roseaux would have resulted only in shaken heads and mutterings that something had to be done about Captain Chamoflet?

It didn't make sense.

Norma was presented the following night, and despite a rather hasty preparation was dazzlingly received. Barbarian soldiers marched, scantily-clothed priestesses cavorted, Druid knives flashed, a mother's Medea-like passion was diverted by the innocence of her children, to the accompaniment of Bellini's soaring "Casta diva" and the somewhat more prosaic interpolation of "Believe Me, If All Those Endearing Young Charms . . ." Even one of the innocent children visibly scratching herself during their "slumbers"—and the fact that someone appeared to have bribed M'sieu Bucher to speed up the music during every one of Madame Montero's arias, so that she had to gasp and stumble hastily through them like patter-songs, eyes blazing with fury—did not mar the general effect.

Mr. Caldwell began to look much cheered.

Two days later, halfway through January's surreptitious morning rehearsal of Euridice's part with Madame Montero, Lorenzo Belaggio returned from Havana.

With him he had his additional cast for *Orfeo ed Euridice:* a massive chorus of forty-five men and five women.

All of them, coincidentally, African.

"It ain't a bad plan," said Abishag Shaw once he'd quit laughing at the sheer audacity of it. "Not a bad plan a-tall. If'n our Navy boys—or the Royal Navy—stops 'em, why, they's just the chorus of Devils. . . ."

"Which is why Belaggio was so insistent on *Orfeo,* of course," muttered January, torn between anger at Shaw for laughing when fifty men and women were about to be sold to the cane plantations, and a desire to laugh himself at the rogue impresario's cleverness. He gestured with one of the posters that had begun to be seen pasted to every fence and building-front in town: *Giant Spectacle Never Before Seen.* "I should have guessed." The garishly printed bill depicted an army of monsters, more like apes or dogs than humans, with fanged mouths and glaring eyes. January's lips hardened with anger and he settled back into the ladder-backed chair Shaw had dragged over from near the sergeant's desk into his own corner of the Cabildo watchroom.

"Well, that is the truth," agreed Shaw with a grin. "What'd Caldwell say?"

"To sum up," said January grimly, *"oh, er,* and *uh.* Of course he guesses what's going on. Now, at least. I don't think he knew ahead of time. And I don't think he knows quite what to do or say, since Belaggio's insisting that these are legitimate members of the opera troupe. . . ."

"Like them poor stage-hands Pedro an' Louis, an' that girl Nina."

January was surprised Shaw remembered their names. He himself had forgotten.

"An' every one of those poor souls is gonna just somehow fade out of sight by the time Belaggio gets to his next engagement in New York. Was this somethin' he set up with Marsan, you think?"

"Has to be," said January. "It may even be the reason the Austrians killed Marsan—or tried to kill Belaggio. To warn him off this. Because, of course, if the Navy caught him, he wouldn't keep his mouth shut. . . ."

You're asking too much of me, Marsan had cried to some member of the Opera Society at the Salle d'Orleans. And, *It's all arranged.* No wonder the other members of the Opera Society were so frantic to stop the duel.

And with the whole Opera Society involved, no wonder the Austrians couldn't do much about it now.

"I'm guessing the money will change hands Thursday night after the performance," said January. "The members of the Opera Society—and whoever else they've told about this scheme—will need to look their 'merchandise' over—" His voice stuck bitterly on the word.

"And Belaggio and La d'Isola are booked on the *Dolley Madison* to New York Friday morning." Shaw folded his long arms and chewed for a moment. His gray eyes—dark-circled now from lack of sleep—cut to the watchroom doors as Guardsmen dragged in a drunk deckhand from one of the steamboats, cursing in a vile mix of Spanish and Greek; noted no immediate danger and moved to the doors that led out into the courtyard, where the wet crack of whips on flesh announced that the usual business of "correction" was in process, sparing urban slave-holders from doing their own violence at the going rate of a dollar a stroke.

Monday morning. Business as usual. The custom of the country.

In the cells someone was ranting, cursing in the voice of a drunkard or a madman, audible even down here. In one of the women's cells a prisoner screamed on and on, a piercing note like a steam whistle. January thought of John Davis, running his faro-bank and hanging on as best he could until his trial. Of Marguerite, sinking deeper into her cold sleep that for four nights now had had no waking. Of Incantobelli, silver hair spread out damp on the boards of the morgue table, and skull glaring through where the crawfish of the canal had eaten away his face.

"How's your singin' voice, Maestro?"

January glanced back at the Kaintuck, reading in that lantern-jawed gargoyle countenance precisely what was in his mind.

"Feel up to treadin' the boards your ownself?"

"I'd have to be slipped in at the last minute." January was already calculating possibilities of how this could be done. "Everyone in the Opera Society knows me, of course. But I've seen the masks backstage, and it's a dark scene. And they have to have everyone on the stage for the performance, because you know the Navy—and probably the British as well—are going to be watching to make sure those people really are part of an 'operatic chorus.' But the buyers are going to want to conclude their bargains and get their property the hell out of town the moment the final curtain rings down. And whoever's behind all this," he said quietly, "I'll see them then."

"I just might sorta mooch on into one of them third-tier boxes this afternoon when you start rehearsin' with that chorus." Shaw spit cheerfully in the direction of the sandbox, adding to the random spatterings of tobacco-juice that befouled the floor all around the box. "Where the gals sit, you know, with the grilles over 'em so's nobody can see who comes callin' on who. Just to have a look at how many friends the members of the Society happen to bring along."

TWENTY·TWO

—◆◆◆—

As Shaw suspected, quite a number of the Opera Society were blessed with friends who were suddenly and inexplicably seized with such a fervor for Gluck's music that they made it a point to attend the first rehearsal with the new chorus. Sitting at the piano, January watched their shadows stir in the dark boxes, listened to the murmur of voices, and felt hot rage rise in him.

Rage at the chicanery of it. At the blithe sidestepping of the laws aimed at ending, at the very least, the kidnapping of slaves from Africa. Rage at the laws themselves, that gave lip-service to sentiments—"Of course we know slavery is evil"—that it had no intention of following through to their logical conclusion.

And rage that they'd use Gluck's music to do it. *My house is a house of prayer, and you have made it a den of robbers,* said Jesus of Nazareth.

Said it to men who—like the two gentlemen sharing Mrs. Redfern's box, and the three who accompanied Mr. Trulove and sat chatting and pointing—were only trying to make a little profit.

From where he sat among the quarter-strength orchestra January could hear them muttering as Belaggio escorted his new "chorus" out onto the stage. As Devils, the Negroes would dance stripped to the waist, the better for the men in the boxes to appraise muscle and skin-tone. And it quickly became clear that they weren't required to do much in the way of dancing, either. Most of the dancing, and the singing of that wild cacophonous chorus that opens Act Two, would be done by Bruno Ponte and his small male troupe, clothed like the prospective slaves in loincloths, tights, and savage-looking paint, crimson instead of black. The slaves themselves had only to sway threateningly, and break into howls, waving red-and-black weapons of light wood and papier-mâché as Orfeo approached the flame and iron and ominous smoke of the gate.

Apollo's sacred lyre in hand, Cavallo stared around him with cold rage in his eyes. The only castrato in New Orleans having been laid to rest last week with one of the largest and most festive funerals January had ever attended, Belaggio had elected to use the 1774 French version of the opera, with Orfeo's crystalline sweetness rewritten for a tenor voice. Cavallo's glance swept the men around him, turned to the spectators in the boxes: "Fellow second from the end, in the yellow," a voice audibly said, "how much is he?"

The tenor's lips tightened. Whatever thoughts of vengeance for his brother had led him to the Carbonari, he had learned enough there—and in America—to genuinely love justice. For a moment January thought he was going to walk over to Belaggio, smash the lyre over his head, and storm off the stage. Then a little of the tension went from him, as if he told himself—as January had—that whether or not he walked out, the half-naked men and women around him would be sold nonetheless.

"And again," urged Belaggio in rough Spanish, shoving aside the nonplussed and dumbfounded Herr Smith. "One, two three, *howl!*"

Backstage, Tiberio lit an experimental flare. A great gout of brightness splashed across the men nearest the gate, showing up their faces: tribal scars, somber eyes, the tight fantastic braids of their hair. And in the back, tall above all the others, the slick-shaved pate of an enormous man, the heavy brow marked with scars gained in the boxing-ring rather than the shaman's hut.

It was Big Lou.

And on his left biceps, as he lifted his arms to howl, January saw a small jagged cut, as if the flesh had been ripped with the broken handle of a china teapot.

January, Shaw, and Hannibal crossed the river early next morning by the steam ferry to Point Algiers. Lying in the back of a small wagon covered with tarpaulins, January heard Shaw's light, scratchy voice as he chatted with the deck-hand, and Hannibal's churchyard cough. ". . . sweetest woman you ever did see, but what does the stupid son of a bitch do but start makin' love to her hairdresser—her *hairdresser,* for the love o' Christ! And ev'ry Thursday afternoon they'd take the ferry an' I'd see her—the hairdresser, I mean—Alice Grantaire, her name was, *an'* no great beauty—all slicked up in lace an' jewels, an' him settin' up in that phaeton. . . . It was a nice phaeton if you like them high-perch types, blue paint an' red wheels, with a smart little bay gelding with one white sock. Now, I heard tell you ought never buy a horse with one white sock 'cause the odd foot makes 'em stumble, but my uncle Finn, he had a white-sock mare—Prettyfoot, her name was, and she had a mouth on her like a iron shovel. . . ."

They were the only travelers that early. There was no way to tell whether they'd been observed or followed, in the first stirrings of the day's traffic. For one moment, last night, January had raised his eyes from Gluck's score to see Big Lou looking down at him from the stage.

"With any luck they'll expect us to try and see M'am Marsan at her brother's first, 'fore going out to Les Roseaux." When the noises of the Algiers waterfront died behind them, January pushed back the oiled canvas sheets, and Shaw reached down for the long rifle that had been concealed beside him. "That's always supposin' M'am Marsan wasn't her husband's partner in the first place."

"A cherub's face," quoted Hannibal, *"a reptile all the rest."* He looked a little better since he'd been squiring Madame Montero, though whether this was from pleasure at the friendship of a fellow artist, or because she was feeding him better, was hard to say.

"I think if she were in on it, she'd have taken enough of the profits to get herself a better dress." January brushed flecks of straw from the wagon-bed out of his hair, and swung around the side of the seat to take the reins. "Her vouching for Cavallo, Ponte, and myself— rather than claiming we were runaway slaves—could have been nothing more than the knowledge that she couldn't get away with it. Aside from the fact that everyone in town saw Cavallo on-stage that night, if her husband was working with Belaggio, Cavallo was too integral a part of the opera to lose just then. But as to whether she's innocent of her husband's death . . ."

"If she ain't, she come across the river that mornin' in some other way than the ferry." Rifle held ready in the crook of his arm, Shaw scanned the wet, low-lying clearings—prairies, the Acadians called them—on either side of the road. "I asked Mr. Break-Jaw back there already about that."

"Anyone who could have been her?" January kept his

voice low in the hush. The stillness, and the winter fog, thick with the scents of woodsmoke and burnt sugar, seemed to cling around them as the wagon drew away from the river. While they followed the shell road between fields of stubble cane he felt safe enough, but the woods were the domain of M'sieu Chamoflet and his men.

It was ridiculous to suppose they didn't know everyone who passed that way.

"Not unless she can turn her color like one of them chameleon-things," replied Shaw. "They was enough folks goin' over in the afternoon that the ferryman can't say for sure. He says he knows M'am Marsan by sight, though I bet he'd miss her on foot in a cheap dress an' bonnet. But she'd have to come back early in the mornin', an' there wasn't a white man or woman returnin' before noon."

January halted the wagon just short of the last thicket before Les Roseaux came into view, for Shaw to step down. Hannibal's personation of a feckless dilettante on the trail of German novels didn't admit the presence of a Kaintuck bodyguard, and in any case, Big Lou—the only person on the plantation itself they had to worry about—was in town. The Big House had a shut-up air in the silvery forenoon, though there was activity around the stables and pig-yards. January could hear, as he drove up, the grinding whir of machinery from the sawmill. As he drew rein before the front steps, the door of Madame Marsan's bedroom opened—like all Creole houses, the women's side of the house was the one upstream from town—and the girl Jocelyn emerged, clothed now in mourning, followed by the respectable Mademoiselle DuClos.

Jocelyn Marsan's black dress looked newer than the

frock she'd worn last month, but still had the air of a hand-me-down, ill-fitting and pale at the seams. January guessed it came from her Dreuze cousins in town. She descended the steps with the calm self-possession she'd earlier shown, and listened to Hannibal's apologies for the intrusion into what he knew was a house of sorrow. But he had heard that M'sieu Marsan had left a number of novels in the German tongue—Hannibal's German accent was a miracle of discretion, considering he was speaking in French.

"M'sieu Knight is taking care of the sale of all my father's things," replied Jocelyn. "But he's busy in town, and nothing has been done so far, if you'd like to come in and have a look." She ascended, Hannibal effusive with thanks on her heels. "There aren't many. I don't think Father even read German. . . ."

January took the wagon around to the back.

Jules recognized him anyway, and Judy, the pleasant-faced cook. And though January guessed they, and all the other slaves on the place, were facing the possibility of sale, and separation from the home they had known, from their friends and families, he thought the two looked more relaxed than they had when last he'd seen them.

"I saw Big Lou in town the other day," he said once he'd traded greetings in the kitchen yard and produced, casually, his tale of being a driver at Desdunes's livery.

"Lord, yes," said Jules as Judy laid a half-loaf of new-baked bread on her willow tray and hurried through the kitchen to where an empty oil-jar was buried neck-deep in the ground behind, a cold-safe for butter and milk. "He was a mean one, Lou—he'd have pounded you up bad, for snoopin' around that jail. M'am Marsan sold him first thing, to pay for Michie Vincent's funeral and keep things going here for a time."

"For a fighter?"

Jules nodded. "At least that's what Michie Knight said. Tillich, he said the feller's name was. Said he saw Big Lou at one of those fights Michie Vincent used to take him to. Thank you, Mamzelle," he added as Judy set a round of fresh-molded butter on a glass plate, and added it, and half a dozen scones, to the tray. He leaned over to give her a peck on the cheek. "What can you cook up that's a little special for lunch? I'm sure Mamzelle Jocelyn's going to ask the white gentleman to have some, 'fore Michie Ben here drives him back to town."

"Why was Big Lou so all-fired anxious that I shouldn't get near that jail?" asked January as he helped Judy bring in apples from the store-room. "I know he said Michie Vincent had given him orders people was to be kept away from it, but you know there's a difference between 'kept away' and 'beat to hash.' "

"It would have been more than beat to hash if you'd been one of the men who worked here," said the cook glumly. Her big hands rolled, floured, folded dough for a lunch tart as unthinkingly as January would have vamped along with a familiar tune. "Big Lou killed a man once— Lionel, his name was, not more than seventeen, nosy as a kitten and just about as harmless. Knocked him down and kicked him, and he pissed blood for two days and died weepin'. . . . Cruel to see." Her brow puckered with remembered distress. "And Michie Vincent didn't do a thing to Lou. Not a whippin', not a scoldin' . . . We'd stayed away from the jail before then, but we *really* stayed away after. Even . . ." She dropped her voice, swallowed hard, with shame and remembered fear. "Even when we heard their voices there, callin' out. The ones they'd sometimes bring up the bayou, and lock up, for Michie Vincent to sell. But it didn't matter whether there was anyone in that jail or not. When Lou killed Lionel, there wasn't even anyone in that jail for him to see."

"Why keep it secret, then?"

She glanced toward the house, and lowered her voice still more, as if Marsan, or Lou, were still there to hear. "I think they used to leave the money there," she said. "Them and the slave-smugglers. All the cells, the keys to the padlocks, was kept in Michie Vincent's office in his desk, but the cells themselves was left open, except, of course, when . . . when Michie Chamoflet and his boys had been by." From its dish set in a greater dish of water—though there were few ants about this time of year—she took the sugar-loaf, brown with molasses, and nipped pieces off, dropping them from the box end of the nippers into a much-stained marble mortar.

"But that one cell on the end, in the corner—that cell was always kept locked up, even when there was nobody there. Michie Vincent would go out to it and let himself in, and you bet the children from the quarters would watch him around corners and from the trees. My own boy David hid in the trees on a dare, and I like to have wore him out, because Michie Vincent, he was an evil man. He wouldn't have stopped at hurtin' a boy, even a child eight or nine years old like David was then. He would even beat his own—" She hesitated, then shook her head and went on. "Anyways, I told him never, *ever* go near that jail."

Kneeling beside the hearth, she prodded the fire, settled the iron griddle into place. "But David told me—and I don't even want to *think* how he came to know—that at night sometimes another man would come down the bayou in a pirogue, or sometimes on a horse down the bayou road. He'd open the lock on that one cell door and let himself in, then let himself out again. He—my David, that is—took me once to the little landin' that the slave-smugglers use, just where the trees hide the jail from the bayou, and showed me the scrape-marks of a boat, and a man's boot-prints. I hauled him away from there fast. I didn't want to know." January handed her the dish of butter—she cut a hunk and it sizzled on the griddle's slick face. "I didn't want him to know. Bring me over those apples, would you, Michie Ben? That's mighty sweet of you to cut them for me. When I whip up this tart, I'll save over enough to make a little one for you. . . ."

"Which I hope," said January, "you and Jules will share with me."

After Judy slipped the tarts into the oven and turned her attention to dressing a couple of pigeons, January strolled to the abandoned jail. He stuck close to the trees for as long as he could, uneasy about walking over the open ground, although, like Judy, he knew Marsan and Big Lou were both gone. The cell doors stood open on all the cells save one. Had Marsan had its key on his person, January wondered, when he'd been cut to pieces in the alley by the theater?

Peering through the judas in the door, he saw only what he had seen before. A bare room with a sort of shelf barely visible at the end. Straining his eyes, he thought he could make out a box on the shelf.

And that was all.

"That's it," said January when he and Hannibal were once more in the wagon, driving away from Les Roseaux. "Tillich is the man who swears he saw Davis at the City Hotel gambling-room. Marsan was definitely part of Belaggio's connection to the Austrians. The slave-smuggling was part of it, the way to both pay Marsan—who as far as I know had no more politics than the average bull in a pasture—and to enlist the services of Captain Chamoflet in keeping a channel of communication open free of observation."

"Leaving aside for a moment why they would think coshing Marguerite over the head, or locking you and Cavallo in a cellar, would prevent Belaggio's affairs from being examined," said Hannibal, "I can tell you what they were handing off to one another in that box. Those books in Marsan's office—they're marked."

"Marked?" January drew rein, scanning the trees for sight of Shaw. The dark-green landscape had a still sameness in the thin light of early afternoon, a birdless quiet that seemed to hold its breath.

"With little ticks in pencil under the words. Not every page, and some pages more than others—I don't think the ticks went down any page more than a paragraph or two—but always from the top of the page. As if someone were counting the words."

January turned, regarding the musician with startled understanding; Hannibal was already digging in the pockets of his shabby coat. "There was a newspaper in the top drawer of the desk, with numbers scribbled in the margins, hundreds of them—always in pencil, like the ticks in the books. Ten/thirty. Forty-five/fifteen. Sixty-three/fifty. That kind of thing. And I helped myself to the blotting-paper. . . ."

January said, "It's a book code."

"Only, I might add, in the German or Italian books. Which leads me to wonder . . ."

January heard the crack of a rifle in the trees at almost the same instant that something hot flicked his face, burning, like a hornet's sting. He dropped with a cry back down to the seat and heard another shot, a bullet burying itself in the side of the wagon, and he thought, *The horse . . .*

He grabbed the reins and lashed wildly at the animal, shouting as the frightened beast leapt forward and a third shot drew blood from its shoulder, sending it well and truly on its way. Hannibal, thrown nearly out of his seat by the lurch, grabbed the seat-back and ducked his head down— "Are they in the woods or across the bayou?" yelled January.

"Woods. At least that's where the muzzle-flashes are. Nothing—damn it!" The horse stumbled, lurching from gallop to trot; January lashed with the reins again, but he saw the blood on the animal's hide and knew it was wounded in earnest now.

"How close?"

"Can't see anyone." Hannibal turned in the seat, looked back at the shell road behind them. "Believe me, they'll be along."

January drew rein, sprang down, and dragged Hannibal after him. "Git!" He tore up a willow-sucker from the water's edge, slapped the horse hard, sending it wildly away up the shell road, then turned and plunged across the water, the fiddler stumbling and panting at his heels.

"I certainly hope you know this part of Jefferson Parish like the back of your hand—"

"I certainly know what happens to people who fall foul of the smugglers and don't get themselves out of the way and under cover," retorted January, dragging the smaller man after him like a half-killed chicken. "They'll search near the bayou, figuring we have to follow it back to the river. I think we'd do better, for the time being, if we took refuge in the swamp."

The marshy lands that lay between the Bayou des

Familles and the Little Barataria Bayou consisted of the usual mix of dry, narrow ridges, most no more than a few feet wide, where old bayous or legs of the river had once lain, and wetter expanses of cypress, palmetto, and smooth-skinned gray magnolias. The spring rise had not yet inundated these stretches, and they lay under a brown layer of last year's leaves, or tangled with vast blankets of new-green elephant-ear, through which cypress-knees poked, like stalagmites displaced from a cave. It was early in the year for snakes, but January used the willow switch to probe ahead for them anyway. Early, too, for mosquitoes. Keeping to the dense belts of palmetto, like head-high forests between the larger trees, they could remain unseen even at a distance of a few feet.

In time they found an Indian shell-mound raised a few feet above the general level of the forest base and grown over with oaks. The spring floods would transform it into an islet—a chênière—and on it, tucked away between the trees, stood the remains of what had been either a trapper's shack or the hideout of a runaway slave.

"Wait here," said January as Hannibal sank down into a corner of this ramshackle structure. It was made of fragments of boards and packing-boxes, re-enforced with brush and moss—invisible at a few yards. "I can't imagine them not killing Shaw if he was too badly wounded to flee, but I have to go back and check. If I'm not back in . . ." He pulled his silver watch from his pocket. "If I'm not back in two hours, there's a landing and a woodlot at Belle Chasse, about ten miles east of here. You'll be able to get a boat back to town. Shaw told them at the Cabildo where he was going. . . ."

"I doubt if, when they send out a posse tomorrow, it will do us much good." Hannibal coughed, one arm wrapped tight around his thin ribs to still both the pain and the sound. "Circumstance may conspire to surprise us, however. We can only hope."

January hesitated, torn with uncertainty. The likelihood that Shaw was alive, wounded, and in need of help was less than that of Hannibal being utterly unable to defend himself should Captain Chamoflet and his swamprats put in an appearance, but he knew he could not simply leave the area without at least making an attempt to find Shaw. It was two, he reflected, stepping cautiously from the shack and carefully re-orienting himself on the group of towering magnolias that dominated the chênière. The sun would set at around five, full darkness settling perhaps half an hour later. . . .

And then, he thought, unless they'd made their way to within a half-mile or so of Belle Chasse, they were doomed indeed.

He worked his way as close to Les Roseaux as he could, through the dense rustling mazes of the palmetto forests and, as he drew closer to the bayou, the old plantation fields choked with overgrown cane and new growths of sapling pine and weeds. The high ground along Bayou des Familles wasn't more than a half-mile deep, barely enough to sustain a plantation. He could smell woodsmoke from somewhere, but heard no sound of the sawmill. Lying in the cane-brake, he caught the furtive rustle of a passing body, and a man called out in the rough archaic French of the Barataria, "Clo? Any sign?"

And a reply, so close to where he lay, January flinched. "No. Curse."

"Keep an eye, eh? They might still try to come back to the house."

"Curse," said Clo again.

January buried his face in his arms and waited, barely

breathing. A huge black ant walked across his arm, and a little later, a small cane-rat. He heard one of the men go, and for a long time strained his ears to detect some sound other than the occasional rain-like rush of wind through the trees. In the stillness a crow cawed. Frogs croaked, first a small tinny chirping, then, elsewhere, another chorus, a deeper and woodier bip-bip-bip: strophe and antistrophe like a Greek play, the sounds distinct as patches of different-colored wildflowers. After a time a rabbit hopped warily from between the dark stalks and sat up, pink nose wiggling, ears slanting one way and another, then scuttled cautiously in the direction from which Clo's voice had come.

Thank you, Compair Lapin. If you think it's safe, I'm game to try it.

Carefully, carefully, January edged out of the cane. No shot rang out. Body bent double, he worked his way back through what had been the field, and into the thick palmettos once more. Listening for some sound. Scanning the ground for track or sign of blood. Then he retreated to the *cipriere* again, and made his way back to the chênière, getting lost twice in the process.

Hannibal was half-unconscious, curled like a ball of bones on the ground. He sat up with a start when January crawled into the shelter, reached for the knife January had left with him, then saw who it was and put a hand over his own lips to still the sound of another cough. He was shivering in the chill afternoon but raised his eyebrows inquiringly; January shook his head.

"Let's go," January breathed. "They're in the woods still, searching, but if we don't start now, we'll be lucky to make Belle Chasse by dark."

"Can these bones live?" inquired Hannibal rhetorically, staggering as he straightened up. January caught his elbow

and wondered how much success he'd have in locating Sam Pickney's farm.

I'd have more luck finding the man if I just walked down the road after dark, of course. . . .

Provided it was Pickney he met.

By the time they reached the river, Hannibal was barely on his feet. They stopped to rest half a dozen times, wherever they could find a deadfall to sit on, and more and more frequently as the afternoon drew on and the spots of brightness on the dark cypress leaves grew higher and brighter with the sinking of the sun. In the closed-in world of the *cipriere,* it was hard to navigate at the best of times, for there was no wind in its shadowy aisles, no movement of water, no rise and fall of land. Sometimes January heard voices far off, and then they stood still in the thick pea-green eternities of palmetto, straining their ears for something beyond the harsh rustling of the fan-like leaves. Once, distantly, he heard a shot.

With the last of the cypress trees' shadows streaming out blue before them, they came into open ground, the bare fields of a sugar plantation, formless in the twilight. The family—relatives of the great Livaudais clan—were in town for Carnival, but the overseer clicked his tongue in shocked disapproval at Hannibal's tale of slave-stealers and attempted murder: "The Army, they try a dozen times to get that Chamoflet," said the fat little fair-haired man, shaking his head in the lamplight of the minuscule gallery before his cottage. "But he got friends in the *cipriere,* crackers, Kaintucks, *animaux—*"

Meaning, January knew, American *animaux.*

"You about a mile and a half down from English Turn. You lucky you didn't get to Belle Chasse." The overseer patted Hannibal's bony shoulder, where the fiddler sat slumped on the bent-willow gallery chair. "Etienne that runs the woodlot there, he's in with Chamoflet. I have the boys put out torches on the landing, there's boats coming past all night."

The *Heroine,* bound upriver from the Belize, didn't dock at the plantation till around eleven. January gave one of the slave-children fifty cents to stand lookout on the levee for it, and spent the next four hours in the cabinet at the back of Michie Tabor's cottage, drinking coffee and reading from the largest collection of old newspapers he'd seen outside Madame Bontemps's attic. Michie Tabor stayed up to chat with Hannibal through supper, then, having ascertained that his guests truly wanted to get on the late boat rather than stay the night, he had a couple of the cane-hands bring a Hitchcock chair and a lamp out to the cabinet, where Hannibal could sit wrapped in blankets until the boat came.

"Winter evenings, there's not a lot to do," said the overseer, scratching the head of the enormous old black-and-white cat that was his chief companion in the cottage. "Sometimes I just go back and read the newspapers to see all these things that I got so angry about ten, fifteen, twenty years ago. And I think, *Well, I lived through all that and I'm fine anyway.* Like watching the boats go by on the river."

"Annihilating all that's made," mused Hannibal as the overseer shut the door that led into the other cottage rooms, *"to a green thought in a green shade.* Look at this— Guerrero and the liberals take over Mexico. I remember my brother thought that was going to be the end of civilization."

"And so it was," murmured January, "for anyone who had ties with the Iturbide regime." It was the first time he'd ever heard Hannibal mention a brother. "What year was that? 'Twenty-seven? About the time Vincent Marsan found himself able to slip slaves through from the Barataria largely unhindered by the Navy."

Hannibal folded the newspaper to his chest and raised his eyebrows. Hot soup and a little bread-and-cheese with their host seemed to have revived him; though he still lay back in his chair like one exhausted, the ragged coughing had ceased, and his thin hands were still.

"Eight years ago," said January softly, "the new Liberal constitution in Mexico—the breakup of newly freed Spanish and Portuguese states in the south—the continuing fighting in New Grenada . . . The Hapsburg government in Vienna gets nervous about who's going to be making alliances with whom, and sends a man to New Orleans to look out for things. Not the first man it's sent, and certainly not the only government to send one— I'm sure the French and the British have their men in town, too, maybe even the Tsar. But our new Hapsburg friend—let's call him Tillich—makes arrangements to get information from across the Gulf, and, probably, to send money to whoever the Emperor thinks ought to be in charge in New Grenada and points south. And since, thanks to Mr. Jackson's increased distrust of the European powers, the Navy is developing an unpleasant tendency to search foreign vessels, those arrangements include information coming in, not upriver past the forts at the Belize, but through Grand Isle and the marshes of the Barataria."

"And since I'm sure Mr. Marsan wasn't willing to commit treason against the United States government for the sake of Mr. Tillich's pretty blue eyes," said Hannibal, "the passage of information was linked to an increase in the smuggling of slaves. A better use of Marsan's property than trying to grow sugar on it, if what I saw on Roseaux is any indication. . . . Bet me our friend Tillich speculated with some of his own money in that trade, too."

"Probably." January lifted half a stack of newspapers, nose prickling at mildew and stirred dust. The *Louisiana Gazette*. August 14, 1820.

He'd been in Paris then. Studying medicine and working in the night clinic.

Playing piano at the Odéon. Walking along the Pont-Neuf hand-in-hand with Marguerite, the Seine molten gold below the railings and hurdy-gurdy grinders pumping out Figaro's opening aria from *The Barber of Seville*. *Ladies and shop-girls / old maids and young girls / Dress this wig / Quick with the beard.* . . .

His throat shut hard and he put the papers down. "When Captain Chamoflet brings in a coffle from Havana or Caracas or wherever the Africa ships put in, he brings other things as well. Messages to leave in the little box on the shelf in one of the cells, the cell that's always kept locked. The cell that no one is allowed to go near. And only one other person has the key."

He lifted another stack of papers. Damp had gotten to them, and they came up in a single piece, like a black brick, breathing mildew. There was a smell of mouse-piss. He half expected to find M'sieu LeMoyne's little blue notebook underneath.

He made out a date, February 9, 1829.

"It's not all that far from town to Les Roseaux," he told Hannibal. "A man can cross the river, ride inconspicuously down to Bayou des Familles in the evening, make his pickup—and leave money—in the darkness while the slaves are having their suppers—did you notice how far the jail is from the quarters?—and be back in town in time for everyone he knows to see him at the opera, or in the gaming-houses, or to make the after-supper set at a ball. Marsan encodes and decodes, if the message is a long one or Tillich is pressed for time. A book code is one of the easiest to use and is unbreakable by someone who doesn't have the specific book."

"And since Marsan doesn't even know German or Italian," remarked Hannibal, "he probably knows nothing and cares less about what is being passed through his jail. All he knows is that he's rich now. Rich enough to convince some other poor girl's mother to sign over her daughter to be his mistress."

"Obviously someone got concerned about the messages being intercepted." January shifted another stack, and, on impulse, sought down through it—the papers were roughly in chronological order, owing probably more to sedimentary action than to any intent—until he found a thick layer of the New Orleans *Abeille* for March 1825. "As I said, there are probably French and English agents working out of the consulate—maybe Carbonari also. Tillich changed books—as you say, always German or Italian, the two main languages spoken in Vienna. And finally, someone at the home office decided that the easiest means of security was to make sure that messages were being transmitted by an unpublished work. Something only those in touch with Belaggio would have."

"*Othello,*" said Hannibal. "No wonder poor Incantobelli was furious."

"Furious enough to risk his life, to avenge his honor." *My house shall be a house of prayer. . . .*

"At a guess," January went on after a moment, "that's what Cavallo saw when we were all in the study together at Les Roseaux. A copy of the libretto, with the words pencil-ticked, as a man will tick them when he counts. That's what he's been looking for in Belaggio's office—

copies of German books that match Marsan's, or of the libretto, similarly marked."

March 5, 1825. *Jefferson Parish planter questioned in connection with the death of a woman. . . .*

March 10, 1825. *The mother of the murdered woman created a scene in court. . . .*

March 12, 1825. *To the editor: A woman of color knows the truth about . . .*

For no reason he could think of, January saw Dominique at the breakfast table, Dominique twelve years old with her soft, thick hair combed down over her back, silky as a white girl's. His mother, he recalled, had always been proud as Lucifer that Dominique's hair wasn't nappy, and never braided it or tied it in strings. She'd dress it with sugar-water so that its reddish highlights gleamed in the sun. Dominique in the flat corsets of girlhood, eating lost bread and listening to her mother's crisp opinions on the case as she read the newspaper.

Dominique sweet-faced and young, with nothing more to worry her than piano lessons and learning to dance gracefully, so that one day she might become placée . . .

"Well, I can see how Marguerite might have stumbled onto some piece of information about all this." Hannibal dropped two chunks of sugar and a dollop of opium into his coffee. "But it still doesn't get us any closer to who's been trying to kill Belaggio. It can't have been Cavallo. He was locked up with you in the cellar at Cornouiller that day."

March 15. *The court today ruled that the woman Sidonie Lalage, and the cab-driver found dead just outside her house, were slain by person or persons unknown. . . .*

"I said," repeated Hannibal, causing January to glance up with a start, "that it can't have been Cavallo who tried to kill Belaggio because he was with you. And I've been checking through everything Concha did, those first two days in town, and I'll swear it wasn't she who hired the Gower boys."

"No," said January, and he folded the newspaper to put in his pocket. He felt curiously calm, and in spite of clothing still damp, and the hot sting of the bullet-graze on his face. In spite of exhaustion and the knowledge that tomorrow night he'd have to deal with Big Lou and, presumably, Mr. Tillich himself when the buyers came after the opera's performance. In spite of all that, he felt at peace.

As if he held one end of a clue of thread in his hand, the other end stretching away into darkness.

"No, it wasn't, I don't think," he told Hannibal softly. "Because from the first it wasn't Belaggio who was the target. It was Marsan all along."

TWENTY THREE

When January and Hannibal limped across the Place d'Armes and into the watchroom of the Cabildo in the small hours of Thursday morning, it was to find Abishag Shaw seated at his desk. In the dirty flare of the oil-lamps, his narrow face had more than ever the appearance of a gargoyle's, bruised and scratched—chipped, one almost might think. A dirty bandage wrapped his left hand and forearm, wet, like his hair, from a hasty dousing in the courtyard trough. He looked up from the report he was scribbling as the door opened, and got hastily to his feet.

"Maestri." A few long strides brought him to them, and he steered Hannibal to one of the benches by the door. "You all right?"

I could play Erecles rarely, responded the fiddler in a conversational tone, *or a part to tear a cat in, to make all split.* A passing indisposition merely, coupled with a far more intimate acquaintance than I ever imagined I could want with the flora and fauna of the bayous. Yourself?"

"Calvert." Shaw gestured to one of the lamplighters. "Might you go over t' the market, see if you can get some coffee for my friend here? Brandy, too, if'n you got it." He held out a couple of silver reales. The man reached for them, then shied back as a rolling mob of City Guards and drunken combatants burst through the door, mud-slathered, bloody, and arguing at the top of their voices in several different tongues. Late as it was, every gambling-den, public house, and brothel in town was doing vigorous business; along the torchlit levee, steamboats off-loaded cargoes and market-women hawked their wares, and the Place d'Armes was as lively as if it were two in the afternoon rather than two in the morning.

When Calvert departed, Shaw went to fetch his grimy coat from his desk, to wrap around Hannibal's shoulders. "Good to see you back. I just got in myself, af-ter checkin' your landlady's, Maestro. I had to backtrail some, 'fore I lost our friends in the swamp—thought as long as I was pullin' foot anyways I might as well split the pursuit. I cut your trail later but lost it again when it got dark. Seemin'ly somebody tattled to Captain Chamoflet that we was headed out to Marsan's after all. You learn anythin'?"

January said, "Oh, yes," and recounted everything he had heard from Jules and Judy, and what Hannibal had found in Marsan's study. He finished with "It has to have been Lou who followed us after Trulove's reception and attacked Marguerite—" *No wonder duCoudreau thought it was me,* he reflected, remembering the prints of those enormous hands. "I still don't know why. But of course he was in town that day, for the fights. As for Mr. Tillich . . ."

"You rat-faced little fyst, who you callin' whore?" bel-lowed one of the women in the mob before the sergeant's desk, and fetched the man next to her a wallop that sent him reeling. Shaw stepped out of the way, still chewing mildly. The man tripped, rolled in a messy white bun-dle—he was clothed as Pierrot, his billowy suit spattered with blood from his streaming nose—and sprang into the fray again, colliding with Madame Montero as she thrust open the watchroom's doors.

"*Corazón!*" Dodging the battle, the soprano strode to Hannibal, a dragonfly glitter of garnet, jet, miles of mantilla, and armloads of sable and plumes. "I have looked all over the town for you. . . ."

Hannibal smiled and extended a hand. "Not all over, I hope, *querida mia.*"

"All over indeed! That disgraceful *puta* who runs the place where you live—"

His eyes widened with alarm. "You went to visit Kentucky Williams?"

"I did indeed, and she told me that you"—she whirled, an accusing finger stabbing up at January—"that *you* had coaxed him away this morning, to who knows what ends, rambling over the countryside like Don Quixote—"

"They had need of a gentleman, Dulcinea," argued Hannibal.

"And you were the best they could do? You have missed the rehearsal, not that there was much to miss, and the Chorus of Hell—bah! As bad as those *imbecilas* of the ballet, and Belaggio letting every friend of the Opera Society come backstage to look at his *diablos* as if they had never seen a *Negro* before. . . ."

Under cover of her account of Belaggio's blatant huckstering, Shaw murmured, "I don't rightly see how Tillich could have bought Big Lou. He's just a clerk, an' lives in lodgin's. Big Lou's livin' in lodgin's on his own, down near the turnin' basin, with a tin-badge pass. If'n we arrest him much 'fore the show tomorrow night, Belaggio's customers won't come backstage to close their deal, much less his Austrian contact to try get his cut of the loot. But I can sure have a man watch him tomorrow. . . ."

"Whose clerk?" asked January.

Shaw smiled slowly, gray eyes twinkling. "Erasmus Knight's," he said. "Now, if'n you please, M'am Montero—it so happens I have a little favor to ask of you. . . ."

Chevalier, January had called to him. He could see himself saying it, distracted between the demands of his work and his concern for John Davis. He'd been switching back and forth between English, French, and Italian all evening, and Chevalier, he recalled, had been the name he'd heard Knight called by on those few occasions he'd seen him in Paris.

It meant the same thing, of course, which made it all the easier to stumble. Not that Chevalier had been his real name in those days, either—at a guess it was actually Ritter. But in Paris, January recalled, he'd been a sort of boulevardier, who made it his business to attend salons and follow the opera and the races and whatever new fashion in cravats or politics came along.

To be in all those places where the politics and plans of the Restoration would be discussed.

Was it so easy? he wondered bitterly, looking down into Marguerite's still face, her cold fingers like the stems of knotted cane.

To Vincent Marsan it would have been nothing when Knight slipped aside and whispered to him, *That man knows me from Paris. Have Big Lou get rid of him.*

Who would search for the casual killer of a black man on a deserted road? In the confusion of Carnival he'd have been lucky if the Guards even investigated. A white woman's body found beside his ("She'll be the one who told him—" He could just imagine Knight saying it, like ordering a dozen eggs for a supper next week) might guarantee that no investigation would be made.

Like *Othello,* something that was unpleasant to think about or view.

For other reasons, it had certainly kept his own friends and family quiet.

Morning light lay cold and silvery on Marguerite's sunken face. From the yard, small, sharp metallic taps as Zizi-Marie hammered a line of tacks into the frame of some rich man's chair. *I should feel triumph,* January thought, turning the thin hand over in his own huge fingers; gently touching the yellowing bruises on her throat. *I know who did this to you, and why. And we'll get him. He won't get away.*

Only, of course, Knight almost certainly would.

Knight would prove his Austrian citizenship; call on the Austrian consul in Havana. Leave his burly, fair-haired, bullyboy of a clerk Tillich to be hanged for treason, and Big Lou, for attacking a white woman, perceived in some circles as the greater crime.

Punish the bullet and smash the gun, but let the man who pulled the trigger go free.

January closed his eyes. *Don't open that door,* he told himself. It's enough to know Knight will be punished by his superiors for fouling up, for being caught.

Warm hands slipped over his shoulder. Like a blind man, he could have identified Rose by touch and scent in the dark: ink and soap and the subtle velvet woman-smell of her body and clothes. She rested her hip against his shoulder and he put his free hand around her skirts, turned his face to rest it against them.

How do men live, he wondered, *who do not have a woman to hold?*

"She woke up late yesterday afternoon," said Rose. "I checked her eyes, and the pupils looked the same size. She knew me—knew where she was. Olympe tells me you know who did it. Who was behind it all."

"That I do," said January, and it was almost the truth. "Marsan's factor, Knight. He's passing money and information between the Austrian government and the counter-revolutionists in New Grenada and Bolivia; using his diplomatic influence to smuggle slaves in from Africa to pay his operatives here. He's kept his name out of it by using Marsan and Tillich as his cat's-paws. No wonder he panicked when I called him by his French alias the other night."

In the yard he heard Gabriel singing as he carried water into the kitchen, light and free and casual. Zizi-Marie called out some remark, and was answered by Olympe's rare, joyous laugh.

How easy to destroy beauty, January thought. To simply say, *Get rid of that person because they might spoil my plans or interfere with the Rights of Man.* Why was happiness always so fragile?

"If he works through Tillich—you mean that stuffed-looking young man who escorted Mademoiselle Flaherty to all those parties?"

"The very same. And who went with Knight to the Hotel Toulouse to search for Incantobelli, and who probably did the horse-riding and torch-throwing the night Big Lou broke in here."

"If he works through Tillich, how are you going to get Knight?"

January sat up, his hand slipping from around Rose's hips to hold on to her fingers, strong and slim and blotched all over with ink and chemicals and dried crusts of glue from Mr. Davis's fireworks. Looking up into her face, with its delicate bones and dusting of freckles and wise, ironic gray-green eyes behind her spectacles, he remembered the desperate warmth of her lips under his, the strength of her arms as they tightened around him.

The memory was in his eyes, because he saw it reflected in hers—and in her slow, secret smile.

And he smiled, too. "Mr. Tillich," he answered, "is going to be taken very sick this afternoon."

"Oh, the poor man," replied Rose, not in the least discomposed. "Was there enough left of whatever Queen Régine's sold to Madame Montero?"

"Oh, yes. Consuela said she didn't dare put much into La d'Isola's soup because she still wasn't sure how strong it was—and given how sick Drusilla got on just that pinch, I think I can assure you that Mr. Tillich is going to be in no shape to go pick up money from Belaggio after tonight's performance. He's due to encounter Kate the Gouger near his rooms in about . . ." He took his watch from his pocket. "About four hours."

"Ah." Rose nodded wisely. "So I expect his lunch isn't the only thing he's going to lose."

No, thought January. Probably, in the long run, he would lose his life.

But sooner or later, everyone does that.

"But if Belaggio was working for Knight," said Rose doubtfully, "why would Knight have had him attacked? Since it was Knight who got him and Marsan together— who killed Marsan? And why?"

Why indeed?

January sighed, and turned back to the bed, to stroke Marguerite's graying hair. She was not, he thought, Knight's only victim. *Kill that man, that woman, to shut them up. Hang that one—or anyone we can find ready to hand—just so that people won't ask about who Belaggio might have been meeting at the theater after hours.*

If it hadn't been John Davis, who was without an alibi, it would have been someone else. Exactly as the desperate Incantobelli had shoved January into a stranger's arms, not caring if he got thrashed or jailed or hanged. But at least Incantobelli had the excuse that he was in fear for his life.

Like Marguerite, he, too, was due his avenging.

He didn't ask Olympe for the information he needed. He wasn't sure she'd tell him. Breakfast, and coffee; a bath in the cabinet behind the parlor and a shave; a little more quiet talk with Rose. The mists were yielding to sunlight sharp as a small knife when he left Olympe's house and made his way to the poorer neighborhood at the back of the old French town.

Only a few of the livery stables along Rue des Ramparts had been there in 1825. As more houses were built, and land became more dear, men who rented out horses and stable-space for a living tended to move across into the Faubourg Tremé. But a handful remained, and by good luck, one of these was the one next door to the cottage of Marie-Pucelle Morriset.

"Yes, he worked out of here," said Romain Faon, in charge of Combeferre's Livery. There was a small house on the front of the property, which extended behind the house almost through to Rue Burgundy. In the big yard, grooms were washing down a cherry-red curricle. The smells of soap mingled with those of horse-piss, clean straw, wet brick. "Rented from Michie Combeferre for ten dollars a month, cab and horses both, plus half his

fares. Nice little bay named Elisá, I recall, good paces but
short in the legs, and a big, tall piebald named Welling-
ton. Treated them well, he did. He'd come in and groom
them, Sunday mornings, while his sister cleaned up the
cab. She'd braid ribbons in their manes, blue for the mare,
red for the gelding. Shameful what happened," he said,
and shook his head. "Shameful."

"You know where he lived?" asked January. "If he had
other family besides the girl?"

"He had no family but the sister," said Faon. "They
lived on Rue de l'Hôpital. Land was owned by the Ursulines then, but they leased to a Madame Fourgette, who
let rooms. God knows if she's still there."

She was. The house was an old one, rambling and
seedy, the smells here of privies long untended, of rooms
long unaired. There was a constant coming and going of
day-laborers in smocks, clerks in checkered trousers and
tight-fitting coats with elbows discreetly patched; young
women more brightly dressed than daytime called for,
even daytime during Carnival. A smell of greasy soup, of
poverty and desperation.

"Oh, I wept for the poor creature." Madame Fourgette clasped big hard hands clotted with rings before her
heavy breasts, but her eyes, set like polished coals in a
thick face framed by an enormous lace-trimmed tignon,
had the dry look of eyes that have shed no tears since
babyhood. "His sister, too, of course, but poor Aucassin!
And him so young! He was only twenty, you know, when
that brute cut him to pieces, only for talking to the
girl. . . ."

"Did he know her?" asked January. "Were they
friends, I mean?"

The woman appeared to be thinking, tongue probing
at the inside of her shut lips, but those hard, dry eyes met

his and January, with the appearance of absent-minded-
ness, jingled the coins in his coat-pocket and took out a
Spanish dollar, turning it over in his gloved hand and
looking at it as if he'd never seen King Ferdinand's face before in his life. The walls of the parlor in which they sat
hadn't been painted, probably, since the house was built;
through the French doors light fell from Rue de l'Hôpital
and showed up the scratched and dulled cypress boards of
the floor. He wondered what white gentleman protector
had given the house to Madame Fourgette, and set her up
with enough money to get her start. And found himself
looking forward to what his mother would say of the
woman when he spoke of this meeting next Sunday at
dinner.

"Well, she only lived over a few streets," said
Madame. "Her cottage was just a house or two from the
livery where he kept his horses, and I know he'd speak to
her sometimes, coming and going from work. Little
Marie—the sister, you know—said once he was walking
home late at night after turning in the cab, and heard her
weeping, and spoke to her through her window. But you
could tell it was only kindness. He'd never come to anything," she added with a touch of condescension, of
scorn, in her tobacco-roughened voice.

She dug a tobacco-pouch from the pocket of her
over-embroidered and none-too-clean silk dress, and with
it stuffed a small ivory pipe. Her clothing, her tignon, the
chairs in the big double parlor, all reeked of old smoke,
and the ceiling was yellow-brown with it around the dead
lights of a dust-covered chandelier.

"He might be light as you please—his mother was
old Charles Hougoumont's placée and near as fair as a
Spaniard herself—but he was nowhere near that poor
Mademoiselle Lalage's class. He could barely sign his

name, and so simple-hearted, you'd take him for a booby. Well, it goes to show, doesn't it?" She walked to the fire, and with a spill from the box by the hearth kindled the pipe, puffing the smoke from the other side of her mouth as she stood beside the marble-painted wooden mantel. "No man in his right mind would go up to a white man's plaçée that way, would he? Not at that time of the night. I don't care if they heard her screaming, let alone just crying—and they do cry a good deal. Don't know when they're well off, I daresay."

The street door opened and two girls came in, hand-in-hand like sisters or friends. But when they stepped clear of the bright incoming light, January saw their faces were like Madame Fourgette's, tired and hard. They might have been thirteen and fourteen years old, but the dresses they wore were styled like women's dresses—cut low despite the earliness of the hour, over small breasts just beginning to bud—and their tignons gaudy with feathers and bows. One of them looked across at her and opened her painted lips to speak, and Madame Fourgette said quickly, "Excuse me a moment, sir," and went to them, holding out her hand.

One of them put some money in it. Madame counted it with a practiced glance and with her free hand lashed out and boxed the girl's ear: "Where's the rest of it?"

"Wasn't no rest of it." The girl rubbed her ear sullenly, and her friend added, "That's all there was."

"Carnival season and every man in town walking around with his pants out in front of him and that's all there was? Little liars!" She shoved the money in her bosom, caught each girl by those thin bare shoulders, and whipped them around, pushed them to the door again. "Don't you come back till you can bring me five dollars apiece, you understand? Five dollars! Lazy little bitches," she added, crossing back to January, her dark eyes ugly with annoyance. "And drunk, and at this time of the day, too." She picked up her pipe again. "They don't care whose money it is."

"No," said January, watching those two flower-bright forms pass the other window, make their way back down Rue de l'Hôpital in the direction of the levee and the taverns of Gallatin Street. "No, I daresay they don't." He looked back at Madame Fourgette. "Is that what happened?" he asked. "Aucassin—"

"Couvent," she said. "Aucassin Couvent."

"Aucassin Couvent heard Sidonie weeping and went around the back to speak to her, to comfort her?"

She shrugged. "It's what he done before, according to that sister of his. I daresay she made it up. She was an ungrateful little creature, stuck-up and pert-mouthed. A thief, too. After he died, I let her stay on here, at my own expense—for they'd no family, their mother being dead, and Old Man Hougoumont, too, by that time—for a month, an entire month! Then she just disappeared, and made not the slightest attempt to pay me back for rent or food or even the clothes on her back. Nothing!"

Aware of the delicate mechanics of owing and paying by which bawds and pimps controlled their girls, of constant debt and earnings that were never quite enough—*five dollars, you understand?*—January guessed what it was that the young cab-driver Aucassin Couvent's twelve-year-old sister had fled. Dominique, at least, he found himself thinking, had the choice of seeking another protector. She had the training, the accomplishments, the social grace to be placée—placed—as a white man's mistress.

Some didn't.

"Do you know what happened to her?" he asked. "Where she went?"

"To hell, I hope." Madame Fourgette viciously knocked the ashes out of her pipe. "Let her sing her little songs for the Devil, and hope he pays her for them."

January paused in the act of rising. "She sang?"

January was late getting to the theater that evening. When he returned to his room at Madame Bontemps's, he found a note from Dominique, and going to her house in the Rue Du Maine, found Thérèse just lacing her into a gown of green and amber, and fastening Henri's pearls around her neck. "He's meeting me at the opera." Dominique angled her head a little to the mirror to touch her lips with rouge. "He says he will not let anything, or anyone, come between us." She fixed small golden pearls into the lobes of her ears, and he saw her hand tremble.

"You believe him?"

Her eyes met his in the mirror, then shifted to her maid. "Thérèse, could you get me a little more coffee? And a cup for my brother? Thank you." She smiled after the woman as she left. When she turned to meet her brother's eyes direct, her face had altered, calm but very still.

"My last period started the twentieth of November," she said. "How long do I have?" She touched her lips with her tongue, pursed them as though fearing for the delicate color there. "Before I have to make up my mind, I mean."

In his mind January saw Henri handing that chill, diamond-perfect girl a cup of negus. Saw Madame Bontemps rubbing her own floors with beeswax. Saw Madame Fourgette in her shiny-elbowed violet plush, knocking ashes into the dirty fireplace of the house some man had given her. "Until Mardi Gras," he replied, and her jaw tightened.

"That's next week," she whispered. "So soon?"

"After that it gets more dangerous with every day that passes," he said. "When will they be married?"

"August."

She was no longer looking at him. Her gaze fixed on the buttons of his waistcoat, holding silence about her like a too-thin shawl against Arctic wind. January put his hands on her shoulders, drew her to him, and kissed her forehead. Held her, trying to give what he'd sought from Rose that morning—the comfort of knowing someone was there.

Everything that he or anyone else might have said—*Henri loves you* or *Everything will be all right*—faded before the fact that there was no way to know. One could only take one's best guess and walk forward in the dark.

"Enjoy the opera," he said, stepping back from her. "The music's beautiful, but very little happens."

Which turned out to be one of the most inaccurate statements he'd ever made.

"But where is she?" Belaggio was demanding when January came up the steps from the prop-room. "I've looked in her dressing-room, in the green room . . ."

Not again, thought January. And then, *Not tonight . . .*

"It was not half an hour ago that I fixed her hair." Madame Rossi still held the curling-tongs, and a handful of hairpins, from preparing the Chorus of Heroes and Heroines; Madame Chiavari, a dressing-gown of violet silk wrapped over the somewhat abbreviated pink costume of Love, trailed her distractedly.

"I've checked in all the dressing-rooms," added Cavallo worriedly. Over flesh-colored tights Orfeo's black tunic looked a little gaudy for mourning—gold laurel-leaves twined its border and sleeves—and in the chill of backstage he wore a decidedly un-Greek blue coat. "Could she have been taken ill again?" He glared pointedly around the backstage, as if expecting to see Consuela Montero emerge from her dressing-room resplendent in Euridice's Act One cerements.

James Caldwell, emerging from the prop-vault behind January with a bull's-eye lantern in hand, cleared his throat diffidently and asked, "Is—er—is Madame Montero on the premises? Not that I'm saying we should cease our search for Mademoiselle d'Isola, of course, but in case something has . . . that is, in case she has been taken ill, and returned to her hotel— *Has* anyone gone to her hotel to look for her?"

"And I suppose she just walked across Camp Street, dressed as she was?" demanded Belaggio sarcastically. He looked shaken. A month ago, January would have been touched at this evidence of concern. As it was, he only reflected, *He still thinks Knight murdered Marsan.*

And why not? It would be like Knight to lie, to put Belaggio off his guard.

"Who'd notice during Carnival?" responded Hannibal, emerging, fiddle in hand, from Hell's twisted gates rather like a down-at-heels Orpheus himself. Tiberio, carefully pouring water into the hidden pans that cradled the fire-pots, glared at him and went on muttering about the thieving ways of the Irish. "To answer your question, sir," the fiddler added, "Madame Montero is, so far as I know, having supper at the Promenade Hotel and then plans to attend the performance of *Fra Diavolo* at the Théâtre d'Orleans."

"Could you . . ." began the theater owner, nervously straightening the outermost and gaudiest of his waistcoats. "Might you . . . that is, do you think she might . . . ?"

"La d'Isola will be found!" Belaggio thundered, raising clenched fists in Jove-like anger.

"Of course she will. Of course she will. Nevertheless . . ."

"I just seen Mr. Knight out front," murmured Abishag Shaw's voice in January's ear. January withdrew from the sextet forming around the Gate of Hell, and stepped to where the policeman slouched in the greenroom door. "Escortin' Marsan's daughter an' a couple of aunts. An' Mr. Tillich is sure-enough indisposed back at his lodgin's. I gather him an' that Kate girl spent half the afternoon there drinkin' champagne."

And helping herself to the contents of Tillich's pockets and bureau, January reflected. Keeping behind the scenery, he made his way to the prop-room under the gallery, where the bloodied desk had been stowed. Hannibal had secreted the ragged tunic, fur-fringed tights, and mask of a member of the Demon Chorus behind the scrims. "What about Big Lou?" From the other side of the wall he could hear the muttering of the rest of the demons, shut up in the rehearsal-room. Locked in, as they'd been locked in before and after rehearsal Monday night and presumably last night as well.

"They wander off, they get lost, they speak no French and no English, either," he had overheard Belaggio explain to the doubtful Caldwell. "Their leader—the big one—he cannot watch over all of them, so to lock them in is the best thing." He wondered if Caldwell accepted the explanation.

"Big Lou busted Labranche and Boechter over the

head and ran for it when they tried to take him," said Shaw grimly, "just as he was comin' here."

He raised the chimney of the oil-lamp he'd snagged from Caldwell's office, but the orange light was little better than a candle's. January was grateful he had only a mask to contend with, and not elaborate make-up.

"Labranche is out yet. My guess is Lou's out of town by this time, but I got my men watchin' the theater for him. You're just about his size, Maestro: with the mask an' all, an' the way they dim down the lights so the fire'll show up, from the front I'm guessin' Knight's gonna think you're him."

January drew on the tights, shook out the tangle of horsehair sewn to the knees and calves, and shivered in the prop-room's stuffy chill. "What happened to d'Isola, do you know?"

"She was here." Shaw proffered a pot of white grease-paint he'd found tucked behind some buckets, with which January marked his chest and arms with signs he'd seen market-women paint on their baskets. "Like the hair-lady said, she got herself all gussied up, then went up to her room to lay down. That's the last anybody saw of her. What with Big Lou absquatulatin', an' Tillich pukin', an' Belaggio pullin' foot in the mornin' for New York, whatever happens, we better get *somebody* on that stage or we lose our chance to hog-tie Knight."

"Wonderful." January put on the mask and tried to get some idea of what he looked like in an ornate mirror. To his own eyes he appeared neither African nor diabolical, only goose-fleshed and rather silly. "Leaving him at large and still nervous about what Marguerite—or I— might remember from our days in Paris. Do you remember if anyone else from the Opera Society was backstage then? Anyone who might also be connected with Knight?"

"They's all in an' out. That Burton fella, an' Trulove—Mrs. Trulove, too, snoopin' around tryin' to catch her husband tradin' the time of day with that Irish—er—damsel. What would Knight have against that little d'Isola gal? She don't sing *that* bad."

What indeed? thought January, and he ducked through the prop-room door again, to find everyone clustered around Consuela Montero as she came up the stairs.

"Bueno, bueno, I will sing," she was saying crossly, shedding sables, bonnet, gloves already as she strode to her dressing-room. "First it is, *O Consuela, you are not as good as that little Neapolitan tart.* Then it is, *O Consuela, you must learn Euridice in the next two days. . . . But oh, so sorry, we shall use this d'Isola after all. . . .* Hannibal? *Corazón?"* She looked around her. *"Ai,* the man is never about when you have need of him!"

The dressing-room door slammed behind her.

From the front, through the curtains, through the flies and scrims and clustered trees of Arcady, January could hear the murmur of voices, the boisterous whoop of some Kaintuck in the stalls, and a woman's coarse, shrill laugh.

Orfeo ed Euridice, before THAT audience. God help us.

January stepped once more into the concealing shadows of the flats as the chorus filed on past him. In the hall the overture had started, beautiful and delicate, muffled by velvet, by bodies, by paper-leaved trees and canvas. Cavallo in his black tunic paused, his broken lyre in hand, to trade a quick whisper with Tiberio—". . . in La Scala," he said, naming the greatest theater in Milan, where presumably the impresarios didn't deal in slaves on the side. The heat of the gas-jets flowed back, the smell thick and gritty. Caldwell's voice echoed in the backstage. "But where could she have gone to?"

The curtain went up.

The first act was, mercifully, short. January gritted his teeth, torn between the grief and beauty of the music and the rising noise of the pit. Conditions were not ideal and Cavallo, who had arrived late with Ponte, was nervous and out of voice, but had Orpheus himself been singing January doubted the Americans would have sat still for it. There was no getting around the fact that for most of the act it was one man in a golden wig alone on-stage singing in a language nobody understood.

"Give that feller a musical saw!" somebody shouted about two verses into "Cerco il mio ben cosi," and was joined by other cries: "Kin you at least juggle them apples?"

In the wings, January understood.

Euridice dead, and yet I breathe . . .
Return her to me, or shut me up in death myself. . . .

Thus his own heart had cried to the dark of the empty Paris streets, those smothering weeks of the cholera, following his wife's death. The dark had not replied.

But no one in the pit, unfortunately, understood Italian. "I like that dress you're wearin'!" "How about singin' 'Sweet Violets'?" Howls, whoops, and whistles greeted the descent of Love from the flies, and January knew exactly why a few moments of quiet greeted the beginning of Madame Chiavari's "Se il dolce suon." *I am that sweetest song. . . .* They were hoping now that something would happen.

And, of course, it didn't.

"Pigs!" Cavallo flung himself off-stage like a man into

battle. "Swine grunting and nosing at the most beautiful music . . ." He sprang out of the way as Paddy and Liam shoved sections of rock past him, and Tiberio ran to join the hosepipes to the gas-jets that would illuminate the fanged and towered doors of Hell. Amid her attendant Nymphs and Heroines, Montero was re-arranging the black curls of her wig and talking impatiently to Bruno Ponte, her ample curves beneath the white grave-robe and bandages the least ghost-like thing imaginable.

"Where has he got to, then? He said he had a thought as to where that provoking girl had got to, and this was the last I saw . . ."

Ponte, transformed from Arcadian shepherd to fuzzy-legged demon, shook his head. "I told him myself I had checked all the boxes, and the attics, though what she would be doing in those places in the first place I cannot imagine. . . ."

Belaggio emerged from his office, glanced around him as if seeking someone—Big Lou, probably, thought January—then hastened to the rehearsal-room door with the air of a man hoping for the best. "On-stage, go, now," he heard the impresario saying in rough Spanish, gesturing to the horrifically-costumed men as they emerged. "Bruno . . ."

Ponte dashed to lead the demons onto the stage. None of the African women, January noted, were in the actual performance—he wondered how Belaggio had explained them to Caldwell. Of course the selected members of the Opera Society would ask for women. Every breeder of new slaves was a plus.

January stepped into the line of demons as they streamed past, and searched out a place for himself as close to the concealing rocks as he could manage. Between the footlights, the firepots, and the gas-jets, the whole stage was like an oven; for a moment all he could think of was that.

Then it came to him that after nearly twenty years of playing in anywhere from two to thirty operas in a year, this was the first time he had ever actually been on a stage. Even in Paris no one hired black men, even for chorus work. For a moment he was seized with an almost unbearable terror, a quaking conviction of nakedness, and a certainty that when the Chorus of Devils leapt forward to surround Orfeo, he, Benjamin January, was going to trip on his own big feet and fall flat on his face in front of everyone in New Orleans.

He wanted to flee to the darkest corner of backstage and vomit.

The ballet dancers blew like bright-colored leaves through the wings to change into Blessed Spirits in double time.

Gluck's unearthly music replaced the Boston Woodcutter's March.

The curtains parted.

Flame glared and burst from the black-and-red gates of stone and iron, and steam billowed from the jets of the machine beneath the stage. The audience—returned to good humor by the ballet—fell silent as the demons surged forward, leaping and cavorting before the doors of Hell.

Given the relatively few actual singers and dancers in the crowd on-stage, January thought the angular, disharmonious Demon Chorus went quite well. The Africans kept to the rocks at the stage's edge, as they'd been instructed, leapt, bounced, strutted, and spun, shouting and shaking their make-believe weapons with the enthusiasm of men who have learned to take each day as it comes. Orfeo, arrayed in white now and clutching Apollo's golden lyre, stepped to the gates and was surrounded, shrieked at, and threatened, while Tiberio laid on greater columns of fire from the gas-jets and Paddy and Liam shook the smoke-painted scrims to catch the filtered crimson light. January had always respected this scene in an opera whose basic premise—the original legend's tragedy of lost trust transformed by a banally happy ending—annoyed him.

When a composer writes about the most brilliant musician in the world, sooner or later in the course of the work he is going to have to come up with music that the audience really believes would gentle the Devils in Hell.

And Gluck did.

The gates of Hell opened. Head bowed, lyre under his arm, Orfeo passed through into shadow. The demons knelt, arms crossed on their breasts in humbled silence as the curtains closed.

An arm like an iron bracket hooked around January's throat from behind, twisting and squeezing with a force strong enough to break his neck.

TWENTY FOUR

There wasn't so much as a half-second that January didn't realize it was Big Lou. He dropped his weight, rolled his shoulder forward, trying to throw the man over, the swollen gray buzzing of blocked carotids already swimming in his head—it was like trying to shift a mountain. He got his foot in front of him and heaved backward with all his strength, and this did topple Big Lou between two columns of rock, jarred loose the strangling grip. January rammed and hammered with his elbows back behind him, beneath him, as he felt Big Lou rise up under him like a whale surfacing. He rolled, tried to get up, to kick, and Lou grabbed him, downed him. He heard the dark rags of his costume rip, his own grunt as the breath was driven from his lungs.

"Shaw!" bellowed January, rolling away from a punch that drove splinters from the stage-boards where his head had been. "Shaw!" And heard only a scream from backstage, and the drumming of panic-driven feet.

And smelled smoke.

Far more smoke than there had been a moment earlier.

It was dark among the flats and plaster rocks, only the red-glassed glare of the gas-jets giving a sort of infernal light. He grabbed Big Lou by the collar, dragged the bald bullet-head down with all his strength as his fist slammed upward. It was like hitting a cannon ball. Two, three times he struck, and rolled his head aside as Lou pounded him again. The man's massive weight pinned him, the smoke-sting in his nostrils he'd thought—prayed—was just the leftover from the Demon Chorus grew worse. As he rolled, finally, to his feet, from the tail of his eye he caught the searing flare of red light from backstage.

And heard someone scream, "FIRE!"

Minou's here! Upstairs, halls crowded, no way to get down . . .

Lou grabbed him, slammed him against the wall. This time January curled his shoulders, head tucked, spun the man's weight into the wall instead. He kneed him hard, slammed his elbow into Lou's throat, his own blood streaming into his eyes where the papier-mâché mask-edge had driven into his brow and cheeks. The shrieking was louder: "Fire! Get the pump . . . DAMN it . . . !"

Out front, too, now, screaming, the crash of benches, trampling.

Damn it, damn it, fire . . . He hammered that can-non-ball head trapped between his own fists and the bricks, frantic to finish this, get out while he could, get out before he burned. *God damn it, damn it, damn . . . !*

Big Lou staggered and January—mask shattered, cos-tume in rags around his gasping body—stepped back to grab the only loose item in the wings heavy enough and hard enough to make any difference, a sandbag counter-weight dangling from one of La Flaherty's dance-wires. His fists were bleeding and Big Lou lunged for him like a wounded bull. He swung the sandbag and connected with the huge man's skull so hard, he felt it through his arm to the shoulder.

Lou stopped, drew himself up, swaying. Red light haloed him, smoke and shrieking. . . .

Fall, God damn you, FALL!

January smote Lou again with every ounce of strength in his body; this time the man's eyeballs rolled up and he went down. Someone knocked a flat over, running toward the door. The wild glare of orange-and-yellow flame spilled among the shadows. January pulled off his belt and the belt from Lou's pants to bind the big man's hands. He heard a man shout something that wasn't *Fire*, incoherent words, and a girl screamed "Don't! No!" but he barely paid attention. Seizing Lou's bound hands, he began to drag the unconscious man back toward the stair, toward the door down into the prop-vault and so outside.

Blinding smoke filled backstage. Through it, January could glimpse the lick and lash of flame. Hot air seared his throat, and he dropped to his knees, crawling, dragging, but at least he could breathe as he crawled. The darkness among the flats confused him. He tried to avoid a blazing wall of trees and found himself lost in a pocket of smoke, walls around him, doors. He'd taken a wrong turn and couldn't tell where he was in the huge cavern of backstage.

Only knew that the theater was burning, that he had to get out or burn, too. . . .

"This way!" A girl's small hand grabbed his wrist. She must have seen the white designs on his chest, gleaming in the churning night of smoke. Coughing, dragging Lou's unconscious weight, he crept after her blindly, writhing along the floor. In the sulfurous glare he saw Vincent Marsan's daughter's narrow, pointed face. Once her skirt caught fire and January dropped Big Lou's hands, tore the burning cloth away from the bodice of her mourning dress. In her petticoats she grabbed Big Lou's arms and the two of them began to drag again. . . .

Stairs, smoke pouring down them into the draft from the door. Lou's heels bumping as January hauled him down. The alley's darkness and the alley's mud, and red light swirling behind the theater windows like the mad gleam in a lunatic's eyes. People churned and heaved in the narrow space, shoving, calling each other's names. Some were fighting to get out of the alley and others fighting to get in with water from the Promenade Hotel. The screams of horses, panicked and terrified by the smoke, from the other side of the wall as the stable-grooms led them away from the danger of the fire. The splash of water, the sudden choking sweet stink of wet hay.

Minou, thought January, *I have to find Minou. . . .*

He shoved Big Lou into the doorway in which the Gower boys had hidden to wait for their prey, and started to lead Jocelyn Marsan down the alley to safety. She balked, pulling back: "Mr. Knight's still in there!" she cried. "The men with guns . . . !"

"What men?" January pulled the girl back against the corner of the cotton-press wall, out of the shoving, shouting crowd that jammed Camp Street from curb to curb. Carriages filled with maskers in Roman armor, Turkish pantaloons, dark evening-dress, and the rough clothes of stevedores and boatmen crammed and mixed and shuffled with them, adding to the sense of nightmare and preventing the pump-wagons from Municipal Engine Company Number Fourteen from getting through. The red flare pouring from the broken front windows showed him her terrified dark eyes.

"Orpheus—the man who played Orpheus, in the gold wig. And one of the Devils . . ."

"Maestro!" Shaw grabbed his arm. "You seen Belaggio?"

"He's in the theater!" gasped Jocelyn Marsan, pointing back at the burning building. "Signor Belaggio and Mr. Knight both! Mr. Knight went backstage, and I followed him through the door at the end of the corridor. . . ."

"Why?"

She looked a little startled that Shaw would demand an explanation, but said, "He was selling slaves. He and my father. He was going to send me to the convent, and I thought if I told him I knew about the slaves, he'd let me go to school in France instead. But when the fire started, the man who'd played Orpheus, and one of the Devils, came out with guns, and made them go up the stairs—"

"Damn it!" Shaw looked back toward the wild Hell of smoke and red-lit windows. "Why the tarnation . . . They'll never get out!"

"They will." Rose Vitrac stepped forward. January saw she was in evening dress—her old yellow tarlatan singed and smoke-blotched—and felt both horror and gratitude that he hadn't known she was in the theater. "The rest of the building's starting to catch now, but only just. That first blaze, the one that drove everyone out . . . I think that was set up."

"Set up?" said January, baffled—flames were beginning to show over the edge of the roof.

Shaw only narrowed his eyes and asked, "You mean they fired the place on purpose?"

"I mean the flame appeared all at the same time in the empty boxes—but *only* in the empty boxes—and in *every* empty box, all the way along. It didn't spread from one to the other, and it didn't catch in the ones in between. And only in the *back* of the boxes, just the flare of firelight. The fire on the stage was all behind the flats, *behind* pieces of scenery. . . ."

"Like that there volcano," said Shaw. He looked back at the flame pouring from the windows. "Sure is goin' good now. . . ."

"But they started it as a controlled burn." January remembered the soaked timbers of the door of Cornouiller, the varnished troughs on Mt. Vesuvius's sides. "To clear the theater." It was probably, he thought, the only reason he and Jocelyn had gotten out alive. "Did anyone see d'Isola?"

"No," said Rose. "Nor Hannibal. Though in this crowd it's hard to tell. He wasn't in the orchestra during the performance. I looked for him from the gallery. Cochon says he was hunting for d'Isola—"

"Cavallo's dressing-room," interrupted January. "Cavallo was the one who searched the dressing-rooms. He's a Carbonaro, he'd have guessed what Belaggio and the Austrians were up to. If d'Isola stumbled on one of the fire-pots in the boxes . . ."

Their eyes met. Then Shaw turned and plunged down the alley, January at his heels, pushing through the crowd that shoved the other way.

"Our friends from Young Italy were one-up on us, looks like," said Shaw, shedding his coat as they reached the stable-yard gate. "They guessed Knight'd have to meet Belaggio to get his money—which the Opera Society folks would hand over for the slaves—the minute they's off the stage, whilst everyone else was watchin' the rest of the dancin'. The slaves all got outa there, by the way, first thing. In them demon-suits they oughta fit right into the crowds all over town tonight. . . ."

The back end of the theater, as Rose had guessed, was dark, the blaze being concentrated around the stage and backstage, where it would drive all witnesses away. Except, of course, thought January, those witnesses who'd chanced upon the fire-pots in their beds of wet clay, the little vessels of paraffin or the hosepipes from the gas-mains set with reflectors, to cast the terrifying glare of fire on the curtains. . . .

He wasn't the only one who had a horror of a theater fire.

The private door into the passway was locked. There wasn't much space in the narrow slot for a run, but January and Shaw were strong men, bracing themselves off the rear wall of the stable-yard to lunge forward against the timbers. The wood of the door gave on the first blow—backing off for the next, January saw the place near-by where the cage of dead rats had lain and thought, *Peanuts. Goobers. Ground-nuts.*

Something no one but the daughter of a plaçée, the sister of a free cab-driver of color, would know that rats loved.

No wonder he'd had the buried conviction that no European had been behind at least some of the crimes.

The next second he and Shaw crashed through the door and literally fell over two bodies, curled and crumpled in the little space at the bottom of the blood-stained stairs.

"What the . . . ?" Shaw held his lantern first high, to show the thick black dribbled trail of blood-stains, then low over the horror of bloated dark features and swarming ants. Though it was hot as a chimney in the stairway, there was little smoke. There were black stains on the walls, on the risers, all the way up and disappearing into shadow.

The men were no one January knew. One had been shot, the other's throat gashed ear to ear with a razor. Neither had been killed here—there was too little blood at the bottom of the stair around the bodies, though the risers were splashed with dull black stains. Both appeared to have been dead for at least a day.

"Well, I will be dipped in shit." Shaw stood up again. "*That's* where they got to."

"*What?*" said January. "Who . . . ?"

"This's the feller got hisself killed yesterday down at the Turkey-Buzzard. I remember that purple jacket." January, who had climbed a step or two up to examine the black satchel that rested on the stairs, came back now to look. "I knowed the boys at the morgue would pull the teeth out'n a corpse if nobody claimed it, or sometimes cut the hair off a likely woman, but a whole body . . . ! An' this must be t'other fella that was missin'. Dr. Ker came in this afternoon, said as how there'd been a break-in at the morgue last night. . . ."

"La Scala," said January, remembering Cavallo's tardy arrival, his nervousness on stage. He pointed to the bodies. "It's Cavallo and Ponte."

"It is not, either. . . ."

"Who will die in the fire, along with the enemies of Italy. I heard Cavallo say to Tiberio, *la scala.* . . . Which is the name of an opera house in Milan, but which also means *the stairway.*" He nodded toward the satchel, halfway up the stair. "And now we know what d'Isola stumbled on that got her taken prisoner."

Shaw and January took the black-stained steps two at a time, passing the other items the conspirators had stowed there—a jar or two of potash, a coil of hosepipe. Metal washtubs and a reflector. And something else, something small that glinted in the juddering lantern-light like a wicked little gold star. . . .

Through the shut door at the top of the steps January heard them: "The man has done us no harm."

"Not yet." The thick Sicilian accent was unmistakable even if January hadn't heard that quick exchange backstage. "The girl—I'll give you the girl. She is a friend of *la patria*. She understands."

Shaw glanced back as January joined him beside the door, gasping in the heat. January mouthed, *Tiberio,* realizing Shaw knew neither Italian nor Sicilian—

Who else but the little maker of fire, to stage this?

"But I do not go to ground and to hiding—I do not destroy my own usefulness to our friends—to give an Irish drunkard another year to drown himself in a gutter. You understand silence, do you not, Signorina?"

She must have whispered "Yes," because Hannibal's weak hoarse voice chimed in with "I assure you gentlemen that I understand silence as well. Why should I concern myself with what becomes of M'sieu Belaggio? *What is he to Hecuba, or Hecuba to him? These our actors were all spirits, and are melted into air, into thin air—*"

He broke off abruptly, and Tiberio's voice continued. "No Irish knows of silence." There was a pause. "Bring the bodies up, then go. I'll make sure of things here, and release the girl when I leave."

Cavallo's voice was chilly polite. "I think we'll take her with us."

"As you please," said Tiberio indifferently. "If you think you can get away unseen in her company through all the crowd in the alley. But I assure you, if she is seen—and she is difficult to miss, since everyone has been seeking her all night—everything we have done here is for naught."

There was silence. Pushing the door open a crack, January saw them, a *tableau vivant* in the amber lamplight of the dressing-room—under whose closed outer door smoke was already beginning to curl. Two jars of paraffin stood near the daybed, on which Drusilla d'Isola lay with her hands and feet bound. Beside her, sitting up but likewise spanceled in the shimmering silk of Princess Elvira's wedding-veils and Princess Isabella's bright gold-and-crimson scarves, Hannibal watched the three Italians warily.

"Don't think you can get away with this," blustered Belaggio. His hands had been not only bound together, but tied to his ankles, leaving him toppled over beside a similarly trussed Knight on the floor. At the small table, Ponte, still furry-limbed and criss-crossed with scarlet paint, was prosaically thrusting things into a small black bag: the libretto of *Othello,* two or three green-covered books January recalled seeing in Belaggio's office. Folded papers, presumably extracted from Knight's pockets. His mask was thrust up onto his forehead and his large dark eyes were cold. "People will wonder, eh? When they find us tied up like this? People will ask questions. . . ."

"And people will find my body, and Bruno's, here beside yours," replied Cavallo. Sweaty and rumpled from the wig, his dark hair hung down over his broad pale forehead, his dark eyes. He'd pulled on trousers, but his feet were bare, as were his arms in Orpheus's sleeveless white tunic. "So who is there to hunt? Drusilla . . ." He stepped over to her, bent to brush her forehead with his lips. "Do not think worse of us, Bruno and myself. Sometimes, to slay the tyrants, the innocent"—he nodded toward Hannibal—"must die, too. As my brother died. Please believe me that if he could be spared, he would be."

Drusilla's glance went from Hannibal to Cavallo, pleading, then moved on to Tiberio's hard little gnome-like face. She wet her lips. "Take me with you now, Silvio. I won't be trouble."

"Don't be afraid, Signorina," said the stage-master in soothing tones. "I'll see you get out safely." Glancing at

Cavallo, Tiberio added, "Shoot them and go. There's no time. I'll see to the girl. . . ."

Or not, thought January, *as the case might be.*

I am terribly sorry, in the dark of the stair she stumbled, she fell, the smoke overcame her. . . .

Cavallo turned toward Knight, a silver-mounted dueling pistol in hand. "As for you," he said quietly, "you Austrian lickspittle; you spy. One day my country and the world will be free of your kind forever. . . ."

As these words came out of Cavallo's mouth, Bruno was already reaching for the handle of the stairway's secret door. But the young man's attention—as always—was on Cavallo, and when January whipped the door open, seized Bruno's wrist, and thrust him into Shaw's grip, Bruno was far too startled to make the slightest resistance.

It was fortunate, too, that they didn't have any great distance to cross from the door, because the moment January opened it, Belaggio's eyes bulged in astonished relief and he cried, "Save us . . . !" causing Cavallo to swing around, gun at the ready. . . .

"Pull that trigger an' he'll still die," said Shaw, one arm hooked around Bruno's throat, his pistol at the young man's head.

January crossed the room in a stride, wrenched the gun from Cavallo's hand, and ducked in the same moment, knowing Tiberio would be armed and would have no hesitation about shooting, and he was right. The Sicilian whipped a pistol from his waistband and fired, not at January, but at Knight, blowing the top of the little man's head off and spraying gore and brains on the green silk of the wall. He flung the empty weapon in January's face as January grabbed at him, then leapt over the daybed, snatched open the door that led onto the gallery, and whipped through like a snake and into the wall of smoke.

"Out of here!" January thrust Cavallo toward the secret stairway door, and fumbled for his knife—which he didn't have, being still clothed in rumpled and bloody demon rags and hair-sewn tights. There were scissors on the dressing-table: he sliced through the scarves that bound d'Isola's feet, then Hannibal's, then Belaggio's as the man bleated wildly.

"Me, too! Don't leave me! *Dio*, I am fainting . . . !"

Flame billowed through the doorway with the draft of the opened door. The heat was unbelievable, a physical blow. Gasping, January dragged the impresario to his feet, shoved him after the others. As he stumbled last from the room, head swimming, he heard the roar of the paraffin jars exploding. Smoke choked the twisting stairway, smoke and hellish bronze light, and when he caught himself against the walls, they were like an oven's, the wood itself pouring out smoke as it spiraled toward catching-heat.

Head throbbing, barely able to see, January half fell down the last steps, tripped on the tangle of corpses, was dragged through the door by hands he could barely see. "Go!" he heard Shaw yell. ". . . Gate . . . Promenade . . ."

The door transformed from blackness to a wall of fire, and January stumbled, chest heaving, into the stable yard's flickering dark.

Somebody threw a wet sheet around his shoulders, guided him to a bench. More water was dumped over his head. He could feel his skin blistering beneath the soaked cloth. Distantly, he was conscious of other people in the fire-streaked gloom; of the gang of men pumping wildly on a fire-engine, spewing water over the wall. Of Belaggio's babbling about how he knew nothing, nothing, of why he'd been dragged up there with that perfidious Austrian spy Knight. Of Hannibal coughing like a dying horse.

Falling timbers crashed—sparks flashed on soaked

dirt and puddles. He opened his eyes and saw, like a black-and-gold painting of Rembrandt, Shaw and two of his men holding Cavallo and Ponte against the side of the stable while a third kept discreetly close behind Belaggio. Cavallo kept shaking his head. "You have no jurisdiction over me. I am not a citizen of your United States."

"You rather I call in them what *do* have jurisdiction over you?" asked Shaw reasonably. "Which I guess would be the Austrian consul in Havana?"

January leaned back against the wall. He turned his head: Drusilla d'Isola sat beside him, ghostly in Euridice's white grave-clothes. "Are you all right?" he asked her.

She nodded. Her face was a mess of half-melted grease-paint and soot, tracked and smeared by tears and sweat. "I heard a noise in the stairway. I was lying down after getting dressed and made up, and I went to see. It was rats, there were . . . there were two dead men down there. I came back to my dressing-room; Silvio was there . . ."

"And you left your satchel," said January. "The satchel you carried the domino in to the Blue Ribbon Ball."

"Oh, you found it there?" Her beautiful brows puckered. "I was looking for it. How it got there . . ."

"It had women's things in it," said January, and she hesitated, her frown deepening.

"How odd," she said.

"It is." From the hip of his ragged tights he unpinned the other thing he'd found in the stair. The tiny topaz, caught at the head of the thin gold shaft, winked again in the reflected glare of the burning theater. "I thought this was even odder."

Her breath caught; she put a hand to her lips.

"You know what it is?" he asked.

"Of course. It was—it was Vincent's." A tear trickled from her eye. "He must have dropped it, one of the nights he came to me."

"Very true," agreed January, holding the toothpick back when she reached to touch it. "But which night?"

Her glance flickered, for one instant, to his face, and there was nothing of grief, nothing of love, in that dark, watchful alertness.

Only a moment. Then she buried her face in her hands.

January took her hands gently and drew them away from her face. "The first time he visited you," he went on, "—the night Belaggio was attacked—he wore mauve, his usual complete ensemble with amethysts on his watch-fob and glove-buttons and toothpick. And the night of the Truloves' ball he wore green. I think the only time he wore a suit of pale yellow—the shade that would go with this topaz—was the night he died. We can check with his valet, of course, and the men in the morgue. That was the night you—and Silvio and Bruno and I—were all lured together out to Bayou des Familles."

"Alas, that I was not there! Daily I have wondered if my foolishness in going out to the countryside . . ." She glanced around her, but Shaw and Cavallo were still arguing in the whirlwind of firelight and shadow. Most of the few spectators in the yard were clustered near the gate.

"I couldn't understand," said January, "why nothing happened to us at La Cornouiller once we were imprisoned. Only when I realized who you had to be did I see that the point of the entire excursion was for us to be imprisoned together. For me to be the witness that your friends Cavallo and Ponte weren't in New Orleans the night Vincent Marsan died. And that you weren't there, either."

"I wasn't!" protested the girl. "This is madness,

Signor! I don't know what you're talking about!" Her lips trembled; tears welled again in her soft eyes, and she tried once more to bring up her hands to hide her face. "Who do I have to be? These—these men, these slave-stealers . . ."

"I think if we show you to the deck-hand on the Algiers ferry," said January gently, "—not dressed in organdy with your hair up, I mean, but in a calico frock and a tignon—he'd recognize the 'li'l nigger gal' who took the ferry into town at seven or eight o'clock Thursday evening. Almost certainly he'd recognize the one who left town as soon as it was light enough for her to travel safely the next morning. And we probably won't have any trouble at all finding the stable in Algiers where you put up M'sieu Desdunes's white-stockinged bay gelding for the night."

D'Isola sat silent, looking at him as he turned the toothpick in his big fingers, catching the firelight in the jewel at its head.

"You waited a long time for him, didn't you?" he asked softly. "And I understand. Killing your brother—a man whose name wasn't even mentioned by the newspaper, a cab-driver even more insignificant to the white jury and the white murderer than the plaçée over whom such fuss was made—did more than rob you of the only person who cared for you. You were twelve. There's few ways a twelve-year-old girl can make her living once the only person who cares for her is gone."

She said nothing, but the reflections of the flames that filled those huge, dark eyes swam again with tears. These, he guessed, were real.

"You sang," said January gently. "Beautifully, according to old M'sieu Faon at the stable, when I went back and asked him. I'm not sure how you managed to reach Naples or who it was who taught you. . . ." She jerked her head aside, but not before he saw the self-loathing in her face, and he remembered Cavallo's words, *She obtained her training in whatever fashion she could.* . . . "It's very easy to pass an Italian as an octoroon, and vice versa, if they don't have the African features. Once you met Belaggio, it was easy. If the Gower boys hadn't made a mistake and attacked the wrong man—and in doing so threw suspicion on your friends—everything would have gone very simply."

He thought she flinched at mention of the Gower boys, but still she said nothing. Only gazed stonily into the leaping shadows of the yard, tears running down her face.

Seeing what? The face of her brother Aucassin Couvent?

The greedy flame in the eyes of Vincent Marsan, just before he died, like Othello, upon a kiss?

"It had nothing to do with me!" Belaggio wailed. "A babe unborn is not more innocent! *Bene,* I had a few harmless dealings with Signor Marsan, but I have no idea why these men would say that *I* took money from the Austrians or anyone else. . . ."

"I don't think anyone would have suspected you," January went on, "or thought to connect you with Aucassin Couvent, dead ten years and buried in some nameless grave. Why should they? You'd been in town only a day or two. You had no connection with M'sieu Knight's skulduggeries, or Incantobelli's schemes of revenge. Putting the blood in the drawer was very good, by the way; a way to attack yourself without coming to any real harm. Unlike the bruises you later put on your own wrists, or the razor-cuts on your fingers. Certainly no connection with Sidonie Lalage."

D'Isola—the Isolated One, the name meant in Italian,

January remembered: the One who is Alone—turned her head back sharply. Had it not been for the two long tear-streaks in the grimed paint on her face, he would never have thought she had wept at Aucassin Couvent's name.

In a very clear, cold voice she said, "Signor, I have no idea what you are talking about. You warned me of Signor Marsan once. Since your sister is a courtesan, I assume she knew of what she spoke, though he was never anything but kind and gentle to me." She drew her hands away from his, but her glance flickered to Shaw, standing a little distance away in the firelight. January saw desperation in her eyes.

"Who these other people are of whom you speak, and why you would imagine that I would have wished to harm a hair of my beautiful Vincent's head, I cannot think. But if you take this ridiculous tale to anyone, I will be forced to . . ."

"Besides," said a girl's voice in halting Italian, and a girl's slim form stepped from the darkness, "you were asleep in the jail-house by the bayou that night. I took you out a blanket, and something to eat, remember? Why did you leave like you did, before it got light?"

For one instant Drusilla d'Isola's eyes widened with shock, staring up into the bright black gaze of Vincent Marsan's daughter. For one instant January saw in her eyes the shaken, almost unbelieving relief he had seen at Trulove's reception, when he'd offered her a simpler song to sing, to save her the humiliation of Anne Trulove's steely gaze. With barely a pause for breath, she said, "I got to thinking that you might be with them—with the men who tied me up and took me away. The place was a—a jail."

"But I told you my father was away," said Jocelyn Marsan, perhaps a little more emphatically than normal conversation required. She cocked her head a little, to regard January. "I didn't tell Mother—didn't tell anyone—that I'd found someone there, because I was afraid I'd be punished. Father had very—distinct—ideas about where girls should and shouldn't go." She hitched around her shoulders the blanket someone had given her, to cover her soot-stained white petticoats: white and black, like her colorless face with its streaks of smoke and grime.

He would even beat his own . . . Judy the cook had started to say, and stopped herself. And January recalled the bruises on Jocelyn's arms.

"She was gone when I went out in the early morning." The girl's voice was matter-of-fact. "But I didn't dare say anything, because of Big Lou."

Big Lou's dark form stood silhouetted by the dimming gold light in the stable-yard gate, swaying a little between two City Guards and two men in soaked and mud-smeared evening-dress. Beyond the wall, the flame could no longer be seen; the smell of fresh smoke had given way to the wet pong of ashes. Somewhere January heard Caldwell talking about fire insurance: "I'm only glad no one was killed. It's almost a miracle so few were injured. Fire usually spreads so fast in theaters. . . ."

The light of cressets, borne into the yard by hotel servants, took the place of the wild flare of the fire, and by it Jocelyn Marsan's thin face looked older, and very calm.

She turned to look down at d'Isola again. "Were you my father's . . . friend?"

"I knew your father, yes," said the singer, still a little hesitant, but settled now into her role. "It is strange that it would be his daughter who helped me that night. I never even thought to ask your name." And she clasped the young girl's hands. "Thank you, Signorina . . . Jocelyn, is it? *Thank you.*"

For a moment their eyes locked.

"And so you see . . ." Jocelyn transferred her gaze to January, bright black eyes like a lizard's, or a bird's. "You must have been mistaken about this person you think killed my father. Because this is the woman who spent that night in the jail-house at Les Roseaux." One hand rested on the white cerement of her shoulder, and the small, pointed chin lifted a little. "She could not possibly have killed my father, sir. And that I will swear in court."

D'Isola's hand stole up and touched those square-ended, stick-thin fingers. The face she turned to January, with its paint smeared and smuts and streaks of ash clinging to her hair, was serene and just the tiniest bit defiant. Susanna facing down Count Almaviva. The lovely Anna defying the evil steward Gaveston to take her castle and her lover away from her. And in Jocelyn's face, equally steady, equally still, January saw the dilapidated house at Les Roseaux, the terror in Madame Marsan's eyes when Big Lou said, *Michie Vincent don't like to be kept waitin'.* The bruises on the faces of the slaves.

Sidonie Lalage—and Aucassin Couvent—had gone unavenged because no white jury would credit the evidence of a person of color against a white. This, too, was in Jocelyn's eyes.

January sighed. "Then I don't think there's anything more to be said." He rose, and nearly fell to his knees. Every limb ached searingly; nausea swept from his blistered shoulders and back. He staggered, and then straightened up. Shaw and Hannibal were coming toward him, as more and more lanterns and torches were brought into the stable yard. More and more men and women in mud-bespattered evening-dress or gaudy and improbable costumes, nursing bruises and abrasions but, January gathered, no burns. He saw Rose slip in through the crowd by the gate, stand looking around for him. Saw Dominique, with a half-dozen of her girlfriends, exclaiming on ruined skirts and ripped petticoats but already beginning to shake their heads and negotiate whose house they'd go to for coffee . . .

Across the yard, a small, pale woman called out Jocelyn's name, and the girl waved, called back, "I'm here, Tante Louise!" She turned back to January and held out her hand. "May I have my father's toothpick? We'll be selling most of his things in order to get along."

January laid it in the small, black-gloved palm.

TWENTY-FIVE

—∞∞∞—

Of the fifty Africans who comprised the Demon Chorus, about two dozen were eventually rounded up in diverse parts of the city. Those members of the St. Mary Opera Society who applied to the Cabildo for recovery of their errant human property—Mrs. Redfern, Fitzhugh Trulove, Jed Burton, and others—swore they'd bought them from Erasmus Knight in good faith, and variously stormed, cursed, and threatened legal action when Shaw informed them that the slaves had been smuggled into the country and would be shipped back to Cuba by the next boat. They were repaid out of the money found in Belaggio's satchel, which Bruno Ponte had had in his hands at the time of his arrest.

The rest of the slaves were never found.

At least, not by anyone who ever reported them so.

Lorenzo Belaggio, Silvio Cavallo, and Bruno Ponte were incarcerated in the Cabildo for two weeks, until an attaché arrived from the Austrian consul in Havana to take them back to that city. John Davis, still awaiting trial in the same cell, was forbearing and affable to his newest roommates but took approximately two hundred dollars in IOUs from Belaggio at faro, for which his lawyer was subsequently forced to sue the Assistant Police Commissioner of Milan. Knight's clerk Tillich, who was also arrested that night at his lodgings near the Circos Market, spent some weeks in the prison before being hanged on charges of attempted murder against Marguerite Scie, accessory to the murder of Orfeo Castorini—known also as Incantobelli— and treason. Big Lou did not testify in court, but as he was sentenced to life imprisonment at hard labor, January assumed that he must have told Shaw enough to put him on the trail of evidence that led to conviction. With the papers found in Knight's brief, there was very little question of Tillich's guilt.

No trace was ever found of Gaio Tiberio, either in the gutted ruin of the American Theater or elsewhere. The theater itself was repaired, and re-opened the following autumn with a complete season of Italian Opera, which was extremely well received. The following year Caldwell opened a second and larger theater immediately behind it on St. Charles Avenue.

Drusilla d'Isola checked quietly out of the City Hotel the day after the theater fire, and took ship for New York.

"It may be that's what hurt her most," said January a few weeks later, when Marguerite Scie asked him about the events surrounding the St. Mary Opera Society's first New Orleans season, "that after she did everything she could to make sure that her two friends had alibis for the night of the murder, they were lukewarm—to say the least—in trying to get her away from Tiberio."

"What did they say about it?" asked Olympe, sewing a pinafore for Chouchou in a blazing halo of work-candles by the parlor fire. Lenten quiet blanketed Rue Douane, and a hard chill; Mardi Gras had fallen early that year, and now in March there was still the possibility of frost. Marguerite, who had continued to rent the rear bedroom during her convalescence, would take ship in the morning for Paris—Gabriel and Olympe between them had cooked a special dinner, and afterward Hannibal had played his fiddle, which Cochon Gardinier had retrieved from the theater when everyone started yelling *Fire*. The children were in bed. It would soon be time to go.

"That they were sorry." January's voice had a dry twist. "But Cavallo said that as a daughter of *la patria*, d'Isola would understand." He had visited the jail that afternoon, after John Davis's trial and acquittal: his general impression in the courtroom, which had been packed with Davis's friends, had been that the jury was overwhelmed by the tangle of conflicting tales of Austrian spies, slave-smugglers, mysterious veiled ladies, nameless hired bravos, Italian politics, and enraged divas to bring in any kind of verdict against a man so universally liked. Prosecutor Greenaway had done his best, but with Tillich's testimony discredited, the case had simply collapsed.

"The man has been in too many operas." Rose's spectacle-lenses flashed gold as she looked up from the hearth where she sat. "Did he really think she wouldn't mind dying, in innocence, for the cause of a united Italy?"

"I don't think he thought much about it at all," said Marguerite. "One doesn't when one's obsession is with higher things. It was enough for Tiberio to say, *I shall make sure she gets out*. Cavallo was absolved. He had done all he could, and he really did need to get on with his own crusade. He could weep about it when he learned the Awful Truth in Act Four, of course. One saw a good deal of that," she added, "in the Revolution."

The ballet mistress had been visited that afternoon by an extremely discreet lawyer, who had taken her deposition regarding her two assaults by Big Lou, had insisted on reimbursing her for her fare back to Paris, and had assured her that she would not be further troubled by representatives of the Vienna regime. "I have no idea who the man was working for," she had remarked over supper. "The name on his card was Dutch. He seemed quite pleased that the connection of Big Lou to Chevalier through Marsan was so clearly established, so there must be trouble in it for the Hapsburgs somewhere." She had sounded pleased.

"If Cavallo and Ponte hadn't fallen under suspicion through their contacts with the Carbonari," said Rose now, "would you still have had to spend the night out in Bayou des Familles?"

"Oh, yes," said January. "I think La d'Isola started looking for a locally knowledgeable witness to establish her alibi the moment she realized her hired bullies had attacked the wrong man. It wouldn't take many inquiries to ascertain that La Cornouiller was deserted, and it was the work of an afternoon to go out and fit the place with new padlocks and hasps. She needed someone who would believe her story of being kidnapped by slave-stealers; having decided to extend the alibi to include her friends, it was, of course, no accident that she 'encountered' them on her way.

"What she didn't count on," he added, "was us getting out from under the house, which she'd cleaned out pretty thoroughly of anything that could be used as a tool. She didn't count on us ending up at Marsan's—and speaking to people who remembered the murder of Sidonie Lalage in any detail—and she couldn't have predicted that I'd have the occasion to learn that most Europeans don't have the slightest idea what a pea-nut is, much less that they're a favorite delicacy of rats."

"White people don't know rats love pea-nuts?" demanded Zizi-Marie, startled.

Then Marguerite asked, "What's a pea-nut?"

"So I knew that it wasn't a European behind the threat against d'Isola. And once I started thinking in terms of what grievance *would* be held by a person of color, I was pretty certain—in spite of all the evidence to the contrary—that it was Marsan who was the original target, not Belaggio at all."

"She was good," said Olympe softly.

Marguerite sniffed. "You obviously never heard her sing."

"Perhaps not," said Hannibal. "But we all saw her *act*. Marsan most of all, I expect—which must have taken the proverbial nerves of steel, to seduce a man whom you not only intend to kill, but who you know is capable of killing you in a jealous rage. *Trifles light as air / are to the jealous confirmations strong / as proofs of holy writ*. . . . As she had more cause than most to know. My God, that would have taken courage."

Looking across at his sister's calm profile in the candle-light, January wondered suddenly if Olympe had guessed. Had realized that the Italian girl was, in fact, what the slave-dealers called a *musterfino*—the child of an octoroon and a white, *with features fine as a Spaniard's,* as old Faon had said. And from that had guessed the rest.

Or did the slight half-smile on her lips mean something else?

"*Could* she have stabbed Marsan," asked Rose reasonably, "without getting blood all over the dressing-room? Whenever I attempt to cook a chicken, the kitchen ends up looking like the St. Bartholomew's Day massacre. And she'd have been caught, surely, the first time someone went up that secret stair. You said it was all splashed with blood, even though Cavallo and Ponte must have just shoved their would-be doubles in through the door at the bottom. You and Hannibal had been up it only a week or so before."

"You gotta take lessons in seduction, girl," remarked Olympe, glancing up from her needlework. "With the whole evening to prepare, and just one or two candles burnin', you think Marsan's gonna notice a couple extra sheets on the floor?"

"Particularly," added Madame Scie wryly, "if La d'Isola were in a sufficiently advanced state of undress at the time."

"Since the stair led down from her room," added January, "Marsan's blood wouldn't have been discovered until after she was gone. Possibly long after, if she made sure the stair was locked at both ends and she lost the key. The sheets themselves would have ended up in the river; there was blood smudged on the lining of her satchel where she carried them. I'm guessing she sent Marsan a note, arranging a meeting in her dressing-room Thursday night—maybe even telling him she wouldn't be at rehearsal, or telling him not to go. The Gower boys having failed her, she wasn't about to trust hirelings again. And she had the knife they'd left in the alley."

There was a little silence, while the log hissed softly between the iron dogs.

"What was her name?" asked Marguerite at last. "Her real name, I mean."

"Marie," said January. "Like every other girl in New Orleans. Marie-Drusille Couvent. God knows what she intends to do with her life now."

"Maybe she doesn't know that herself," said Olympe softly. "Some people can fight to the death as warriors, but then they can't let the war be won. When there's a chance at peace, they get edgy. They pick fights with everyone around 'em, and finally go look for another war.

In a lot of ways, war is easier than loving, and learning to live day to day."

"Maybe that explains Marsan," said Paul, who up until this time had not spoken.

And maybe, thought January, it explained Othello as well.

He and Rose parted from Hannibal where Rue Douane crossed Rue Chartres, Hannibal turning his steps toward the City Hotel. Consuela was leaving the day after tomorrow, bound for Mexico City, where an Easter opera season was being readied for the grandees who made up a little court around the flamboyant dictator Santa Anna. John Davis, with whom January had spoken briefly after the trial that afternoon, had plans for another tour of the North—Philadelphia, New York, Boston—but looking at that haggard face, the exhaustion in his eyes, January wondered whether the little man would ever fully recover from his month in the cells of the Cabildo.

But at least he was free. He had clasped January's hand in thanks before his white Creole friends and well-wishers had crowded around him. January had known when to step away.

Rose's hand slipped quietly into his. After a moment, the streets being deserted, he put his arm around her shoulders, and she leaned a little into him, like a wild bird settling, hesitantly, onto a human hand.

Walking back, late, from seeing Rose to Rue des Victoires, January passed the levee, and saw gold-threaded in the torchlight of the wharves not only the clumsy stacks of the steamboats, but the masts of the tall clippers, the squatter funnels of the ocean-going packets that would take Marguerite back to her home. Such were the turns of fate—especially given the fact that he himself was forty-two now, and she fifty-seven—that there was a chance he would never see her again.

But he would know she was there, he thought. Alive in that gray-walled city, with its twisting cobblestone streets and pewter river, instructing her bright-haired little rats at the Odéon, or shopping in Les Halles with its reek of fish and wet pavement when the chestnut trees along the boulevards put out their leaves. For two years now he'd walked the muddy brick banquettes of this pastel town beside the vast brown Mississippi flood, and had nearly forgotten Paris, and what it was like to be close to the heartbeat of something beyond sugar cane and money.

Hannibal was right, he thought. There was a miasma here that made you forget.

It was good to remember again.

Another thought came to him, and instead of turning up Rue des Ursulines when he came to it, he went two more streets to Rue Du Maine. For three days now, cold winds had flowed down over the town as if vengeful northern gods were trying to punish the gentler world for its Mardi Gras excess; January's breath smoked as he passed beneath the iron lamps, burning on their crossed chains above the crossed streets. But he could tell this was the last of the winter. By next week the city would blaze with azaleas.

The pink cottage on Rue Du Maine was quiet. Through gauzy curtains he saw a woman sitting alone in the bedroom, coiffed and jeweled, and immaculately dressed.

Waiting, as Desdemona had waited. As all women wait who give their lives over into the hands of men.

Women who hope against their better knowledge and judgment that things will change, and be all right.

He knocked gently at the French door and saw the woman startle. "It's me, Minou. Ben." She gathered her cashmere shawl from the chair, hurried to open the door.

"I can't stay," he said, meaning, *You don't have to worry about me lingering, in case Henri arrives.*

"It's all right." Her smile was tired. In the Place d'Armes, the Cathedral clock spoke eleven.

He asked, "Are you all right?"

"Do you mean, have I made up my mind?" Her hand stroked her belly as her velvet eyes playfully mocked. He lifted his hand in a fencer's gesture, acknowledging a hit. "Or is it already too late?"

"You tell me."

The mockery melted to a genuine smile of grateful friendship, of warmth at being understood. "I have a note for you." She went back and fetched it from the dressing-table where her open book lay. "Your friend Shaw brought it here, not knowing where to find you. I said you'd probably be by. To check on me, if nothing else."

I was in the court today, it said without salutation, without date or address or any kind of identification, but he knew the hand. He had last seen it on a note informing him that the writer was on her way out to Cornouiller Plantation on Bayou des Familles.

> *I don't think you saw me, though I was within a few feet of you. It is surprising what a tignon and a beaten look can accomplish. As I have reason to know.*
>
> *I wanted you to know that if they had convicted Mr. Davis of the crime, I would have spoken. I*

*would rather get away free, as Vincent Marsan did
for my brother's murder, but not if another had to
take my place on the scaffold. I'm not sorry for
what I did, nor would you blame me, if you knew
the life I endured, after Aucassin's death. Mlle.
Jocelyn will have hardship, and I'm sorry to do that
to her, and to her mother, for they are blameless. As
I was.*

*You were good to me. More faithful even than
Silvio and Bruno. You came back into the burning
theater to help me, who was a stranger to you, and
whom you already knew to have done murder. I try
to remember things like that, when Marsan's face
comes to me in dreams—or Silvio's. I thank you.*

*Maybe one day I will have the freedom to be
that kind of friend.*

January folded the note and tucked it into the pocket of
his coat. Unsigned, and written in French—a language
she would deny she wrote.

War is easier than loving. Did Marie-Drusille Couvent
have the courage to live in peace?

He looked up at his sister on the doorsill above him,
arms folded beneath the blue-and-ruby gorgeousness of
her shawl. "Thank you," he said. And then, "Don't let one
of your friends tell you that it isn't too late. If you change
your mind about what you've decided, speak to me—and
only to me."

"I won't change my mind." Her breath was a cloud of
diamond in the soft gold light from the room behind her.
"I love him, and he loves me."

Do you believe that makes any difference?

Instead, he said, "Go to bed. He isn't coming."

"I will." But after she closed the door, she left the

heavy curtains open, so that the light would fall welcoming through. He saw her go back to her dressing-table again, and pick up her book.

My mother hath a maid called Barbary, Desdemona says to Emilia as she prepares herself for the coming of her lord. *She was in love, and he she lov'd prov'd mad, and did forsake her. . . .*

Like Desdemona's willow song, the music would not leave January's mind as he walked back down Rue Du Maine. Sidonie Lalage had waited, he thought. And Drusilla d'Isola. There were more ways than the violence of passion, for love to wound; more ways than one, to die upon a kiss.

From the corner of Rue Dauphine he glanced behind him, and saw the gold light of Dominique's window still lying on the wet pavement, keeping faith with Henri in the raw blackness of the night.

In the eighteenth and nineteenth centuries, opera held a position in popular entertainment almost equivalent to motion pictures today. There were wonderful operas, there were bad operas, and there were god-awful silly operas, and in the early nineteenth century New Orleans had probably the most active opera and opera following in the United States.

John Davis—to whose shade I extend my sincerest apologies for making him a suspect (although by all accounts he probably would have been tickled: he seems to have been that kind of man)—not only produced operas of close to European standards, but took his company on successful tours of the northern cities for several years running. There actually were "opera wars" of the kind I've described once James Caldwell opened a rival opera house on Camp Street, including putting on competing productions of the same opera in the same season. The original American Theater did not burn down as I've described in the book, though its successor did. In fact, incendiary destruction seems to have been the fate of most theaters in that era of gas lighting and nonexistent safety laws.

All the operas mentioned in the text, with the exception of Incantobelli's *Othello,* actually existed, although it's difficult to find recordings of some of them. The 1830s were years of transition, from Classic Opera into full-blown Grand Opera, with elaborate sets and over-the-top special effects. In this period neither Verdi nor Puccini had written yet, and many of their predecessors— like Auber and Meyerbeer—are far less well known today. (I looked very hard for a video of the ghosts of the mad dancing nuns.)

German opera was only just beginning to come into its own, and only one piece—Weber's *Der Freischütz*— seems to have been popular in New Orleans.

Prior to Verdi's 1887 rendition of Shakespeare's *Othello,* there was at least one other opera of the play, by Rossini in 1816. (The tragic ending was rewritten because audiences in Rome found it too much of a downer.) (Rossini wasn't the first composer to put Beaumarchais's play *The Barber of Seville* into operatic form, for that matter.) It was not un-known for producers to insert other music or popular songs into operas, or to tinker with the texts—in Italy it was not uncommon for the performance to be discontinued after the death-throes of the star, since nobody really wanted to see the rest of the piece anyway. I have done my best to give a sense of what opera must have been like at this era: grandiose, overblown, politically hot, sometimes silly but enormous fun.

Since blocked toe-shoes did not come into use until the 1840s, ballerinas really did do pointe-work supported by wires. Apparently some of the most famous actually worked on pointe without wires, with nothing more than lambswool stuffing and extra stitching on the toes of their shoes. They must have stayed on full pointe for relatively short periods of time, and must have had astonishingly strong feet.

Mostly, the object of the opera ballet was to provide a

leg-show to .the young bucks in the audience, many of whom had girlfriends in the corps: the dancers seem to have been a lot closer to Broadway chorus ponies than to the artists of today.

No plan of the original American Theater exists. I have based my reconstruction of the building on contemporary descriptions of it, and on the plans of other theaters in existence at the time. Likewise, I have tried to reconstruct pre-electric—and pre-Argand—stage lighting and effects as well as I could, from such histories as are available.

As always, I have tried to tell a story to the best of my ability, without doing violence to what I've been able to find out about a time, a place, and attitudes very different from our own.

ABOUT THE AUTHOR

———◆◆◆———

BARBARA HAMBLY attended the University of California and spent a year at the University of Bordeaux, France, obtaining a master's degree in medieval history. She has worked as both a teacher and a technical editor, but her first love has always been history. Ms. Hambly lives in Los Angeles, where she is at work on the sixth Benjamin January novel, *Wet Grave*.

If you enjoyed Barbara Hambly's

DIE UPON A KISS

you won't want to miss any

of the superb mysteries in the

Benjamin January series.

Look for

SOLD DOWN THE RIVER

and

GRAVEYARD DUST

at your favorite bookseller's.

And don't miss

WET GRAVE

the latest Benjamin January novel, available

in hardcover in July 2002!